# Blood Herring

Bob; Susan

As the CEO of an Investment Firm, I've gotten to know Jim and Bernstein quite well over the past twenty years. I can assure you that you're working with the very best

I hope you enjoy my novel.

Regards,

Duncan

# Blood Herring

## A Novel

# Douglas C. Eby

Cartouche

## Cartouche

Published by Cartouche

Washington, D.C. U.S.A.
www.cartouchecorp.com

First Printing November 2014

Copyright @ 2015 by Douglas C. Eby

All rights reserved.

ISBN: 978-0-692-32289-5

Cartouche Registered Trademark

Printed in the United States of America

1 3 5 7 9 10 8 6 4 2

Set in Times New Roman

*Designed by* Marsha Cohen / Parallelogram Graphics

COVER:
# Gulfstream 550

## Aircraft Specifications

Manufacturer—Gulfstream Aerospace, a General Dynamics Company
Twin Engines—Rolls Royce 700-710C4-11, 15,385 lb Thrust (each)
Avionics—Honeywell PlaneView™ Flight Director
Maximum Operating Speed (MACH)—0.885
Range—12 hours, 6,750 Nautical Miles, 12,501 Kilometers
Takeoff Distance—5,910 feet
Landing Distance—2,770 feet
Maximum Cruise Altitude—51,600 feet
Length—96 feet, 5 inches
Height—25 feet, 10 inches
Wing Span—93 feet, 6 inches
Windows—14
Interior Configuration—18-seat capacity
Maximum Takeoff Weight—91,000 lb

## Non-Stop Flight Capability

Shanghai—Los Angeles (0.80 MACH)
New York City—Dubai (0.80 MACH)
London—Tokyo (0.85 MACH)
London—Los Angeles (0.85 MACH)

## Exterior Paint

Upper Fuselage—Snow White
Lower Fuselage—Balboa Blue
Striping—Omaha Orange, Rojo Red, Kingston Gray

## Price New - $60,000,000

For my Mother and late Father,
whose unconditional love and unwavering
support has always put a smile on my face
and given me the strength and
self-confidence to embrace life.

# Author's Note

My inspiration for writing *Blood Herring* came from a dinner at one of Europe's most distinguished establishments, London's Reform Club. During the summer of 2013, England was experiencing an almost unprecedented heat wave, one that saw temperatures exceed ninety-four degrees for nineteen straight days. On the night of July 16th, with the index approaching one hundred, the formal and tradition-rich Reform Club, renowned for its persnicketiness, waived the jacket and tie requirement in the main dining room—for the first time in a long time.

In anticipation of the dinner with Dr. Paul Woolley, an esteemed economist at the London School of Economics, I reread Jules Verne's novel *Around the World in Eighty Days*, which opens in the Reform Club's card room. In the classic, some of the gentlemen at the table were remarking how, with the advent of the railroad, the world had changed but earth's physical shape had not. Phileas Fogg, Verne's protagonist, rebuts his contemporaries who say the planet remains unchanged as to its size. He pipes up and says that in fact the world is now smaller, and to prove his point he proposes to circumnavigate the Earth in eighty days—one-tenth the time required a century before. One hundred and forty-one years, dozens of reprints and millions of copies later, the rest, as they say, is history.

The exhilarating discussion with my host, predominately focused on the foolishness associated with the efficient market theory, the world-class economist's work attempting to rewrite the laws of financial theory and even whether the "railroad" of the day—the Internet—had compressed the world again. After several hours, I floated onto Pall Mall Street, located in central London's clubland. While hailing one of the United Kingdom's incomparable cabs, with my mind buzzing like a bumblebee from the stimulating intellectual experience, I was drawn to a storefront window directly across the street from the Italian Renaissance–styled Reform Club.

Capturing my attention was a detailed model of a magnificent Feadship under the sign of the Burgess Super Yacht Company. I thought to myself how Phileas Fogg would have leapt for joy if Burgess had been located opposite the Reform Club when he walked out in 1872 to commence his odyssey. With cruising speeds approaching twenty knots per hour, Fogg would have most likely only needed fifty days to circumnavigate the globe—not eighty – in one of Burgess' floating "Ritz Carltons."

Nestled in the back of the taxi in London, one of the grandest and most important cities in the world, while en route back to the Caledonian Club in Belgrave Square, I opened my iPhone to the photograph of the yacht I had snapped earlier. To my surprise, Burgess' storefront glass window was acting as a mirror casting an ethereal reflection of the august Reform Club in the background. In a flash the idea to write a modern-day version of this beguiling story came to me in the heat of the English night. Following my philosophy of informative entertainment, the book relies heavily on my perspectives gained through extensive international travel, years of business and Wall Street experience and personal studies of history motivated by a love of humanity's past.

Life's circumstances change, but the essence of life—man's experience—remains stubbornly frozen in time. In *Blood Herring*, my protagonist, Christian Robinson Roos, may be flying around the world in jet aircraft, but his struggles to weave through humanity are timeless, as he attempts to prove to a few of his fellow Winged Foot members that safe global travel is alive and well and that, in fact, the world has not gone mad.

A special thank you to Helen McInnis for her dedication and commitment to seeing *Blood Herring* matriculate, from ideas bouncing around an author's wide-eyed mind to a published novel. Balancing a thoughtful approach and sound counsel with unwavering journalistic principles, Ms. McInnis exhibited the requisite, and often elusive, vital skills in shepherding creativity ever so gracefully into a literary work.

My naturally optimistic personality is full of hope that the enjoyment you derive from reading *Blood Herring* equals the gratification I achieved from writing the book. If true, you will have a feast—I promise.

*"It is good to have an end to journey toward; but it is the journey that matters, in the end."*

—ERNEST HEMINGWAY

# Contents

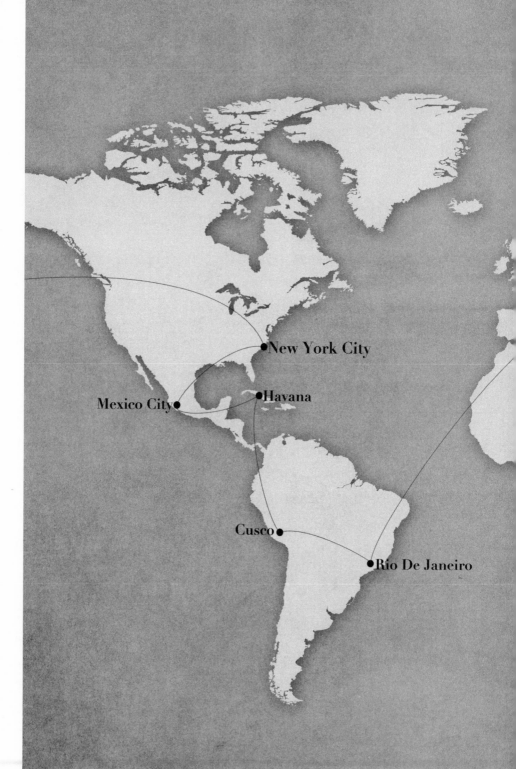

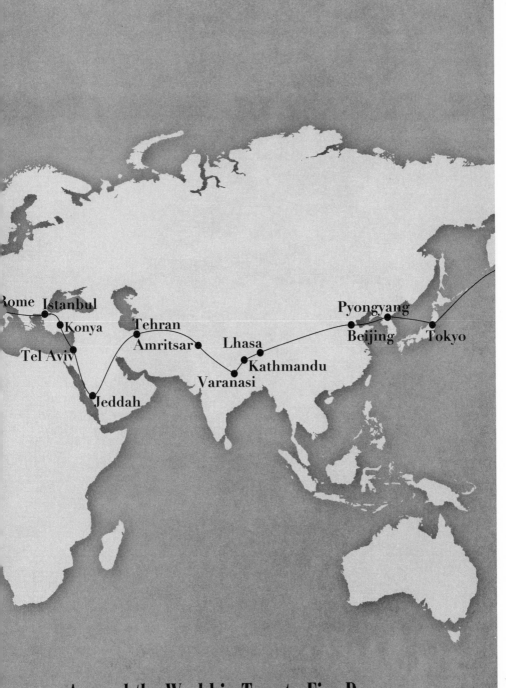

**Around the World in Twenty-Five Days**

# Blood Herring

# Prologue

*"The fox knows many things; but the hedgehog just one big thing."*
—ARCHILOCHUS

L ife is the supreme red herring, a fascinating non-elective journey, which is never as it appears for it is far too occupied providing camouflage for reality.

Born in the seventh century B.C. on the Greek island of Paros, Archilochus was the second western poet after arch-poet Homer. The trailblazing Renaissance man, who lived over two millennia before the world knew of the term, used these words to describe himself: *I am comrade henchman of the Ares the Enylaian King. Also understanding the lovely gift of the muses.* The soldier and poet understood both the art of war and the beauty of the word, a combination fatefully lost on modern-day warriors. One of his most famous lines, *The fox knows many things; but the hedgehog just one big thing*, surely has many meanings. Exactly what was percolating through Archilochus' mind when he wrote those words in circa 650 B.C. will never be known—nor should it be—for the beauty of his message resides in the power of transcendence.

But that has not stopped many from trying to interpret their meaning over the centuries. And why not? Imagining Archilochus, with a brightly colored tunic made from homespun fabric and leather sandals and his long hair flowing in the gentle breezes blowing through the Aegean Sea, is romanticism and mystery personified. While singing his latest poem, the preferred mode of the day, to a fervent bevy of Greek women, his attention is suddenly diverted by an impending attack—by

1

a fox—not the Greek archrival Persians. Through rolling hills overlooking the blue waters of the Aegean, an unsuspecting and seemingly defenseless hedgehog is going about his daily business foraging for insects, mushrooms and grassroots. Sensing his own dinner, the fox circles his prey causing the hedgehog to brace himself for the impending assault. In a brilliant defensive move, the animal curls up into a tight ball with only his spines exposed in all directions. Fearing this—his last tango on Paros—the hedgehog waits in terror as the fox approaches. The red tailed fox, known around the world for his unmatched cleverness, is buffaloed in the most uncustomary of ways by his opponent's shape-shifting. After several failed attempts to unfurl the animal by pawing the medieval-flail-looking spine ball, the frustrated fox slinks away and Archilochus resumes his singing.

In his famous 1953 essay, *The Fox and the Hedgehog*, British philosopher Isaiah Berlin's interpretation of Archilochus' poem appears to be the universally accepted elucidation—one that has produced an epic metaphor. Extrapolating the animals' behavior, Berlin concluded that the world is made up of two types of individuals: those like the fox, who accept their reality and are contented with the idea that knowledge of life's ultimate singular meaning escapes them, while the hedgehog lives with an insatiable quest to discover the true meaning of life. Solving life's riddle through the big answer that explains human existence is the elusive and sometimes perilous goal of the hedgehog. Reality is granted acceptance by the fox but soundly rejected by the hedgehog, who requires an explanation for what he sees and feels—a reason for his world. Iconic graphic artist M.C. Escher humbly yet insightfully, and in all likelihood coincidentally, illuminated Berlin's metaphor when he said, "To have peace with this peculiar life; to accept what we do not understand; to wait calmly for what awaits us, you have to be wiser than I am."

The quest to understand the human experience, through the studies of the humanities, provides an important connection to our past, present and future. It helps to put life's unique journey in proper perspective and provides meaning to human existence. Knowledge of the humanities—

philosophy, literature, art, music, history and language—makes the world go around—at least in the eyes of the foxes. But the hedgehogs insatiably thirst for more and grab for the Gatorade of reality, a drink with many flavors—religion being the most popular. In his book, *A Brief History of Time*, Stephen Hawking preaches to the hedgehog-stacked choir, "Ever since the dawn of civilization people have not been content to see events as unconnected and inexplicable. They have craved an understanding of the underlying order in the world."

Ironically, the phrase a *red herring*, something that distracts from the real issues, has proved to be a red herring itself, producing one of the English language's ultimate double entendre—an autological one.

Red herring has been used for centuries to describe fish. John Heywood's 1546 glossary, *A dialogue containing the number in effect of all the proverbes in the English tongue*, which includes thousands of popular sayings in Old English during the sixteenth century, most certainly includes the expression: *She is nother fyshe nor flesh, nor good red hearing*.

The clergy ate fish such as salmon, tuna and cod. Tasty venison, lamb and cattle flesh were consumed by the wealthy and the dried and smoked herring, with its questionable culinary qualities was eaten by the poor. Capturing all classes of society, the list of foods serves as a brilliant metaphor for encompassing all possible eventualities.

The meanings of words, which derive wholly from the commonly accepted usage of the day, naturally change over time. The interpretation of a red herring has morphed from a single reference to fish to also include the definition of a clue that is intended to be misleading or distracting. Driving this change was the seventeenth-century practice of using the pungent scent of a kipper fish in the training of bloodhounds by foxhunters and by criminals attempting to elude the likes of Sherlock Holmes.

The first written example of red herring as a training scent for foxhunters is found in Nicholas Cox's 1686, *The Sportsman's Dictionary: Or The Gentleman's Companion*. Modern-day foxhunters rarely track down the live furry red animals, opting instead to use a red herring scent, which may mean a scent other than a fox or an actual herring, the fish. In either event it is definitely something other than the real issue.

Christian Robinson Roos, a trusting man who believes life is an angling adventure for the goodness in humanity, will find himself dangerously entangled with a red herring. For twenty-five days, as he travels around the world, Roos will be both hooked and setting the hook in a real-life deadly fishing expedition.

A true *Blood Herring*.

# The Wager

Ensconced in the powerful Grille Room of the exclusive Winged Foot Golf Club, Charles MacCormick, peering up from *The New York Times*, muttered out loud, "The world has gone mad."

The Club, simply known as The Foot by the membership, is a virtual who's who of the New York cognoscenti. Despite being located just twenty-five miles north of New York City in Mamaroneck, New York, in the heart of wealthy Westchester County, The Foot feels like another world. The chaos of Manhattan is lost in its serenity, which oozes from every fiber of the magnificent clubhouse and every blade of grass on the two golf courses designed by Albert Warren Tillinghast. Tillie, as he was referred to, created his Winged Foot masterpieces in the 1920's, on his way to becoming the greatest golf course architect of the twentieth century.

Famous composer George M. Cohan summed up the juxtaposition between one of the most dynamic cities in the world during the roaring 1920's and Westchester in his lead song from his musical, *Forty-Five Minutes From Broadway*. *"Only forty-five minutes from Broadway. Think of the changes it brings. For the short time it takes. What a difference it makes in the ways of the people and things."*

The Foot, host to five United States Open Golf Championships, stands only behind Oakmont, Oakland Hills and Baltusrol as the United States Golf Association's most popular venue. Considered one of the greatest golfers in history, Bobby Jones won his first U.S. Open at Winged Foot in dramatic fashion in 1929. The Foot is a special place. All members understand how fortunate they are to know the four-digit code to the entrance gates, which are closed to the public.

The magisterial clubhouse is a combination of Tudor and Norman design, the signature of architect Clifford Charles Wendehack. The structure makes brilliant use of brick and stone set under a massive slate roof sporting multiple chimneys and prominent gables with gracious entryways. The visual is one of permanence yet warmth, which at first glance appears to be an optical illusion. Rising from the earth like a Tudor England fortress, not dissimilar to Henry VIII's Hampton Court, the clubhouse takes the breath away before it takes you back in time. How could something be so visually intimidating and yet at the same time so warm and inviting?

Many might say the same about Charles "Mac" MacCormick. At six foot four and pushing two hundred and forty pounds, Mac was an imposing man. Now in his late sixties, Mac had been the Chief Executive Officer of Springer and Waldron, without question the most powerful investment bank in the world. He joined the firm straight out of Harvard, where he received his undergraduate degree in history. Mac's path to Wall Street was all but predetermined. His grandfather, Seamus, immigrated in the early part of the twentieth century to New York from the family's hometown of Cork, located in the southernmost Irish province of Munster. Shortly after his arrival, Seamus landed a job as a runner for one of the major specialists of the day, kicking off a seventy-five year string of MacCormicks working on the floor of the mighty New York Stock Exchange. Following in his ancestor's footsteps, Mac started on the NYSE as a floor broker, where he quickly displayed a unique talent for trading. Fierce and quick of foot, like the famous Cork and Kerry Irish hurlers of his homeland, he became a star overnight. Then came the Getty Oil trade.

After proving his skill in executing orders for the firm's clients, Mac was promoted to head of the firm's proprietary trading operations. Running the prop desk meant that he was making investment decisions with millions of dollars of the partner's personal capital.

J. Paul Getty's last will and testament placed his shares in Getty Oil, approximately forty percent of the outstanding shares of the company, in the Sarah C. Getty Trust. The two trustees were his son Gordon P. Getty and his longtime lawyer, Lansing Hays Jr. When Hays passed away in 1982, Gordon P. Getty became the sole successor trustee of the trust. With bloody chum in the water, the sharks on the Street started circling. Investment bankers, led by Martin Siegel at Kidder Peabody, began floating potential deals to sell Getty Oil, whose major shareholder was Gordon P. Getty, an aspiring musician, who was making no secret of his feelings that the company was delivering insufficient shareholder returns under the management of the Chief Executive Officer, Sidney Petersen. Shares of Getty began to rise in anticipation of a takeover.

The dynamic was certainly not lost on Mac as he started building a position in Getty. In late December of 1983, Mac was able to acquire one million shares at forty-two dollars per share. Committing forty-two million dollars of the firm's capital was the largest position that the young trader had ever taken. In a single trade with the wave of a hand, Mac had taken the biggest gamble of his young life. Ninety minutes later the unimaginable happened. Pennzoil announced a bid just shy of ten billion dollars for Getty after the close of the market, a price equal to one hundred dollars per share. In after-hours trading, shares of Getty more than doubled, creating a paper profit of fifty million dollars on Mac's trade.

Someone lost that fifty million on paper. The interesting world of trading is many things, but without a doubt, first and foremost it is a zero-sum game in the short term. Someone is always on the other side of the trade. And the person on the other side of Mac's Getty trade reneged. The exact story is unknown; however, the argument appeared to be like the drunken guy at the high-end art auction who scratches his nose at just the wrong time.

Despite the explosion in electronic communication driven by Internet protocol, much of the trillion-dollar trading in equities is done by hand. A wink here, a flash there, the floor brokers, who are responsible for a majority of the trading, all operate under a strict code of honor.

Reneging on a trade is a career ender. Despite the time-honored code, discrepancies occasionally arise and the exchange has a system to deal with them quickly. After the close of trading at 4 P.M., the disputing parties meet in the room located just off of the floor, where they are joined by an adjudicating exchange official. Each side tells their side of the story, after which the official makes a binding final determination. No questions asked.

Upon hearing this in the dispute room, the exchange official turned to Mac and asked him for his side of the story. Mac, displaying masterful aplomb, approached the much smaller man, leaned forward and glared at him with his crystal blues for several minutes without so much as saying a word. Sensing true fear, the trader acquiesced to the trade. Young traders today still talk in awe of the day Mac became the "Man."

The Getty trade took Mac's already rising star and sent it into the stratosphere. He was quickly promoted to Global Head of Equities, elected to the Board of Directors and ultimately appointed as the Chairman and Chief Executive Officer of Springer and Waldron at the young age of forty-five.

"What do you mean, the world has gone mad?" asked John Francis, a fellow member who was seated to the right of Mac in the Grille Room, a wood-paneled piece of heaven on earth. The long rectangular room is filled with four top tables leading up to a handsome bar on one end and a grand fireplace on the other. On one side is a flag-stoned terrace overlooking the eighteenth holes of both golf courses. The main entrance to the club is opposite, where the tenth hole green sits elevated like a St. Patrick's Day birthday cake. Walking off of the tenth green, players march through the clubhouse, grab a beverage and continue on through to the eleventh tee box, like good Christian soldiers.

"I will tell you what I mean." Mac began recalling from a *New York Times* article, "As foreign fighters pour into Syria at an increasing clip, extremist groups are carving out pockets of territory that are becoming havens for Islamist militants, posing what United States and Western intelligence officials say may be developing into one of the biggest terrorist threats in the world today." Mac continued with his own thoughts: "The world has changed since 9/11. Gone are the days when Americans can travel the globe with safety and security. Religious extremism has reached the tipping point, God help us all."

Parker Collins, the powerful head of FIG investment banking at Coopers & Waters, seated to the left of Mac at the four top, echoed his sentiments. "I read recently the interim government of Egypt, fresh from ousting Mohammed Morsi, declared a state of emergency for a month, which includes a 7 P.M. curfew. The Ministry of Health announced more than two hundred dead on the streets of Cairo as violence continues to spin out of control. Egyptian's security forces, determined to crackdown on the Muslim Brotherhood and other opposition groups, unleashed a fury of military firepower on largely unarmed civilians."

John Francis, portfolio manager of Kraft Advisors' flagship Permanent Value Fund, now understanding where Mac was going with his initial statement, chimed in, "British Parliament voted down the use of military force in retaliation for the Syrian's government's use of chemical weapons killing innocent women and children in the thousands. In a painfully open debate the Brits rejected Prime Minister Cameron's proposal to attack by just thirteen votes, two hundred eighty to two hundred seventy-two. And now the president, clearly shaken by our strongest ally's no vote, changed his plans of a Syrian airstrike and decided to put the decision up to a vote. Congress said no. Gentlemen, it sure sounds like déjà vu all over again. Our president is backing down, creating an image of weakness not seen at 1600 Pennsylvania Avenue since Jimmy Carter."

Mac, a man used to dominating the conversation, came back in for another bite at the apple. "How about Nigeria's militant Islamist group Boko Harem? They abduct over two hundred Nigerian schoolgirls and offer their return in exchange for the release of some of their incarcerated comrades. Adding insult to injury, the name Boko Harem means Western education is forbidden in the local Hausa language. How appropriate for such a crime against humanity."

9

Working himself up into a folly-fallen lather, Mac continued to argue his case, "Imagine Russian President Putin invading Crimea before most of the Sochi Olympic athletes have even unpacked their medals. Or Russian Separatists shooting down a Malaysian commercial airliner, killing almost three hundred innocent civilians over eastern Ukraine. Consider Israel eradicating Hamas spelunkers from Gaza tunnels with air raids with a swath wide enough to murder women and children, some who were already in hospitals. Gentlemen, the world is sinking into chaos. To borrow a phrase from Ross Perot, that giant sucking sound you hear is not NAFTA this time around, rather it is the United States' status as hegemon evaporating. The rest of the world, full of mistrust, is adjusting to the vacuum created by our acquiescence of global domination under the current administration. The uncertainty, which has been created by our hegemon hedging is cheered by our enemies and feared by our allies. Case in point, gentlemen, I am sure you read Prime Minister Abe recently succeeded in amending the Japanese Constitution giving more powers to their military forces. They don't want to have to rely on America."

Parker Collins, with both of his hands firmly grasping onto Mac's bandwagon, piled on. "Agreed. China has developed a new class of ballistic missiles with a frightening range of almost a thousand miles, which threatens to alter the balance of naval power in the East Pacific. Named the Dong Feng, Chinese for east winds, the DF-21D missile is capable of sinking one of our aircraft carriers from beyond the range of our military jets. The weapon is literally blowing our boats east from Japan. China's saber rattling over the disputed Senkaku Islands in the East China Sea and the DF-21D are certainly no coincidence. No wonder the Japanese are nervous. And speaking of new weapons, how long before Iran is packing nukes?"

Not to be outdone, John Francis fired back, "We should focus more on our own borders. Has it occurred to anyone that Americans can't log onto the ObamaCare website because of the traffic, both cyber and now physical, coming from Central America?"

Shaking his head in dismissive disgust, Mac elevated his line of patriotic musings. "Hell, most people are not even familiar with the concept of hegemony. I was glad to hear Governor Chris Christie say that America must represent the strongest military and economic power and the strongest moral power for what is good and right in the world."

The fourth gentleman at the table, seated directly across from Mac, took an extended sip of his Ketel One dry martini, his signature tickle-brained cocktail, before gently placing the drink on the table, the glass landing like a butterfly with sore feet, so softly the lemon twist barely moved in the clear liquid. Executing such a move, with that level of precision, requires significant deft, which only comes with years of practice. Christian Robinson Roos had plenty. Leaning forward, addressing everyone, but clearly focusing his remarks directly across the table to Mac, Roos deferentially yet forcefully joined the conversation. "With all due respect, gentlemen, I disagree."

A subtle yet profound air of tension floated over the table, like an American drone, which nobody can see but everyone knows is there. Christian Roos, hailing from his hometown of Washington, D.C., was a longtime member of The Foot. An affable man, he had a gregarious personality and a keen intellect, qualities that Roos spent most of his waking hours trying to camouflage with healthy doses of humor and humility. Admired and respected, Roos fit into The Foot like a Scotsman in a tweed coat. He was by all accounts an unfathomable character. His friends have often claimed Roos, rhyming with goose, was one of the most unusual people they had ever met.

Active in thought, simmering with vexations and lacking the ability to suffer fools, Roos was prone to playing the featherhead with his occasional hooch-fueled outbursts. Ironically, it was his non-confrontational style that precluded him from heading issues off at the proverbial pass before they became flammable. Thankfully Roos' "ski bindings" were set at three plus. An incorrigible bon vivant, his zest and passion for life sometimes crossed the line, an illusory demarcation developed by the moral powers that be, containing more zigzags than the International Date Line. But his heart was always in the right place, something that could not always be said for some of his other precious organs.

Roos' self-understanding, the necessary dynamic required for a sense of self-identity, obfuscated by his early success, percolated to the surface of his emotional radar, commensurate with middle age and life's inevitable setbacks. Talk of accepting who you are had previously fallen on deaf ears to Roos, a man who questioned this valueless advice based on the simple fact that one could not yield to the unknown. The mindful financial analyst at heart never thought much of the analysis of the beating and reasoning organs. Preferring to leave the subject to the types who liked to talk about the weather, Roos sidestepped the issue at every opportunity by quoting Oscar Wilde, "Be yourself, everyone else is already taken." While most men succumb at the hands of the maturing eventualities of graduation, careers, marriage and fatherhood, Roos, despite being in this normal slipstream of life, stubbornly clung to his youth. It wasn't until he experienced events, once thought unimaginable, that Roos begrudgingly acquiesced to the true state of adulthood.

Christian Roos was of Swiss descent, the Bern region, specifically the Emmental Valley. As the thirteenth-generation Roos in the United States on his father's side, Christian was fond of saying, "Well, that may sound impressive to you, but it feels decidedly unlucky to me." The derivation of the name Roos is from a house in Switzerland, one with a rose in front. In Dutch the name means simply rose. Either way, Christian, whose family crest included two roses, was unable to escape his genes, as his trademark move was always to send his female acquaintances the iconic red flower.

During the Dutch Golden Era in the seventeenth century, a trading mania in tulips, and to a lesser extent in roses, swept through Europe. Considered to be the first example of an economic bubble, the speculation in flowers saw their individual prices inflate to that of ten times the annual wages of a skilled laborer. Benjamin Roos, at the time, was the largest individual importer of Dutch flowers into Switzerland. By all accounts a smart, respectable businessman, sadly he became engulfed in the bubble along with most of the higher society of Europe of the day, which stretched north from the Netherlands and south to Spain. Typical of market peaks, fear fades and greed surfaces just at the wrong time. Benjamin Roos was caught with a huge inventory of a very short-lived asset, which promptly proceeded to decline in price by over ninety-eight percent in just a few months. Ultimately, Benjamin Roos ended up being pricked by the Dutch and their beautiful but thorny flowers. It took the Roos family three generations to recover from Benjamin's financial collapse. Christian Theodorous Roos started a clock-making company in Bern in the late seventeenth century, which finally brought the roses back on the front door.

Fast-forward to the bull market of the 1990's when Christian Roos and his partner built a powerhouse investment advisory firm, which at the peak was managing ten billion dollars in equities for large institutional clients as well as individuals through a publicly traded mutual fund. A master of the universe, Roos had succeeded financially, professionally and personally beyond his wildest expectations. He was just thirty-five.

"Please explain your position, Christian." Mac's request was the kind one did not take lightly. Surrounded by quintessential sycophants for most of his career at Springer and Waldron, Mac was a man unaccustomed to being challenged, even in the most benign of ways. Besides his business prowess and personal fortune, he was one of the most influential members of The Foot. As a member of the board and a past president, Mac wielded significant power. Mac and Roos were acquaintances, occasional golf partners, but by no means close friends. Roos' previous investment firm, Value Partners, was a relatively small client of Springer and Waldron, and over the years the pair had met during industry functions from time to time. But other than that, the men were simply fellow members of The Foot, who put their pants on one leg at a time.

Roos stepped into the waters. "Religious differences, which so often have boiled over into full-blown warfare, have existed since the beginning of time. For most of recorded history, individual aspirations were subject to the vagaries of warlords, kings and tyrants. Divisions of race, religion and tribe were settled through violence on the battlefield. The concept of a negotiated diplomacy, where humanity would come together in peace to solve their disputes, in lieu of war, was unimaginable. I believe man's internal struggle to deal with his own mortality has created an insatiable desire to explain life, its meaning, its purpose. Seeking answers to the unanswerable has been and will always be the obsession of man. These obsessions, inextricably linked to religious beliefs, are humanity's Achilles' heel. Problems surface when a select few hedgehogs think they have solved the riddle, which, is almost always linked to religion. Forcefully imposing religious beliefs or constraints on others is the magic formula for eternal conflict, which, I'm afraid, is perpetual. If this makes the world mad, get used to it, Mac. It was mad long before you were here and will be mad long after you are gone."

Mac grumbled, "Religion has been the cause of the majority of bloodshed, suffering and death on this planet—since day one. Need we look any further than the spineless bunch of demonic zealots who dare call themselves the Islamic State? Gutless pariahs who are hellbent on sinking the world in Armageddon with their barbaric tactics, which include grotesque beheadings of innocent civilians."

Roos, impervious to Mac's powerful bearing, continued, "Agree completely, Mac. Some wars have been fought out of a desire to be free from oppressive regimes, others over defining issues like slavery and even a few over the love of a woman. But you are correct—they are few and far between when compared to religious-based conflicts. Please indulge me by allowing a question. We know of the wars that happened, of course, and can trace their root cause. But what of the wars that didn't happen on account of religious beliefs that almost always preach against violence? How many millions would have been killed over the millennia if these wars actually happened? After all, Mac, you surely don't believe that the world would be a safer place if everyone were an atheist? Do you? Just imagine living in that nethermost world for a moment."

The table tensed, like a cardiovascular system processing a Marlboro Red.

Mac took a sip of his Grey Goose and soda, pushed back from the table, breathed deeply, exhaled and said, "I don't live in a world of proving negatives. I deal with facts and make deductions based upon reality.

But please continue, Christian. This beats discussing a three putt on the eighteenth hole—for now."

Roos went on, "It looks like trends will continue unabated according to the president's statement during his recent speech to the United Nations, where he forcefully stated that the U.S. stands ready to do our part to prevent atrocities throughout the world and to protect human rights. The president clearly acknowledged the hostility that our engagement in the region has engendered throughout the Muslim world. But according to the president, backing out now would create a void unlikely to be filled by another country."

Over-talking, a technique the retired CEO of Springer and Waldron was no stranger to, Mac interjected, "Well the president talks the talk but he doesn't come close to walking the walk."

Mac, a stout man capable of brute force, often overwhelmed his adversaries by hitting below the intellectual belt with brute reason, an aggressive and unbearable technique.

Roos unfazed continued, "I love our country, but sometimes I wish Americans possessed a more enlightened historical perspective of the world. When you drive out of The Foot tonight, take special notice of the magnificent rocks, which are indigenous to this region of the country." Roos, a voracious reader and a student of history with a tenacious memory, then proceeded to recall facts from a New York Historical Society publication on the subject. "New York City is the site of ancient earth-shaking events. The bedrock that anchors the city's skyscrapers tells a story of a place going back more than a billion years. Think about that, gentlemen, a billion years. The island of Manhattan is built on three strata known as the Manhattan Schist, Inwood Marble and Fordham Gneiss. It is the latter that is so prominently displayed on the lush grounds here at Winged Foot. Think about the rocks surrounding the green on hole number three east or the large rock formation lining the left side of the par-five twelfth hole on west course. These are examples of billion-year-old Fordham Gneiss. Our clubhouse is built with the material as well."

After withstanding a barrage from his three fellow Foot members, Roos' normal indefatigable patience was suddenly wearing thin.

Feeling exasperated and fearful of his ability to remain composed, Roos found himself perilously close to the tipping point. A place of no return, which a younger Roos would have enthusiastically navigated headfirst, but experiencing life's inevitable peaks and valleys had matured him. Analyzing Mac's body language and demeanor, Roos sensed an opportunity to capitalize on the Wall Street legend's overzealous discourse. Merging the fortuitous coincidence of his preplanned odyssey to circumnavigate the world and the spirited discussion on the overnight demise of civilization in its current form, Roos interjected, "Gentlemen, I believe that there exists more in this world that connects us than divides us. Despite the chaos, the world is safer now, on a relative basis, than at any other time in history. I am prepared to circle the globe in order to prove it, by visiting humankind's most important spiritual sites—many of which are located in the planet's most socially inhospitable, hostile and dangerous places. Besides the widely considered 'safe' destinations of New York City, Cusco, Rome, Kathmandu, Lhasa, Beijing and Tokyo, I will venture into the heart of the Mexican drug trade in Mexico City, the kidnapping capital of South America, Rio de Janeiro, Communist-infested Havana, Cuba, and Pyongyang, North Korea. My route will also include the recent site of rioting, Istanbul, Turkey, the home of Islam, Mecca, Saudi Arabia, the Iranian capital, Tehran, along with perennial hot spots Jerusalem and India. In my quest to establish that not only has humanity survived the millennia—but in fact it is flourishing—I will be incorporating the appropriate balance of the safe and the dangerous. And I will do it in twenty-five days."

"Twenty-five days!" scoffed John Francis. "A commercial jet can circumnavigate the globe in just under fifty hours. A military jet takes less than twenty hours to travel the approximate twenty-five thousand miles."

"Hell, Phileas Fogg took only eighty days to travel around the world in 1872 before aviation even existed." Parker Collins was, of course, referring to the main character in Jules Verne's novel *Around the World in Eighty Days*.

"Yes, of course I understand the dynamics of aviation," rebutted Roos. "I am not intending to sit in an F-18 with an oxygen mask on, or burying myself in the hold of some steamship. Rather, I intend on interacting with the different cultures and religions of the world and bringing back experiences to prove my point that the planet is still predominately filled with goodness and humanity. One that can be safely traveled."

Roos, feeling the need to amend John Francis' statement, continued, "And by the way, John, Gulfstream's latest masterpiece, the G650 just set the around-the-world speed record for a non-supersonic jet. The plane took off and landed back in San Diego after forty-one hours and seven minutes, averaging five hundred sixty-eight miles an hour to travel the twenty thousand three hundred ten miles. The flight made stops in Guam, Dubai and Cape Verde."

Intrigued, Mac queried, "Christian, please tell us more about your proposed travels."

With his typical flare and strict attention to detail, Roos reached into his trademark blue blazer and to everyone's amazement pulled out a typed itinerary. It included thirty of the most famous spiritual sites in twenty-two cities spread across fifteen countries located on five continents.

Incredulously, John Francis inquired, "How in the world is it possible that you just happen to have a typed itinerary on your person?"

The gentlemen seated at the table were unaware of Roos' mood of late. In light of some significant changes in his life, Roos' state of mind was decidedly reflective, causing bouts of deeply introspective thoughts. Those close to Roos knew his condition, which began to heighten over the summer, was doing nothing but intensifying. A dinner at one of Europe's most prestigious social clubs, England's Reform Club, sent Roos' soul searching skyward. On a steamy July evening, which saw temperatures reaching historic levels, the persnickety Reform Club was forced to abandon their required coat rule—for the first time in over one hundred years. His host for the evening was Dr. St. John Smythe, a world-famous English economist attempting to rewrite the laws of finance, while leaving the efficient market theory in his wake. Dr. Smythe's denouncing the long-held belief that all public information is known, therefore no value added can be gained by fundamental research in investment analysis—the creed of the lemming-like momentum fund managers—had a profound impact on Christian Roos. The man with a deep intellectual curiosity wondered if Smythe's hypothesis had implications for other aspects of life, such as political science and human relationships.

Roos answered, "Well, I must confess that I have been planning this trip for a wee bit now, obviously. What better way to gain some proper perspective on life than with an around-the-world adventure, one that hits many important spiritual sites and touches the hearts of the people on five continents."

Roos began spouting off the logic behind his itinerary: "The spiritual destinations on the itinerary incorporate the four largest faiths: Christianity, Islam, Hinduism and Buddhism, as defined by numbers of followers. Of the approximate seven billion human beings on earth, two billion one hundred million or thirty percent of the world's total population claim to be Christian, the one and a half billion Muslims make up twenty-one percent, Hinduism counts one billion members representing fourteen percent. The fourth, Buddhism, is difficult to count. Why? Because everything in China is hard to count, that is why it is difficult to gauge an accurate estimate of the religion's followers. Conservative estimates are in the five hundred million range, while more aggressive tallies exceed one and a half billion. What is not in dispute is that Buddhism is the world's fastest-growing religion. A simple midpoint approach has the current population of Buddhists at one billion or fourteen percent of the world's total. Of course it would be an oversight to leave out the rather large one billion one hundred million individuals who consider themselves to be atheist, agnostic or non-religious. No doubt my route will create many encounters with non-believers along the way. Some quick math shows that of these five major categories, approximately six billion six hundred million people representing ninety-six percent of the world's population are accounted for. Despite the small population of approximately thirty million, Judaism remains an extremely important religion in the world today, and as such has representation on my itinerary."

| Scheduled Itinerary | |
|---|---|
| 1 | St. Patrick's Cathedral, New York, New York, USA |
| 2 | Our Lady of Guadalupe, Mexico City, Mexico |
| 3 | Cathedral of Havana, Havana, Cuba |
| 4 | Machu Picchu, Cusco, Peru |
| 5 | Christ the Redeemer, Rio de Janeiro, Brazil |
| 6 | St. Peter's Basilica, Rome, Italy |
| 7 | Suleymaniye Mosque, Istanbul, Turkey |
| 8 | Sultan Ahmed Mosque, Istanbul, Turkey |
| 9 | Shrine of Rumi, Konya, Turkey |
| 10 | Western Wall, Jerusalem, Israel |
| 11 | Church of the Holy Sepulchre, Jerusalem, Israel |
| 12 | Church of the Nativity, Bethlehem, Israel |
| 13 | Al Haram Mosque, Mecca, Saudi Arabia |
| 14 | Treasury of National Jewels, Tehran, Iran |
| 15 | Mount Hira, Mecca, Saudi Arabia |
| 16 | Vaishnodevi Temple, Jammu and Kashmir, India |
| 17 | Golden Temple, Amritsar, India |
| 18 | River Ganges, Varanasi, India |
| 19 | Bodhi Tree, Bodhgaya, India |
| 20 | Pashupatinath Temple, Kathmandu, Nepal |
| 21 | Potala Palace, Lhasa, Tibet |
| 22 | Jokhang Temple, Lhasa, Tibet |
| 23 | Temple of Heaven, Beijing, China |
| 24 | Great Wall, Beijing, China |
| 25 | The Forbidden City, Beijing, China |
| 26 | Lama Temple, Beijing, China |
| 27 | Tiananmen Square, Beijing, China |
| 28 | Ryugyong Hotel, Pyongyang, North Korea |
| 29 | Meiji Shrine, Tokyo, Japan |
| 30 | Sensoji Temple, Tokyo, Japan |

"Well, I can see this apparently is a topic that has crossed your fertile mind before today," Mac mused out loud as he continued to analyze the itinerary with acumen that could easily and quickly draw judgments and assess risk from data. Mac continued, "No doubt you have calculated the total distance of the odyssey."

Roos immediately responded, "Why yes, Mac. The distance between all of the airports on my itinerary is exactly 30,760 nautical miles. Look on the back of the page: I have listed all of the flights, cities, airports and corresponding distances."

With the document now reversed and firm in his rock-steady hands, Mac's analytical mind was busy processing the data appearing on Roos' air travel itinerary.

| Scheduled Flight Itinerary | | | | | |
|---|---|---|---|---|---|
| Flight | Departure City | Airport Code | Arrival City | Airport Code | Nautical Miles |
| 1 | New York City | JFK | Mexico City | MEX | 1,821 |
| 2 | Mexico City | MEX | Havana | HAV | 960 |
| 3 | Havana | HAV | Cusco | CUZ | 2,283 |
| 4 | Cusco | CUZ | Rio de Janeiro | GIG | 1,730 |
| 5 | Rio de Janeiro | GIG | Rome | FCO | 4,967 |
| 6 | Rome | FCO | Istanbul | IST | 749 |
| 7 | Istanbul | IST | Konya | KYA | 250 |
| 8 | Konya | KYA | Tel Aviv | TLV | 378 |
| 9 | Tel Aviv | TLV | Jeddah | JED | 671 |
| 10 | Jeddah | JED | Tehran | IKA | 2,638 |
| 11 | Tehran | IKA | Jammu Kashmir | IXJ | 4,649 |
| 12 | Jammu Kashmir | IXJ | Amritsar | ATQ | 59 |
| 13 | Amritsar | ATQ | Varanasi | VNS | 568 |
| 14 | Varanasi | VNS | Gaya | GAY | 121 |
| 15 | Gaya | GAY | Kathmandu | KTM | 180 |
| 16 | Kathmandu | KTM | Lhasa | LXA | 328 |
| 17 | Lhasa | LXA | Beijing | PEK | 1,396 |
| 18 | Beijing | PEK | Pyongyang | FNJ | 430 |
| 19 | Pyongyang | FNJ | Tokyo | NRT | 722 |
| 20 | Tokyo | NRT | New York City | JFK | 5,860 |
| | | | Total | | 30,760 |

After a few minutes, Mac inquired, as he passed the itinerary along to the other two gentlemen at the table, "Are you serious, Christian?"

"Absolutely. I am prepared to depart tomorrow at noon, from right here at The Foot and I will return by noon on the twenty-fifth day."

"Well, I think you are crazy, but far be it from me to try to dissuade you from your ambitious goal. Would you be willing to place a wager on the outcome?" Mac was never a man to pass up a little action, especially at this stage in his life. This type of an opportunity was heaven-sent and completely irresistible for a gambler such as Charles MacCormick—a man not accustomed to losing. And Roos knew it. But Roos also knew that Mac never took an uncalculated risk and that surely—like him—he was already improvising with a clever scheme.

"Sure, what do you have in mind?" Roos asked.

"Whatever makes you nervous would be my inclination," deadpanned Mac.

The time had reached 6:30 P.M. and the Grille Room was packed. Sensing something important was transpiring, a crowd starting gathering around the table.

Calling his bluff and displaying intestinal fortitude buried deep within his psyche, Roos calmly invited, "You name it."

Mac leaned across the table, smiled, flashed his steely blue Irish eyes, looking like the day he became the "Man," and with a slight nod, in his trademark deep voice said, "Twenty-five million dollars. The money needs to be escrowed prior to your departure and a simple one-page agreement prepared and executed."

An audible gasp was heard in the room. Roos was a man not unfamiliar with this kind of money. At his peak, with a net worth exceeding eight figures, raising twenty-five million on twenty-four hours' notice would require some maneuvering, but would be infinitely manageable. The peak was far from sight for Christian Roos, the result of a divorce from his wife and another from a business partner, and living through the largest financial collapse in history along with the real estate meltdown—all had exacted a substantial economic toll on him. The man who preferred steam showers ended up on the receiving end of a bone-chilling bath, administered by the ones closest to him.

Roos finished his third martini with a strong pull, rose from his chair, extended his hand and said, "You have a deal, with one exception. I need another day to raise the necessary funds. I presume you will draw up the agreement. Shall we meet here at The Foot for lunch in two days?"

As he squeezed Roos' hand, Mac smiled. "Don't forget the French iconic fashion designer Coco Chanel, a woman proudly occupying a spot on *Time* magazine's list of *Most 100 Influential People of the Twentieth Century*, and her famous line, 'The best things in life are free, the second best are very expensive.' As I see it, there are only two possibilities for you, first or second place. The former will be free and the latter expensive beyond even your wild imagination."

Mac's words hit home with Roos, but the younger man, who was well known for wearing his heart on his sleeve, tried to camouflage his emotions. "Oh one more thing, I will need a travel assistant. You know, someone to keep records, schedules, take photographs, and to make notification in case of an emergency. However, please be assured that our agreement will stipulate that I and I alone must cross the finish line, after connecting all of the dots on the itinerary. Is that satisfactory?"

Noticeably curious, Mac nonetheless said, "Naturally, I will send you a draft of the agreement tomorrow."

"Speaking of crossing the finish line, one last thing, Mac. A life-long dream of mine has been to run the Great Wall Marathon. As luck would have it, I will be in Beijing on day twenty-two of my trip, which is when the race is scheduled. So you can throw that in your agreement as well, which I will be awaiting with great anticipation."

As he walked out of the Grille Room, passing the eighteenth green, the scene of so much triumph and so much failure, the setting sun was casting beautiful long shadows. The grass was glistening, the sand traps sparkling like South Beach on a clear summer day and the magisterial oak trees were standing like terracotta soldiers guarding the sacred golfing grounds of Winged Foot. One could almost see Phil Mickleson walking off the green after a disastrous double bogey that ended up costing him the 2006 United States Open. Other images of past triumphs and failure arose: Fuzzy Zoeller's waving the white towel as he stood in disbe-lief watching Greg Norman sink a seventy-five-foot putt to force a play-off in the 1984 Championship, and Bobby Jones on his way to winning the 1929 U.S. Open in a thirty-six-hole Monday playoff. Caught in the moment, Roos fondly remembered the heaven-sent rainbow that magi-cally appeared over the clubhouse as Davis Love III was walking up to the eighteenth en route to winning the 1997 Professional Golf Association Championship. Love's father, a longtime golf professional, had passed away earlier in the year.

Despite the magnificence of the scene, all Christian Roos could think of was Katherine Mandu.

# The Set

*"One day everything will be well, that is our hope.*
*Everything's fine today, that is our illusion."*

—VOLTAIRE

Roos arrived at his longtime friend's house in Rye, New York. Frank Harrison's spectacular Long Island Sound waterfront mansion was Roos' home away from home during his visits to Winged Foot.

As Roos walked in the door, Harrison, in his thick New York Italian accent, boomed, "CR, have you lost your mind?" From the moment they met twenty years ago, Harrison could never spit out Christian Roos, it just sounded so ridiculous to him. So Roos became CR to Harrison and only him.

Even though it is a twenty-minute ride from Winged Foot to Harrison's house, the news had already reached him. Traveling like a magic carpet riding a zephyr, the details of the wager crashed upon the shores of the Long Island Sound, washed up on the lawn and stormed into the kitchen, where Harrison was enjoying tequila on the rocks.

"You can't raise that kind of cash in forty-eight hours, and even if you could why take such a risk on such an uncertain outcome."

Roos bellowed, "Frank, Jupiter aligned with Mars. I threw some bait in the water and Mac took it hook, line and sinker. We have him!"

Harrison fired back, "I don't think Jupiter is a planet anymore."

Harrison was probably right and Roos knew it; however, it was one of those rare moments in life. Spontaneously he decided to make a daring proposal and was not about to back down at this point. Emphatically he laid out the logistics, explaining how the trip could easily be done in twenty days. Roos was a devotee of Warren Buffett, who quoted his mentor, Benjamin Graham, at every opportunity. Always invest with a margin of safety. The wager calls for circumnavigating the globe in twenty-five days, which by CR's math provided five days or a twenty percent margin of safety.

Assuming time risk was off of the table, an issue not conceded by Harrison, according to CR, the risks were threefold: sickness, kidnapping or death. The latter could be managed through a twenty-five-million-dollar term life insurance policy. Kidnapping insurance was an active market, which could also be utilized. CR became an expert in the insurance industry through his longtime service as an independent director of a major global public insurance company. Roos knew the risk of sickness was real and inescapable, despite the fact that all necessary precautions would be taken, such as vaccinations, exercise, limited alcohol consumption and proper sleep.

"How are you going to secure a twenty-five-million-dollar life insurance policy, raise the cash for the bet and get vaccinated in forty-eight hours?" asked an incredulous Harrison. "And are you going by yourself? And what about transportation arrangements and necessary visas?"

Roos changed the subject. "How was your night, Frank?"

"Okay. I attended the Irish Catholic Charities fundraiser dinner tonight at St. Murphy's."

Roos, a Catholic with non-Irish roots, was a frequent visitor of the magical Emerald Isle. Playing out of Lahinch and Ballybunion, two of the best golf courses in Ireland, Roos owned a deep and strong affection for Ireland and was utterly disgusted by the severity of the Catholic Church's current unmentionable problems.

"Frank, in all of the years that I have been visiting Ireland, I have never seen a worse situation, one with such open disdain by Catholics for the Church. Do you think it has hit bottom yet?"

"The subject didn't arise," was all that Harrison could come up with in between gulps of tequila.

Roos, still avoiding Frank's direct and troublesome questions, attempted to throw his longtime friend off once more. "Walking up to your door just now, I saw Ajay Jamir next door. I chatted with him briefly."

Bluntly Harrison growled, "Yeah, he moved in a few years ago."

Roos incredulously asked, "Do you know who he is?"

Harrison responded, "My neighbor?"

"You must be joking, Frank. Surely you know that Jamir is Walter Bramble's right-hand man. Someone the Prophet of Peoria, one of the richest men in the world, has described on numerous occasions as the world's smartest mind in the insurance business. He is widely thought to be the person who will ultimately succeed Bramble at the Breckenridge Corporation, a guy, who from scratch less than twenty years ago built the largest insurance company at Breckenridge with assets over thirty-five billion dollars. Jamir is the god of the global insurance world."

Harrison replied, "Well, we were arguing over the fence between our properties, but now everything is cool. He is a great guy. Now stop evading my questions about your bet with Mac."

Back to Frank's original question, CR explained that he could make it happen and of course he would go over the exact itinerary day by day with Harrison, but he needed to move fast. He first had to make a series of phone calls. In the meantime he asked Harrison to start thinking of a syndicate who could invest in the wager and the terms required to get the deal done. If anyone could make this happen it was Harrison. An ex–floor broker, sell-side-coverage trader turned hedge fund manager, Harrison was wired into the New York City investment world better than anyone. Extremely successful, respected and well liked, Harrison was a pro's pro. Roos always thought that if there was someone with a bigger heart than Harrison, someone with a more friendly personality, someone more generous, it was just that he had never met that person. Character is revealed through adversity. Harrison "checked" his divorce, heart attack and business setbacks in the proverbial coat closet and charged on with unabated optimism, confidence and fortitude. Greatness oozed from Harrison like Haut Brion from a Graves Pessac-Leognan Bordeaux grape.

CR plugged in his iPhone charger and went to work.

Christian Roos' first call was to one of his closest girlfriends in Washington, Katherine Mandu. Friends and family nicknamed her Katmandu on account of her birthplace and synergistic name, but Roos affectionately referred to her as simply Kat. The two met several years ago in Washington, D.C. at the twentieth-anniversary celebration of Café Milano. The vogue Georgetown restaurant was anointed as "the place to be" by the apathetic social connoisseurs of the nation's capital, a city traditionally more interested in pork. Every city has one. Which comes first, the chicken or the egg? Are places like Café Milano popular because of the food and ambiance? Or is it the popularity that draws the crowds? Unclear, but what is not, is Minori-born-owner Franco Nuschese's dedication to serving exquisite southern Italian coastal cuisine paired with the finest of Italian wines in a chic setting, plumb with an ultra professional waitstaff. Rain or shine, Café Milano never fails to produce an au courant scene. The evening of November 3, 2012, was certainly no exception. The restaurant was packed liked herrings in a small tin can with D.C. business and political dignitaries and of course beautiful women — of all ages — dressed in skimpy cocktail dresses with plunging necklines and five-plus-inch stilettos protruding from shoes made by the finest Italian craftsman.

As Washington Mayor Vincent Gray handed Franco the keys to his city and proclaimed the date as Café Milano Day, Laurent Menoud, the consummate professional maître de was holding court at the restaurant's tasteful yet modest entrance. Who sat where and when, both of equal importance to the image-conscious patrons, was determined in Laurent's sole judgment. The restaurants premier seating began at table 100, a venue which was located directly in the revelers' sights as they turned right from the reception area and passed the beginning of the famed flamingo-shaped bar on their way into the main dining room. Roos was seated at his usual spot — table 101 — the second along the reputed wall, which contained six prized tables. Joining him that evening were several of his play-hard-work-hard Georgetown friends: Washington and Dallas bar maven McFadden Boycor, insurance executive Tom Cavan and D.C. club proprietor, Tom Kostarelos, the owner of chic local nightclubs, Towns and Gaze. Rounding out the group were: Elgin Link, a crackerjack golf tour guide specializing in the British Isles, chef and proprietor of the trendy W Street Grille, Andrion "Sockeye" Stevens, and big data analytics ace, Razor Bell.

Menoud's top lieutenant, Hector Galvez, was busy spinning home-made tagliatelle bathed in a cream sauce inside a tableside fire-burnt barrel of pecorino topped with Sicily's version of poor man's caviar, *bottarga,* a dense cured fish roe. The socialite crowd slobbered to see and be seen in Café Milano, whereas the menu-savvy locals salivated for the food—one of the restaurant's best-kept secrets.

Kat sauntered into Café Milano solo and sans a reservation, wearing a form-fitting black cocktail dress with matching high heels. Sensing the scene developing, an art form, which he had developed into a science, Franco with a wave of his hand transformed Roos' seven top into an eight top—a magic trick performed nightly at Café Milano. Roos was instantly captivated by Kat's mysterious personality, one he sensed quickly was filled to the brim with charisma and style, but also with intrigue packed tighter than the streets of Le Pre-Saint-Gervais.

From this night on, Kat and Roos became quite close friends, which led to dating and ultimately an intimate yet nonconforming relationship. Frustrated by what he described to friends as unrequited love, Roos became convinced that Kat, the maverick with an unbounded free spirit, was in fact gay. Maybe he was insecure, jealous or just a little gun shy after some rough patches with the female sex, or possibly all three, but it was the inescapable conclusion he reached—in his own mind at least. Roos would soon learn that Kat's unconventional childhood, something she rarely discussed, had created challenging psychological issues. While manageable, they would uniquely and profoundly shape her as an adult.

Roos, a man who spent most of his adult life married, was clearly not familiar with the modern version of the ancient art of dating—and it showed. Being thrown into the belly of the beast upon his relocation to Georgetown threw him for a loop, which took years—and counting—to recover from.

He learned quickly that Kat, a voluptuous blonde with runway model looks, was a wild child of a unique flavor. Always the life of the party, she turned heads in a Mike Tyson right-hand kind of way. A Times New Roman in the streets and a Wingdings in the sheets, she was a rare bird indeed, a true font of all knowledge. A perfect blend of high jinks and stability, hatched and molded in the foothills of the Himalayan Mountains. An expert in the ancient art of yoga, Kat's body could twist, bend and contort in the most beautiful and erotic of ways. Her breathtaking physical creations surely would have made Caligula blush. Roos' favorite move by the yoga star was, without question, the handstand shot. To the amazement and delight of a crowd, or just Roos, Kat would place a shot glass on the floor filled with Petron Anejo, glass circled with salt, sporting a lime. Posing in a full-on handstand, with her beautiful blonde hair inverted, draping her head like an Armani wedding dress, she would tilt her mouth backwards, biting the glass upwards. After licking the salt in a counterclockwise motion with her inestimable tongue, Kat would quaff the tequila, capture the lime with her Marilyn Monroe lips, flick the glass and, with a thrust, jump kick off of her hands to a full standing position. They say tequila has mystical powers and everyone who has seen the Katmandu handstand shot indubitably agrees. Roos needed a travel partner and Kat Mandu was the perfect candidate. Not only was she Roos' number one choice, the woman named Kat Mandu, hailing from the Nepalese capital, prominently held the positions of numbers two and three.

Born in the capital city of Nepal to an English father and an Irish mother, Katherine Mandu's childhood was far from ordinary. Her mother, Aoibheann (pronounced *eve—een*) descended from the family of Saint Edna of Aran, an Irish Saint in the Roman Catholic Church. The patriarch settled in the sixth century in Galway City in the west of Ireland. Increasingly dissatisfied by the Catholic Church, Aoibheann rejected her family's religion of choice for centuries. She fled the Emerald Isle to Kathmandu, the home of Gautama Buddha, the founder of Buddhism. After an intense spiritual experience, Aoibheann found herself, in short order, to be a yoga practitioner and instructor as well as a practicing Buddhist.

In Kathmandu, she would meet and quickly marry Malcolm Mandu, his name modified slightly from his real surname of Mander. As a member of the elite Special Boat Services, the United Kingdom's military equivalent of the Navy SEALs, Mandu saw action in the Falkland Islands campaign off the Argentinean coast. The experience traumatized Mandu, who fled the UK after his service to settle in remote Nepal where he quickly became obsessed with mountain climbing and hunting. Katherine was born the following year.

Tragedy struck the Mandu family in the 1990's. Climbing the South Col route to the top of Mount Everest, Malcolm Mandu reached the south summit at twenty-eight thousand five hundred feet where the team established their base camp for the night. In the morning they planned to take the Hillary Step before making the final ascent to the summit. Malcolm Mandu and his accompanying two-man expedition, positioned less than seven hundred feet from the highest peak in the world, were blindsided by a sudden change in weather. Within minutes the climbers were engulfed in dark storm clouds, fifty-mile-per-hour winds and temperatures that plummeted to thirty-five degrees below zero. In an instant, visibility vanished, as an ominous veil of darkness enveloped Everest like a marine body bag. Trapped in isolation, devastatingly lonely and frightening, the experienced climbers instantly understood the implications of their predicament—an emotion described by Johnny Cash in *Long Black Veil: "Nobody Knows, Nobody Sees, Nobody Knows But Me."* The song was written by Lefty Frizzell but made famous by the Cimmerian musical genius who wore his demons on his guitar pick to the delight of his obsessed die-hard fans, dichotomous devotees unsure whether to shed tears of joy or sorrow for their beloved hero.

The climbers were pinned down in the corpse-lined death zone. In the oxygen deprived one-mile stretch separating the South Col from the summit, the shivering climbers were dragooned into waiting for hypothermia to set in. Unable to offset the loss of body heat, the climber's temperatures quickly dropped below ninety-five degrees Fahrenheit, a level which causes a lack of energy, shallow breathing, slurred speech, clumsiness and poor judgment—characteristics clearly not ideal for extricating oneself from the peak of the tallest mountain in the world. The only redeeming dynamic was the fact that hypothermia creates extreme apathy and, ironically, a lack of concern for one's dire circumstances. Hard to image that dying would feel so peaceful. The three climbers froze within hours and solemnly joined the hundreds of other hopefuls who are buried on Mount Everest like human popsicles.

Understandably traumatized by the death of her husband, Aoibheann and her daughter abruptly left Nepal. Her sister lived in Washington, D.C., which appeared to be the logical destination for the two Mandu women, who never really recovered from the death of Malcolm. The image of Mount Everest haunts Katherine to this day, a place to which she never returned.

Roos reached Kat on the *Schuang Fei*, a luxury yacht anchored in the Washington, D.C. harbor on the Potomac River. Stationed within plain view of the nearby infamous Watergate apartment and office building, the yacht was chockablock full of beautiful girls who were too young to have heard of Richard Nixon, let alone the break-in, which toppled the first United States president in history. The noise of the party precluded voice communication.

Built in Brisbane, Australia, at the Warren Yacht Shipyard, the eighty-seven-foot yacht is generally considered to be the finest sporting boat in the yachting world. Her owners: Mr. Mobile Powers, a tech visionary billionaire who runs mPower, a leading global provider of enterprise software platforms for business intelligence, mobile intelligence and network applications; and Dodge Caverman, another Washington billionaire industrialist who owned Current, an electrical engineering design and build company. Powers and Caverman, close friends, ran a highly organized and exceedingly generous party program for their massive fanatical boosters in the nation's capital. With one colossal gratis fete after the next, the Powers and Caverman well-oiled wingding machine chugged on with literally no end in sight, to the absolute delectation of the Washington, D.C. merrymakers.

On this particular evening, the bow area of the *Schuang Fei* was especially flush with a bevy of bikini-clad smoke shows. Nightly the yacht features women grasping Veuve Clicquot champagne flutes with the tenacity of an American soldier clutching a water bottle on the Bataan Death March, creating the optics of backstage at the Miss Universe Pageant during the swimsuit competition.

In lieu of talking, Roos sent the following text: "Kat, listen carefully. I'm taking you home to the Pashupatinath Temple in Kathmandu! About to embark on an around-the-world trip, which clearly sounds crazy, and I need a sidekick. Will explain the details tomorrow, but if interested get off that boat and on the next train to NYC. Bring your passport, an open mind, and prepare for the trip of a lifetime. A toothbrush and some comfortable shoes might help as well. Let me know if you're coming ASAP. Will have a car pick you up at Penn Station."

Roos' second call was to Bennedict Boulstridge, his longtime friend and main contact in the London insurance industry.

"Bennedict, it's Christian. I don't have a lot of time, but I need to discuss some business with you. Circumstances have arisen suddenly which necessitate a twenty-five-million-dollar term life insurance policy on yours truly, and a similar amount of kidnap coverage on two individuals. Lastly, I need to bind the coverage within thirty-six hours."

Bennedict Boulstridge was a partner in Boulstridge Insurance, a family firm dating to the late eighteenth century, now a global public insurance company. Always a successful diversified underwriter, things changed in the early twentieth century when Boulstridge acquired one of the coveted Lloyd's of London syndicates, along with a management license giving the firm full operating control over a pool of capital. Having a "seat" at the most important insurance "table" in the world launched Boulstridge, and Bennedict, into the upper echelons of the global insurance world.

Based in the insurance center of London's old financial district, Lloyd's of London is the world's specialist insurance market. Unlike many other insurance brands, Lloyd's is not a company; it's a market where members join together as syndicates to insure risks. The origins of Lloyd's date back three hundred and twenty-five years to 1688 and a small coffee shop on Lombard Street run by Edward Lloyd. His shop, down by the Thames River, quickly became the meeting place of ship captains, where the inevitable discussions about insuring ships and cargo blossomed. To this day most global maritime shipping and cargo is insured through one or likely many of the Lloyd's syndicates. Over the years Lloyd's has developed a unique reputation as a result of their enviable performance record. Lloyd's proudly states that in their entire three-hundred-and-twenty-five-year history that none of the syndicates has ever failed to pay a claim. Known as the place where anything can be insured for a price, Lloyd's has written policies for just about everything: Keith Richard's hands, a wine taster's nose, a supermodel's legs, Bruce Springsteen's voice, a footballer's legs and even private space travel. You name it, and Lloyd's has insured it.

"Crikey, Christian, do you realize it is 4 A.M. here in London?" boomed Bennedict. "Why do you require such large and sudden coverage? Is your ex-wife preparing another assault? Or, God forbid, is there a new woman on the scene, who has taken a turn for the worse? Maybe you are sideways with the bookmakers or skipping out on bail? Je t'en prie."

Bennedict, clearly at first peeved by being awakened at such an early hour, was now mind abuzz with the endless possibilities that could be responsible for his dear friend's rather bizarre request.

Even half asleep, Bennedict's superior intellect and wit was on full display as he halfheartedly teased his longtime friend. Trained at Cambridge, then going straight into the business, Bennedict through hard work and determination worked his way up through the corporate ladder at Boulstridge Insurance to the powerful position of Chief Underwriter. How much risk his firm will take and how much they will lay off through other syndicates is a function of how good the transaction looks to the all-important underwriter.

Christian knew that Bennedict would have the authority and limits necessary to place the insurance coverage he needed. So, he anxiously explained the proposition that he and Mac had agreed to at The Foot. Ben's response was concise and extremely logical, as he listed five required items to process the application. "First, a full medical exam performed tomorrow (today in England) with complete blood panel, chest X-ray, EKG, all body vitals and stats, along with the notes from your past two annual physicals. Second, a copy of your itinerary, required for the K and R coverage. Third, the named beneficiaries of the twenty-five-million-dollar life insurance—I assume these will be your investors along with yourself. Fourth, a copy of the wager agreement between you and Mac. Finally, evidence of all required vaccinations."

"Email this material by 10:00 P.M. London time. In the meantime, I will put together a package and start making some calls." Bennedict then eased out, "You are aware of the way kidnap ransom coverage works, correct?"

Roos' insurance company, where he sits as an independent director, was one of the pioneers of this type of coverage in the United States. In the 1980's as the world's economies started opening up for global trade, kidnapping took off as a business. Thousands of executives from United States companies traveling into developing countries posed a huge security risk, a risk that that they would pay dearly to have someone else take. Roos' firm hired several retired CIA agents, Special Forces Army Rangers and Navy SEALs and formed a subsidiary insurance company, which provided the new kidnap policies. During an early meeting, Roos remembered hearing one of the CIA agents responding to a question: "You really do not want to know how we operate. Just trust us when we say we can extract people from anywhere on the planet. The less you know, the better this business will work."

"Bennedict, please hold the line, I have another call coming in."

At that moment the personalized ringtone, Scorpion's monster hit *Rock Me Like a Hurricane* chimed in on Roos' phone. Of course this could only be Kat. Roos grinned as he read the following text:

"I'm on the 10 P.M. Acela arriving Penn Station at 12:43 A.M. See you soon. Have my toothbrush and mind wide open. By the way, I see that Louboutin is having a sale tomorrow. Love"

Roos' chubby fingers pounded out, "Car with the sign Katmandu will be waiting for you at Penn Station"

Back to business with Bennedict, Roos heard that while the process usually takes two to three months, for Christian Robinson Roos, as

Bennedict always referred to him, he would move heaven and earth to make it happen. Appreciative of the effort, Roos, who was ruthlessly knowledgeable about the insurance business, chuckled at the support. Friendship aside, Roos knew from personal experience the lucrative nature of such a policy—after all, he had had fifty million dollars of coverage for years. Roos' quick back-of-the-envelope calculation showed that for a forty-two-year-old male, non-smoker, slightly overweight—well a little more than slightly—twenty-five million of term coverage would cost approximately two hundred thousand dollars per year. The underwriter would normally pay one hundred percent of the first year's premium to the broker. Good for Bennedict, thought Roos. For better or worse, in good times or bad, Roos always believed in supporting friends and he did so without reservation.

Bennedict's last instructions were to stop drinking to minimize the blood-alcohol level and the damage to cognitive ability, both of which would be tested tomorrow in New York. The pair discussed the medical examination, required for such a large amount of coverage.

Bennedict elaborated, "Our carriers will most likely require a psychological examination. They will need to assure themselves that this is not some sort of suicide mission. This can be done over the phone. I will arrange a call tomorrow afternoon with my psychiatrist friend, Dr. Rory Slip. Please control your personal views of psychiatry, which you have shared with me on multiple occasions over drinks, and take the interview seriously, Christian. Regarding the medical exam, are you still in touch with your old roommate?"

Bennedict was referring to Esperanza Roohullah. Of course he was. The two had just returned from Tuscany, where they celebrated her thirtieth birthday. Roos' mind drifted instantly to the gentle rolling hills of the Italian wine country, drenched in brilliant sunshine, the spectacular food and wine and the wonderful company of Dr. Roohullah.

With a Pakistani father and a Venezuelan mother, Esperanza Roohullah was a self-proclaimed "Pakizuelan." A highly intelligent and stunning woman, Roo, as Roos lovingly and tongue-in-cheek called her, was truly unique.

Roos placed his third call and was lucky to catch the second-year resident at Mount Sinai Medical Center, acclaimed internationally for excellence in clinical care. "Good evening, Roo, it's me. I know you're busy, so I'll be brief. What time can you schedule an insurance physical tomorrow? Don't ask, I will explain when I see you. The morning would be better for me."

Esperanza, a woman who chose her words wisely, without ambiguity, responded, "10:30 A.M. No fluids or food, starting now."

The time had reached 1:00 A.M., and Roos' mind refocused on the investment syndicate, which he hoped Harrison was mulling over. There were days when investment managers would scoff at the notion of investing in such a ridiculous security. But this was the twenty-first century and times had changed. Preaching concepts to unsuspecting investors like uncorrelated events, risk-free alpha, hedged barbells and absolute return strategies, the hedge fund managers of the day were busy morphing into shadow bankers who were financing everything imaginable outside of the governing purview of the keystone regulators. Hiding in plain sight, the shadow banking industry, thought to be largely responsible for the 2008 global financial crisis, was marching forward unabatedly. Recently a confused Federal Reserve Bank president candidly responded to a question about the future safety of global financial markets by quoting the Green Hornet, a masked vigilante created by George Trendle and Fran Striker in the 1930's, "Only the shadow knows."

Heading down the upstairs hallway, which in the dark felt like it stretched eternally, Roos only heard the snarl of a wolverine as he approached Harrison's room. The uber–hedge fund star was down for the night. While Roos was debating with himself about whether Harrison had commenced discussions with potential investment partners or not, a text came in from Kat.

"Ten minutes out"

Christian chased Kat up the stairs and into one of the many bedrooms, closed the door and began to catch up with the yoga star.

# 3

## The Deal

*"Always do sober what you said you would do drunk.
That will teach you to keep your mouth shut."*

—ERNEST HEMINGWAY

s Christian rose, the sun was working its way up over the Atlantic Ocean, projecting brilliant sunlight onto Long Island Sound, which peered through his guest bedroom window. Glistening off of Kat's blonde hair, the light illuminated her like an angel on fire as she appeared to float above the sheets. Roos thought for an instant to stay put and blow off his schedule for the day, which included a tour of St. Patrick's Cathedral, a physical and psychological examination, reviewing the agreement coming from Mac, securing around-the-world travel arrangements, including necessary visas, and raising twenty-five million dollars of capital to fund the wager with Mac. But commitments were commitments and, after all, people were hopefully going to be betting substantial sums of money on him. He would learn soon enough that people were betting equally large sums against him.

From the back seat of the car, while cruising down the Hutchinson River Parkway, Roos called Colin Murphy, an American expat from Boston currently residing in Havana, Cuba. Murphy was the retired chief of the State Department's Office of American Citizens Services and Crisis Management (ACS), and the administrator of the Consular Information Program, which informs the public of conditions abroad that may affect their safety and security. Having served in this capacity for ten years, Murphy had a Rolodex brimming with the most important United States Foreign Service contacts around the globe. Post-retirement, Murphy operated a People to People license issued by the Treasury Department's Office of Foreign Assets Control (OFAC). Instituted by President Clinton in the 1990's, revoked by President George W. Bush and eventually reinstated by President Obama, People to People licenses legal travel for United States citizens to Cuba. The license requires travel with a purpose such as education, journalism, or healthcare. Americans interested in tanning while sipping rum on the famous beaches of Playa Paraiso and Playa Sirena, need to make a stop in Mexico City or Montreal before arriving on Fidel Castro's private Idaho.

Last year, Roos spent a week in Havana with Murphy—the most enthralling trip in his lifetime, to the most unique country he had ever seen, as Roos is quick to tell anyone who asks.

"Hey, Christian, what's up?" Colin Murphy said in his thick Boston accent.

"Need a favor, Murph. I have some unexpected travel that has surfaced on extremely short notice. Departing tomorrow for the following countries: Mexico, Cuba, Peru, Brazil, Italy, Turkey, Israel, Saudi Arabia, Iran, India, Nepal, Tibet, of course part of China but not sure if a separate visa is required, China, North Korea and Japan. I will email you the exact itinerary after we hang up, and the passport information for my associate, Katherine Mandu (no middle name), who will be traveling with me. She was born in Kathmandu, Nepal, on August 1, 1984, but she is currently a United States citizen. I realize this is huge, but I need you to work your magic, like only you can, and secure the necessary visas for these countries. We should be okay through Israel, where we are scheduled to arrive on day ten. Slight issue might be Cuba, which we visit on day two of our itinerary. I assume this call finds you on the ground in Havana. We can discuss the situation in more detail in person over some mojitos at the Floridita. One last request, do you think a meeting with Bermudez could be arranged? I know you are close friends with his son."

Roos was referring to the fifty-three-year-old electrical engineer who joined the Cuban Revolutionary Armed Forces and was recently appointed to the position of First Vice President of the Council of

State of Cuba. Since transition in power is something that usually happens through revolution in Cuba, the significance of the appointment is not immediately clear. Cuban President Raul Castro, Fidel's younger eighty-two-year-old brother, announced "No mas" at the time of Bermudez's appointment. Raul will retire after his current presidential term ends in 2018. If Bermudez can convince Fidel that he is still a true believer in the Revolution, it looks like he will succeed Raul to become the first leader of Cuba in the post-Castro era.

Hurricanes begin thousands of miles from land out in the middle of the world's oceans with just a puff, then a zephyr, before gaining strength into a squall and ultimately matriculating into a devastating force on terra firma with the power to change the landscape. For the sake of the long-suffering Cuban people, Roos hoped that Bermudez was the leader who could transform a puff into the majestic winds of freedom. Fascinated by the elusive island whose beauty is hard to see but easy to feel, Roos wondered if Cuba's kaleidoscope was preparing for the mother of all turns? Time will tell, he thought.

"Only you could make such an outlandish and eccentric request, with a straight face, I might add. Of course you know that I will do anything for you, Roos, but realistically the Bermudez meeting is going to be difficult. Possibly I can arrange a meeting with some of his lieutenants and his son. Surely you understand the sensitivity of Bermudez's situation. Travel visas for North Korea and Iran, on such short notice, are going to be extremely challenging. The rest shouldn't be a problem. Naturally, I can't wait to hear the back-story." Murphy's response was schizophrenically interspersed with incredulity and laughter.

Katherine and Christian popped out of the car in Midtown on Fifth Avenue and ducked into the nearest Starbucks. After ordering, Roos made the following observation: "Washington seems so small compared to New York City. If you want to change your life in my hometown, one needs to leave the city limits. But here, all one needs to do is migrate to the next Starbucks."

Kat, gulping a chai tea latte and about to head out on foot up Fifth Avenue on a shopping spree, reached for Roos' Black Card. "Pick me up at Roberto Cavalli around 2 P.M.?"

"Perfect, please remember to get me some casual, nondescript gear—the kind of clothing that will blend in in a duck blind—like an Eastern Shore of Maryland's hunter's camouflage."

Leaving Starbucks, Roos walked into New York City's haven of Christianity, occupying the corner of Fifth Avenue and 50th Street like no other structure could in the money-crazed city. One of the most important Catholic sanctuaries in the United States, St. Patrick's Cathedral stands, in the words of Cardinal Timothy Dolan, the Archbishop of New York, as a "supernatural home, where people of all faiths are welcome to drop in for a hit of the divine."

In the mid-nineteenth century, the only Roman Catholic Church in the New World, Prince of the Apostles, St. Peter, was located on Barclay Street in downtown Manhattan. St. Peter's was built in 1785, a time that counted two hundred Catholics and one priest. The idea to build a new Cathedral was the brainchild of Archbishop John Hughes. Hard to imagine, but in 1850 the plan for St. Patrick's was dubbed "Hughes' Folly" on account of the near-wilderness location on what would become Fifth Avenue and 50th. Despite being so far from the city, the cathedral, designed by James Renwick, opened for "business" in 1879, a mere six hundred and eighty-nine years after the original St. Patrick's Cathedral in Dublin celebrated its first mass. Or nine hundred and eighty-nine years after the first church was built on St. Patrick's site in the capital city of the Republic of Ireland, one thousand four hundred and twenty-nine years after the fifth-century Romano-British Christian missionary, St. Patrick, first baptized a person at the address which would eventually become Eight St. Patrick's Close in Dublin, Ireland.

Having been to St. Patrick's in Dublin on numerous occasions, Roos could not help but reflect on the stark contrast in the timelines of the Catholic Church's experience in Europe and America. This thought did not linger long, and as per usual, was quickly excommunicated as Roos' mind focused on how St. Patrick's had deteriorated since his last visit, slightly over five years ago. Roos flashed back to the only time a Pope has ever visited St. Patrick's in New York. Seated in the last pew of the church, the perfect figurative location for the divorced member of the Catholic Church, Roos recalled listening to His Holiness Pope Benedict XVI, on April 19, 2008, call upon everyone present to become a Herald of Hope. As he walked down the marble aisle toward the altar, Roos mused how prescient the Pope's mandate was in relation to his wager with Mac.

The roof was leaking, the exterior was crusted with grit, the magnificent stained-glass windows splitting, the plumbing, air and electrical systems all failing and the bricks were literally cracking. St. Patrick's was showing her age and, in the words of Cardinal Dolan, was crumbling with her survival at stake. Continuing down the aisle Roos took a slight detour and stopped by the donation box adorned by the Virgin Mary and became a Cathedral Builder as he pulled out his wallet and wrote a five-thousand-dollar check, payable to the St. Patrick's Cathedral Restoration Fund. Always a fan of mathematic, Roos calculated his contribution to be one thirty-five thousandth of the one hundred and seventy-five-million-dollar target. "Need some more believers, preferably with some cash." Roos' murmuring could be heard echoing off of the cathedral's spires looming above, like an eagle's talons seconds before touching down on an unsuspecting soon-to-be corpse. After, all St. Peter's in Rome was neither built in a day nor without the assistance of the creation of purgatory. Talk about marketing.

As Roos continued to make his way down St. Patrick's well-worn center aisle, he noticed a sole person sitting in the first pew. The woman's posture was perfect, something rarely seen in American religious houses of worship, certainly not in a Catholic Church, Roos thought. Her head was motionless as she stared at St. Patrick's majestic altar, almost as if the guest—unsure of either proper etiquette or appropriate custom—was being respectful in the only way she knew how, utter deference. As Roos approached the first pew he turned slowly to his left and made eye contact with one of the most beautiful women he had ever seen. For most of his life, Roos erroneously focused almost exclusively on one of two definitions of beauty—the quality of being physically attractive. Several expensive and emotional trips down this branch of lovers' lane had finally broadened Roos' thought process to incorporate the other infinitely more important definition of beauty—the qualities in a person that give pleasure to the senses or the mind.

The woman sitting before him owned both in spades—Roos knew it. He felt and saw something foreign to him. Just like the woman who was paying respect, Roos stood motionless and speechless himself, opting to stare not at the altar, but rather into the Japanese woman's captivating dark eyes. Unquestionably she was the product of the homogeneous Japanese gene pool—thousands of years in the making, a distinctly proud culture, witness to turbulence and bloody conflict for much of her history. None of this was evident in the woman's peaceful demeanor, which displayed eye-of-the-hurricane characteristics. Roos marveled at the woman's magnificence—exquisitely refined and perfected through generations of a civilization who pulled through incalculable adversity and hardship. But who doesn't suffer on this cruel planet, Roos asked himself. He answered his own question: nobody does so with the stoicism, unified resolve and solidarity of the Japanese people. Ringing in his ears were his father's words: "Determination, intelligence and hard work win out."

"My name is Christian Roos. Whom do I have the pleasure of meeting?"

Like a blossoming flower, the woman rose, showcasing her conservative oxblood Burberry translucent vinyl dress and black grainy calf Jimmy Choo leather boots. Her honey-colored Burberry gabardine vinyl trench coat and cashmere classic Burberry checked scarf were draped over her left sleeveless arm. She extended her right arm toward Roos, who wasted little time in clasping his less than steady hand around her petite delicate fingers, which looked almost too fragile to hold. Feeling nothing but warmth and safety, Roos squeezed on, eliciting an exquisite sound so lovely and sweet it brought a pacific smile to his face, music to his ears and a sense of enchantment to his mind.

"My name is Sakura Nagasawa. It is very nice to meet you, Mr. Roos."

"Please call me Christian."

Sakura, whose English was clearly not too strong, bowed her head in embarrassment. "Mr. Roos, I did not intend on calling you another religion. Please accept my apologies."

Roos immediately interjected, "Not at all. My first name is Christian—it just happens to be a name of a religion. Nothing more—nothing less. Does that make sense?"

Sakura smiled so broadly that the bridge of her nose crinkled up in the cutest manner. She continued in her increasingly soft and quiet voice, "Yes, Christian, I now understand."

Sakura Nagasawa was born in Kyoto, Japan, a uniquely mystical city that was the Imperial Capital of the Japanese Empire for nearly one thousand years up until the late nineteenth century. Located in the middle of the country, Kyoto is not far from either the Sea of Japan or the Pacific Ocean. The city is known for an abundance of cherry blossoms—the most sacred of all Japanese treasures and the meaning of Sakura's name—and for the prestigious Kyoto University, widely considered the greatest research institute in all of Japan. Its famous ancient sites and temples attract people from all over the world. Kinkakuji, a Shogun retirement community turned Zen Buddhist temple, stands prodigiously among two thousand other revered sites as the unquestioned master. Sakura's father, Takakazu Nagasawa, earned his undergraduate and PhD in Polymer Science from Kyoto University and went on to a distinguished career at Osaka-based Takeda Pharmaceuticals, where he was instrumental in developing polymer coatings used in sustained-release drug-delivery systems. Following in her father's footsteps, Sakura studied engineering at Kyoto University. Graduating near the top of her class was sufficient to land a prominent position in Sony Corporation's management training program in Tokyo.

"What brings you to NYC?" Roos inquired.

Sakura politely responded, "I am on vacation. Two nights in Washington and two in New York City. Flying back to Tokyo tomorrow."

Roos curiously asked, "By yourself?"

The woman with lustrous long black hair, porcelain skin and a perfectly shaped face, which exuded pride, honor and goodness replied, "Yes."

Roos thought quickly. "I have some meetings this morning but should be finished by noon. Would you like to have lunch with me?"

Sakura's nose crinkled again and she followed up enthusiastically, "Christian, I would very much be honored to join you for lunch."

"Great. Meet me at Le Bernardin at 155 West 51st Street at noon. The restaurant is located just three blocks from St. Patrick's. I assume you eat seafood?"

Sakura deferentially replied, "Yes I do. I will go back to my hotel room and change."

Roos, giggling to himself, let out a big smile and said, "Sakura Nagasawa, you are impeccably dressed and perfectly appropriate for Le Bernardin. But, I will need to throw on a coat and tie, which I will absolutely do. Looking forward to lunch and hearing all about your trip."

And with that, Roos gave Sakura a hug followed by the European two-cheek kiss, which left his new friend in a state of confusion. Was she thinking of crying, slapping Roos or just being happy? In the formal ancient ways of the Japanese, one simply never knows the correct protocol. But Sakura appeared okay with the situation, at least in Roos' distinctly American mind.

Roos' final comment, "See you at noon," could be heard echoing throughout the church as he triumphantly marched down the aisle—again.

On the street corner, Roos pulled out his iPhone, scrolled through his contacts and hit send when Ben's named surfaced. As the longtime maître de of Le Bernardin, one of the toughest reservations to secure in New York City, or the world for that matter, Ben wielded herculean power among the sophisticated and demanding New York City dining crowd.

"Hi, Ben. Christian Roos here. How are you, my friend?"

Never one to chitchat, Ben tersely but politely responded, "Very well. When would you like to come in?"

Roos floated, "Noon today for lunch."

Unfazed, Ben responded, "Christian, it is 9:30 A.M. But for you I will make it happen, of course. I assume it will be you and a beautiful exotic lady."

Roos knew Ben really didn't care too much about him. Why should he, after all it was just business to him. Sure, slipping him a Jackson, Grant or Benjamin, depending upon the desperate nature of the circumstances, helped to ingratiate himself. But, Roos thought, make no mistake, life is all about the value added. Roos ordered nice bottles of wine, stuff waiters may care about, but with Ben it was all about the eye candy.

"Yes, Ben. I will be joined by Sakura Nagasawa, who is visiting from Tokyo."

As he walked out of St. Patrick's onto Fifth Avenue, a call came in from Harrison: "Here's the deal. I have three hedge funds, Net Neutrality Holdings, Wolfram Global Partners and Sixty Two Thousand LLC, in for five million each. My fund will throw in five million as well. You must round out the twenty-five million by putting up five million personally and arrange for the twenty-five million in life insurance with each of the five parties named as equal beneficiaries. No need for the kidnapping and or ransom insurance on our part. But, please knock yourself out. The investment group will give you the industry-standard twenty percent promote, an additional five million, payable upon a successful victory in the wager against Mac. Of course we will need to see the agreement between you and Mac, which must list the four hedge funds as participants. Lastly, the group requires daily updates on your progress, delivered to me via WhatsApp. We trust that confidentiality is a given. Please let us know if these terms are acceptable."

Roos responded, "Deal is perfectly acceptable. I will forward the draft agreement along with wire instructions. Thank you." Anyone within earshot would have heard Roos laughing as he muttered, "Standard twenty percent promote? What has happened to the investment industry?"

Dr. Roohullah greeted Roos with a huge smile and hug, which the excitable patient converted into a deep French kiss. Wasting little time, Roos was rolling, rubbing and probing his lips and tongue all over the beautiful Pakizuelan, passing through her luscious lips and slightly oversized mouth. If Allergan, the manufacturers of Botox, ever needed a cover girl to showcase their product, it was Roohullah. But then again Ezperanza's lips were natural, so more deception in advertising will just have to take a number. Pushing Roos away and reminding him that this was not Tuscany, Esperanza proceeded to bark orders at him. "Strip down to your boxers."

"Where should I put my clothes, doctor?" asked Roos.

Roohullah responded with an inside joke the two shared, "Oh, over there in the corner on top of mine." The two had lived together in Georgetown while Esperanza was finishing her fourth year at Georgetown Medical School and in short order developed an unconventional relationship, filled with high jinks.

"Heart sounds perfect, blood pressure 115 over 74 is nice, cannot feel any organs, at least the ones I am looking for. Roos, don't start. Stomach feels soft, no swelling in your ankles, eyes and skin look clear with a strong color, lastly your weight is down 15 pounds to 180, which is much better given your 70-inch height. Up on the table and roll to your right. Prostate feels smooth, good. Any problems with the plumbing?"

"Well the scope of my plums are quite inconsequential, oh well alright, where should I begin?"

Shaking her head as she walked out of the room, Esperanza instructed the nurse to take blood, administer an EKG, chest X-ray and give the appropriate vaccination shots. "I have your last two annual physical results and will email the blood work, chest tests and my exam notes over to Bennedict Boulstridge in a few hours."

Roos thought to himself, women! His endless analysis and fascination with the female sex was a dangerous obsession that had created so much happiness and so much sadness for him over the years. Roos wondered to himself just how in the world it was all going to end up. The unknown was both intriguing and scary. Grasping for solidarity,

Roos was reminded of a quote from Freud, "The great question that has never been answered, and which I have not yet been able to answer, despite my thirty years of research into the feminine soul, is 'What does a woman want?'"

His daily internal debate on the subject would have to wait. The anticipated phone call from psychiatrist Dr. Rory Slip, reached Roos.

"Good afternoon, Christian Roos, this is Dr. Slip. I trust that Bennedict Boulstridge told you about the psychological examination that the insurance company is requiring as a part of your application for a rather large and sudden amount of life insurance."

"Yes, of course. As you can image, I am in a bit of a rush, so if we could do this as quickly as possible I would be most appreciative." Roos' voice sounded irritated, as he normally did when faced with these types of situations. It is certainly no secret that men are chronically under-treated for mental illness versus women. The reason is simple. Men see mental illness as a weakness or failing, while women correctly under-stand that mental illness is in fact a disease, which can be successfully treated with medication. Unquestionably, Roos was deeply rooted in the male camp on this issue.

The doctor then proceeded to ask Roos a series of questions.

Slip, "Are you thinking and or talking about killing yourself?"

Roos, "No."

Slip, "Are you writing and or talking about death in general?"

Roos, "No, but in the course of writing my online magazine, from time to time the subject of death does come up."

Slip, "I see. Do you own a gun?"

Roos, "Not since the divorce when I sold the Eastern Shore of Maryland estate, which housed a small arsenal of shotguns, handguns and rifles."

Slip, "Where are they now?"

Roos, "No idea, along with many other lost items."

Slip, "What medications are you currently taking?"

Roos, "Other than a baby aspirin daily, none on a regular basis. But I do travel internationally quite often, when I take Ambien 12.5 mg SR.

Occasionally, I pop a 20 mg Cialis," Roos said, winking, "It gives me something to talk about on the golf course from time to time."

Slip, "Have you been the victim of abuse?"

Roos, "No, but I have been married."

Slip, "Have you ever been treated for depression or bipolar disorder?"

Roos, "Do my ex-wife's armchair diagnoses and suggestions count?"

Slip, laughing for the first time, "Well I guess it depends upon what she came up with."

Roos, "Nothing worth repeating. Dr. Slip, the answer to your question is definitely no."

Slip, "Do you suffer from alcohol dependence?"

Roos, "Only when I stop drinking."

Slip: "Ever attended Alcoholics Anonymous?"

Roos, "No."

Slip, "Do you have feelings of hopelessness?"

Roos, "No."

Slip, "Are you withdrawing from others?"

Roos, "I assume traveling around the world in twenty-five days does not count? No, I am definitely not withdrawing from humanity. I am fortunate to have so many wonderful friendships with a very diverse group of individuals. These relationships have proved to be extremely helpful during my transition over the past five years."

Slip, "Tell me about your transition."

Roos kicked himself for not just answering "no." How many lawyers had told him, just before a deposition, to answer the questions with as few words as possible. And never discuss things outside of the scope of the question. "I sold my business in 2008, a year which saw my new business fail. Sold my caboodle of homes around the country, sold the Gulfstream and reconnoitered back to my roots in Washington, D.C. I am sure some would say the adjustment would have killed most people. I disagree, and besides, I am not most people."

Slip, "Have you or any family member ever attempted suicide?"

Roos, "No."

Slip, "Last question, Mr. Roos. Why did you enter into this wager calling for you to travel the world in twenty-five days, while visiting some extremely dangerous destinations?"

Roos, "Well, certainly not for the money, not to say winning ten million dollars would not be a kick. Let me put it this way. As a result of my own extraordinary personal life experiences, which have included both good and evil, honesty and dishonesty, joy and sorrow, success and failure, love and hate, I need to believe in the formers, all of them, to make sense of the world that I find myself living in. Honestly, at this point in my life, I do not really know how I want to spend my remaining years. My hope is that this trip will provide the perfect answer to this important question, which I have been struggling to find an answer to. Besides, it will be an experience of a lifetime, one that I hopefully can use to educate my fellow Americans about the overwhelming goodness of humanity, which I believe still exists in the world. Lastly, unquestionably it will make for a great story, one which yours truly will no doubt tell to anyone who will listen."

Slip, "Good luck, Christian Roos. If you need to talk, please call my cell phone."

Clean from his medical examinations, Roos hopped in a cab and headed straight for Michelin Three-Star Le Bernardin's fishpond, where iconic seafood chef Eric Ripert continues to break new ground underwater. Having recently undergone a makeover, the Parisian seafood restaurant opened in 1986 by the Le Coze brothers, later taken over by Frenchman Ripert who added Spanish and Asian flavors, was looking and smelling better than ever as Roos and Sakura breached the entrance.·

The renovated interior's *pièce de résistance* is an oil on canvas triptych painting covering the entire west side of the restaurant. Titled *Deep Water #1*, Brooklyn-based artist Ral Ortner's brilliant piece depicting a stormy ocean siphons patrons from their steel-framed brown leather chairs out to sea like a rip tide. One almost hears the squawks of seagulls as the flock circles a deep-sea fishing vessel, searching for scraps. The scene brilliantly sets the stage for an epic culinary seafood experience.

Shortly after the couple was seated, the waiter brought a complimentary pre-lunch tidbit trio comprised of candied walnuts, caramelized popcorn and traditional Japanese rice crackers wrapped in seaweed. Roos braced himself as Sakura passed one of the crackers through her natural pale pink plump lips. Chewing completed, Sakura leaned inward across the table and whispered, "I never believed I could taste such a lovely Japanese delicacy in America."

Roos just stared in disbelief at both the excruciating details which restaurants like Le Bernardin perfect and to Sakura's sincere but surprising revelation about a cracker.

Roos explained to Sakura over lunch his bet with Mac and his upcoming schedule. "I plan on being in Tokyo by the end of the month. By chance will you be there?"

Not needing to look at her calendar Sakura responded, "Yes."

A confident Roos stated, "Well then, I will reach out to you prior to my arrival."

After dining on Beausoleil oysters, Nantucket Bay scallops with sea urchin and poached halibut, Roos paid the check and the couple exited the restaurant. Roos again attempted his compulsory hugging and kissing. This time Sakura preempted Roos with a soft handshake. After exchanging contact information, Roos offered Sakura the first cab that pulled up, but she refused, insisting that Christian take it. As the cab pulled into traffic, Roos looked on in amazement as Sakura stood at attention on the sidewalk, simply watching as he disappeared into the Manhattan mayhem. Only her head moved, following the movement of the vehicle.

As Sakura Nagasawa's image faded in the distance, Roos' mind morphed into a pinball machine with his thoughts the pinball.

Breaking the silence with a full tilt was the gruff New York cab driver who asked, "Where to?" Roos responded, "Roberto Cavalli, 63rd and Madison, please."

As promised, Mac emailed Roos the one-page wager agreement, with the itinerary as the sole exhibit. After a quick scan, Roos forwarded the document to Harrison, who in turn sent it on to the three participating hedge funds. Roos also copied his longtime lawyer, Kevin Kinsale, on the email. The only part of the agreement that caught Roos' attention was the arbitration clause. Mac astutely anticipated the potential differences of opinion as to the wager's outcome and shrewdly included the following language: "All parties unconditionally agree that the certification of the successful completion of the itinerary listed in Exhibit A will be determined by the Honorable Henry A. Hebblethwaite. He, in his sole judgment, will certify the winner and loser of the wager."

As a member of the Winged Foot Golf Club, Roos knew the retired Chief Justice of the United States Court of Appeals for the Second Circuit and could personally attest that the Judge was a highly distinguished man of unquestionable integrity who possessed an unassailable character. Judge Hebblethwaite was a top candidate to matriculate to the United States Supreme Court, but unfortunately the ultraconservative jurist fell victim to Machiavellianism, the unwritten code of honor in the nation's capital. Showcasing a healthy dose of class and dignity, Hebblethwaite took the high road—the road less traveled in Washington, D.C.—and wrote a letter to the president announcing the withdrawal of his name for consideration to an appointment to the highest court in the land. The Judge presided over thousands of important cases during his celebrated career, but the one which popped into Roos' mind as the decision he is best known for was the overturning of a lower court's acquittal of Antonio "The Widowmaker" DeFilippo. A mobster who was tried on three capital murder charges, the "Widowmaker" was rumored to have killed over one hundred men during his career as a professional assassin. The Judge in the lower court that acquitted DeFilippo made a critical evidentiary ruling. DeFilippo confessed to the crimes in a legally binding sworn statement. When asked if he killed the three victims in cold blood with a sawed-off shotgun, "The Widowmaker" answered, "Yeah I whacked the bastards. They had it coming and each one knew why. I could see it in their hugger-mugger eyes busy blinking panic and guilt. I am a hit man, that is what I do for a living."

At trial, DeFilippo's attorney moved to suppress the confession. He produced a psychiatrist who convinced the Judge that DeFilippo suffered from a severe case of Dissociative Identity Disorder, DID (previously known as multiple personality disorder). The disease is characterized by the presence of two or more distinct or split identities or personality states that continually have power over the person's behavior. The Judge agreed that the defendant was the victim of extreme abuse at the hands of his alcoholic father and suffered from DID, and he bought the argument that the defendant's confession was made by one of his other personalities. He threw out the confession. With the district attorney's key piece of evidence gone, the jury deadlocked and DeFilippo walked. The State of New York appealed the decision to the United States Court of Appeals for the Second Circuit. Judge Hepplethwaite cast the deciding third vote reversing the lower court's throwing out of the confession, and wrote the majority opinion, which stands today as the highest standing precedent on DID. DeFilippo was convicted at the retrial. The United States Supreme Court refused to grant DeFilippo's request for certiorari. He is currently serving three life sentences, without the possibility of parole.

In his mid-seventies, the Judge now spends his days with family, reading and writing books, giving speeches, mainly to law schools · around the country, and playing golf at his beloved Foot. Roos felt safe with this choice as the ultimate arbitrator of the wager and was confident that his partners would be as well. Besides stamped passports and visas, Roos planned to take both a photograph and video of himself in front of each of the thirty sacred sites. To him it was cut and dried.

Roos called his longtime broker Daniel DaRosso. "Hey, Dan, I need some cash. Please send five million dollars out of my margin account to Continent Bank. I will text you the wire instructions."

Bennedict Boulstridge, sporting the required jacket and tie, walked into the grand entrance to Lloyd's of London bright and early. The building, an interesting combination of concrete, steel and glass, has a three-story atrium running through a majority of the footprint. The epicenter of the old-line British insurance industry, stocked with open escalators and exposed ductwork, looks and feels befitting for a California social media company's headquarters. Bennedict walked past the famous Lutine Bell named after the French frigate that surrendered to the British at Toulon in 1793, shortly before sinking with an estimated one million pound sterling cargo onboard. Lloyd's had insured the ship and paid the claim. In 1859, a salvage attempt recovered the ship's bell, which was moved to Lloyd's of London, where it is rung to signify significant events and losses, though relegated to ceremonial status these days. Bennedict made his way to the second floor, where he approached the chief underwriter of Buckingham Insurance, Beardsley Cripplegate.

"Morning, Mr. Cripplegate." Bennedict always took a formal approach with Lloyd's of London syndicates such as Buckingham.

"It is indeed, Mr. Boulstridge," was the elder statesman's, quid pro quo.

"I have an interesting risk for your consideration. My firm is taking half of the twenty-five-million-dollar term insurance and an equal ratio of the kidnap and ransom coverage, which carries the same face. I would like to offer you the balance."

Cripplegate put down his spot of tea and *Financial Times*, swirled in his chair around to his desk, his prodigious stomach just barely missing kissing the burled mahogany and began reading the package. Within three minutes, Cripplegate swung back to face Bennedict, an obligatory pivot the swag-bellied Englishman needed to fine-tune over the years to accommodate for his girth, which grew proportional to his bank account and sense of self-importance.

"We will take the twelve and a half million dollars of term insurance in exchange for a one-hundred-thousand-dollar premium, with the following stipulation: coverage is excluded in Iran and North Korea. We will pass on the kidnap and ransom piece. Besides paltry premiums, I just find the business unworthy and disreputably tawdry. We do not want to be involved in negotiating with kidnappers and or terrorists, period—end of sentence. I am assuming you are okay with our participation on the life piece alone?"

"Of course, thank you. We will take the entire piece. Easier that way, if the unfortunate happens. Certainly do not need too many cooks in the kitchen when talking to some of these unsavory characters."

With that, Cripplegate swung back to his desk, grabbed his syndicate's official stamp and with an authoritarian move, he stripped the package. An old-school, yet mandatory move, which bound his firm to the insurance contract, a financial commitment which has been honored by Lloyd's of London—without exception—for almost four centuries.

# The Launch

Quashing any second thoughts, an emotional Roos reached out of the back window of the Uber car and punched the four-digit code into the box attached to the black wrought-iron gates guarding the north entrance to the Winged Foot Golf Club. As the car slowly proceeded toward the clubhouse, Roos marveled at the huge stone boulders made of Fordham Gneiss that lined the driveway along the east course, imagining what they had seen over the years.

Lost in thought, Roos inadvertently spit out, "Dinosaurs and Titleist Pro V1 golf balls, but not at the same time."

The list of attendees at the deal-closing lunch at Winged Foot began to expand. Besides Roos and Mac, several others were piling out of cars in the Winged Foot parking lot: Judge Hebblethwaite, Frank Harrison and representatives from the three hedge funds—Greg Powers from Net Neutrality Holdings LLC, Stone Baxter from Wolfram Global Partners and Mark Elliott from Sixty Two Thousand Capital, all friends of Harrison. The headcount was seven, before the lawyers. With the exception of the Judge, who braved the meeting alone, everyone else brought legal counsel. Mac and Roos knew that thirteen people signing documents in the Grille Room, possibly arguing, would be potential grounds for expulsion from the club. Therefore, the pair arranged for a private room where the deal could be sealed.

After the standard greetings, the parties all executed the document in quick fashion. The only major change was the addition of the twenty-five-million-dollar life insurance policy, which was marked as Exhibit B. Of course the lawyers felt compelled to request a few tweaks here and a few twists there. Everyone was satisfied with Judge Hebblethwaite, but the group insisted the factors that he would utilize in reaching his determination be written out in the agreement. So the photograph and video, each with Apple's iPhone time signature along with the stamped passport and visas, became memorialized in the document as the evidence required for the Judge's decision.

Roos' lawyer, Kevin Kinsale, added the twenty percent promote, which his client would earn upon a successful completion. He also added language for the purpose of the avoidance of doubt, stating that any and all modes of transportation were allowable and no movement by any means was restricted.

Kinsale, who had known his client and friend for over three decades, announced to the group, "You may not know Roos as well as I do. This man is an extreme competitor. I could see him on a camel, elephant, submarine or even one of Richard Branson's spaceships if that is what it takes to get back here in twenty-five days. Just making sure we are all on the same page, gentlemen."

Roos laughed, thanked Kinsale and threw out, "One last thing. Mac, while I was in the city yesterday for my insurance physical, I visited St. Patrick's Cathedral, the number one spiritual destination on my itinerary. I trust you are okay with the day-ahead start?" Roos was a little uncomfortable asking such a patently obvious rhetorical question, but confirmation of this potentially deal-threatening technical issue was of paramount importance.

Rising from the table, Mac extended his hand and said, "Of course, Christian. By the way, I have already told Cardinal Dolan that I plan on donating my winnings, a sum of twelve and one-half million dollars, to the Church's renovation fund. But please do not despair, he promised me that neither God nor he would be rooting against you."

Roos' mathematical mind asked, "Twelve and a half million? Don't you mean twenty-five million?"

"What? Are you the only one allowed to have a partner?" Mac asked.

Roos, clearly curious and somewhat concerned by Mac's disclosure, returned to the question of God and the Cardinal rooting against him, "Well if they are, no doubt they will be mistakenly rooting against one of my doppelgängers." And with that quip, Christian Robinson Roos vanished from The Foot like a whirling dervish, hearing the faint last words from Mac: "Don't drink the water, Christian, I hear it clashes with the Kool-Aid."

Charles MacCormick, channeling Clark Kent, dashed for the nearest phone booth. Cell phone usage was strictly prohibited at Winged Foot, except in the phone booths located in the clubhouse's front lobby. How ironic that the only place one can make a cell phone call is in a phone booth equipped with a working telephone. Mac, who was instrumental in passing the regulation during his tenure as president, wondered to himself as he pulled on the door, what next? Only reading the newspaper in the bathroom?

Scrolling through his contacts, Mac hit call when Carl Strange's name appeared.

A distinctly British voice, one that conveyed confidence and intelligence, instantly answered, "Strange here."

"It's Mac, I have a business proposition for you. Meet me at Jimmy's Pizza in an hour."

The nondescript Mamaroneck restaurant was as far from The Foot as possibly imagined. The food was excellent and the atmosphere beyond discreet, a perfect setting for an important clandestine meeting. And besides, despite his sophistication and worldliness, Mac knew all too well that his longtime friend and business associate was not a club man.

Carl Strange grew up in the north of England, during the late 1950's and 1960's. Life in Britain during this unfortunate time was nasty, brutish and short. Strange, when growing up, liked to coin a phrase, in fact it was the nearest he got to any sort of coins at all, for there wasn't any money, anywhere. World War II had left the country bankrupt and, in addition, the emerging economies had destroyed the industrial base of his hometown. The once thriving industries of iron and steel, coal mining and shipbuilding, were gone or almost gone.

Strange's family could not escape this grinding poverty. His mother, a bookmaker, purchased the family's clothes from a grimy Army and Navy store. Until he was seventeen, Strange attended school dressed either as a Japanese admiral, kamikaze pilot or German SS officer, which painfully left deep permanent psychological scars.

By his late teens, Strange quickly appreciated that the best thing to come out of his birthplace was the motorway to London where he knew, by common consent, the streets were paved with gold. Despite gold's ridiculously low prevailing price of the day, Strange knew that London was immeasurably a wealthier town than his birthplace, and once he arrived there, it was going to take a legion of wild horses to drag him back.

During the dark and lonely days of his childhood in Newcastle, Strange sought refuge in music. Sitting alone in his cramped below-ground bedroom, he managed to teach himself how to play the guitar. His driving influence was the new band from Liverpool, featuring four mop-haired lads wearing jackets and ties, who called themselves the Beatles. When Strange hit the streets of London in the 1960's, he made his way to pop central Soho, where he formed the rock band, Coin Jam. Struggling and sorely needing money to pay the bills, Strange temporarily found work as an actor and model. Experiencing a moment of clarity, Strange applied and was accepted to Oxford University, where he studied economics. Upon graduation he joined the London office of Springer and Waldron as a junior credit analyst. Equipped with a strong work ethic, superior intelligence and a tremendous instinct for the financial markets, Strange quickly rose up the ranks at the investment bank. Positions of senior credit analyst, head of U.K. fixed income and chief economist for Europe fell like dominoes at the feet of the idiosyncratic and extraordinary man from the north of England.

But his big break came in 1978. Strange's roommate at Oxford was an Iranian named Pooria Namdar, the son of a prominent cleric and a close friend of Shah Mohammad Reza Pahlavi, better known as the Shah of Iran. Strange had the interesting opportunity to visit with Namdar and his family in Tehran on several occasions during his years at Oxford. By chance of the freshman room assignment lottery, Strange became intimately familiar with the mysterious Persian powerhouse. It was through this store of knowledge that Strange was able to appreciate the significance and ultimate consequences of the unrest, which began to build in 1977. Demonstrations, which began in the hundreds, quickly spread to the thousands in the country's capital city of Tehran. Ultimately the conflict would spin out of control leading to the Iranian Revolution in 1978, which brought Ayatollah Khomeini to power, sending the Shah packing. Anticipating the coup, Strange keenly understood the uncertainty that would be created in the marketplace by such an event. At the time, Iran ranked third in the world for oil reserves and production. Strange flew to New York City to meet with the powerful investment committee of his firm and boldly recommended buying oil. In less than fifteen months between 1978 and 1979, oil tripled in price from fifteen to forty-five dollars a barrel. As 444 Americans were held hostage in Tehran, Springer and Waldron, along with their clients, profited wildly. Strange was handsomely rewarded with total compensation of three million dollars in 1979, by a factor of five, his best year ever.

Shortly afterwards, Strange was tapped to become the firm's Global Chief Investment Strategist, a plum position located in New York City at Springer and Waldron's global headquarters. The kid from Newcastle, who was now able to phrase more than coin, was on the move again.

His market calls became the stuff of legend. In 1982 he predicted the peak in interest rates, sending a buy signal on the global fixed income and equity markets. While vacationing in the Galapagos Islands in late September of 1987, unable to access phone service, Strange commandeered an Ecuadorian fisherman to hand deliver his recommendation to sell equities. Traveling by ferry, car and ultimately airplane out of Quito, the journey to New York City took eight days. The fisherman, looking like an overanxious Halloween trick-or-treater, arrived at the Wall Street headquarters of Springer and Waldron less than a month before the famous October crash, which saw the Dow Jones Industrial Average drop over twenty percent in a single day.

But it was his prediction of the peak in the U.S. equity markets in 2000 that immortalized Carl Strange. As a result of his call he was invited to deliver the 2001 keynote speech at the World Economic Forum in Davos, Switzerland, the most prestigious gathering of the globe's financial mavens. On account of the Forum taking place during the peak snow month of January every year, in typical fashion, Strange skydived into the town, wearing a *Sgt. Pepper's Lonely Heart's Club Band* bodysuit, streaming red, white and blue smoke. When asked about his exploit, Strange matter-of-factly answered with a question, "Have you seen the traffic?"

His feats outside of his professional life were equally mercurial and impressive. Raising money for 9/11 victims, Strange swam the twenty-eight and a half miles around Manhattan Island, in a clockwise circum-navigation—against the tide—in less than twenty-four hours. When Hurricane Katrina devastated the southeastern United States, Strange played in a seventy-two-hour marathon charity polo match at the West Palm Polo Club, going through eight horses in the process.

Inside the halls of the mighty Springer and Waldron, Strange out-landishly became known as the World's Most Interesting Man of Finance. Despite his success and notoriety, Strange remained a mysterious man who kept to himself, never discussing his personal life. Rarely seen outside of the office, religiously shunning the press, most of his colleagues did not even know if he was married.

Tired of the pressures and responsibilities inherent in his position as Chief Investment Strategist, one day he abruptly called it quits. Despite being rich beyond his dreams, the kid from depressed northern England could not shake the demons buried deep within his brilliant mind. MacCormick, Springer and Waldron's CEO at the time begrudgingly accepted his resignation; however, he was successful in convincing Strange to stay in his personal employ. Strange's major responsibility was managing MacCormick's sizeable investment portfolio, estimated to be north of five hundred million dollars. When Mac retired, he and Strange formed a business partnership that controlled both private and public investments. The mutual respect and trust the two men shared were extraordinary.

Seeing MacCormick walking into Mamaroneck Pizza brought a huge grin to Strange's face. "What's up, Mac?"

MacCormick described the conversation with Roos and the subsequent wager, which brought a sly smile to the face of Strange.

"I hope you don't mind, but I committed our partnership to the wager. My plan is for you to follow Christian Roos on his voyage around the world, report back on his progress and certify his route. Of course, I trust Christian, but it might be a good idea to adopt the spirit of President Ronald Reagan. During the nuclear weapons negotiations with the Soviet Union at the height of the Cold War, the Gipper reminded the Soviet President, Mikhail Gorbachev, of the old Russian proverb, 'Doveryai no Proveryai,'—'Trust but Verify.'"

Having worked together for decades, the two men could figuratively and literally read each other's minds. Married couples talk of a similar dynamic, but in the "time-invested category," work associates like Mac and Strange spend far more time together than the average husband and wife. The result was an unparalleled bonding experiencing. Mac and Carl were truly unique in this respect.

"Understand completely" was Strange's immediate response. Continuing, "I assume the twenty-five million dollars is a red herring to the real action, which no doubt you want me to arrange." Strange's sharp and clever mind instantly recognized Mac's plan and his deployment of the red herring, a metaphor which served as a double entendre to boot, was simply brilliant. In addition, the phrase, meaning something that distracts attention from the real issue, is the nickname used by the investment industry to describe a preliminary prospectus. How many the two men have read over their illustrious careers would be incalculable.

Strange continued: "My thought would be to create a tradable derivative security, which we would dominate through our perfect information flow. The hedgies will love the product. With the risk-free return at historic lows, pools of capital are salivating for uncorrelated investment opportunities. One of my buddies at Bolt On Capital recently told me that his firm has invested over three hundred million dollars of capital into tranches of super catastrophe insurance pools, which include the likes of Japanese quakes and North American East Coast wind. Through our partnership we can trade the synthetic product, both long and short. Besides short-term trading profits based on the inevitable ups and downs of Roos' travels, which we will be a part of, I will make sure we are hedged, guaranteeing a profit regardless of what happens to Christian Roos. A smooth and uneventful trip will translate into minimal profit, but no loss of our principal. If all hell breaks loose for Roos, this could be one of our better plays in decades. Touché, Mac, brilliant idea."

"More than just a pretty face," Mac beamed to his longtime, short-fused partner. "We will show these young Masters of the Universe that we older guys still have some serious game left. I suggest you contact James Hawker to prepare the derivative security this afternoon." Mac was referring to the longtime head of the derivative desk at Springer and Waldron, a man simply known in the world of derivative trading as the Hawk.

James Hawker descended from a long line of English nobility, but left all pretenses of gentlemanly behavior far behind in the British Isles. Cutthroat to the bone, the Hawk was notorious for his ruthless trading prowess and a perennial source of enormous profits for Springer and Waldron. The Hawk would end the daily morning global call with his derivative trading team with a quote from Maximus in the film *Gladiator*, "Brothers, what we do in life, echoes in eternity."

After one particularly strong year in which the Hawk generated over one billion dollars in pre-tax profits, Mac honored him at the firm's holiday party. After a warm toast bestowing great praise on the young trader, Mac motioned to the tech team to start the YouTube video. A montage of hawk kill scenes rolled across the makeshift screen in the Midtown Four Seasons ballroom. One had a red-tailed hawk swooping down in the Arizona Sonoran Desert with his talons exposed, like Iron Man about to grab Pepper Potts, snatching a coiled diamondback rattlesnake. Without missing a beat, the hawk proceeded to soar virtually straight up into the sky as it simultaneously began to devour his prey. Only on the Street—a greed-sanctioned den of iniquity where one eats what he kills—could this visual bring the house down at a holiday party.

As DB flight number 34 from John F. Kennedy Airport to Mexico City lifted off, Christian Roos and Katherine Mandu were nestled into seats A and B in row ten. Roos had just washed down a twelve and a half milligram sustained release Ambien with some distilled water, while Mandu was on her second glass of Sauvignon blanc. Unbeknownst to either, just four rows back in seat A was Carl Strange, calmly poring over the stock quotes in the *Financial Times*.

With the plane breaking through the heavy cloud cover blanketing the New York metropolitan area and the fast-acting sleep agent beginning to take effect, Christian Robinson Roos reflected upon the challenges he would undoubtedly confront on the trip around the world. Popping into his mind was the 1942 song, *Coming in on a Wing and a Prayer*, written by Harold Adamson and composed by Jimmy McHugh. The tune was written about a World War II fighter plane struggling home after a bombing raid.

*Coming in on a Wing and a Prayer* became an instant hit, entering the lexicon almost immediately. The phrase is primarily used to describe desperate situations that cause victims to rely on hope and hope alone to survive. Sounds too scary and depressing, thought Roos, a man who embraced life with an almost insatiable enthusiasm, optimism and passion. With a grin and a wink of his blue eyes, Roos leaned inward toward Kat and whispered, "Welcome to my *Wingding and a Prayer*. Thanks for believing in me. I promise to get you home safely."

Observing Roos' emotional side blossoming, as it always did in response to sleeping agents and alcohol, Kat sensed the opportune moment to bring up a subject that she had been continuously mulling over since his call—money.

"Of course I believe in you, Christian. If I did not trust your abilities, I certainly would not be sitting next to you at this very moment. By the way, how much will you win, if you complete the journey in twenty-five days or less?" Kat asked in a flirtatiously innocent tone, which always came off as serious and sincere at critical moments, a mystical combination that few adult people could pull off with men of Roos' caliber. She mastered the technique at an early age.

Roos' math was unaffected by the Ambien. He responded, "Ten million." Restraining from bursting out laughing and in full comprehension of where the conversation was headed, Roos continued matter-of-factly, "Why do you ask?"

Kat's answer was one of the many sources of intense attraction for Roos. Tilting her head back and right toward Roos' aisle seat caused her hair to float off her neck, a visual she knew he loved. Flashing an adorable serious smile, one that he could never resist, and lacking any pretense of presumption and in a suave and sophisticated manner, she continued to discuss the "unknown" subject. "Well I have been thinking about compensation for my assistance on your trip. You said that you could not do this alone."

Roos cut her off. "I am receiving an industry standard twenty percent promote upon the successful completion of the trip. If you complete the entire trip with me, I will offer you the same terms. Twenty percent of ten million equals two million for you, Kat. By the way, please accept my apologies for making you broach this awkward subject. No doubt you must feel uncomfortable. Please understand it was my intent to offer this all along. I just have been so busy, as you know. Is this acceptable?"

Kat's answer, which supplanted words with action, came in the form of a groin tingling kiss, sensually stimulating on a level that miraculously left the accomplished value investor uncharacteristically satiated.

Eyes shut, Roos nearly asleep, adroitly slurred, "Best two-million-dollar kiss ever!"

"Good night, Roos, you clever man."

# 5

## Central American High Jinks

*"I love to travel, but hate to arrive."*
—HERNANDO CORTEZ

he Airbus A300 touched down in Mexico City's main international airport named after Benito Juarez, after making the five-hour journey, at 9:00 P.M. Juarez served five terms as the president of Mexico during the turbulent post-war years with the United States from 1858 to 1872. As a full-blooded Zapotec, Juarez was the only native to ever hold the office of the Mexican presidency. Originating in the Oaxaca Valley, the pre-Colombian civilization dated back two thousand five hundred years.

Roos and Katmandu hopped in a cab and headed for Our Lady of Guadalupe Basilica, located just ten kilometers from the airport—a ride that could take hours during the midday rush. Mexico City's population of twenty million within the metropolitan region ranked it as the tenth-largest city in the world. To Roos, the only thing worse than the traffic was the pollution. After a fifteen-minute ride, counterclockwise on the Circuito Interior, the car pulled up in front of the Basilica, one of the most sacred and the most visited Catholic shrines in the world.

In 1531, ten years after the Aztec Empire fell to Spanish forces, a lady from heaven appeared in Tepeyac, a hill north of what is now Mexico City. She identified herself as the Ever Virgin Mary, Mother of true God for whom we live, of the Creator of all things, Lord of Heaven and the Earth.

As Roos entered, he inveterately genuflected, placed his right hand fingertips on his forehead, "in nomine Patris" (in the name of the Father) lowered his hand pressing his fingertips into his breast bone, "et Filii" (and of the Son) finally touching his left shoulder followed by his right shoulder, "et spiritus sancti" (and of the Holy Ghost).

Roos read the inscription under the statue of the Virgin Mary:

*"I wish that a temple be erected here quickly, so I may therein exhibit and give all my love, compassion, help, and protection. Because I am your merciful mother, to you, and to all the inhabitants on this land and all the rest who love me, invoke and confide in me; to listen there to their lamentations, and remedy all their miseries, afflictions and sorrows. And to accomplish what my clemency pretends, go to the palace of the bishop of Mexico, and you will say to him that I manifest my great desire, that here on this plain a temple be built to me."*

"Well, Kat, our Merciful Mother's plan worked. Within ten years, nine million inhabitants of the land, who professed for centuries a polytheistic and human sacrificing religion, were converted to Christianity. If you ask me, that is absolutely astonishing."

"I am a Buddhist, remember. Looks like a spaceship," giggled Kat. "I was expecting more of a St. Peter's architectural design."

Roos responded as the pair walked into the Basilica, "The circular design allows for three-hundred-and-sixty-degree unobstructed views of the Virgin Mary from anywhere in the church. I plan on doing the same in our place, assuming you will ever move in. The Jeff Koons bronze *Katmandu* sculpture will be the focal point of the house, just like the Virgin Mary is here. I am thinking of commissioning you in the Scorpion yoga position."

Kat responded flippantly, "Isn't one marriage enough for one lifetime, Christian? I love Koons' work. It is all so brilliantly interesting and creative. My favorite is his terrier *Puppy*, standing at a height of forty feet, constructed of stainless steel, wood and live flowers. One was at Rockefeller in New York a while ago. Have you seen it, Christian?"

Grousing to himself, Roos gave a begrudging touché to the only woman he knew who could answer a question about commitment with a comment and question about a grass terrier puppy. Jeff Koons is reasonably well known, but for Kat to pull out that response was, well, vintage Kat.

"Of course, baby. Partial to his *Esquiline Venus Gazing Ball* myself, though."

The current Basilica, constructed in 1976, replaced the original structure built in the sixteenth century, celebrates Mass continuously from 6 A.M. to 9 P.M., three hundred and sixty-five days a year. Deceptively large, the Basilica has the space to accommodate fifty thousand worshipers.

"Not very impressive looking," Kat probed.

Roos' agreed. "Budgetary constraints here in Mexico. It may be somewhat pedestrian looking, but quite efficient in spreading the word. Ninety-three million people, eighty-three percent of the Mexican population, are members of the Catholic Church. Only Brazil has more Catholics. But the numbers are down. Twenty years ago, ninety-seven percent of Mexicans were Catholic. Twenty-five Popes have celebrated Mass here, including four visits by Pope John Paul II. A few more than St. Patrick's in New York City, for sure."

As the pair flagged a taxi, Kat screamed, "Roos, the photograph and video!"

"Brilliant, I can see you are already earning your two-million-dollar fee. Well done, baby."

After a quick cameo in Kat's newly established Instagram and Vimeo accounts, both titled, *Wingdings and a Prayer*, Roos instructed the driver, "Back to the airport."

"Airport? I thought we were staying in Mexico City tonight." Kat expressed confusion at the development.

Roos responded, "Change in plans. We are flying to Havana tonight."

She was clearly not happy. "Roos, I am exhausted. Unlike you, I cannot sleep on planes. How long is the flight?"

"Relax. I have arranged for an AirJets Citation X to fly us there. Too complicated flying commercial into Havana. Last time it took me three hours to make it through customs, and that was only after Colin bribed a few officials. Flight time is around two hours and forty-five minutes, but in an X, the trip should not take more than one hundred and thirty-five minutes. You can sleep in tomorrow."

At that moment, the circa-1975 Chevy preparing to exit onto the Mexico City beltway struck a pedestrian who was inexplicably crossing the motorway's entrance. The force of the collision, which thankfully happened at a speed of less than thirty miles per hour, propelled the young man off of the bumper, careening into the windshield, bouncing on the roof several times, and barrel rolling on the coarse pavement before ultimately landing twenty yards down the street. In a car unequipped with seatbelts, Roos and Kat were helplessly thrown into the immoveable backs of the car's front seats. As the vehicle came to a stop on the shoulder, she shouted, "What in the hell just happened?"

Collecting himself, Roos embraced her. "Are you okay?"

Surprisingly calm given the severity of the accident, Kat responded, "Yes. How are you, Christian? Let's get out of here."

"Okay too, but let me check on the pedestrian." The taxi driver restrained by his seatbelt remained unharmed behind the wheel. As Roos approached the man, crumbled up in a ball on the side of road, he could hear police and ambulance sirens approaching. The man, in his early twenties, to Roos' amazement stood straight upright, and began demanding money in the King's English, which would make the Fowler brothers proud. Speechless, Roos' look of disbelief was emblazoned on his face like Hawaiian Tropic suntan lotion on a South Beach Botox queen. By the time the emergency vehicles arrived on the scene, the taxi driver was out of his car, ranting and raving and pointing to the passengers. Having traveled in Mexico previously, Roos, smelling a rat, correctly anticipated what was about to happen next.

As the police approached the visibly shaken passengers, Roos reached into his wallet, peeled off ten Benjamins and handed two to each police officer, two to the taxi driver, two to the pedestrian, and the remaining two to the ambulance driver. The latter was tied to a ride to the airport. The participants, sans the passengers, formed a huddle and began arguing in a tone and cadence remarkable even for Mexicans, a culture known for their enthusiastic discourse. After several minutes, the lead police officer demanded one hundred from the pedestrian and one hundred from the ambulance driver. After receiving a larger slice of the pie, the police motioned to Roos and Kat to get in the ambulance.

While bouncing around in the back of the circa-1970 ambulance, Roos was musing about the staged car crash hierarchy. The participant most at risk — the pedestrian — receives the lowest payout along with the ambulance driver. Next is the car owner who has sustained damage to his car, which must be repaired, and lastly the police who received three hundred each equal to sixty percent of the total bribe. Roos' request for oxycodone was met with blank stares from both paramedics and a definitive, *"No se."*

Pulling up to the General Aviation field of Benito Juarez International in an ambulance was virgin territory for sure. The dimly lit Fixed Base Operator (FBO), where the Citation X's Rolls Royce twin jet engines packing over seven thousand pounds of thrust, were purring, looked like the Pearly Gates to Kat and Roos. Walking onto the tarmac, Roos recalled how he always was surprised that buyers would pay the twenty-three-million price tag for a plane with such little curb appeal. Sure it was the fastest midsized plane in the sky, but it decidedly did not look that way on the ground. Besides, in the egotistical world of private aviation, most people counterintuitively want the flight to last longer, not shorter. Preying upon the vanity of deep-pocketed, narcissistic customers, AirJets was able to craft a business which would never exist according to Nobel Prize winning economist, Franco Modigliani, who believed that all consumers act rational at all times. Able to climb to fifty-one thousand feet and hit tops speeds seven hundred eighteen miles per hour, approaching .935 MACH, the speed of sound, the Citation X is a true Ferrari in the sky.

With the Citation rolling down the runway, Roos typed the first of what he hoped would be twenty-five daily updates on WhatsApp to Frank Harrison, as stipulated in the investment group's agreement.

"Frank, Day 1, Our Lady of Guadalupe done. En route to Havana, already a day ahead of schedule, but slightly behind budget. Thank

God for the Virgin Mary, both literally and figuratively. Without her visit here who knows what the bughouse menagerie stuffed with twenty million residents fused by throes, known as Mexico City, would have become. CR"

In less than sixty seconds, Harrison's text hit Roos' iPhone. "CR, Word of your wager with Mac is spreading like wildfire through the hedge fund community. The Hawk, over at Springer and Waldron, has called me three times tonight. Tomorrow, he plans on opening trading in a derivative product, a binary bet on either side of your wager with Mac. He is calling the security the RoosCaboose. Too damn funny, if you ask me. Don't forget to keep in touch daily, and not a word to anyone. I plan on being an active player in the position. Godspeed, CR. Frank"

Seated at the bar in the swank Four Seasons Hotel on Paseo de la Reforma, located in the high-end Federal District of Mexico City, was Carl Strange. Mac's partner skipped the visit to Our Lady of Guadalupe Basilica for two reasons. First, he did not want to risk being seen by Roos, a man who would not instantly recognize him, but would come around in short order. Second, he knew Roos had booked a room at the Four Seasons for tonight. One of his old friends at the banking institution that issued Roos' credit card did him a huge favor by agreeing to provide limited access to charges made. Never much of a religious man, Strange would rather spend the time drinking and socializing with women.

Several hours and multiple drinks later, Strange checked and to his consternation saw no credit card charges at the Four Seasons being recorded by Roos. Strange, without saying a word to his new Mexican female acquaintance, stood up and walked out front of the hotel.

"Mac, Strange here. Sorry for the late call, but I have a bit of bad news. I have lost Roos."

Mac, reacting to his partner's ephemeral shadowing, said, "Jesus Christ, Strange, it's the first day. How could this happen? Where the hell are you?"

"Four Seasons in Mexico City. They booked a room here for tonight, but cancelled. No record of another hotel booking in the city. They must be en route to Havana, via private aviation. The last commercial flight left at 3:30 P.M. At this point, I don't see any advantage in going to Havana. My thought is to meet them in Cusco, Peru, in two days."

Mac agreed. "I spoke with the Hawk. Trading starts tomorrow in the derivative, which he has coined the RoosCaboose. Looks like we will be in the dark, along with everyone else." Shocked that his partner's train had been decoupled from the caboose while sitting in the station, he continued, "Strange, get your ass back in the game and don't forget, we didn't become rich by trading on public information alone. Somehow I seriously doubt it will start now."

In a veiled attempt to assuage his humiliation, Strange walked back into the hotel bar, motioned to his newly found female companion still seated with her margarita and checked into the honeymoon suite. He wasted little time in deploying his eponymous sexual move, which his friends called *Busting a Strange*. Carl Strange simply had no time for the awkward moment shared by a man and a woman, when each person is wondering what is going to be happening from an intimacy perspective. *Busting a Strange* was Carl's aggressive and effective way of defusing the uncertainty. He was fond of saying, "All they can say is no. What is so difficult to understand about that?"

Heading due east, cruising at six hundred fifty miles per hour at forty-one thousand feet over the Gulf of Mexico, Roos and Kat were locked in a titanic backgammon match. As the X landed on the main runway at the Martí International Airport, she rolled boxcars, producing a gammon, to her delight and Roos' all-too-familiar backgammon chagrin.

"Wheels up at 5 P.M. tomorrow for Cusco, Peru," Roos instructed the pilots.

José Martí founded the Cuban Revolutionary Party in the 1892. The Father of the Revolution, Martí was the leader of the Cuban independence movement from Spain at the end of the nineteenth century.

Martí, also known as the Apostle of Freedom, a true champion of human rights, is visible all over Cuba. Besides the airport, there are statues, photographs and busts of the Apostle in just about every park, school and library. Martí led the end of slavery in Cuba and started the movement toward independence. Shot and killed by Spanish snipers in 1895, Martí was neither able to live to see his dream of a free Cuba come true nor the eventual return to oppression under the Castro dictatorship.

Spain's involvement in Cuba dates to Christopher Columbus's landing on the island on October 28, 1492, when he promptly announced the discovery of China and dispatched his lieutenants to find the Chinese Emperor. Columbus declared the island to be "the most beautiful place yet to be seen on earth." Of course, Columbus did not actually discover what has come to be known as Cuba. By the time he arrived, the Taoina Indians had been occupying the island for over four thousand years. In short order, the Spanish slaughtered the Taoina Indians, all but expunging the race from the history books in the process.

Roos mused to Kat, "Can you imagine being on a fifteenth-century vessel and mistaking Cuba for China, a land mass eighty-six times larger, located over seven thousand nautical miles to the east? What I find so intriguing about antique maps is the fact that they were really just the best guesses of what the smartest people in the world thought the earth looked like at the time."

Kat's response brought laughter to Roos, "Hopefully we will not find out. Let's stick with the X, Christian."

A quote from Martí is boldly written across the main entrance to the airport: *"Those who have you, O Liberty, do not know you. Those who do not have you should not speak of you, but win you."* How ironic, thought Roos, for a country that deprives its citizens of Internet service.

Colin Murphy was waiting for the pair outside of the airport in his 1952 bubblegum-pink Chevy, a car which would stand out in most places, but not here in Cuba, where the streets are crammed with vintage 1950's American and Russian clunkers. Lacking replacement parts and not being able to afford them if they were available, most Cubans have replaced the original engines with what are essentially lawn mower engines. Maxing out at top speeds of thirty miles per hour, completely underpowered, huffing and puffing, the cars cruising the streets of Havana appear to be caught in a time warp.

"I see the sign is still up." Roos was referring to the large billboard directly opposite the airport exit that read, *Bloque el genocidio mas largo de la historia*, translated as *Blockade the largest mass genocide in history*. The billboard has an image of a rope noose strangling the island of Cuba, like a bad debt you cannot pay.

"Where do you have us staying tonight, Colin?" Christian asked his good friend.

"Nice private house down by the Hotel Nacional, owned by Dr. Garcia. I believe you stayed with him last year, Christian." Colin knew Roos would like that.

Roos, "Yes of course, I remember Raul well. Is that really good club just a few blocks from his house still open?"

Castro made a decision early on in his leadership of Cuba to invest heavily into healthcare and education. Both decisions were wise and have paid huge dividends over the decades. Cuba is a major force in the Central and South American healthcare industry. Cuban medical professionals, treating patients, teaching doctors and medical students, can be found from Mexico down to Argentina. Castro sends doctors to Venezuela and receives daily oil shipments in return. The Cuban resolve, centered on barter and a large underground economy, miraculously manages to keep everyone alive. You paint my house and I will fix your car. Teach my son English and I will drive you to work.

Roos began, "Colin, when I tell people in the States that Dr. Raul Garcia, an experienced ear, nose and throat (ENT) doctor, who performs cancer surgeries weekly, earns four hundred and fifty-two dollars a year, they simply stare at me with a patronizing incredulity. I remember Dr. Garcia telling me about the inverted compensation pyramid in the Cuban economy, where professionals earn less than unskilled workers. Why, I asked him. 'Healthcare is free; therefore, I receive no bribes. But the gas station attendant, that is another story.'"

Colin agreed. "I experience the same disbelief. I am surprised how unaware and frankly insensitive Americans are to the plight of the Cuban people, living just ninety miles off the Florida coast. I get the sense that if Cuba could do something for America, the human rights violations, which are so appalling, would suddenly become horribly unacceptable. The invasion would begin in a matter of days. But enough of that, yes the Coco Playa is still rocking, just drop you gear off and we will walk over."

Kat, surprised by the accommodations, asked, "Christian, don't they have hotels here in Havana? I thought you raved about the something called the Hotel Nacional?"

"Of course, but the best way to experience Havana is unquestionably through the eyes of the wonderful locals. Most of them in this neighborhood rent rooms in their homes for much needed extra cash. But it is not all about the money with the Cubans. They are proud people, anxious to share their culture with foreigners. Almost a 'look here, we are normal, don't believe everything you read,' pervades their mentality." With Colin nodding affirmatively, Roos continued, "Cubans are highly educated and intelligent people, with a strong work ethic and immense national pride. When asked about the Castro Communist Regime, most Cubans simply shrug their shoulders and say what can you do. They have resigned themselves to the situation, believing that it will never change. The attitude is similar to a short person who desires to be tall or a brown-eyed girl who dreams of crystal baby blues. Why worry about things that are out of your control?"

With his passion for the Cuban people kicking into high gear, Roos thought to himself that, love him or hate him, nobody could deny that Castro's propaganda machine of over fifty years, during the collapse of Communism worldwide, was second to none.

Roos' mind flashed back to a late-night conversation with Dr. Garcia in which they discussed Cuba, seeing it as a kaleidoscope whose turns bring happiness and sadness, pleasure and pain, hope and fear. Communism and the twenty-first century may make for strange bedfellows, but not here on the island of elusive beauty where everyone is under the sheets of "resolver." Just as in golf where every shot makes someone happy, every twist of the Cuban kaleidoscope brings joy in some corner. In the movie *Midnight in Paris,* the main character, Gil, toggles back and forth between present-day and early-twentieth-century Paris. The contrast is stark and magical. One needs neither movie sets nor actors to achieve the same sensation in Havana, where there is simply no modern day. Walking the streets of Havana, a city described by Winston Churchill as "one where almost anything can happen," creates the sensation of being trapped in a time machine. The situation that exists in Cuba is just so crazy; it is not believable unless seen firsthand. A local Cuban woman in describing her hometown says it all, "Baby, it's Havana!"

Cruising down toward the Malecon, the long stretch of sea wall in the center of town, one half expects 1950's mob boss Meyer Lansky to pull up in a 1954 DeSoto at the Hotel Nacional for the mafia's annual meeting, with a beautiful woman on each arm, surrounded by henchmen sporting machine guns. A sighting of Cuban citizen Ernest Hemingway feels strangely in the cards. Hemingway's masterpiece *The Old Man and the Sea* takes place in Cojimar just one hour from Havana. Upon receiving the Cuban flag, Papa kissed the hem. When asked to do it again for the cameras, Hemingway boomed, "I said I was a Cuban not an actor" (per Carlos Baker's biography of Hemingway). The Spanish are famous for their *dichos* or, as they say, proverbs. "The spirit always returns to where one was happiest on earth" probably explains why so many ghosts are running through the streets of Havana, including Hemingway's.

Or how about Fidel Castro's revolutionary sidekick Che Guevara, voted one of the most influential persons of the twentieth century. One can almost see him riding down Presidente Street in a jeep waving a machine gun to adoring crowds. One's mind cannot be fully Cuba-engaged without imagining secret Soviet warships arriving in 1960 at the port of Havana stocked with medium-range nuclear missiles. Imagine the phone call between Khrushchev and Castro. The maniacal Russian leader was probably in a secret below-ground bunker on a triple encrypted phone. Thirty-four-year-old Castro, fresh off his big win in the Revolution and wearing his traditional green uniform, was probably gawking at the cargo from the dock on a pay phone, smoking a Cohiba. No doubt he was already scheming how to acquire the launch codes. Sounds of Desi Arnaz, aka Ricky Ricardo, singing *Babalu* at the legendary nightclub, The Tropicana, echo through the crowded Havana streets. Ricardo gives that awkward, tight-lipped smile of his as he sees Marilyn Monroe, sporting full cleavage, and Joe DiMaggio arriving at their front-row table.

Roos' daydreaming ceased as he marveled at the scene in downtown Havana late in the wee hours: "No drugs, no guns, no crime in Havana. One could walk naked through these streets unharmed. Communism is horrible, but I will give the Castro regime high marks for safety."

Colin added, "People live such a daily struggle, they don't have time for anything else. Religion included."

# 6

## RoosCaboose

*"An investment in knowledge pays the best interest."*
—BENJAMIN FRANKLIN

Bright-eyed and bushy-tailed at 6 A.M. sharp, James Hawker was poised at his desk on Springer and Waldron's massive thirty-five-thousand-square-foot trading floor—a venue not for the faint of heart, where some the of world's brightest minds convened to play the ultimate game of Monopoly. Preparing to commence trading in the derivative security, which he and his firm had crafted, the Hawk was feeling particularly hyped-up. Before most people had awakened, the merciless trader had already fired two of his team members—one over the phone, and the other in cold blood. Violating two of the most important unwritten rules of the Street—calling in sick with a bogus illness and putting one's own interest before that of clients—cost them their choice positions. The stone-faced team witnessed the Hawk ripping apart one of their own for his shameless request to have his dowry-surfeited wife participate in the first trade in the RoosCaboose for her personal account. Marrying for money might be what other unbookish milksops do, but not on the Street, where veins ran hot with virility and devoid of such pathetic intellectual vaporousness. Without so much as missing a beat, the Englishman opened up his daily morning call by putting some stick about with a rabble-rousing call to arms on the RoosCaboose product. "Tell your clients this type of creativity and originality is what makes Springer and Waldron unique."

The Hawk's disdain for lawyers was immense, matched only by his contempt for charlatans masquerading as trophy husbands, but he knew that due to the unusual nature of the RoosCaboose that a careful document had to be drafted. Spending hours with the legal team of Springer and Waldron was Chinese water torture to the man who ran the derivatives desk with unyielding power. Crossing t's and dotting i's were things that other people did, something that did not interest him in the slightest. But he sat there like a schoolboy for most of the afternoon yesterday, as the legal team quizzed him on the transaction. Sealing the deal was the consent of all signatures to the wager agreement, permitting the disclosure of Judge Hebblethwaite's ruling to Springer and Waldron's general counsel.

The firm would be acting as both agent and principal with regards to trading positions, but the Hawk made it clear that all trades had to be personally approved by him.

"Million-dollar-minimum position sizes, without exception. We want to discourage retail investor participation. Focus on our hedge fund clients, who are looking for uncorrelated risk. The ones who have shown a propensity for esoteric products in the past."

The first trade in the RoosCaboose contract occurred just before noon at a price of one hundred ten dollars, a ten percent premium to the initial par price of one hundred dollars. A hedge fund out of Greenwich, Connecticut, took a five-million-dollar long position, which would net a profit just over four and one-half million dollars if Roos completed the itinerary within the allotted twenty-five days. Hawk executed the trade as a principal and shorted the position to the firm's longtime client. A short position takes place when a seller of a security does not own the underlying position. Prior to the expiration of the derivative contract, a short seller must purchase the position in order to eventually deliver to the buyer or simply pay the cash differential upon the expiration of the contract. The RoosCaboose was a zero-sum game, every dollar of profit would be lost by someone. The treacherous game of derivative trading was played on dangerous landscape, where the master Hawk excelled.

He preached to his team daily, "Remember gentlemen, we are playing chess, not checkers."

The Hawk continued to short positions during the day, as the price climbed steadily, ultimately reaching one hundred and fifty dollars.

Without question the consensus among the participants in the early going was that Roos would easily succeed. One young analyst, who went long the contract on behalf of his fund, told the Hawk, "Roos has significant skin in the game providing sufficient incentive, capital at his disposal and more than enough time to navigate the itinerary. It is a no brainer. You would have to be crazy to bet against him."

Hubris is the oxygen of the hedge fund world, a place where the meek were weeded out, like salmon in a grizzly bear's jaws.

The Hawk was sure the rising price would bring out both long buyers and short sellers. He craved both and was willing to commit the firm's capital in the early stages, as a loss leader, to accomplish his objective. By throwing out some early small-sized chum in the murky waters of the Street, the Hawk's limitless pound line hit paydirt.

The three hedge funds in Harrison's investment syndicate, Net Neutrality Holdings, Wolfram Global Partners and Sixty-Two Thousand LLC, all sold their individual five-million-dollar positions by the end of the day, inking a nifty profit of fifty percent on their brief investment. Sitting back in his chair at the end of the day, Hawk reviewed the day's trading results with the firm's powerful head of the investment committee.

"Trading volume was one hundred and thirty-five million. Our average spread was two points, generating two million seven hundred thousand dollars in commissions. I committed sixty-five million of our capital, closed the day flat the position, with a six-million-dollar trading profit. Total outstanding in the RoosCaboose, including Mac's initial twenty-five million, is one hundred sixty million."

The Hawk thought that the day could not have gone any better. Then a huge smile lightened his face as he saw the caller identification on his cell phone.

"Good afternoon, James, Alexei Romanov here. Do you have a moment to discuss the RoosCaboose contract?"

Romanov, a Russian immigrant from Moscow, ran Vengeance Capital, one of the largest hedge funds in the world. With twenty-five billion dollars under management, Vengeance was a powerful force within the investment universe, the proverbial eight-hundred-pound gorilla in the truest of senses. By all accounts, Romanov was an oppressive, brutal man with a scandalous past.

When Alexei was seven years of age his father, Boris Romanov, caught his wife having an affair. The sight of not one but two young men in bed with his wife, Anna, sent the older Romanov into a rage. With his bare hands, Boris killed her two lovers, while Anna trembled with fear under the covers pulled up to her nose. As he approached her, Boris brandished a six-and-a-half-inch steel-bladed Kizlyar Korshun military knife. At the trial, which lasted less than a day and saw no defense presented, the coroner testified that in his forty-year medical career he had never seen such a disfigured face.

Boris Romanov was given a life sentence without the possibility of parole in Russia's infamous Black Dolphin Prison. Located in the Orenburg region near the border of Kazakhstan and named for a statue of a black dolphin made by the inmates, the prison is home to seven hundred of the country's most brutal criminals. Black Dolphin is a final resting place of sorts for the serial murderers, cannibals and terrorists who sit in their prison cells within cells under twenty-four-hour surveillance. Built over two hundred and fifty years ago in 1773, the prison's security track record is unblemished. With no escapes and only one prisoner released upon appeal in its entire history, the only realistic way out of Black Dolphin, a prison restricted to life-sentenced inmates, is in a body bag.

From the moment inmates arrive at Black Dolphin they are taught the "position." Forced to bend over with their hands cuffed behind their backs and blindfolded, the prisoners never see their surroundings.

With no cafeteria, all meals are taken in cells—the only sights the men see during the rest of their entire lives. Inmates, confined in triple-barred cells with another inmate with less than fifty square feet of living space for more than twenty-two hours a day, are prohibited from sitting on their bunks, must sleep with the lights on and are subjected to cell searches every fifteen minutes—every day of the year—including Christmas. Whenever on the move, in the mandatory position resembling a dolphin jumping out of the water, Caucasian Mountain

Shepherd guard dogs bark and growl by their sides. Tipping out at over two hundred pounds and standing over six feet tall, the Mountain Shepherd is the fiercest canine on the planet. Able to strike with the force of a 45-caliber gun, the animal evokes fear—even in blindfolded prisoners.

Asked about conditions in the prison, the lieutenant guard in charge of Black Dolphin had this to say, "To call the prisoners people makes your tongue fall backwards, just to say it. I have never felt any sympathies toward them."

With his parents suddenly gone, Romanov was sent to the local orphanage in downtown Moscow. The three ways of departure from the orphanage were in the arms of an American adoption family, a hearse or escape. Romanov chose the latter. Escaping after ten years, Romanov found himself on the streets of Moscow looking for work.

The collapse of Soviet Union sent arctic winds of change blowing through the decimated empire. As Gorbachev's machine crumbled, a perfect storm of corruption engulfed the streets of Moscow, sweeping up government officials, members of the military and criminals, who were all jockeying for position in the new cash-crazed dissolute society locked in the greedy grip of organized crime. Romanov, witnessing the swell of greenbacks firsthand, wanted in badly.

His initial expressions of interest to local mob players were rebuffed. Feeling stymied but undaunted, Romanov befriended the bouncer at the Marika Club. Located at Ulitsa Petrovaka 21 Street between the Moskva and Yanza Rivers in the central Moscow District of Tagansky, the Marika was one of Russia's first and most successful high-end disco clubs. Brimming with supermodels nightly, the Marika, which was housed in an eighteenth-century mansion, was also an established recruiting ground for future Russian mobsters from the old Soviet Communist regime. After securing Scorpion, Foreigner and Journey albums for the bouncer, Romanov was finally admitted entrance to the Club, where he instantly gained favor.

At six foot four inches, weighing over two hundred pounds with a fight-scarred face, Romanov did not look seventeen. He could easily pass for a man ten years older. A prodigious fighter, Romanov developed an early reputation as one of the toughest enforcers on the dark and seedy crime-infested streets of the Russian capital. His early assignments with the mob were focused on the organization's loan sharking operation. Collecting money from people crumbling under the pressure from usurious interest rates was a natural fit for the ruthless and pugnacious Romanov.

While paying a visit to one of his customers, a local bar owner, Romanov's young life careened out of control. The owner was deeply in debt, owing sixty-five thousand in dollar equivalent Russian rubles, an amount increasing by ten thousand per month, based on the annualized interest rate of one hundred and eighty percent. Frustrated by the borrower's inability to produce the necessary cash for the week, Romanov lost it. He grabbed the man by the throat, slammed him to the top of the bar and reached for a weapon. Unfortunately for the bar owner, the closest instrument was a full bottle of Smirnoff vodka, which Romanov clutched and proceeded to strike down on the man with all his fury. The blood spatter, gushing from the cranium, which was literally split in half from the nose upward, would have even confused the likes of Dexter Morgan.

Upon learning that the bar owner's brother was a "made" member of a rival crime organization, Romanov fled Russia within hours. He caught a train to Odessa, Ukraine, on the northern shores of the Black Sea, grabbed a ferry to Istanbul, where he traveled the historic Silk Road, through Bagdad, Tehran, and ultimately ending up in Beijing.

Alexei descended from the House of Romanov, rulers of Russia during the sixteenth and seventeenth century. His bloodline afforded Romanov with strong DNA, his father notwithstanding. Possessing an abundance of intestinal fortitude and an uncommon intelligence, Romanov was a man with unlimited potential, as long as he could keep his haunting rage contained. Working as a dim sum short-order cook by day, Romanov enrolled in night school at the prestigious Tsinghua University in Beijing, often referred to as China's "MIT." Deploying his steely determination and computer-like mind, Romanov excelled at an unconventional pace, mastering an advanced mathematic and finance curriculum. Romanov exhibited an uncanny ability to understand complex mathematical concepts. The ex-mobster's mind was opened to a previously unknown world of finance, one gushing with a new type of money—legal tender.

Finishing his undergraduate degree in less than four years, Romanov turned his sights toward America. The year was 1997 and the United States economy and financial markets were rocking. In the midst of experiencing the greatest run in the history of the country, America looked like the Star of David shining over Bethlehem to the young, ambitious Romanov, who desperately wanted in on the action—again. One of his mathematic professors at Tsinghua University had taken a shine to Romanov. Professor Wu Zheng marveled at her student, who possessed mathematic skill the likes of which she had not seen before in her twenty years of teaching. After endless cajoling and some adventuresome late-night sessions in the bedroom, Zheng agreed to introduce Romanov to her brother, Tien Zheng, who worked in the credit structuring division of a mid-level Wall Street investment banking firm. Zheng interviewed Romanov over the phone several times, becoming increasingly impressed after each successive conversation. Zheng offered Romanov an internship, which the Russian mathematic wizard accepted instantly.

One of the oldest and most profound sayings on the Street is *When the ducks are quacking, feed them.* The sound of the gaggle was deafening at the turn of the century. Interest rates at historic lows and the stock market at historic highs sent fear packing. The new sheriff in town was greed, spreading like cholera spawned from an 1850's London water pump. Wall Street seized on the moment, as the institution always does. The new game this time around was securitizing credit. Any and all types of debt backed by assets such as cars, credit cards, student loans, and real estate mortgages, both residential and commercial, were packaged in Collateral Debt Obligations (CDOs) then sliced and diced and sold off in tranches to an unsuspecting investor base. Romanov, leveraging his command of mathematic, mastered the new science of structured finance, where one plus one created the optical illusion of equaling three, in short order. Within three years, the ex–Russian mob money collector was collecting money again, this time on Wall Street where he became a "made" man. Unsatisfied with his compensation,

Romanov branched out on his own, forming Vengeance Capital with several associates and just five million of capital under management. Riding the market up, Vengeance reversed course, ultimately placing a huge leveraged bet against the housing market. The clients of Vengeance scored a once-in-a-lifetime hit, sending Romanov into rarified air in the hedge fund community. The firm soared. Then things got better.

As a multibillionaire, running one of the world's largest hedge funds, Romanov was a man living the American dream. At his beck and call were a bevy of trappings consistent with the uber wealthy: a fleet of private planes such as the Global Express 6000 and Gulfstream V, a beachfront mansion in the Hamptons, villas in Monaco and Tuscany, and a penthouse co-op in the luxury cooperative located at 740 Park Avenue. The property, considered one of the most expensive and exclusive addresses in New York City, was built in 1929 by Jacqueline Kennedy Onassis' grandfather. Home to Blackstone founder Steve Schwarzman, oil baron David Koch and other luminaries, the 740 obsessively finicky co-op board was rumored to have turned down would-be buyers Barbra Streisand and Russian billionaire Leo Blavanik. Romanov, under normal circumstances, would have had a snowball's chance in hell of being accepted for residence in 740. But Romanov's power preceded his co-op application, which was accepted instantaneously. Romanov, along with many Russian oligarchs, also kept a residence in One Hyde Park, reported to be the most expensive real estate in the world. Shrouded in secrecy the shadowy residents included mainly Nigerian, Russian and Arab billionaires all availing themselves of the attractive tax treatment of foreign nationals afforded by the English government. Dubbed the world's safest tax haven, real estate prices in the building have crested the twelve-thousand-dollars-per-square-foot barrier. Although controversy continues to plague the property as evidenced by a recent statement in the House of Commons made by Peter Badcock, an extremely liberal Labour Party Member of Parliament:

> "The tax fraud that is One Hyde Park has to be the greatest double entendre in the English language. The Right Honourable gentleman must know that the word *Hyde*, a derivation of *hide* derives from the

Anglo-Saxon word hid, which traces its meaning to the amount of rent due from land, and did indeed matriculate into a unit of taxation for all public obligation. Foreign billionaires 'parking' money tax-free while 'hiding' in their One Hyde Park residences overlooking Hyde Park is the height of hypocrisy, one matched only by the spectacle of a Henry VIII wedding ceremony. The Right Honourable gentleman also is no doubt aware that Henry VIII confiscated the 350 acres constituting Hyde Park from the Monks of Westminster Abbey in 1536 to use as his personal hunting grounds. 'Hides' of another kind, yet again."

Tall, dark and brutally handsome to boot, Romanov graced the lists of the world's most eligible bachelor—usually near the top—if not number one.

But old habits die hard—and some not at all. Unable to shake either his roots or pernicious proclivities, the hedge fund star began slipping into his dark past. It started with a simple call from Russian President Fyodor Rasputin. The two men shared a family history together at the highest levels of Russian governmental power. Rasputin's great-grandfather was a trusted private advisor to the ruling House of Romanovs at the turn of the nineteenth century. With Russia locked in a close race with Australia and South Korea to host the 2014 Winter Olympics, Rasputin called in a marker by asking Romanov to sprinkle the International Olympic Committee "infield" with cash bribes in order to swing the games to Sochi. Romanov was all too happy to oblige his homeland's leader.

Romanov's dirty Vengeance Capital money rained around the globe, ultimately swinging enough votes for a slim but sufficient 51 to 47 Russian victory over Pyeongchang, South Korea, on the final ballot. His payback was an equity piece of the rigged construction bids for hundreds of billions of dollars of infrastructure projects including roads, airports, hotels, housing and Olympic venues to be built for the games. Most normal men would ask for the release of their father from prison as a reward. Still tormented from his father's jarring ironhearted murder of his mother, the thought never crossed Romanov's mind. The murder aside, Romanov wasn't close to being normal. The equity stakes were categorized on Vengeance Capital's financial statements under the heading Minority Equity Positions in Construction Companies—BRICS.

The acronym stood for Brazil, Russia, India, China and South Africa, the world's five emerging economic powers.

Romanov was a genius in the collateralized debt markets, but he quickly realized that there was easier money to be made in the murky world of shadow banking. Looking like the terrifying but harmless fangtooth, a deep-sea creature with disproportionately large teeth, most hedge fund managers were busy diving into Wall Street's dark pools contaminated with high-frequency traders. As the regulator's nets began to close in on the illegal HFT "fisherman," Romanov—a man who preferred swimming against the tide—shunned the crowded stygian waters. He opted instead to develop a new investment concept—one which transcended shadow banking—ghost banking. Shadow bankers merely circumvented financial regulations, while ghost bankers took the law into their own hands, a concept not foreign to the ex–Russian mob debt-collector Romanov. The difference between the two—bad things happened to those who couldn't repay the ghoul. Vengeance Capital's ghost banking practices spread quickly outside of the BRICS into the Middle East and beyond construction-related businesses into the technology and defense industries.

Despite the constant flow of ghastly rumors circling the firm, Vengeance Capital's clients gladly checked their morality at the front door of the hedge fund's massive Midtown Park Avenue offices. Greedy investors clamoring to be part of Vengeance's outsized investment returns looked the other way when discussions of Romanov's abhorrent history and current practices surfaced. The elite of New York literally begged to throw capital at the firm, producing annualized returns of thirty-two percent, net of all fees, for ten straight years. The mathematic of this feat turns a dollar into twenty-four, an experience reveled in by Vengeance's initial investors. Romanov's new vigorish was the legal two-and-twenty fee structure of the hedge fund world.

Romanov politely asked, "Would you please explain the basic terms of the RoosCaboose contract to me?" After hearing the Hawk's concise pitch, Romanov continued, "Can you email me the contractual agreement?

Where did the position close today? What is the liquidity? I would never ask you to violate any confidences, but could you characterize the players in the contract? Will Springer and Waldron stand behind the position?"

As if playing a game of rock, paper and scissors with a golden poison dart frog, the Hawk's response was, "Email already sent, one forty-five was the close, outstanding of one hundred sixty million, I will make a market in the position for you, of course cannot comment on the players. Have I ever failed to stand by my positions with you?"

The Hawk's largest client by a wide margin, the ex–Russian mobster turned hedge fund superstar's response was, "I will call you first thing in the morning."

After hanging up, the Hawk scrolled through his contacts, excitedly smashing send when Charles MacCormick's name appeared.

"Mac, Hawk here. Can we meet for dinner tonight? How does Piccola Vinezia at say 8:30 sound?"

"See you there," was Mac's instantaneous response. After all, it was his favorite Italian restaurant in America, a slice of heaven on earth, buried in the nondescript streets of Astoria Queens, just fifteen minutes from LaGuardia Airport. The restaurant sported old-school Italian red-checked tablecloths with matching curtains. Experienced old-school waiters carved parmigiano reggiano out of huge barrels, while pouring the grandest of Tuscan wines, with meats, fish and vegetables that would make a Sicilian salivate. Mac's favorite dish was the Dover sole, filleted tableside, served as an entire fish lightly sautéed in a white wine and butter sauce. The onetime Chief Executive Officer of Springer and Waldron was fond of saying that it tingled his senses in such a delectable way that he would turn down sex for the dish. Devouring pasta in a corner table, a patron might not express too much surprise if a mob hit went down. It was the kind of place that if you did not know about, you simply were not in on the deal. When it came to Piccola Vinezia, there were those who didn't know or didn't know that they didn't know. And of course, he knew the Hawk had important business to discuss. A Wall Street titan requesting a dinner meeting on two hours' notice, outside of the city, was a tell of the grandest proportions.

When Mac arrived, he was escorted to a back corner table where the Hawk was already seated, anxiously washing down olives with a 2004 Piero Antinori Tignanello. Made in the rolling hills forty kilometers south of Florence, in the heart of Tuscany, Tig was the wine of choice for the smart rollers. Only thing better is the select premium Solaia, made with the best grapes in Piero Antinori's entire six-thousand-acre estate.

After perfunctory pleasantries, the Hawk focused on business. "Mac, we have known each other professionally and socially for over twenty years. I respect you without reservation. Of course, I would never ask you to compromise your integrity, but I need to discuss your wager with Christian Roos. Your associate, Carl Strange, approached Springer and Waldron with the transaction. I have created a derivative product, which traded over one hundred million dollars today. On day one."

"Yes, yes, of course, it was my idea to have Strange contact you. Please get to the point," Mac huffed as only he could, a man who never suffered fools very well. Unimaginable as it was, in the eyes of one of the greatest Wall Street stars of the past one hundred years, the Hawk appeared infinitely mortal.

"Romanov called me today. He is sniffing around the derivative contract. I may be mistaken, but knowing him the way I do, my instincts tell me he is contemplating a short position. You will recall, given their massive assets under management (AUM), Vengeance Capital's minimal position size is in the two hundred and fifty million dollar range." The Hawk leaned in closely, nearly placing his elbows in the olive oil, and continued, "Mac, I smell blood on this one. A sniff in the deep-nine-figure territory. Off the record, do you have any advice for me? What is the backdrop on the bet? I understand that boozing at Winged Foot can get at little carried away, but twenty-five million dollars on a trip around the world? Please elaborate."

"It was not premeditated, the cards simply fell in a certain pattern the other day. Christian Roos stuck his neck out, and I seized the moment. I have Carl Strange tailing him at this very moment. Surely you recall Strange from back in the day?"

The Hawk was slightly miffed at the condescending question, which he normally wouldn't answer. However, Mac wasn't normal and he had designs. "Of course. Who doesn't remember Strange?"

Mac continued, "They are in Mexico City as we speak. This, by the way, is completely legal. You and your associates are all 'big boys' who structured the contract, simply at our suggestion. Maybe you could be a little more specific? And why do you think a man of Romanov's intelligence and power would be willing to place such a large bet on Roos' failure?"

"Let's partner up," was the Hawk's immediate retort. "You provide timely progress reports from Strange on Roos' goings, and I'll trade the living hell out of the contract, which I've named the RoosCaboose. Naturally, you will have first priority on any and all trading opportunities. If Romanov wants to short Roos, I'll go to a quarter of a billion. If need be, with the amount of money at stake, we can hire the United States military to escort him home safely."

Unaccustomedly, the Hawk asked, "Do we have a deal?"

Mac boomed, "Yes. But you deal with Strange directly. He is handling the trading in the Caboose for our partnership."

"Understood. From this point, I think it best that we limit our traceable communications. Text me and we can meet here to discuss any future developments. However, in the meantime," the Hawk cautioned, "if you learn of significant troubles facing Roos, immediately send me the following text, *Train Derailed*. As to Romanov's motivation, I have no clue. But if five percent of the rumors about him are true, we need to remain focused on Roos' safety. If this goes down, I will reach out to some of my contacts in the intelligence world."

"Not necessary, Strange and I already have. He purchased Kidnap and Ransom insurance from a company we know very well, which is staffed with a bunch of ex-CIA, Special Forces and Navy SEALs types. You just focus your attention on maximizing the outstanding value in the contract. We will take good care of Christian Roos. Higher volume translates into better liquidity, which will make it easier for us to trade the position based upon the inevitable volatility of Roos' travels, which we will have perfect information on."

Earlier in the day, traveling east along the Malecon, on the north side of Havana, a four-lane road separating the city from the Gulf of Mexico, Roos and Colin were headed to Old Havana. Kat, catching up on some beauty sleep, decided to skip the visit to the Havana Cathedral. The scene on the Malecon is a tale of two cities. To the north is the beautiful clear blue water of the Gulf of Mexico for as far as the eye can see. The water crashes upon the steel-and-rock embankment, occasionally sending huge sprays onto the people and cars passing by. Never a boat in sight, which means no water sports, no fishing, and no catch of the day in the local restaurants. On the south side of the Malecon sit decrepit, largely vacant buildings ranging between three to six stories. As the old real estate axiom goes, *The three most important things about real estate are location, location and location.* Without question the real estate lining the Malecon is located in the absolute prime spots in Havana. Every international hotel company in the world must have a plan, already crafted, just waiting to spring into action if Cuba ever really opens up to free market capitalism. The management teams of Four Seasons, Ritz Carlton and Marriott, along with many others, surely must have their spots already selected. Describing the existing structures as decrepit is really quite an understatement. The situation that exists today is far worse. Hardly a week goes by without a building or house literally crumbling in Havana.

Built in 1777, two hundred and thirty-six years ago, the Cathedral of Havana is located on San Ignacio Street in a beautiful Spanish-style square, overlooking Parque Cespedes named after the leader of the first Cuban independence movement, which culminated in the Ten Years War with Spain in 1868. On the eastern side of the Parque is the narrow, one-thousand-foot-wide Canal de Entrada, a swiftly moving waterway connecting the Gulf of Mexico to the deep water Port of Havana. Heavily protected from the unpredictable storms in the Gulf, the Cuban Port was a safe haven for ships stuffed with gold and treasures from the New World to the north. On the eastern side of the entrance to the Canal sits the imposing Castle Morro, built by the Spanish immediately after their conquest of Cuba in 1589. Named after the biblical Magi, the Three Wise Men, the fortress has successfully guarded the interest to the Havana Harbor for centuries.

Cuban citizen Ernest Hemingway wrote an article titled *Marlin off the Morro*, published in the first-ever edition of *Esquire* magazine in the fall of 1933. The Gulf Stream moves water through the Florida Straits and Gulf of Mexico at thirty million cubic meters per second. In the *Esquire* piece, Hemingway vividly describes his fishing exploits aboard his beloved boat, the *Pilar*. Readers can almost feel their muscles burning from the strong and relentless pull of the marlin, described in excruciating detail by one of the greatest writers of the twentieth century.

Roos and Murphy approached the baroque Cathedral's entrance, Roos marveling at the imposing nature of the structure: "The right tower is noticeably larger than the left one creating an interesting asymmetrical look, both intriguing and intimidating. Almost like a stripper with a poor boob job."

Murphy laughed. "The two bells in the larger breast have gold and silver mixed in with the bronze, which the Spanish thought created a sweeter sound when rung. Look up close at the stone and you can sea coral imprints of marine flora and fauna, like an archeological dig site, above ground. The Spanish dubbed the cathedral 'music cast into stone'."

Inside, they observed the centerpiece of the Cathedral, a Martin Andujar sculpture of Havana's patron saint, St. Christopher. Colin took the requisite video and photo of Roos at the Cathedral, and Roos texted Frank on WhatsApp: "Day 2, the Cathedral of Havana, completed. Off to Cusco tonight."

Back in the bubblegum Chevy headed to the airport, Colin handed Roos a thick envelope.

"In the package you will find visas for both you and Katherine for Brazil, China, Iran, India, Saudi Arabia and Nepal. The other countries on your itinerary—Peru, Italy, Turkey, Israel and Japan—do not require visas for the length of your visits. We need to discuss the one country I have not mentioned, North Korea. As you are aware, the communist dictatorship operates in absolute secrecy. There is no formal visa application process; essentially you have to be invited, like Dennis Rodman recently was."

Roos responded emphatically, "Colin, I have to get into North Korea or I lose the bet. It is as simple as that."

Colin, "I understand, that is why I went ahead with my idea. On short notice, I had no time to gain preclearance from you. Rather, I assumed it was an at-all-costs type of assignment."

With the last statement, Colin pulled the car off to the side of the road, cut the engine and began to explain his plan to get Christian and Katherine into North Korea.

"As you can imagine, Cuba and North Korea share a very close relationship, which begins at the highest of levels. Metaphorically speaking, the countries are the last two Cheerios clinging together in a raging sea of milk, by some yet to be discovered scientific form of *Cheeriomagnetism*. Cuban government officials have strong contacts with their counterparts over in Pyongyang. I'm sure you have seen the reports, unconfirmed of course, that Fidel Castro has amassed a portfolio in excess of one billion dollars. I'm not sure of the exact amount, but I assure you that a majority of the cash is not in Cuba. Most likely the bulk of the assets are held in Swiss banks. It is widely believed that Kim Jong-il passed the majority of his four-billion-dollar estate, accumulated through six decades of the Kim dynasty raping and pillaging North Korea, to his son, Kim Jong-un. The young tyrant, obsessed by wealth and power, is determined to expand his ill-gotten gains through a sophisticated global investment strategy. Naturally his first call on the subject was to Fidel Castro. It is believed that the world's leading dictators have routine investment conversations, which debate the merits of different strategies and even swap stock tips, plummeting hypocrisy to a depth that would even give Brutus consternation. Through my deep contacts within the Central Bank of Cuba, I've been able to arrange a meeting for you in Pyongyang with the Cabinet level Minister of Finance, Hyun-woo Rhee. In the package you will find visas and passports with the names Mr. Remy Zaugg and Ms. Zoe Zubriggen. You are both Swiss citizens, but in order to efficiently service your important high-level accounts in Cuba, you hold a dual citizenship with Cuba, hence the Cuban passport. Remy Zaugg is a senior portfolio manager with Aebi Bank and Trust Company, one of the oldest and most prestigious financial institutions in Switzerland. Headquartered in Zurich, the five-hundred-year-old company, which epitomizes privacy and confidentiality, is the financial home to the some of the most powerful families in the world. Zoe Zubriggen works for the organization as a client service representative. In all likelihood neither the Minister nor his close associates in attendance will be conversant in either English or Spanish. God help you if someone speaks German. Standard practice calls for the use of interpreters during these types of meetings. Don't be surprised if you are treated to an elaborate formal dinner afterwards. Send me your flight information into North Korea and I will forward to my contact. Don't worry about being googled, they don't use the Internet in North Korea. They operate in a very old-school manner, relying heavily on word of mouth recommendations and referrals, like the one I've arranged for you both. In the off chance that a Google search is used, simply tell them that it is part of the organization's philosophy of absolute discretion, which is so deeply engrained in the culture of your bank. In case it comes up, and I'd be very surprised if it did, the gentleman here in the Cuban government who set up the meeting is named Javier Castellanos."

Kat, feeling a bit concerned, asked Colin, "What if we are uncovered?"

Matter-of-factly Colin responded, "Well, that would be decidedly unfortunate. They would assume you both to be enemy spies and most likely ship you off to join the other million residents in one of the country's infamous prison work camps. But, of course, please call me if something goes wrong. I'll do everything in my power to straighten out the situation. You will find William Donovan's contact information in the package. He's the head of the United States Interest Section in Pyongyang, located within the Embassy of Sweden. He would be the best person to call in case of emergency."

An eerie sense of dead calm suddenly permeated the vehicle.

Roos quickly interjected, "Completely understand. Great work on the travel documents. Please email me the bill. What is the word on the Street regarding Bermudez?"

Murphy responded with a grin. "Sorry, I was unable to arrange any meetings with his staff. I'm sure you understand the sensitivity associated with any publicity at this stage of Bermudez's political career. Walking on eggshells would not even begin to capture the dynamic. Well, Christian, as to his image it can be summed up by Chinese communist revolutionary politician Mao Zedong's response when asked in 1955 what he thought of the French Revolution. 'Too soon to tell.' The Cubans have been oppressed for so long, naturally a wait-and-see attitude is ingrained in their souls. I am sure you saw that Cuban President Raul Castro, Fidel's younger eighty-two-year-old brother, announced 'No mas' coincident with Bermudez's appointment. He is retiring after his current presidential term ends in 2018. If Bermudez can convince Fidel that he is still a true believer in the Revolution, it looks like he will succeed Raul to become the first leader of Cuba in the post-Castro era. Good luck with the rest of your travels. It was a pleasure meeting you, Katherine. Keep an eye on Christian for us both."

"Both eyes for sure. The pleasure was all mine. See you in Washington on your next visit." Kat continued, "You mentioned the need for Bermudez to convince Fidel that he is still on board. Colin, do you think Fidel is still a true believer in the Revolution and socialism? Or is he just another hypocritical opportunistic political leader?"

Without hesitation Colin confirmed, "He is one hundred percent committed to the cause. People in the States make a career out of analyzing Fidel's motives. Whether one agrees or disagrees with his policies, nobody here in Cuba questions where Fidel stands."

The traveling duo was greeted by the X pilots. The distance from Havana to Cusco was just over two thousand five hundred miles, which the pilots estimated would take four hours. Picking up an hour due to the time change, the chief pilot forecasted an 8:30 P.M. arrival.

Before dozing off, Roos informed a weary Kat, "Long day tomorrow. Flying commercial to Rio de Janeiro the following day. In Rio we can relax. I hear there is a mini-carnival happening in the city. Sound good?"

"Roger, Roos."

# 7

## The Puma Sleeps Tonight

James Hawker's trading desk line lit up precisely at 7 A.M.

"Good morning, James, Alexei here. Following up on the RoosCaboose contract. Vengeance would like to initiate a short position. What type of size can you offer us? I assume Springer and Waldron would be acting as a principal in the trade? Or would you act as an agent, or combination? I guess it really does not make a difference to me, as long as Vengeance settles directly with you. I am not interested in assuming a credit risk on this unusual position."

"Good morning indeed." The Hawk was feeling strong. "We can go twice the outstanding of one hundred sixty million, meaning I can short you three hundred and twenty million, as a principal. But my legal department needs an executed document in place before a trade of that volume can be inked. I can have a courier deliver one within the hour. Please advise how you would like me to proceed."

"Of course, let's discuss price. You indicated the contract closed at one forty-five. I will do the three hundred twenty million at par. Please confirm trades in the Caboose are private third-party transactions, which are not printed publicly." Romanov was clearly asking a rhetorical question.

The Hawk countered, "Yes. Listen, Alexei, we are not taking an opinion in this trade. As you no doubt can surmise, I am trading the contract on a very short-term basis and collecting commissions. I am okay with the size, as I previously indicated, however, the difference between par and one forty-five is huge. I can offer you two options: print the entire trade at one twenty-five, or allow me to work it off in smaller pieces at one forty-five. Say, four trades of eighty million at a time. As my largest client, I want to accommodate you. By the way, what do you see here? What do you say?"

Romanov ignored the Hawk's probing and asked, "How long will it take you to do the four trades?"

"Not sure, give me the word and I will go to work," the Hawk replied without taking a breath.

"Confirmed but only a day order." Romanov then requested the paperwork.

"On the way as soon as we hang up. In addition, we need one hundred percent margin on this one, Alexei." Nearly audibly gulping, the Hawk knew how the Russian hedge fund maven would dislike this request.

"Yeah, okay. But only a point spread, understand?"

"Deal."

After hanging up with Romanov, the Hawk immediately called Mac with the news.

"What is the latest with Carl Strange? We're going to need him now more than ever."

Mac grumbled, "Let me find out."

"Good morning. Welcome to the Four Seasons Mexico City, how may I assist you?"

Mac's request was noticeably irritable, "I am trying to reach one of your hotel guests, Mr. Carl Strange."

"Connecting you now, have a nice day."

The phone in the honeymoon suite rang eight times before being answered by the Mexican woman Strange had met two nights earlier at the hotel bar,

"Hola, buenos días."

"Mac here, I am trying to reach Carl Strange."

"Uno minuto. Papi! Llamada telefónica. Es Mac."

In his trademark English accent, he said, "Morning, Mac."

"Carl. Sorry to interrupt in the middle of your *Busting a Strange*, but I have important business to discuss. I just got off the phone with the Hawk. Do you know Alexei Romanov over at Vengeance Capital?"

"Of course. I'm the one gave him the call to short the United States housing market back in 2008. The bastard never even sent me a Christmas card." Strange sounded miffed.

"I had dinner with the Hawk last night. We struck a deal to partner up. The Hawk thinks that Romanov wants to short three hundred and twenty million of the Caboose contract today. The Hawk agreed to the trade based somewhat, I would imagine, on our agreement." Mac bellowed. "So why the hell are you still in Mexico City? And don't forget you are supposed to be trading our position in the Caboose with the Hawk."

"Calm down, Mac. I have everything under control." Strange knew just how to deal with his longtime strongman partner. "We discussed skipping Havana, remember? Roos is hiking the trail tomorrow. I saw he charged two nights at the Hotel Monasterio in Cusco on his credit card, as well as two commercial airline tickets to Rio de Janeiro for the day after tomorrow. So I would recommend that I head directly to Rio."

Mac retorted, "Carl, have you ever been to Machu Picchu?"

Strange answered negatively.

Mac, increasingly annoyed, said, "I didn't think so. The hike from Cusco is fifty-five miles, which on average takes seven days. By the time you reach the ruins, the elevation is over thirteen thousand feet. Christ, Mary dragged my ass down there ten years ago. I damn near died on that trail. To this day, I accuse my wife of attempted murder. There is no possibility that Christian Roos is hiking from Cusco to Machu Picchu. The bet requires him to visit the site. We need to know what is happening today. If he skips Machu Picchu, and we know it, we can make a fortune."

Strange deadpanned, "That is why I never married. I have always preferred to curl up in bed with a Trollope."

Mac's laughter was deep and heartfelt for his longtime friend and business associate who always knew how to say the correct thing at just the right time.

Strange calmly made a suggestion to Mac: "Let me check with Peru Travel. I read a few years ago about a new helicopter service the company is offering. Apparently the trip takes thirty minutes to reach the ruins from Cusco."

"Let me know. I promised the Hawk updates based upon your intelligence. La mujer sounds incredibly sexy. Text me some pictures when you have a moment." Mac, calmed down by this time, was laughing and reminiscing about some of the great times he and Carl shared together *Busting Stranges* all over the world.

The predominantly southern heading from Havana took Roos and Kat over the Caribbean Sea, until they hit the northern coast of South America at Cartagena, Colombia. Continuing due south, the plane flew over the Colombian and Peruvian portion of the Andes mountain range, a terrain flush with some of the world's most dense and lush jungles. Containing over one million three hundred thousand square miles and stretching north to south for four thousand three hundred miles, the Andes is the longest and largest continental mountain range in the world. The setting sun provided dramatic views out of the right side of the airplane for most of the nearly five-hour flight. Around 8:30 P.M. the Citation X entered its final approach to the Alejandro Velasco Astete International Airport at Cusco, Peru, named after the first pilot to cross the Andes in 1925. The field sits just below eleven thousand feet of elevation, ranking it the twelfth highest in the world. Outside of China, only El Alto in Bolivia, Inca Manco Capac and Andahuaylas, both of which are located within Peru, present higher altitude landings than Alejandro Velasco Astete. On final descent into the field's sole runway, the setting sun looked like an orange fireball blasting magnificent light across the blue waters of the Pacific Ocean.

Roos glanced at the in-flight monitor, which was flashing a variety of intelligence. Catching his eye were two key weather indicators, the local temperature of forty-two degrees Fahrenheit and humidity of sixty-two percent. The equator cuts through the northern border of Peru, effectively separating the country from Colombia. Despite Cusco sitting just nine hundred and thirty miles south of the equator, the temperatures are relatively moderate on account of the high altitude. Airplanes generally do not like high altitudes, at least when they are attempting to takeoff or land. The higher the better when cruising at altitude, but when the ground comes into play pilots spend significant training time studying the effects of an aerodynamic phenomenon known as high-density altitude, which decreases aircraft performance. The air is naturally thinner at higher altitudes, creating the need for longer runways for landings and takeoffs and adjusted approach and climb angles. Exacerbating the effects of high-density altitude are heat and humidity. Thankfully, for passengers flying into Cusco, the mountains provide an offset to the deleterious effect of high altitude with a cool climate and moderate humidity for most of the year. The subtropical highlands climate rarely sends temperatures below twenty and above seventy degrees. As the wheels were touching down, Roos thought about the old saying "things that can't happen won't." Certainly, if the temperatures in Cusco were in the nineties with equal levels of humidity, at eleven thousand feet, passengers landing at Alejandro Velasco Astete International might still be welcomed by Spanish conquerors.

Roos and Kat hopped in a crew car furnished by the FBO for the short drive to the Hotel Monasterio located in the historic Plaza de Arms section of downtown Cusco. Built in 1595 on the site of Inca Amaru Qhala's Palace, the magnificent hotel bleeds Peruvian and Incan history. Captured by the Spanish three years later in 1598, the hotel was converted into the Seminary Antonio Abad. The signature of the property, which for centuries served as an active monastery, is the cloistered courtyard anchored by a three-hundred-year-old cedar tree. Looking like a large piece of broccoli standing on its stem, the tree is breathtaking. Its legend grew as the tree survived the massive earthquake of 1650, which destroyed much of the monastery along with most of Cusco. During the earthquake, locals paraded a dark statue of Jesus Christ through the streets, which according to myth, brought about the end of the tremors. The statue came to be known as the Cristo de los Temolores and is venerated at the Cathedral-Basilica of Cusco.

After checking into the Monasterio, the couple walked out into the Plaza de Arms, so named by the Spanish after their conquest of the lands. Originally the Incas called the venue Plaza Huacaypata, an area that became the center of Incan life. Full of restaurants, bars, and stores, today the plaza is ground zero for both locals and tourists.

"Christian," said Kat, "I read that the Incas, who were deep into animal mythology, designed the plaza in the shape of a puma, the animal sitting proudly atop the food chain. Sounds like a fitting image for the Incan capital. But standing here, I don't see it. Do you?"

Roos, trying to recall what a puma looks like and struggling to gain proper perspective from ground level, just shook his head. Seeing a friendly looking local, Roos approached the man. "Perdóneme. Buenos noches. Habla Inglés, por favor?"

The elderly man with dark leathery skin, deep-set brown eyes, long black hair and clothes draping him like cellophane, answered, "Yes, of course."

Roos inquired, "Is the Plaza de Arms designed in the shape of a puma?"

Laughing, the man responded, "No, but the city of Cusco is." Reaching into his pocket, the man pulled out a map and handed it to Kat.

"Ah yes, look at this, Christian. You can see the puma's tail working up highway 3S from the east, which builds into the torso. Then at highway Carreter a Paruro, which heads south, the peninsula area of the town forms the animal's legs, which are slightly bent almost as if in full sprint. Lastly, farther west out 3S, the puma's head is formed."

Roos agreed. "Brilliant depiction. Must have had a strict zoning commission chairman back in the day."

Handing the gentleman back his map, Roos and Kat randomly walked into the Limo Restaurant located on the plaza. The unofficial national cuisine of Peru is *ceviche*, a dish composed of various combinations of white fish, prawns and squid, marinated in lime juice, chili, salt and red onion. The icy Humboldt Current, which originates in Aukland,

New Zealand, and runs across the Pacific Ocean up the South American coastline, creates a rich seafood industry for Peruvians. Roos was busy washing down the fresh *ceviche* with the famous Peruvian cocktail, a pisco sour—a staple of Peruvian life made from mixing pisco, tart key limes, an egg white and Angostura bitters and served on the rocks. Pisco originated from the Spanish wine trade. Homesick for wine, the Spanish conquerors imported grape vines and began producing their favorite liquid refreshment. The locals learned how to recycle the grapes lacking sufficient quality for winemaking. Through a process of distilling fermented grape juice, the Peruvians were able to turn the useless grapes, from a wine perspective, into a high-potency brandy, which ranged from sixty to one hundred proof in alcohol. Despite its strength, pisco goes down quite smoothly, which can lead to trouble.

Always a fan of street food, Roos was unable to pass by the mobile *polleria* stand in the Plaza de Arms. The other unofficial national cuisine of Peru, Polla al Brasia, is sold throughout the country in thousands of establishments referred to as *pollerias*. The chicken is marinated for days in a mixture of soy sauce, lime juice, garlic, cumin, paprika, oregano, and pepper, before a slow spit roasting over an open flame. The blackened chicken is served over rice. On the eve of hiking one of the seven wonders of the world, feeling the heightened effects of excessive pisco consumption at high altitude, standing on five-hundred-year-old stones in an ancient Incan plaza, staring up into the crystal-clear starlit Peruvian sky and devouring the best chicken he had ever tasted, Roos looked over at Kat and said in his quintessential alcohol-inflamed emotional voice, "This is one of those rare moments in life which so few individuals will ever experience but should. Imagine standing here in the early sixteenth century, during the peak of the Incan empire, when the population of Cusco was less than five thousand. All of them believed strongly in an afterlife and would mummify their dead who were believed to be able to communicate with the living. The religion encouraged human sacrifice to the gods, including the purest of the population, young children. And then their whole world came crashing down at the hands of less than two hundred Spaniards wielding swords, riding on horseback. You almost get the sense that if neither the Spanish nor anyone else came conquering, the Incas would still be here believing that eclipses were signs of angry gods, which could only be appeased by sacrificing their own people. But they wouldn't have pisco sours, and that would just be a crying shame."

"Just remember, Christian, 'The city is the puma, not the plaza!'"

Roos was disgusted. "I find it embarrassingly loathsome to be perpetuating the image of the idiot American tourist. Thankfully it is not something I do often." Roos, laughing now, said, "Can you imagine the mileage that nice man is getting out of my question about the plaza's shape?"

Ensconced back in the Hotel Monasterio, Kat jumped into the shower. Roos' curious mind had him rummaging through reading material on the desk in their room. His eyes lit on a description of the intensity of the sun in Peru, specifically Cusco. He walked into the bathroom where Kat's naked saturated silhouette shown through the beveled glass shower door like that of an enchanting goddess.

"Baby, listen to this." Roos began to read from a pamphlet.

"Cusco, Peru, is the site where the highest level of ultraviolet (UV) rays occur on Earth. The strength of UV radiation is measured in terms of the UV index. Typically, on this scale, UVI readings over ten are considered dangerous to even somewhat prolonged exposure. In an area with a UVI rate of ten, a fair-complexioned person will typically begin to experience sunburn after half an hour. Cusco has a measured peak UVI of twenty-five, considered extremely hazardous to exposed skin. Peru has the third-highest skin cancer rate in South America; the rate in Cusco is roughly eight percent higher than the rest of the country. Exposure to UV rays is a significant contributor to the formation of skin cancer."

Roos injected his own opinions. "Obviously the high elevation here combined with the three-hundred-a-year-plus brilliant sunshine days and a depleted ozone in this part of the world have all come together to create this intense ultraviolet environment. The Urumbamba Valley, which is protected on all sides by the mighty Andes Mountains, creates a safe haven from clouds, apparently a concept not lost on the Incas, who chose Cusco as the capital of their empire from the thirteenth to sixteenth centuries." Pisco talk coming forth, "Think about the intensity of the sun. The sun's unimaginable power, ninety-three-million miles from earth, is affected by the climb up to Cusco, a mere eleven thousand feet from sea level. An apparent insignificant distance dramatically alters the ultraviolet exposure, thereby increasing the chance of skin cancer. Doesn't sound possible."

Roos' southern European heritage had darkened him up considerably over the centuries. On the other hand, Kat, the biologic product of an Irish mother and an English father, was a fair-skinned blonde prone to sunburn.

"We need to gear up for tomorrow's adventure to Machu Picchu." As Roos was throwing off his clothes and grabbing some lotion, he blurted out, "As a matter of fact, let's get started now," as he opened the door and stepped into the steamy shower.

Carl Strange checked out of the Four Seasons in Mexico City and headed for the airport, calling his partner en route. "Evening, Mac. I've confirmed that Roos has arranged a helicopter to take him up to Machu Picchu tomorrow. He's overnight again in Cusco tomorrow, then heading to Rio on the morning flight. I don't see any purpose in going to Peru at this point, so I'm traveling directly from Mexico City to Rio tonight."

Mac's response displayed pragmatism, a trait that had served him well over the years, "Sounds logical. Safe travels."

The bright Peruvian sunlight burst through the hotel room window, waking Roos at the unwanted time of 5:30 A.M. Feeling groggy and desirous of more sleep, Roos knew himself all too well. Falling back to sleep, at eleven thousand feet of elevation, was not an option. While Kat slept, Roos reconfirmed the day's schedule with the hotel's concierge: a short taxi ride to meet the helicopter for a 9 A.M. takeoff, followed by a thirty-minute ride up the valley to a three-thousand-feet elevation, to a landing zone within an hour's hike to the ancient city, Machu Picchu. The return flight was scheduled for 5 P.M. Roos was imagining the anticipated spectacle visible from the helicopter. Aghast and appalled hikers, who were religiously and painfully traveling the fifty-five-mile route one environmental step at a time, would surely be horrified by the sight of a helicopter dropping American tourists into the sacred Incan site. But time was of the essence. Trying to assuage his conscience, Roos deceptively told himself that on his next visit he would hike the route, which builds with once-in-a-lifetime-awe-inspiring anticipation. In all likelihood, there would never be another visit, but as Freud preached, a little self-denial is a necessary healthy mechanism to help man cope with reality.

The helicopter took off, exactly at 9 A.M., from a helipad just southeast of Cusco. On a northwest heading, the bird began climbing over the ancient Incan capital. Mimicking a backward stepping patron lost in translation at the famed Musée d'Orsay in Paris while studying an Impressionist painting from too close a vantage point, as the bird rose in altitude, Kat screamed out, "Christian, look at the puma!"

Sure enough, the outline of one of the animal kingdom's most powerful predators came into crystalline view.

Roos recalled a description of a puma from literature he read over breakfast: "The puma's distinctively mighty hind legs are capable of propelling the big cat twelve feet in the air, at a forty-five-degree angle, a distance of twenty feet, reaching speeds of thirty miles per hour."

As the direction of Machu Picchu became clearer as the bird continued rising, Kat astutely observed: "The puma is in full sprint attack mode and appears to be lunging in the exact direction of Machu Picchu. Could that be a coincidence? The member of the big cat family even appears to be a jumping at a forty-five-degree angle. Over five hundred years ago, the Incas positioned the most powerful animal known to them as a guard warding off evil spirits and protecting their most revered sacred site."

Roos, bursting internally both metaphorically and literally with pride at Kat's sheer brilliance, simply stared at one of the most beautiful women he had ever laid eyes upon, and said with a distinct tone of amo-rousness, "Intelligence is the most powerful aphrodisiac on the planet."

The helicopter landed in the parking lot of Gringo Bill's Hotel in the small town of Auguas Calientes, located at the base of Machu Picchu along the Urubamba River. Christian and Kat jumped on two mules, who looked like they had seen better days, and headed for the beginning of the final stretch of the Inca Trail, which started just over the river. Dismounting, the couple embarked on the switchback two-mile trail to the ancient ruins. In order to limit damage to the trail, a maximum of five hundred tickets, at forty-seven dollars each, are sold daily. Thankfully the Incas were master builders. The trail's stone design is intricate and solid, leaving the feeling of permanence. Discovered in 1911 by Yale historian Hiram Bingham, the site built in 1450 is thought to have been an estate for Incan emperor Pachacuti. But after a cursory look, one comes quickly to understand that the one-hundred-and-twenty-five-square-mile complex containing mul-tiple ancient ruins was much more than a man's castle. Machu Picchu was the religious epicenter of the Incan civilization. Surrounded by steep cliffs, virtually on all sides, the site was unrivaled as a defensive position.

Passing through a subtropical rainforest surrounded by the soaring Andes Mountains, highlighted by the twenty-thousand-five-hundred-foot Mount Salcantay peak, hikers are transported back in time. Crest-ing the final ridge of the trail, at the eight thousand peak of Machu Pic-chu, Kat dropped to her knees and simply stared, speechless. Collecting herself, she remarked, "Christian, this is the most beautiful and tranquil place that I have ever witnessed. Absolutely magnificent and magical, in a deeply spiritual sense."

Roos nodded and added, "I agree but I also feel darkness. Don't know what death is like, but this place is a good start. Very eerie."

The couple sat for hours in awe of the scene. Before departing, Kat took a photo and video of Roos. Back in the Hotel Monasterio, Roos checked in with Harrison via WhatsApp. "Frank, CR here. Day 3: We hiked Machu Picchu today. The experience has left me at a loss for words. Heading to Rio in the morning, where I will no doubt get my rap back."

Out over the South Atlantic Ocean, the plane banked hard left on a north-west heading, putting the Boeing 737 on a course over the entrance of Guanabara Bay, toward Villegagnon Island, home to Rio de Janeiro / Galeao International Airport. Peering out of his window seat on the left side of the plane, Roos saw the sprawling metropolis of Rio de Janeiro stuffed to the gills with twelve million people, over ninety percent of whom call themselves members of the Catholic Church. Standing out in a city of this magnitude is difficult. One hundred thirty feet atop Corcovado, a two-thousand-three hundred-foot mountain peak at the southeastern tip of Rio de Janeiro, the statue of Christ the Redeemer, rises magisterially to the challenge. Watching over the citizens of Rio de Janeiro since the 1920's, the world's largest art deco statue defines the skyline here in more dramatic fashion than anywhere in the world. Named as one of the modern Seven Wonders of the World, Christ the Redeemer brings goodness to the largest concentration of believers in the Catholic Church, three hundred and sixty-five days a year.

As the plane entered its final approach, positioned just twelve miles due south of the airport, another Rio de Janeiro icon popped into view, Estádio do Maracanã, officially named Estádio Jornalista Mário Filho. Looking like the eye of a giant Cyclops, the stadium is arguably the most important venue of the most popular sport in the world. Brazil, the world's most successful football nation, has captured five World Cups.

Despite Brazil's economic success, the majority of the country's citizens live in poverty, which is extreme in many cases. Forty million Brazilians, one in five, live in slum-like conditions in one of the more than a thousand *favelas* throughout the country. Progress, which is painful and inevitably threatening to egalitarianism, has led to much bloodshed throughout the centuries as civilizations struggle with ascension.

Bringing Christian back to reality, Kat asked, "Baby, where are we staying tonight?"

Roos replied, "My business school roommate at Wharton, Gabriel Santos, lives here. I hope you don't mind but he is insisting we stay with him. Trust me, you will like him. He is classy gentleman stuffed with an outsized dose of charisma. After graduation, he spent a few years at McKinsey & Company as a consultant, afterwards he moved back home to Rio and joined his father's advertising company. Gabriel is credited with moving the firm into the Internet space. Today, Xsantos is one of the largest social media advertising companies in South America. His father, who still doesn't use email, ceded the Chief Executive Officer position to Gabriel earlier this year."

"Can't wait to meet him," Kat replied. "Where does he live?"

"On his yacht, which he keeps down in Ipanema, one of the most exclusive parts of Rio, located just south of Christ the Redeemer on the Atlantic Ocean."

The spectacular Ipanema Beach is a bastion for luxury shopping, restaurants, hotels and street carnivals. But the place is best known for the beautiful bikini-clad Brazilian women. Old Blue Eyes, Frank Sinatra himself, crooned about the girls in Antonio Carlos Jobim's 1965 Grammy winning song, *The Girl From Ipanema: "Tall and thin and young and lovely, the girl from Ipanema goes walking."* The talented Cariocan is considered to be the primary force behind the Bossa Nova movement and one of the most influential Latin American musicians of the second half of the twentieth century.

"Kat, the plan for today is as follows: head straight from the airport down to Gabriel's yacht, *Xsantos*. Hang out for the day in the wonderful Brazilian sun, walk the beach, maybe take in a little shopping. Gabriel is hosting an all-day party on the boat; don't worry, it's not in our honor. Tomorrow afternoon we will tour Christ the Redeemer on the way to the airport, where we are catching a non-stop overnight eleven-hour commercial flight to Rome."

"Is that all you got?" teased Kat.

The *Xsantos* tender was waiting at the dock when Roos and Kat arrived.

*Xsantos* was designed and constructed in 2011 in Amsterdam by the premier Dutch shipbuilder VanHootchlande, whose eponymous founder, Storm VanHootchlande is a direct descendent of Jan van Riebeeck, the man who started the Dutch East Indies Company (VOC) in 1602. Granted semi-governmental powers, the VOC was granted a charter to control trade with Asia. The Dutch, masters of both sail and sword, quickly crushed the Portuguese and dominated the seas with their massive war ships. In short order, VOC became the largest corporation in the world.

Powered by her twin CAT 3512C diesel engines with a sixteen-thousand-liter fuel capacity, *Xsantos*, hosting twelve guests and a crew of fifteen, is capable of cruising at fourteen knots for five thousand nautical miles. No port is out of the floating resort's sights.

As the tender approached the bow of *Xsantos*, anchored off the famous Ipanema Beach, she crossed the bow and traversed the two-hundred-and-three-foot starboard side before docking on the stern. The cocktail party was in full swing on the first of three aft decks, which spanned the thirty-four-foot beam. A perforated conical stand on the teak swim stern platform, looking like a Christmas tree decorated with Jimmy Choo, Christian Louboutin and Manolo Blahnik ornaments, welcomed guests as they boarded. Naturally, the highly original shoe stand was painted green, yellow and blue, the national colors of Brazil. Roos nonchalantly kicked off his anonymous brown loafers into the men's bucket, while Katmandu carefully stuck her spikes down two holes on the upper part of the shoe tree. Always a perfectionist, she utilized part of the blue section, thinking it would go better with her orange-hued Jimmy Choo Avril flame elaphe pointy-toe pumps.

Observing Roos' state of fixation with his dreaming eyes locked in the most obsessive of ways on the numerous pairs of women's high-heeled stilettos impaled on the Brazilian shoe cone, Kat joked, "You look like a disciple of Nicolas-Edme Retif."

Roos was caught unaware of the eighteenth-century French novelist who was known both as a social realist and a sexual fantasist. A man whose dearth of morals, proclivity for sexual gratification, which earned him the nickname "Voltaire of the chambermaids," and his Brobdingnagian ego, enabled him to stand out amongst the virtuous decay which was Paris back in the day. He replied inquisitively, "Come again?"

Kat, realizing she had caught Christian clueless for a change, responded confidently, "He was a Frenchman who wrote beautifully about women's footwear. So much so, he was credited as being the father of shoe fetishism, a mania later coined *retifism* in Retif's honor. Judging from your besetting preoccupation with the pumps, I would say you have a pretty severe case of retifism. In my non-medical professional opinion, that is."

Roos' nonchalant retort: "Sounds like quite a guy."

While Roos was scanning for his friend and old roommate in a sea of beautiful Brazilian woman dressed in a mixture of thong bikinis, tee shirts and sundresses, he was instantly reminded just how much women love yachts. Especially gorgeous women, he thought. As Fleet Admiral of the United States Navy, Chester William Nimitz said, "A ship is always referred to as a 'she' because it costs so much to keep her in paint and powder." As someone who had lived both on the port and the starboard sides of life, Roos had a theory on the subject, which he felt compelled to run up Kat's flagpole as they sipped on caipirinhas, the unofficial national drink of Brazil. The simple yet powerful drink is made from cachaca, the local version of rum, mixed with sugar and lime, occasionally with some fruit thrown in the glass, served over rocks.

"Women with the requisite beauty factor, ones who are legitimate players in the game, are naturally drawn to money and power. Interestingly relevant outside of the scientific laboratory, Isaac Newton's Third Law of Physics, which states that for every action there is an equal and opposite reaction, powerful men with money are drawn to beautiful women. This phenomenon is a bright-line truism that dates back to the beginning of time. But unlike the unbending laws of physics, the relationship inherent in the Human Third Law is supported mainly by unpredictability and disingenuousness. Cuban drug lord, Tony Montana, played by Al Pacino in the movie *Scarface*, sums up the dynamic quite succinctly, 'In this country, first jou get the money, then jou get the power, then jou get the women.' The ultimate symbols of money and power in society today are private planes and yachts. Why is the latter so much more compelling in the eyes of women? But think about private planes. Sure a ride on a Gulfstream is exciting. However, after the novelty wears off, which it inevitably does, the experience is not significantly distinguishable from a commercial airline flight, particularly if you factor in first or business class. But yachts are entirely a different story, for three reasons, which give rise to my theory as to why women love them so much. First of all you cannot be 'seen' on a plane, except by the passengers, who presumably already know your whereabouts. Of course, 'selfies' on the tarmac in front of the plane or on the airstairs, which find themselves narcissistically onto social media sites, are mandatory. But those are in the past. Only the line crew see passengers board the plane live. Secondly, unlike aviation, there really exists no substitute for the yacht experience. Canoes at camp as kids, water skiing on a twenty-foot center console outboard, sailing on a J30, fishing in a forty-five-foot Hatteras, are off of most girls' bucket lists by the time they reach college. Sure you can take a ride on a Carnival Cruise, but one might as well be in a gaudy Las Vegas hotel. Yachts provide a truly unique experience. Lastly, a woman's territorial instincts become inflamed on large boats. Most anyone can get into a club if they wait in line long enough, or can crash a party, which appears to be socially accepted behavior these days. Absent swimming, there exists only one way to board a luxury yacht and that is by being waved through by security and walking the gangway, in full view of bystanders on the dock. What do you think of my theory?"

Kat deadpanned, "Let's go find your friend."

Roos continued: "If I were a chick, I would go for intelligence, which I have told you on multiple occasions is the ultimate in sex appeal. I see Gabriel, he is the one surrounded by women up on the third-level deck."

Before retiring for the night, Roos texted Harrison: "Frank, Day 4: a day off in Rio, heading to Rome tomorrow. CR"

# Constantine's Slipstream

*"Do not go where the path may lead,*
*go instead where there is no path and leave a trail."*
—Constantine the Great

Fearful of traffic lines, something that Roos spent considerable time and effort avoiding, he and Kat, fully rested from ten hours of sleep in the luxurious state cabin, boarded the *Xsantos* tender at 7 A.M. sharp. The eight-seat craft was already flush with women who were just leaving the party, piled higgledy-piggledy against each other. The foregoing revelry was obfuscated by vapid stares from the speechless roisterers now clutching their high heels and iPhones with equal horsepower. As the tender motored toward the Ipanema Beach dock, the girls were busy posting, friending, tagging, texting, emailing and listening to voice messages, a process, which Christian Roos tongue-in-cheek christened years before as *Symbiosexting*.

The twenty-minute ride on the Corcovado eco train travels through the Tijuca National Park to the top of the mountain where Christ the Redeemer stands in wondrous magnificence. During the ride deep within the world's largest urban hand-planted forest, passengers are serenaded by the soft sweet sounds of singing toco toucans and macaw parrots. Once at the peak, visitors are welcomed by breathtaking unobstructed three-hundred-sixty-degree views of Rio de Janeiro.

Kat made sure the Instagram photograph and Vimeo video were taken to the south, capturing the illusory sight of *Xsantos* floating in the beautiful warm blue waters of the Atlantic Ocean.

As the airplane, headed for Rome, taxied from the gate, Roos sent a text on WhatsApp to Harrison, "Frank, Day 5 in Rio with Christ the Redeemer. Who would have thought that Art Deco could provide such comfort and joy to so many people. Now taking off for the overnight flight to Rome. CR"

In the middle of the fourth century A.D., Constantine, the first Christian emperor of Rome, ordered the construction of a basilica on Vatican Hill in Rome, the likely site of St. Peter's tomb. Consecrated in the year three hundred twenty-six A.D. and completed in the year three hundred forty nine, St. Peter's Basilica was the most important structure in Europe, without question. In the eyes of the Catholic Church, the Romans and their home Christendom had indeed come a long way in the four hundred years since Pontius Pilate executed Jesus Christ.

Eleven centuries later, in the year 1506, one of the most aggressive Popes in the history of the Catholic Church, Julius II, would lay the cornerstone at daybreak on April eighteenth for what would become the greatest structure the world had ever seen. A bull of man, possessing an incomprehensible thirst for greatness, Julius II, referred to as *iL Terribilis* by the people of Rome, was just not satisfied with the current Basilica. The wear and tear of a millennium took its toll on St. Peter's for sure, but it was the mighty desire of Julius II to show the world the power of the Rome, which drove the Pope to raise the original St. Peter's. Riding the wave of the Renaissance with the fall of the Roman Empire safely in the rearview mirror, Julius II was determined to raise the bar to a level so high it would pierce the newly formed Purgatory, created to help finance the massive building project, before it was all done.

Before completion, the new Basilica would outlast seven architects over one hundred and twenty years—including the incomparable Michelangelo Buonarroti, who despite his genius was fired and sentenced to go paint the ceiling—a staggering twenty-eight Popes and fifty million ducats.

Light rain was falling as Roos hopped in a taxi. Unable to rest on the overnight flight from Rio de Janeiro, Katherine opted for sleep, leaving Roos on his own to visit St. Peter's Basilica. Noticing the Christian Cross, the instrument of the Crucifixion of Jesus Christ, hanging from the taxi's rearview mirror, Roos asked the driver if the rain would cancel the weekly Wednesday Papal Audience held outdoors in St. Peter's Square. He was relieved to hear that in the rain His Holiness moves his audience indoors to the Hall of Pope Paul VI, located in St. Peter's Basilica. With his free ticket in hand, Roos walked through the massive square, passing the statues of Catholic Saints, turned left and entered the hall. The weekly Papal Audience is open to the public on a first-come basis. The first several rows of the six-thousand-three-hundred-seat-capacity hall are reserved for ticket holders. Roos was able to secured one of the coveted front row seats through his relationship with Cardinal Dolan in New York City. The hall looks like an airplane hangar with a complete skylight ceiling creating natural lighting from above. By the time Roos arrived, the room was almost filled to capacity. Escorted to the front row by a Vatican employee, Roos took his assigned seat near the center. The audience is separated from the stage by nine marble steps, which run the entire length of the hall. Just one large white cushioned chair sat empty on the stage flanked by two colorful members of the Swiss Guard. Dominating the hall's stage is the magnificent sculpture of a Risen Christ, hair and beard blowing in the wind, symbolizing the Resurrection and completed by Italian artist Perice Fazzini in 1977.

His Holiness Pope Francis, Jorge Mario Bergoglio, the first Jesuit to lead the Church and the first from the Americas, walked onto the stage with arms waving. Quickly seated, His Holiness spoke to the crowd. He began by defining members of the Catholic Church who do not take sanctification seriously as Christians at "half speed." Explaining that as Christians we are holy, justified, sanctified by the blood of Christ, His Holiness preached to the "choir" as he encouraged everyone to carry this message forward, especially to the "lukewarm" Christians. Pope Francis reflected that authentic prayer involves knocking "at the heart" of God with a strong, unwavering faith that he will respond. The Pontiff reminded the audience that when all of us were baptized, our parents made the act of faith in our name, because we were just children. It is a second creation!

If before the whole of our life—our body, our soul, our habits—were on the road of sin and iniquity; after this re-creation we must make the effort to walk on the path of righteousness, sanctification and holiness.

After ninety minutes the Pope closed his Audience with a prayer, which began, "I believe in Jesus Christ, who has forgiven us our sins, I believe in Jesus Christ."

Visible from every inch of the city, Michelangelo's magnificent dome atop St. Peter's is the symbol of Rome and of the Catholic Church. Designed in 1505 by the genius, eighty-five years later it would be completed by architect Giacomo della Porta. Michelangelo would die before seeing his creation grace the Roman skyline. He lived only to see the drum base completed, a structure that would end up supporting over six hundred thousand tons. The tip of the cross rises four hundred fifty-two feet from the ground. A dome of this size had never before been attempted. Once completed it would be three times the size of the Pantheon's dome and dwarf Filippo Brunelleschi's Duomo Cathedral in Florence.

Roos commandeered a tourist to take his photo and video in front of St. Peter's and sent Frank a text on WhatsApp: "Day 6 at the incomparable St. Peter's. It was comforting to hear His Holiness speak of the need to be committed."

In his fluffy bed the following morning at The Inn near the Spanish Steps, Roos embarked on a scavenger hunt. The treasure was his iPhone. Finding the device at the foot of the bed, Roos walked out onto the balcony overlooking the one hundred and thirty stone and cement steps connecting Piazza di Spagna and Piazza dei Monti. A huge smile rolled across his face as he read his most recent email, sent late last night.

"Good evening, Mr. Roos. My name is Veronica Mazzoni. I am the Director of Public Relations for Tenuta Tignanello. I understand from Mr. Piero Antinori that you would like a tour of our vineyard tomorrow. We would be delighted to receive you. Please let me know what time would be convenient for you. Additionally, kindly inform me of the number of guests in your party. Directions to Tenuta Tignanello are attached. Ciao, Veronica Mazzoni"

Roos excitedly awakened Kat. "Wake up, baby. There has been a change in plans."

"Again? Christian, it is only 7 A.M.!"

"Several years ago I did a favor for one of my restaurant friends in Pebble Beach. He had an important business associate in town who wanted to play Cypress Point Club."

Kat interrupted him: "You are not a member of Cypress."

"Correct," said Roos. "But living in the area afforded me the opportunity to make the acquaintance of several Cypress members. The club allows eight unaccompanied foursomes, who have been introduced by a member of the course, Monday through Thursday mornings. The course receives such little play, the club allows the guests in order to keep the caddy program alive. Pay your fee, bypass the practice range, proceed straight to the first tee and scoot off the property after you putt out on the eighteenth green."

"Who was the player?" she asked.

"The one and only Marchese Piero Antinori."

Kat said matter-of-factly, "Never heard of him. Who is he?"

"Piero is either the most or second-most important winemaker in Italy, making him top ten in the world. In my opinion, the five first growths in Bordeaux, Haut Brion, Lafitte Rothschild, Mouton Rothschild, Latour and Margaux and Ornellaia in Italy are the only ones that rival Antinori."

Fully awake now, Kat asked, "What are his brands? How did you arrange the tour on such short notice?"

"His flagship red wines are Solaia and Tignanello. The vineyard is located thirty miles south of Florence. We should be able to make the drive in two hours. We can catch a flight to Istanbul from the Florence airport. If we have time after the vineyard tour, we'll have lunch in Florence. I sent Piero a text yesterday — he is in Pebble Beach of all coincidences — and he put me in touch with his executive assistant, who contacted Veronica Mazzoni at the vineyard."

Roos sent an RSVP to Veronica Mazzoni. "Thank you, Veronica. Katherine Mandu and I would love to visit with you at Tentu Tignanello. We are departing by car from Rome within the hour and should arrive by 11 A.M. Thank you for the prompt and accommodative response. Christian Roos"

Roos called the front desk for a porter and asked for their rental car and a taxi, explaining that he was heading to Florence and needed to follow the taxi out of Rome. Paris is a snap, Tokyo a breeze for the man, but Roos struggled mightily behind the wheel in the frenetic Italian capital, aka motocross track. The taxi driver looked back a few times only to be motioned to continue by Roos. Finally feeling comfortable, Roos passed the taxi and pulled over to the side of the road. He approached and handed the perplexed Italian driver forty euros.

The drive to Florence through the rolling hills of Tuscany is romanticism itself. Passing the unique Tuscan towns built on top of ancient rock formations takes the visitor back into the glory days of the Roman Empire. Historically impenetrable, now towns like Montefiascone, Orvietto and San Gimignano welcome visitors to their perched havens of wine, cheese and pasta. The wonderful people of Tuscany celebrate life in a sophisticated yet unpretentious way. Exhibiting grandeur, which would make their ancestors proud, Tuscan style is intoxicating and spellbindingly addictive.

Nobody displays these characteristics better than Marchese Piero Antinori himself, whose family started making wine in Florence in the year 1385. In all likelihood, the man who started the six-hundred-year grape dynasty, Arte Fiorentina, borrowed money from a local Florentine banker named Cosimo d'Medici to help get his new wine business off the ground. Piero checks in as the twenty-sixth-generation Antinori to make wine, which Galileo Galilei referred to as "sunlight held together by water." Piero lives in Florence in the fifty-room Palazzo Antinori, built in 1461, which has served as the office for Antinori's wine company since 1506.

Roos remarked to Kat about the stark contrast between Tuscany and France's epicenter of wine, Bordeaux, a place he had never visited until recently. "While attending this year's Vinexpo, the uber Super Bowl of the wine industry, I was really struck by Bordeaux's out-of-the-way nature. I imagined that the small towns and vine-lined roads would be populated with adorable bed & breakfasts, wine & cheese shops, and cafes. That mind's eye could not have been more incorrect. Bordeaux is all about business, all about maximizing the value of their big earthy wines. The illusory glamour of winemaking, so prevalent around the world, simply does not exist in Bordeaux. To the geniuses surrounding the Garonne, Gironde and Dordogne Rivers, winemaking is just farming, after all."

Kat asked, "So not like Napa Valley or here in Tuscany?"

Roos continued. "Nothing like it. For starters Bordeaux is essentially closed to the public. Tastings are by invitation only to people in the trade, the press and VIPs of the wine world. When you have the best there is little need for marketing. After a brilliant private tasting at Chateau Latour, I found myself hungry and quite frankly in the mood for a little more wine. Contrary to consensus thought, the French are not indulgent people and definitely not voracious drinkers. Latour is up on the west bank of the Gironde, a slow going fifty miles on some tough roads from our hotel, Les Sources De Caudalie in Graves. On the drive back, to my consternation, I was unable to find a venue to pop in for some much needed wine and cheese. Growing increasingly impatient, I was forced to pull into a gas station in the tiny town of Listrac Medoc, where I could only find a baguette of French bread, some cheese, salome and great French mustard. But no wine."

She giggled at the image. "What did you do?"

"Back in the Peugeot rental car."

"Peugeot, I thought those were bicycles," said Kat, overtalking.

"They are, but it is also a French automotive company. You might know it by the logo, which looks like Michael Jackson dressed in a lion costume dancing in the music video *Thriller*."

"Ah yes, I know it," she replied.

Roos continued. "I started back on the road, but not before splitting the French baguette lengthwise with the car key and stuffing in the cheese, meat and lathering the mustard from tip to tip, using the rental car agreement as a knife. Driving, eating and laughing, the sandwich never tasted better, but the situation was sorely lacking a Bordeaux. At that point out of the corner of my right eye, I saw the bottle of Latour 1996, which the director of the Chateaux had given to me as gift. A staring contest ensued for fifteen minutes and ended with me waving the figurative white flag."

"Was that a good year?" she asked.

Roos emphatically responded, "The uber wine critic, Robert Parker, arguably the most influential kibitzer on any subject in the world, gave the vintage ninety-nine points on his legendary one hundred point scale. A bottle will set you back seven hundred fifty dollars at Sherry Lehman in NYC. I tried to pay, but unlike any other wine regions that I have ever visited Bordeaux has no gift shops in the chateaus!"

Kat was hysterical at this point. "Don't tell me, you didn't, did you? Oh my God, you did."

"Gnawing on a crusty French baguette stuffed with cheese and salome purchased in a gas station, listening to Def Leopard's monster hit, *Pour some sugar on me*, while driving through the left bank grapes of the gods, attending Vinexpo as a journalist, visiting Chateau Mouton Rothschild, Chateau Haut Brion and Chateau Margaux, drinking one of the greatest vintages, from one of five first growths of Bordeaux, a 1996 Latour out of the bottle in a rental car.........Priceless."

Kat quipped, "How did you open the bottle?"

Roos, who was left puzzling over what was worse—drinking a '96 Latour out of the bottle solo or literally drinking and driving, something he never did, responded, "With the affinity opener given to me at Chateau Latour, which means 'tower' in French. The piece is shaped like a tower, just like the one in the wine fields." Roos continued on his Bordeaux analysis, "But Kat, I will tell you, if the French army were as disciplined and as organized as the caterers in Bordeaux, the German army would never have captured France. In my lifetime, I have neither seen such exquisite service nor mouthwatering food served with such precision to so many people in efficiency that would make a Swiss train schedule look sketchy. At Chateau Mouton Rothschild, music accompanied each course. The experience was simply breathtaking."

The gates to Tenuta Tignanello opened like the Pearly Gates to Heaven. Perched atop a hill, the vineyard enjoyed stunning views of the surrounding hillsides flush with grapevines. Roos was reminded of the two aspects of vineyards that never ceased to amaze him. How can so few people produce so much wine, and how do the winemakers know the exact vines, which produce the highest-quality grapes, were questions, which endlessly puzzled him over the years. Antiniori's operation counted just sixty full-time workers, inclusive of grape pickers in high demand during the fall seasonal harvest. When asked where the best grapes were growing, Veronica Mazzoni wasted little time in pointing to a ten-hectare southwest-facing steep slope located just south of the perched winery. Named Solaia, meaning 'sunny one,' Antinori's flagship wine is produced from Cabernet Sauvignon grapes basking in the constant sunlight drenching the hillside. Ms. Mazzoni explained that shade is just not possible in this golden nugget located in the vast Antinori empire. But the majority of Antinori wines are made from sangiovese grapes indigenous to Tuscany that require significant grade to flourish. Efforts to grow sangiovese grapes in Antinori's California vineyard on top of Atlas Peak Mountain have so far proved unsuccessful. Just not steep enough.

During the mandatory tasting, ensconced in the seventeenth-century Tuscan villa adjacent to the winery, Roos and Kat, already pleasantly aware of the magnificent Tignanello and Solaia wines, were treated to the "sleeper" Badia a Passignano. Antinori's third label, named for the adjacent Abbey of Passignano, an ancient monastery established by the Archbishop of Florence in the fourth century A.D. Badia a Passignano requires little blending as the wine is made from one hundred percent sangiovese grapes from the Chianti region of Tuscany, the heart and soul of Marchese Piero Antinori's terroir.

After the tour of the vineyard, Roos and Kat lunched at Piero's Florentine restaurant in Palazzo Antinori, Cantinetta Antinori, where the couple gorged on Tuscan tomato and bread soup, pasta Bolognese, entrecote of beef on the grill from Tuscany with roast potato, assortment of cheeses from Castello Della Sala and warm pear pie with mascarpone cheese. All washed down with a 2008 Badia a Passignano and a 2004 Solaia.

To Roos' consternation, there existed no nonstop flights to Istanbul from Florence. Surveying the options, Roos selected a quick spin over the Italian Alps, with a short layover in Munich, before heading east toward the ancient eastern capital of the Roman Empire. Next he sent Harrison a text about Day 7: They had spent part of it in Italy and were on the way to Turkey.

Roos and Kat arrived in Istanbul in early evening. Later, walking through the streets of the medieval town of Constantinople, modern-day Istanbul, Christian Roos was drawn to a man sitting on a wooden box. With the magnificent fourteenth-century Galata Tower looming at the end of Buyuk Hendek Street, looking like a smaller but a more prodigious vertical Tower of Pisa, Roos focused his attention on the man who was sitting by himself sporting a demeanor of forlornness. His methodical yet random rolls of a pair of dice back and forth onto the backgammon board in front of him, resting atop of a cardboard box, looked like a fisherman pulling in his catch of mackerel from the nearby Bosphoros River. The middle-aged Turk, dressed in nondescript dark clothing, clearly lacked a command of the English language, but that did not preclude him from successfully motioning for Roos to join him. The internationally known wave of his hand was all that was required.

After shaking hands, Osman suggested gambling stakes of five Turkish lire a point on the doubling cube. Backgammon, a class of board game that includes go, chess and checkers, dating back five thousand years to Mesopotamia, survived for four thousand nine hundred and ten of those years before the Americans made a slight adjustment, and a great one. America's contribution to the ancient game was the doubling cube, a six-sided cube, containing the numbers two, four, eight, sixteen, thirty-two, and sixty-four. Each player, before his turn, assuming he has possession of the cube that switches back and forth after each player's deployment, may increase the bet by doubling the stakes, represented in multiples of the figure shown on the cube. This feature, added in the early twentieth century by gambling aficionados in New York City, gave backgammon the moniker the Cruelest Game. Sensing vulnerability, a player can squeeze his opponent by turning the doubling cube, forcing a pay to play dynamic from a compromised position. Unlike chess, backgammon is a game that includes a healthy dose of chance. The doubling cube, chance's governor, is the weapon of the skillful player, who rides statistical analysis all the way to the bank in a game, which the average player believes is nothing but luck. If not for this human emotional flaw, Las Vegas would still be a desert, passed over by the Mormons. An average player can beat a world champion in backgammon routinely. However, over a thousand games, involving the infamous gambling cube, the champion will prevail in overwhelming fashion. Who would ever bet a chess master? Nobody, but the deceptive allure of the gambling tables and the backgammon board are a different story, truly the work of marketing geniuses.

Stabling himself on the wooden Kurukahveci Mehmet Efendi Coffee box, Roos began preparing his board of white pieces. How ironic, he thought, to be in the shadows of the Galata Tower, the historic symbol of the Roman Empire, while pressing his rear on the name of the man who conquered the city. Mehmet II, The Conqueror, a devil of a man according to Pope Nicholas V, defeated the Romans in 1453, starting a five-century run of the Ottoman Empire.

As customary for street backgammon, a small crowd gathered around the two men. Unbeknownst to Roos was the fact that Osman was a notorious hustler and local backgammon champion. "Hustler," either verbose or redundant, in the Turkish world is a cavalier term that is bantered around quite frequently through the ancient streets of the Istanbul. Wonderful and friendly, the Turks are world famous for their aggressive personalities. Their proclivity for negotiating is legendary. A quick spin through the Grand Bazaar exposes the culture of Turkey more vividly than any tour guide tutorial possible. Dating back to the fifteenth century, the Bazaar is one of the largest and oldest trading centers in the world. Over five thousand merchants, populating a labyrinth of makeshift shops, hawk everything from hand-painted ceramics, rugs, candy, antiques, spices, gold jewelry to embroideries under sixty covered streets to their prey, which exceeds a quarter of a million people—daily.

The last of five games ended with Osman, channeling a small child, knocking the board over and spilling the pieces onto the ancient cobblestone street, felled like Roman soldiers at the sword of Mehmet's vehement army.

Roos, sensing the humiliation he had inflicted, refused Osman's insufficient offer of cash. Osman gave a limp handshake and motioned for Roos to follow him. Along with Kat, the two men entered a three-story building, walked two flights of stairs and entered into a large open room encompassing the entire floor. All four walls were stacked with rugs, from floor to ceiling. Osman gestured to Kat and Roos to sit. A small man approached with traditional Turkish tea served in petite ornate porcelain cups. As they were drinking the tea, the man, who looked as if he weighed one hundred and twenty pounds dripping wet, began pulling rolled rugs from the shelves and unfurled them onto the floor in a singular motioned. At this well-choreographed moment, Osman's brother Murat entered the room and said, "Which of the four do you like the best?"

Kat pointed to the black-and-gold run containing red flowers set against an intricate pattern similar to an intaglio design.

The man removed the three discarded by Kat and threw three more out. Roos, not particularly interested in the rugs, was stupefied by the man's athletic prowess. He figured a nine-by-twelve Turkish rug would weigh in the neighborhood of one hundred pounds. After repeating the process several more times, Kat's black-and-gold handmade Turkish rug continued to survive the cuts.

Roos finished his third cup of tea and asked, "How much?"

Murat went through his predetermined routine with precision. Flipping over one corner of the rug and looking back at Roos, the Turkish rug salesman feigning indecision responded, "For you, I could do six thousand dollars?"

Roos asked incredulously, "U.S. dollars?"

"Yes," was Murat's immediate response.

Roos mulled the situation over, looked at Kat, then glanced back at Murat, "I will pay three hundred."

Unfazed despite the ninety-five percent discount offered, Murat, clearly a man accustomed to such haggling countered, "Six hundred."

Roos shot back: "Four fifty."

Murat, "Okay, but no shipping."

"How am I supposed to get it home?"

With that the little man proceeded to fold the rug like a marine handling the United States flag as he prepares to hand Old Glory to a crying widow.

Roos handed his new Turkish friend four hundred and fifty dollars. "We have a deal only if you ship the rug. Slow boat to China is okay. Kat, please give Murat your address."

Murat smiled and shook Roos' hand. "Let's go have some drink and food."

The trio hopped into a taxi for the short ride to Taksim Square, a bastion of decadence dating back centuries. In atypical Muslim fashion the streets contain a cornucopia of bars and restaurants fanning from the center of Taksim, in such magnitude, a pedestrian trolley system was built in order to facilitate logistics.

In a clannish sense, Taksim is segregated by type of retail establishment. Backgammon shops on one street, sports bars on another. Off to the left are seafood restaurants, to the right hookah lounges. Down the center sit dance clubs, adjacent to traditional Turkish retail stores. The unifying theme, which unites all establishments in the Beyoglu district, is an open-for-business mentality at all times. Twenty-four-seven, three hundred sixty-five days a year, one of the largest parties in the world never sleeps. On an unimaginable scale, which puts Mardi Gras to shame, Taksim truly rocks around the sleepless clock.

Murat led Roos and Kat through a crowded Taksim street to an insider's right-hand turn down an unsuspecting Arcadian alley. With a knock on the door followed by some brief local rap, the trio were granted entrance and passed through the psychedelic beads hanging from the ceiling to the floor.

With hookahs aflame, visibility in the smoke-filled room was minimal. The club was clearly a local's destination. Looking like human locomotive steam engines the crowd was sucking and blowing on long tubes connected to ornate hookahs made of colorful glass. The confluence of the different charcoals created a fragrance something between perfume, incense and sex. At first, Roos thought their new Turkish friend had taken them to a strip club. But a quick glance around the room showed no women.

After talking with the maître d', the party was shown to a low couch located next to the elevated stage. A musical ensemble, including a drummer, guitarist and tambourine player, assembled on the stage and began playing an enchanting Arabian tune. Joining in short order were three whirling dervishes dressed in all white, who began spinning in controlled repetitive motion. According to Sufi history the whirling is a form a physical meditation meant to spread peace and happiness through God.

Back in the hotel the time had reached 5:42 A.M. and the unique voice of the Adhan could be heard through the streets intoning the Muadhan.

*Allahu Akbar, Allahu Akbar (God is the greatest, God is the greatest)*
*Allahu Akbar, Allahu Akbar (God is the greatest, God is the greatest)*

Roos peered from his hotel room window and saw locals pouring onto the streets heading to the nearest mosque to pray.

Two of the most visually dominating structures on the Istanbul skyline are the Suleymaniye Mosque and the Sultan Ahmed Mosque, better known as the Blue Mosque. Roos and Kat needed to visit both before catching their quick flight to Konya.

In the taxi, Kat recalled reading an article about the opening of the underwater tunnel connecting the eastern and western sides shores of the Bosphorus River in 2013. At a cost of four billion dollars, twenty-five percent paid for by Japan, the eight-and-a-half-mile tunnel sits fifty-five meters below the surface of the mighty Bosphorus River that connects the Black Sea to the Sea of Marmara, a body of water that ultimately morphs into the Mediterranean Sea. The mile crossing is designed to ease traffic and pollution, while opening up an important passageway from Asia to Europe. Istanbul, literally the point where the East meets the West, holds significant strategic importance to worldwide trade and the Japanese wanted a seat at the table.

Kat recalled that the project, which commenced in 2005 and was slated for a 2009 opening, was delayed for five years on account of an important archaeological discovery.

Roos, staring out on the historic Istanbul streets, passageways witness to invading armies from the east and the west, priests and imams and Greeks and Romans, asked, "What did they find?"

Kat answered, "A fourth-century A.D. Byzantine port. Amazing!"

Roos replied, "Can you imagine the look on the construction crew's faces on the day when the underwater drill hit that scene?"

First up was the sixteenth-century mosque built by the Sultan Suleiman. Showcasing emblematic Ottoman palatine architecture, the largest mosque in Istanbul is designed with a square dome. From the floor of the mosque staring up at the dome, Roos commented, "Incredibly impressive, but only one-third the size of Michelangelo's dome in St. Peter's Basilica."

Kat asked, "Do all mosques have carpets?"

Roos, "Indeed."

Next up was the Blue Mosque, built in the early part of the seventeenth century and widely considered the last of the great mosques erected in the classical period. Utilizing a combination of Byzantine and traditional Islamic architecture, the beautiful structure has a main dome, eight secondary domes and six minarets, which are used by the muezzin to call people to prayer. The interior walls are covered in blue tile.

Before leaving for the airport, Kat took the requisite photo and video of Roos before each of the mosques.

The flight from Istanbul's Ataturk Airport, named for the leader credited with creating the Republic of Turkey in the early twentieth century, to Konya was less than an hour and they arrived there in the early afternoon. Konya, called Iconium when it was part of the Roman Empire, is known for many things. The city is home of the Whirling Dervishes who date back eight hundred years. Their inspirational leader was Rumi, who interpreted and converted the Koran into one big message of love. The Dervishes became his messengers, traveling the world to spread his love. With hands in the air reaching toward heaven, one foot on the figurative Koran and the other spinning symbolizing their travels, the Dervishes turned like tops. Other interpretations claim the Dervishes spinning represents the planets orbiting the sun. Either way they go on and on.

Konya is also the site of the prehistoric Neolithic settlement of Catal Huyuk, which dates back to the year 7,500 B.C., making it one of the oldest-known human communities. But it is Jelaleddin Rumi who makes Konya an international tourist destination. The tomb of the influential Persian poet and one of the greatest spiritual teachers and thinkers of the thirteenth century, who died on December 17, 1273, is sheltered in the Mevlana Museum in downtown Konya. Immortalized in surroundings that would make an Egyptian Pharaoh jealous and roll over in his pyramid, Rumi's remains are showcased in ornate grandeur in the Shrine of Rumi.

While standing in front of the tomb, Roos, the hopeless romantic, turned to Kat and whispered, "Rumi was the greatest love poet of all time. I am not embarrassed to say that I have read his works over the years. Always illuminating, insightful and poignant, his writings have been so soothing to me. My favorite comes from his work entitled *Essential Rumi*."

Kat responded, "Let's hear it."

Roos began reciting from memory a poem from Rumi, which always brought a smile to his face,

*Let the lover be disgraceful, crazy, absentminded.*
*Someone sober will worry about things going badly. Let the lover be.*

Roos continued, "If written last year, I would still love the poem. But the fact that Rumi wrote this masterpiece, in my mind, over seven hundred and fifty years ago, is simply amazing. We may have planes, cell phones, the Internet and sliced bread these days, but the important things in life, one of which is love, never really change. Do they, Kat?"

She simply shrugged her shoulders and laughed at her Christian.

Kat recorded the visit in photo and video, and Roos texted Frank: "Day 8, Visited all the sites in Turkey: the two Istanbul mosques and the Shrine of Rumi in Konya. CR"

The couple visited the ancient settlement of Catal Huyuk, located just outside of Konya. It may have taken over seven thousand years, but in the late 1950's archeologists discovered the settlement, which at the peak boasted a population of six thousand. Mud huts, arranged in a rectangle formation, are easily visible, contain hand-painted geometric patterns on the walls, hand tools and even bull's heads with horns frozen into the rocks for thousands of years.

Audibling, Roos decided to stay overnight in Konya.

# 9

$$\rule{2cm}{0.4pt} \;\text{≫≫≪≪}\; \rule{2cm}{0.4pt}$$

# The Little Engine That Could

*"The future starts today, not tomorrow."*
—POPE JOHN PAUL II

I n the morning the couple continued south by car toward the Turkish coastline. The one hundred and sixty miles separating Konya and the small Mediterranean seaside town of Side, Turkey, are distinguished by a barren landscape. As the beautiful waters of the Mediterranean approach, a small mountain range runs east-west along the southern Turkish coast. The resort town of Side is situated on a small peninsula, which juts out in the Mediterranean like a Maine lobster with its claws extended, forming a protected harbor. Before one can make it to either of the beautiful white sand beaches flanking both sides of Side, they must go through a gauntlet of Roman and Greek ruins. Alexander the Great captured Side with little difficulty in the year three hundred thirty-three B.C. The Roman General Pompey would bring in his legendary army in the first century B.C. and claim Side as part of the Roman Empire. Still standing as testimonials to two of the greatest Empires in history are a twenty-thousand-seat theater, an aqueduct, multiple temples, a fifth-century hospital, and of course Roman baths. For her magisterial beauty and important history, Side is appropriately named the "Pearl of the Mediterranean."

Understanding the geography of the Mediterranean and more importantly the thought process of Christian Roos, Kat began putting things together as the pair made their way onto the large dock, peppered with marinas and boats of all shapes and sizes. "Christian, what is the plan now?"

Roos, with eyes darting back and forth, surveyed the scene, "Charter a boat to take us across the northeast corner of the Med, around the island of Cyprus to Tel Aviv."

"You can't be serious. How far is that?" Kat asked.

"Oh, I would estimate four hundred nautical miles. Around twelve hours in a boat that can cruise at thirty knots. Don't worry, I am an experienced captain and the trip will be insanely beautiful. Besides, the cruise will provide a much needed break from airline travel."

Roos noticed a Royal Denship yacht in the first slip of Turkish Charters. Once a powerhouse Danish shipbuilder, the company is now going through a financial reorganization. But not before building mega yachts, *Force Blue, Princess Mariana* and *Turmoil*, along with some of the sharpest-looking and best-performing mid-size boats. One of the company's more successful lines were the eighty-two-foot yacht cruisers, famous for their dark blue hulls and silver top sides. The sleek open designs maximized sun decks, a critical requirement in the mid-size yacht market. The global bear market exacted a huge toll on the yacht industry, which saw orders plummet and individual bankruptcies wreck havoc on the resale market. Yachts previously selling quickly in the twenty-million-dollar range suddenly were trading hands below five million dollars. Others were sinking under the most mysterious of circumstances. Royal Denship's financial woes were not of particular significance, from a spare part or service perspective, to their existing worldwide floating fleet. But in the world of big money, individuals had choices and plenty of them. The market value of existing Royal Denship yachts dropped more than most. Just too difficult to explain at cocktail parties why the builder of your yacht is out of business.

The couple was greeted by a representative of Turkish Charters, Turguy Cenk.

Roos, glancing at the nameplate on the stern, saw *AKREP*, introduced himself and inquired as to the meaning of the boat's name.

Cenk answered, "*Akrep* is Turkish for Scorpion."

Roos asked for a tour and Cenk was happy to oblige.

The eighty-two-foot yacht was in decent shape, considering her eighteen-year age. Clearly, *Akrep* was well cared for during her lifetime. Most likely the boat spent her entire existence bouncing around the Med, cruising the Greek Islands, the southwestern coast of Turkey, the South of France and the Spanish island of Ibiza. Roos imagined the beautiful bikini-clad women who had no doubt graced *Akrep* over the years. Roos read from the boat's laminated fact sheet:

Cruising Speed: 28 Knots
Maximum Speed: 40 Knots
Fuel Capacity: 2,000 liters
Range: 450 Nautical Miles
Powerplant: Twin Cat C32 1900 HP Engines
Length: 82 Feet
Draw: 5 Feet
Beam: 20 Feet
Cabins: 4 – 2 VIP State Rooms (bathroom enclosed),
    2 Double Bedrooms
Price: $3,000,000

Roos surfaced from below where he was inspecting the sleeping quarters, approached Cenk and asked, "Is *Akrep* available for charter?"

Cenk replied, "Yes, but the captain has taken ill. We are looking for a substitute at the moment. The boat is available for fifty thousand U.S. dollars per the week minimum."

Roos said that they did not need a captain and only wanted it for a couple of days.

Cenk asked, "When would you be returning the boat?"

When Roos told him he wanted to drop her in Jeddah, Saudi Arabia, Cenk laughed out loud. "Absolutely not. The boat would have to be returned here. With no captain or crew, we would need a substantial deposit from you as well."

"Who owns the boat? How long has she been on the market?" Roos asked.

"A gentleman from Cyprus is the owner," Cenk replied. "I believe she has been for sale several years now."

Roos naturally assumed the owner must have become ensnared in the financial crisis that had brought the Cypriot banks to their knees.

As a result, mostly likely he was forced to relinquish his assets, probably ownership in oil and gas fields, which are popping up between Cyprus and Israel like breaching whales. Cyprus was a financial mess and bargains were to be had in all sorts of asset classes including vacation homes, Ferraris and luxury boats.

Kat asked, "What type of navigational systems does she have? How about sonar-based, forward-looking collision avoidance systems like NOAS?"

Cenk replied, "Have not a clue, but please have a look for yourself. All of the boat's technical information is on the bridge."

As Roos and Kat made their way to the bridge, Roos inquired curiously, "Where did that question come from, may I ask?"

"Well I didn't spend five years as a Naval Officer without picking up a few bits of knowledge about boats here and there," she replied.

"You were in the Navy? When?"

"I joined directly from the United States Naval Academy." As she was studying the communication and navigational specifications, she continued, "I could operate this yacht blindfolded."

Roos burst out laughing. "A Midshipman, who knew?"

Rejoining Cenk on the lower aft deck, Roos asked, "I presume charter regulations in Turkey require periodic inspections. When was *Akrep's* last one?"

"Two months ago." Cenk continued, "The full report is on the bridge as well."

Roos called out to Kat, who was still buried in technical paperwork on the bridge, to check out the inspection report and turned back to Cenk."Assuming everything checks out, I will offer one million United States dollars for the boat. Cash today. Assuming the offer is acceptable, we will need a local attorney to draw up a bill of sale and perform a title search."

Cenk nodded, reached for his cell phone and called the owner of *Akrep.*

It took less than an hour to finalize the transaction. The title search showed a nine hundred thousand dollar first lien held by a Cypriot bank. Kat was satisfied with the recent inspection report by the Turkish Marine Ministry. Funds were wired. Roos emailed Bennedict Boulstridge with the details of the transaction, hull number and instructions to bind property and casualty insurance on the vessel. Roos dropped off the rental car, while Kat secured provisions in town.

Both back on the dock, Roos used his credit card to top off the two-thousand-liter diesel fuel tanks. Kat put her arms around Christian, leaned in close and whispered into his ear, "It might be a good idea to secure some firepower for the voyage."

"I have plenty of Cialis. Exactly what do you have in mind?"

She answered, "Well we should be fine, although I am sure there are some unsavory characters out there in the deep blue sea. The Mediterranean Sea is very safe. The Red Sea as far down as Jeddah, our destination, along the shores of Saudi Arabia, Egypt and Sudan is reasonably safe. The real danger begins when ships pass southward through the four-mile-wide Straits of Tiran, the point of intersection between the Red Sea and the Gulf of Aden on the shores of Yemen and Djibouti. On the southwest coast of Africa, just past the Straits of Tiran, sits Somalia, looking like a rhinoceros, protruding symbolically and out into the Gulf of Aden. It is in these waters where most of the world's ship hijackings occur at the hands of the treacherous Somali pirates. It is my understanding the pirates tend to shy away from the heavily secure Suez Canal. They generally wait until ships are out in the Gulf of Aden and the Arabian Sea before attacking, two places we will definitely not be cruising through. But over the past several years, the Yemenis have jumped into the lucrative pirate business. The northwest part of Yemen borders the Red Sea. These waters have seen a dramatic rise in hijackings. Again, it shouldn't be a problem, but safety first, Christian, isn't that what you always say? Trust me when I say a few guns would be wise items to have on board as we make our way south."

Dumbfounded, Roos asked Kat, "How do you know so much about this part of the world?

Proudly she responded, "I was deployed on the USS *George Washington*, a nuclear-powered supercarrier, in the Persian Gulf shortly after the Gulf War II broke out. While not involved with the military effort over in the Gulf of Aden, through osmosis I learned about the enormous problem posed to the world's shipping industry by the Somali pirates. Christian, the world is a messy place and there are few venues as lawless and hopeless as Somalia."

Roos agreed completely. "I read a recent United Nations report that detailed the monumental humanitarian crisis that has engulfed Somali. Human suffering caused by disease, starvation and violence, all of which have reached proportions defined as epidemicities, have thrown the country into a state of Armageddon."

"During my tour of duty," Kat recalled, "I remember hearing a captured Somali pirate, through an interpreter, defiantly say that he is dead to the world. Left with no hope, he and his fellow pirates will continue to attack ships without reservation or trepidation. If you think about it, Christian, the level of desperation is so great that it is forcing Somalis to bear arms, board small vessels and take on the world's naval powers that be. And they are winning. Over five years ago, twenty countries formed an alliance to protect Somali waters. During this time, thirty of the most sophisticated naval vessels sailing the waters have been deployed to the region. The result? Hijackings, costs and ransom have all increased."

"How much ransom is being paid?" Roos asked.

"Difficult to know. For obvious reasons, shipping companies are reticent to disclose the figures. No one likes to be a curve wrecker after all. But reliable sources, many tied to the insurance industry, place the annual figure around fifty million. The crazy thing is that the cost to provide military support is in the eight-billion-dollar range, per year. The collective governments and the shipping industry would be infinitely better off if they would simply hire the Somali pirates to be the region's security for fifty million and send the war ships back to port, saving seven billion nine hundred fifty million per year. Hell, pay them a hundred million."

Roos, injecting his thoughts on what he considered to be one of the most glaring examples of Western hypocrisy, said, "With refugee camps overflowing and children under the age of five dying in the tens of thousands by the month, how many of the world's hunters and gatherers would just sit on the beach and watch trillions of dollars piled sky high on tankers for all to see, literally float by their shores, without doing something. As their wives and children die on the streets by the day, these men are doing the only thing they know. Arguably the situation may be the worst in world. Global indifference is only rivaled by the atrocity itself."

Kat continued. "The Somalis claim that international boats have illegally invaded their waters and squeezed out the local fishing industry. Word on the streets throughout Somalia is that all the pirates, who are held in extremely high esteem, are ex-fisherman. To quote one pirate, the hostages are the new fish."

Roos returned to the guns. "Where would one secure those types of weapons here in the Pearl of the Mediterranean, dear?"

Katherine replied, "Oh, my guess would be to start with Cenk, assuming he has not taken his sixty-thousand-dollar commission and fled the country."

After some haggling and a few phone calls, a black truck pulled up to the dock. The driver hopped out, circled to the bed, pulled back a tarp and exposed a prodigious armament. To Roos' amazement, Kat jumped up on the truck's rear hatch and began rummaging through the assortment of handguns, rifles and shotguns. She selected an AK47 assault rifle with a standard steel thirty-round banana clip, a Glock G30S pistol with a ten round magazine forty-five caliber clip and a Benelli Super Black Eagle, three mag, twenty-six inch shotgun—all for the shockingly low price of one thousand U.S. dollars, ammunition included.

Roos, tongue in cheek, asked Kat, "Do you know how to handle these things?"

In a flash, Kat fired back, "Oh yeah!"

"Did you learn to shoot in the Navy?"

"Way before then," replied Kat. "My dad was a member of the Special Boat Service, an elite unit within the UK Special Forces. The equivalent in America would be the Navy SEALs. He was a highly decorated sniper, earning the Order of Merit for his performance in the Falkland Islands campaign in the early 1980's. Unfortunately, the experience left my father disillusioned. Shortly after the war, he ran off to the edge of the earth, Kathmandu, Nepal."

"So he taught you to shoot?" asked Roos.

"At age six. My mom hated it, but every week for most of my childhood, my dad and I would go shooting. We started out on the range, then moved to the outdoors, where we would hunt all sorts of wild animals. We would travel to the western part of the country where the Dhorpatan Hunting Preserve, the only licensed area in Nepal, is located."

Roos asked, "What would you hunt?"

"Birds, at first, mostly the Koklass and Impeyan pheasant. As I got older, we matriculated to black bear, wild boar and musk deer. But eventually our prey was the trophy animal, which people travel from all over the world to Dhorpatan, the Blue Sheep. Initially, I hated it. The preserve is located about one hundred and twenty miles northwest of Kathmandu at the base of the Dhaulagirl Mountains. The days would be so long, cold and somewhat scary for a little girl. But my dad was amazing. I loved him so much. I really miss him."

"He died too young," said Roos. "My father passed away eight years ago. I understand and can relate to your feelings."

Leaving that topic, Kat went on. "The altitude of the preserve ranges from nine to eighteen thousand feet. Growing up in Nepal really develops a person's lung capacity. My resting heart rate is a ridiculously low thirty-eight beats per minute. Steady hands are the key to shooting. Also helps in yoga and in the sack."

"Was there a shooting program at the United States Naval Academy?" asked Roos.

"Of course. I joined the school's rifle team. In 1999, my sophomore year, we were finalists in the NCAA Championships. I was the number three shooter on that squad and the top marksman in my senior year. You think I am good in bed. Wait until you see me shoot, Christian!"

"Well, with all due respect, I would rather not. Especially not from the stern of the *Akrep*."

Roos mapped out the course using the GPS navigational system: They would cruise from Turkey and refuel and dock overnight on the southern coast of Cyprus, the approximate halfway point, between Side and Tel Aviv. The Saint Raphael Resort and Marina in the town of Limassol looked ideal. He figured the trip to Tel Aviv would take twelve hours, in two equal six-hour shifts.

The historical significance of the Mediterranean Sea, the cradle of civilization, is rivaled only by her mysterious beauty. The first several hours of the cruise reminded Roos just how much he loved the water. Coming into view was the six-thousand-four-hundred-foot peak of Mount Olympus, the highest point on the Troodos Mountain range on the tiny island of Cyprus. With the setting sun casting long streams of light, the *Akrep* sheared through the crystal-clear blue waters of the Med.

From the bridge, Roos saw Kat walking alongside the starboard railing, heading up to the bow. Wearing just a pair of size two Lululemon Boogie Short Silver black yoga shorts and a pink Flow Y Bra IV, Kat with mat in tow, took center stage on the bow of the *Akrep*. Her blonde hair was furled under a white baseball cap, which she must have found below. The image of a pink scorpion was printed on the cap's crown, with the name *Akrep* written in pink Rockwell extra bold font on the back. In anticipation of a yoga show, Roos pulled back on the twin screws, slowing *Akrep's* speed from twenty-eight knots to fifteen. Kat opened with the classic Warrior pose, which she held motionless despite the boat's natural heaving and swaying in the reasonably calm waters of the Mediterranean. Starting with some basic moves, Kat sat upright facing the bridge and began taking large breaths through her nose, holding for a count of four, then releasing. Through each of the ten cycles, her breasts were stretching the mesh paneling of her sports bra, designed to evaporate sweat quickly.

She then went through a series of stretching exercises. Extremely limber, the yoga expert within minutes was loosened to the point of placing both her palms flat on the deck with unbent legs. Turning back to the bridge, she grabbed opposite elbows, releasing back and neck tension in a bent over pose. Holding for ten seconds before standing up, shaking her head no and nodding yes, she would repeat the routine ten times. As Roos observed Kat's firm rear, which was jam-packed in her black pants, he began to fantasize. The tight gear hermetically sealed the most erotic part of her body, creating a mud flap silhouette of every square inch, curve and muscle from her upper thighs to just below her bellybutton. Unnecessarily, her Lululemon shorts were equipped with the brand's Silverscent Technology designed to help inhibit the growth of odor-causing bacteria. It was something Roos, a man of who enjoyed all five of his God given senses, definitely preferred she do without. The Silverscent aside, Roos was partial to the too see-through material in the Groove and Astro Lululemon yoga pants, which had been recalled by the company. As Kat continued to bend, contort and twist on the bow, her exposed midriff displayed subtle ripples, badges of honor earned from years of sacrificial core exercise. Roos' mind irresistibly morphed into flagrante delicto thought.

With the sun now almost below the horizon, Kat, from a full upright standing position with palms facing towards the heavens, launched into a handstand. After holding an erect vertical position for over thirty seconds, she slowly began arching her back and lowering her legs backwards into the symbolic scorpion yoga pose. One more time, Roos throttled back on both engine screws, slowing the boat to a sailing crawl. From the scorpion pose, she began tilting her head backwards and gently placing her face down on the mat. Arching her spine, she lowered her legs until they were flush from the knee down on the mat, where she grabbed her toes. Her groin was thrust skyward, along with her breasts, as she remained motionless in the iconic camel pose, floating like an Arabian desert-like heavenly mirage in the Mediterranean Sea.

From behind the windshield on the bridge, Roos who was laser beam focused on Kat practicing the ancient art of yoga, became increasingly aroused, as one erotic pose followed the next. Unable to contain himself any longer, the makeshift captain killed *Akrep's* engines, switched on the boat's night lights, kicked off his flip flops and scurried up the port side railing towards an awaiting Kat, who met him with an embrace. She pulled back, stared into his blue eyes and started massaging his temples in a sensual circular motion. She lowered him down onto his back and proceeded to rip off his shirt and khakis, leaving him wearing just a grey pair of Polo mid-rise four-pack underwear. Laying there, staring up at the brightly lit stars, the same ones which have watched over the Mediterranean for all of time, Roos was more than happy to acquiesce to his new role as a human yoga mat.

Kat climbed aboard in a reverse cowboy position, leaned forward and grabbed Christian's thighs with her muscular yet smooth hands. Extending her legs over her tricep muscles, she rose into the firefly pose. After holding the position for several minutes, she bent her right leg, lowered her arms, twisted her torso to the right and placed her left foot onto the shelf created by her left arm. From Roos' viewing angle the dragonfly pose was exceptionally sensual.

Unable to resist, Roos grabbed Kat, rolled her over and began kissing her plump soft lips. Sliding down her sweaty body, Roos removed her top, exposing her exceptional natural breasts. She escaped with a Mongolian reversal, flipping Christian back onto the mat. Grabbing his wrists, she extended her body perfectly horizontal to his and bent her legs at the knees until they were flush with her thighs. Roos was astonished at the leg position she was able to achieve in the peacock variation yoga pose. With her naked body, except for a small pair of shorts, parallel to his, Kat playfully imitated the live animal as she nodded her head down and kissed him passionately. An erotic sensation of suspension engulfed Roos, making him feel safe yet helpless at the same time. If a stripper pole could talk, surely it would express the same emotion, thought Roos as he tried to remain in control as his heart began to palpitate. As stimulatingly torturous as the show was, he instinctively knew he wanted more. Lots more. The couple began a playful banter.

Kat started: "Sailor, yoga class is ninety minutes today, I hope you don't mind. Just so you know, we are just warming up."

Roos responded, "I have cleared my calendar."

"Sailor, you're a long way from home. What would your mommy

think of you now?"

"She warned me there would be moments like this," he replied.

"If needed can you man the decks?"

"Heavy artillery is loaded, only need a match," he said. "Do you smoke?"

"Never looked. I want to fly some propaganda up you flagpole. How much can she hold?"

"It depends are how strong the winds are blowing!"

By this time, Kat was working up quite a sweat. The salty droplets were streaming down her face and neck before ultimately dripping off her breasts onto Roos, like hot wax from a candle. She crooned, "Sailor, you best batten down the hatches and brace yourself for a storm."

Sensing that her partner was approaching the breaking point, Kat slowly came out of her pose and slid down Roos' trembling body, removing his underwear in a seamless motion. With her hands on Roos' pelvic bones, Kat extended her legs assuming a variation of the firefly pose. Placing the soles of her feet on the submissive face of her prey, she sat down on the excited captain. After ten minutes of "parallel bar" dips, Roos screamed out in ecstasy.

The scorpion christened the *Akrep*, leaving Christian in the wake of blissful satiety, aboard his new pleasure dome.

An energized Kat dismounted and exclaimed, "I will take the helm from here and bring *Akrep* into safe harbor on Cyprus. Sailor, get in the crow's nest and watch out for pirates!"

Roos, temporarily paralyzed, simply grinned as he lay motionless on his back staring into the mesmerizing Mediterranean sky and gave an, "Aye, aye, Captain."

In darkness only slightly mitigated by the clear starry skies, Kat skillfully navigated the boat around the southwestern tip of Cyprus. The sparkling town of Akrotiri served as a natural lighthouse demarcating the small peninsula jutting southward into the Mediterranean Sea. The land provided a natural safe harbor for the Saint Raphael Marina, located just up along Cyprus' southern coast in the town of Limassol. Kat grabbed the radio: "Saint Raphael Marina, this is the

*Akrep.* Over."

Operator, "Saint Raphael Marina control here. Over."

Kat continued, "Requesting overnight docking and fuel for an eighty-two-foot yacht, drawing five feet. Over."

Operator, "Permission granted. Proceed to the port side of the main entrance marked by buoy number three. Dock in slot sixty-four. What is your ETA? Over."

"Five minutes out. Over."

Operator, "Marina personnel will be on site to assist with the docking. Over."

Too exhausted to join in the revelry at the marina's main restaurant and bar, the couple passed out in the main stateroom to the sounds of circa 1980's American rock bands, Journey and Foreigner, blasting in typical European fashion from the outdoor party.

Roos sent off a message to Harrison via WhatsApp: "Frank, Day 9, overnight in Cyprus en route to Tel Aviv tomorrow. Have a new toy. CR" Attached was a photo of the *Akrep.*

Harrison texted back within seconds with one of his trademark sayings, "Nice!"

"Hi, Mac, Strange here. Just touched down in Tel Aviv."

Mac, happy to hear from his partner, replied, "Carl, how are you holding up? The schedule sounds grueling."

Having heard perfunctory language like this before from Mac for decades, Strange, like a longtime spouse accustomed to pointless questions, knew instinctively just how to proceed with the details at hand. "I think we have another issue potentially brewing. As you know, I was in Istanbul with Roos and Mandu. His itinerary had him flying to Konya to visit the grave of Rumi, after which he is heading to Tel Aviv. I am sure you agree that there was little point in me joining the party in Konya."

Mac, growing impatient, interrupted, "So what is the problem?"

Strange answered, "Well, I checked in with my contact at the bank, you know the gentleman who is giving me updates on the purchases made on Roos' credit card."

"Yes," Mac said, "but it is my understanding that Roos has several cards issued by more than one banking institution."

"Correct, but I have access to his main card, which showed a one thousand three hundred dollar purchase of diesel fuel at a marina in Side, Turkey."

"What do you make of this?" asked Mac.

"My initial thought is that Roos drove from Konya to Side, gained access to a boat, and is somewhere on the Mediterranean Sea heading toward Tel Aviv via water. Don't worry, I will figure it out."

Mac just grumbled.

Carl Strange was lounging on the rooftop pool of the Marina Tel Aviv, an upscale hotel and marina complex located in downtown Tel Aviv. A Pimm's No. 1 cocktail was in one hand and a pair of high-powered American-made Brunton Eterna ELO 15 X 51 roof prism binoculars was in the other. His intelligence from the bank indicated that Roos had booked a slip in the hotel's marina for tonight.

Shortly before 1 P.M., Strange observed a yacht flying the bright red Turkish flag with a white crescent and star, both symbols of the Holy Koran, which he would eventually determine to be the *Akrep*, approaching the Marina Tel Aviv. With his hands "Pimm's No. 1" steady, Strange noticed an official-looking vessel making a beeline toward the *Akrep*. Focusing the binoculars, he could read the writing on the side of the boat, *Israeli Border Police*. The tiny country of Israel, with her eight million inhabitants, all of whom are surrounded by Arab countries, has not survived by being complacent about security. The approximate one-hundred-and-twenty-five-mile Mediterranean coastline presents a huge security challenge and as such is heavily patrolled by the Magev, the Hebrew word for Border Police. It is widely believed that the HaYamas unit within the Magev has the most advanced urban warfare capabilities in the world. Keeping order in areas such as the volatile and dangerous

West Bank and Gaza Strip, as well as the coastline, requires sophisticated counterintelligence, skilled military personnel and advanced weaponry. The Magev are world leaders in all of these categories.

Holding a bullhorn to his mouth, the officer wearing dark green pants and shirt, similar color beret and black boots, instructed Roos to kill his engines and prepare to be boarded. Members of the Magev threw lines over the *Akrep*, securing her stern to their center console rubber rimmed thirty foot boat. Three officers carrying Colt M4 Carbine rifles, known for their lightweight and potent firepower capability, and Jericho 941 SL semi-automatic handguns, boarded the aft deck of the *Akrep*. By their side were two red black German shepherd detection K-9s. Both self-assured animals were sporting their breed's trademark large erect Dr. Spock–looking ears.

Kat astutely had all of the boat's paperwork arranged in a folder, along with the couple's passports and visas. And more importantly she secured the guns down below in an obscure spot, out of sight but not out of a sniff. After examining the paperwork, one of the officers initiated a line of questioning. "I see you purchased the vessel yesterday in Side, Turkey. Impulse decision or just a bizarre coincidence?"

"The former. We were looking for a charter, but the price was right on the *Akrep*," replied Roos.

"I see," the officer remarked. "The Turks are notorious negotiators or hustlers, depending upon your point of view. I seriously doubt you took anyone from Side to the cleaners. How long do you intend to stay in Tel Aviv and what is the nature of your visit?"

"Just one night," said Roos. "We are booked for a slip at the Marina Tel Aviv. We plan to visit the Western Wall and Holy Sepulchre in Jerusalem and the Church of the Nativity in Bethlehem tomorrow. Afterwards we will be departing."

"Where is your next destination?" the officer asked.

"Jeddah."

"Through the Suez Canal?" asked the officer.

Roos, "Unless you have a better route."

Officer, "Alright. Your paperwork is in order. I must notify you that your vessel is floating in official Israeli territorial waters and therefore subject to search and seizure."

At this point the officer motioned to his two team members to commence a search of the *Akrep*. Each holding a leash, the officers separated. One went onto the boat's bridge, while the other made a heading toward the bow via the starboard side. The lead officer remained on the aft deck, where he radioed his Tel Aviv command post with an update of the happenings aboard the *Akrep*. After ten minutes, the officer below deck called out to his commander, who immediately made his way toward his underling. Katherine and Roos followed quickly behind. The officer was standing in a closet-lined hallway leading to the aft main stateroom. The German shepherd was crouched in an alert position with his elongated nose pointing toward the door directly in front of him.

During a case involving the Fourth Amendment to the United States Constitution, the Chief Justice of the Supreme Court, the Honorable John Roberts, asked a litigant the following question, "So you don't know whether, in other words, are dogs good at sniffing things, or are they, can they be good at bombs, but not good at meth?"

The answer is yes. The most common application of a dog's nose, thought to be thousands of times more powerful than a human's sniffer, is illegal drugs. But other smells, equally as important, yet not as common, are money, weapons like bombs and humans.

The dog in front of Roos and Kat was trained in the detection of firearms and bombs. Specifically, during training the canines are exposed to the smell of C-4, dynamite, Tovex, gunpowder, TNT and potassium chlorate, as well as oils and resins used to clean firearms.

The commanding officer asked what would be found when the door to the closet was opened. Kat interjected, "An AK47 assault rifle, a Glock G30S pistol and a Benelli Super Black Eagle Shotgun."

Upon hearing the answer, the officer motioned to his partner to open the door, exposing the cache. The officer explained Israeli law, which requires individuals to have a license in order to carry firearms in the country. He further elaborated the types of usage that qualify for a license. Security workers, people who transport valuables or explosives, residents of the West Bank and hunters are the only constituencies who need apply. With a success rate less of sixty percent, Israel has the highest rejection rate in the Western world.

The officer then announced, "These weapons are illegal. We will have to confiscate them. They will be returned to you upon your departure tomorrow."

The marina provided Roos and Kat with a rental car for the drive to Jerusalem, just a short fifty-mile trip from Tel Aviv. The couple planned to visit the Old Walled City and the Church of the Holy Sepulchre, universally defined as both the Crucifixion and burial site of Jesus. Within a stones throw of the Church was the Western Wall, sometimes referred to as the Wailing Wall, where Christians and Muslims have come in pilgrimage for thousands of years, to pray, fight, scream and cry.

Jerusalem exudes spirituality. It is the place where Judaism, Christianity and Islam all lay claim to religious sites of great importance to them and to other religions as well. It is also a city of significant historical and archeological sites whose landscape is dominated by the glorious golden Dome of the Rock, an Islamic shrine dating to about 691 A.D., which sits atop the Temple Mount within the Old City of Jerusalem. Outside the walls of the Old City is the vibrant and prosperous city of modern-day Jerusalem where people of all faiths live, work and pray, mostly in harmony.

The couple entered the Old Walled City through Jaffa Gate and walked into the Christian Quarter and part of the Via Dolorosa on their way to the Church of the Holy Sepulcre. One of the holiest sites in the Christian world and dating from the twelfth century, the Church marks the site of the Crucifixion and burial of Jesus. Inside, the Church is a complex of a number of sites and chapels including the Chapel of Golgotha, where Christ was crucified, and the Stone of Anointing, where pilgrims kneel, pray and kiss the place where Jesus' body was prepared for burial. The tomb of Jesus is located in a chapel under the main rotunda, and pilgrims come from many distances to experience the tremendous spirituality within its walls. Roos and Kat stood motionless and speechless in a state of absolute wonderment. After several minutes, Roos moved into a position of genuflection before praying. Kat followed suit.

From the Church, Roos and Kat made their way through the narrow streets and lanes to the great space occupied by the Western Wall, the holiest spot for Jews within the Old City. Built originally as a retaining wall to shore up the mighty Temple Mount erected by Herod, it is referred to also as the "Wailing Wall" where Jews came to lament the loss of the Temple in 70 A.D. from which they were expelled by the Romans. Jews, Christians, Muslims and people of other faiths converge on the Western Wall, clearly divided into two sections—for men on one side and women on the other—to offer prayers, thanks and supplication. Many place handwritten notes with prayers and entreaties within the cracks of the old wall.

Roos made his way to the area for men—the larger of the two sections—said his prayers and made his entreaties alongside the many men in the black coats and garb of Orthodox Jews. Kat paid her respects in the smaller area reserved for women, many of them in the headscarves and head coverings worn by Jewish women and Muslim women. Neither knew if the other left a note of supplication within the cracks of the Western Wall.

Staring at the ancient wall after their visit, Kat asked Christian, "This appears to be a decidedly significant destination for people of many faiths. What is the conflict between Judaism, Christianity and Islam?"

Roos replied, "It's a very complex religious/political situation. All three religions lay claim to various sites within Jerusalem. Israel, of course, has claim to Jerusalem as a result of the Six-Day War with Jordan in 1967. We've seen the Western Wall, sacred to Judaism, and the Church of the Holy Sepulcre, sacred to Christianity, and both religions have other sacred sites within Jerusalem. So, too, do the Muslims. After Mecca and Medina, Jerusalem is the third holiest of destinations in the Muslim religion. Back in the seventh century, when Mohammed was experiencing revelations down in Mecca, he was awakened one night and brought here to the site of the Dome of the Rock where he rode a winged horse up into the heavens before returning, making this a very controversial venue in the process. Over a millennium later, the situation has not worked itself out. The Dome and Temple Rock, now under the control of Jordan and the Palestinian Authority, stand in the midst of East Jerusalem in the state of Israel, which controls access to it. So pilgrims from the Muslim religion come to visit their holy site, as do Christians from all over the world to visit their sacred sites, all in the heart of the Israeli state. It's all very complex and amazing that it works at all.

"Unfortunately," Roos continued, "a similar controversy exists in Bethlehem, the birthplace of Jesus, where we are headed next. In the fourth century A.D., Constantine commissioned the Church of the Nativity to be constructed in present-day Palestinian territory. The site is thought to be located above the caves where Jesus was born, an area which holds tremendous significance for both Christians and Muslims."

"While Bethlehem is just six miles and a short fifteen-minute drive from Jerusalem, it is in another political world as part of the Palestinian West Bank," he explained. "A center of Palestinian culture, it is the capital of the Bethlehem Governorate of the Palestinian National Authority and it is bound on all sides by Israeli territory. Visitors have to go through an Israeli military checkpoint at the border crossing between Jerusalem and the West Bank."

Roos and Kat hired a taxi and after being checked through the military checkpoint, they arrived in Bethlehem and made their way to Manger Square and the Church of the Nativity, another sacred site in Christendom and one of the oldest continuously operating churches in the world. The Roman Catholic, Greek Orthodox and Armenian churches jointly administer the site. Within the Church is the Grotto of the Nativity, an underground cave beneath the basilica that enshrines the spot where Jesus was born. Beneath a small altar lies a fourteen-pointed star that marks the site of the birth. Roos and Kat visited the Grotto before hiring a taxi for the ride back through the Israeli checkpoint and on to Tel Aviv.

Back aboard the *Akrep* in their slip at the Marina Tel Aviv, they watched a spectacular view of the setting sun over the Mediterranean Sea. The vibrant nightlife of Israel's second-largest city was already starting to percolate.

Sitting on the aft deck with a cocktail, Kat remarked to Roos, "If the world wants to eradicate Somali pirates, they should give the assignment to the Israeli military. Those guys do not fool around; they would have the situation under control within a year."

Before retiring, Roos sent Frank his daily text update: "Day 10: In Israel. Visited the Church of the Holy Sepulchre, the Western Wall and the Church of the Nativity. CR"

# 10

## The Jeddah Night

*"Sleep is the brother of death."*
—Prophet Muhammad

U p early the next day, Roos and Kat prepared for the long journey to Jeddah, Saudi Arabia. Their ultimate destination was the Park Hyatt Jeddah Marina Club and Spa. But the two-day voyage would require an overnight stop. What better place than Hurghada, thought Roos. Egypt's second-largest city was beautifully situated on the western shores of the Red Sea. Up until the early twentieth century, Hurghada remained a small fishing village. That has all changed. Now a hot-spot party destination for Europe, the town is flush with chic shopping, restaurants and nightclubs stocked with revelers galore. Relaxing on the breathtaking beaches by day and dancing in clubs by night is the move in Hurghada for the European jet-set crowd.

Kat, upon hearing the itinerary, commented, "Christian, I read recently that the British Foreign Office issued a warning to their citizens traveling to Hurghada to not leave the resort grounds. This was in response to recent violence."

"Isn't this why you bought those guns?"

"Seriously," she replied. "Christian, I don't like the sound of the plan."

"We are staying at the newly constructed Hurghada Marina, located just outside of town. The venue boasts high security and one-stop shopping for restaurants, bars and hotels. Other than a quick spin through the resort, grabbing some food and a quick drink at one of the numerous clubs, I anticipate staying on the pleasure dome at all times."

The route was an arduous one, but on the *Akrep*, the couple was quickly learning that given the yacht's comforts, nothing was too difficult to endure. The four hundred and thirty-one nautical mile trip to Jeddah would require navigating the Suez Canal. The one hundred and thirty mile passageway connecting the Mediterranean Sea to the Red Sea, built on the backs of Egyptian labor over a period of ten years, opened for business in 1869. The waterway brings the East and West significantly closer to each other, as a result of bypassing the Cape of Good Hope, the most southwestern point of the African continent, and by offering an alternative to the Panama Canal. The old lighthouse perched on Cape Point, a rocky headland on the Atlantic Ocean, has stood guard in the shadows of Cape Town's majestic Table Mountain for centuries. She has seen fewer ships pass since the opening of the shorter Egyptian passageway. The shortest route from East to West by water offers up tremendous savings to shipping companies. Tokyo to Rotterdam through the Suez Canal is three thousand five hundred nautical miles shorter than the route around Cape Hope. New York to Singapore through the Panama Canal tacks on almost three thousand nautical miles. Shorter trips from Southeast Asia to Europe are cut in half by the Suez Canal. It is easy to understand why seventeen thousand ships pass through the Port of Said every day of the year, risks in the region notwithstanding.

Cruising at twenty-eight knots, the *Akrep* reached Port of Said, the entrance to the Suez Canal, in just under five hours. The time was 1 P.M. Roos maneuvered the boat into the tollbooth. An official-looking man, dressed in traditional Egyptian clothing, boarded the *Akrep* and handed Roos a stack of paperwork. In perfect English, he explained some basic information about the passageway. "The Canal is single lane for one hundred and thirteen kilometers. There are four double-lane zones and six bypass zones, which total eighty kilometers. With a boat of your size, you don't want to get stuck behind an oil tanker. It will take you forever to get to the Gulf of Suez, therefore please make use of the passing lanes. The minimum speed is fourteen kilometers per hour. Minimum. If you drop below by a kilometer the fine is ten percent of the tolls, six kilometers below the minimum speed results in a fine equal to one hundred sixty percent. Maintain speed at all times. Mooring bollards are placed every one hundred and twenty-five kilometers for emergency docking only. The fee based upon your gross weight of twenty-nine tons is seven thousand six hundred and fifty SDR's. How would you like to pay?"

"What is an SDR?" Roos asked.

Officer, "An index made up of a basket of four currencies, the dollar, pound, euro and yen. What currency will you be paying in?"

Roos replied, "United States dollars."

The officer pulled out a calculator and started punching away. "The exchange rate is point six four seven for the U.S. dollar. Total fee for the Akrep will be nine thousand nine hundred and fifty-six U.S. dollars. But this is your lucky day. I am running a special."

The officer extended his left hand, which was holding a small handbag, toward Roos, and continued, "For you just three thousand U.S. dollars."

Kat quickly usurped Roos' bafflement by heading below to the safe. Emerging in minutes, she grabbed the handbag and placed forty Benjamins and handed it back to the smiling officer.

Roos paid the official bill of three thousand U.S. dollars by credit card and headed south through the Isthmus of Suez. Roos calculated the passage would take twelve hours and another six hours to travel the one hundred and eighty-six nautical miles to Hurghada. He and Kat agreed to work in three six-hour shifts. Roos would take the first and last.

Kat kissed Roos and headed for *Akrep's* master stateroom. As she was departing from the bridge, she turned to Christian and stated, "I bet you don't know who first built this canal."

Roos, "I think it was the Egyptian leader Pasha Said who teamed up with the French and their diplomat and engineer Vicomte Ferdinand Marie de Lesseps. Around the 1860 timeframe."

"Close with the year, but I am afraid you have mixed up your Anno Domini and Before Christ, my dear. You are correct about Said and Lesseps, but they were the ones who reopened the canal. By the way, it has been reopened and closed a half a dozen or so times over the course of history. The Egyptian Pharaoh, Senausert III, in 1874—B.C., was the man who first built the canal. Think about that, Christian. Almost four thousand years ago, boats were making this journey."

Roos, feeling his pyramid begin to tense up, joked to his partner, "Cleopatra, you know I'd walk a mile for a camel."

Roos quickly found the *Akrep* behind a large container ship. Through his binoculars Roos could read the ship's name, *Ebba*, flying under the Danish flag. The letters MAERSK were plastered all over her mighty blue hull. A subsidiary of the diversified Danish conglomerate, AP Moller Group, Maersk is the world's largest shipping company, by a considerable margin. Acquisitions over the past decade, of United States–based Sealand and P & O Nedlyon of the United Kingdom, have put additional distance between Maersk and its competitors. With a fleet of six hundred and forty-six ships, approximately a third owned and two-thirds chartered, Maersk generates revenues over sixty billion US dollars, which puts the company in control of fifteen percent of the global shipping industry. Roos quickly googled the *Ebba* and learned that the vessel was the fifth-largest cargo ship in the world. As a matter of fact, the top seven ships all fly the Danish flag and proudly sport the powerful Maersk logo. Roos marveled at the *Ebba's* statistics, as he continued reading from the Maersk website. Built in 2007 with a length of three hundred ninety-seven feet and beam of one hundred eighty-three, Roos' beloved hometown Washington Redskins could play their dreaded rivals, the Dallas Cowboys, on the deck of the *Ebba*, and still have plenty of room on all sides for cheerleaders and spectators. The *Ebba* is able to carry fifteen thousand twenty foot equivalent units (TEU), up to seventy thousand tons, an astonishing weight, which converts into one hundred forty million pounds. Roos thought out loud that the brightly colored containers stacked on the deck looked like a LEGO creation under a suburban Christmas tree. Roos wondered what was more impressive, the fact that a ship of such enormous size could actually float and make it through the shallow-looking canal, an image of water runoff cutting a path through an Atlantic Ocean beach, or the fact that the *Ebba* was manned by a crew of just thirteen.

Able to cruise at twenty knots and max out at twenty-five, Roos was pleasantly surprised at the speed the *Ebba* was able to maintain as the two vessels headed south through the Suez Canal. However, he was not disappointed to see the markings for the first of six passing zones approaching. In the Port Said bypass, which extends for forty kilometers, Roos was able to giddy up the *Akrep* and pass a dozen cargo ships. Snapping his iPhone camera, Roos captured images of ships from Swiss's Mediterranean Shipping Company, China's COSCO, France's CMA CGM, Taiwan's Evergreen and the German company Hapag-Lloyd. A virtual United Nations, transporting the world's GDP, floating down Pharaoh's man-made canal cut through a desert, was truly a sight to behold.

After six hours, with approximately half of the canal behind them, Kat relieved Roos behind the wheel of the *Akrep*. Before he went to sleep, he sent Frank a text on WhatsApp: "Day 11 spent sailing on the *Akrep* on the way to Hurghada. CR"

As the Egyptian clock struck midnight, the *Akrep*, under the steady control of Kat, passed the Egyptian town of Suez and poked into the Red Sea. Recent reports indicated that the Muslim Brotherhood were targeting the southern entrance to the Suez Canal in retaliation for Egyptian President Mohammed Morsi's forceful removal from office by the Egyptian military. The town and waters were crawling with the same military forces staked out seemingly in every drop of the critical waterway. Roos relieved Kat of her captain duties after her six hours. After briefing Roos on *Akrep's* progress, she repaired to the stateroom for another round of much needed sleep.

As Roos cruised the yacht toward Hurghada, the sun was rising over the Arabian Desert to the east occupying almost the entire Arabian Peninsula. The sand, surprisingly red, was made more so by the bright morning sunlight, which danced across the calm blue waters of the Red

Sea before ultimately reflecting off of the *Akrep's* blue hull. The city of Hurghada lies just south of the Gulf of Suez on the northwestern shores of the majestic and historic Red Sea—a body of water, which must feel wholly inadequate over the millennium as popular opinion has always held that she just did not extend far enough to the north, specifically to the strategically located Mediterranean Sea, which enjoyed coveted borders with the West. As the *Akrep* made her way along the shoreline, Roos could see revelers pouring out of the nightclubs, bars and restaurants that populate the twenty-four-mile shoreline defining the round-the-clock party town of Hurghada. Roos maneuvered the yacht into the harbor and joined Kat below in the main stateroom where the couple slept until midday.

Sitting on a urine-stained concrete floor, Mooge Abdikarim stared day after day at the names and phone numbers etched on his prison cell's walls—walls which if they could talk would speak of a century of horror, pain and suffering. His home away from home was a prison built in 1884 during the Ottoman Empire in Berbara, the capital city of the breakaway self-declared Republic of Somaliland and now internationally recognized autonomous state. Abdikarim and his crew were picked up in his skiff approximately fifty miles off of the coast of Berbara, in the pirate-infested waters of the Gulf of Aden, known eerily as the Somali Basin. Despite their "independence," Somaliland is an impoverished country struggling to survive. The only hope for the future lies in the Port of Berbara, a strategically import venue for shipping between east Africa and Arabia. Naturally, pirates hijacking shipping vessels have a deleterious effect on attempts to grow the Port of Berbara's business. The government recently announced an effort to curb piracy, which involves a rag-tag Coast Guard whose mission is to patrol the waters of Somaliland's coast and capture the pirates. Distinguishing the pirates from the Coast Guard is only made possible by identifying a skiff's flag. Pirates, of course, fly a version of the Jolly Roger, while the Coast Guard hoists the Somaliland national flag, containing three horizontal stripes: red—reflecting blood and sacrifice;

black—emblematic of the country's dark past; and white—symbolizing the new country's bright future—a future that everyone hopes is coming but nobody really believes or thinks is.

Abdikarim claimed he was fishing when the Coast Guard boarded his skiff. But the officers found neither fishing nets nor equipment, only a global positioning system. When asked to explain, Abdikarim claimed that they had to find the fish first. Unable to sell his preposterous story, Mooge Abdikarim was sent to prison—the old one. Appalled by the wretched inhumane living conditions at the prison, the United Nations stepped in and built a new prison in the neighboring city of Hargeisa. The new facility, which can house four hundred prisoners, proudly boasts cots, bathrooms and a medical facility. Unfortunately for Abdikarim, given the state of anarchy in his country, the prison sold out almost immediately, and therefore was unable to accommodate the "fisherman" turned pirate.

With the court system backed up, Abdikarim was facing at least two years before he would have his day in front of a judge. Given the poor quality of life in the country, Abdikarim's life expectancy was short. An insurance actuary would forecast that the thirty-year-old man would not live to see his fifty-fifth birthday. Desperate to escape, Mooge enlisted his father, who cut a deal with a prison guard. The good news was that in the corrupt country, where the average income was measured in hundreds of dollars, the cost of bribing a prison guard was both possible and manageable. Macoow Abdikarim, Mooge's father, paid in kind for his son's release. The price was two camels—the animal, not the cigarette. With a "desert" value of approximately five hundred dollars, Macoow's bribe equated to almost five years of salary for the prison guard, who was more than willing to consent to the transaction. All Mooge had to do was walk out of his unlocked prison cell dressed as a guard.

In the parched, sun-baked country of Somaliland, the camel was a revered animal. Equipped with a unique physiology, which includes a three-chamber stomach, a self-controlled internal body temperature and the ability to store water in its bloodstream, the camel absolutely gets it done in the desert. The animal has been so important to the herding culture of East Africans and Arabians and appropriately was accorded special status in the Muslim religion by the Prophet Muhammad himself when he chose to deliver his valedictory sermon from the back of one of the humped creatures.

Told to get out of town upon his clandestine release, Mooge assembled a new six-man pirate crew, none of whom were over the age of twenty-one, boarded the *Malik* (Arabic for "King") his twenty-foot wooden skiff, started the single outboard Mercury 200L Opti Max Pro XS engine and headed north. The recent arrest of alleged Somali pirate kingpin, Mohammed Abdi Hassan, known as "Big Mouth" and "Afweyn" who was allegedly Mooge's boss and the mastermind behind many of hijackings over the past ten years, shook up the Jolly Roger camp. Belgian authorities, still smarting from the seventy-day hostage taking of the crew of the container ship the *Pompei* in 2009, were determined to catch the notorious pirate. Deploying a brilliant narcissistic-laced red herring, the Belgian prosecutors lured "Big Mouth" to Brussels by posing as a movie company that wanted to interview him for an upcoming documentary film about the life of one of the most famous Somali pirates of all time. Big Mouth was arrested immediately upon his landing in Brussels and now awaits trial in a Bruges prison.

The combination of his ties to Big Mouth's network being severed and his recent arrest meant that Mooge's street value had plummeted. Suffering from a massive credibility cleavage, with his days of roaming off of the Somali coast over, the pirate decided to plumb the ancient waters of the beguiling Red Sea. His new destination was Port Sudan, the capital of the Red Sea State of the Republic of Sudan, a town constructed in the early twentieth century by the British who needed a venue for a new railway station connecting the Red Sea to the Nile River. Over the past one hundred years, the town had seen its share of sesame seed, sorghum and cotton from the fertile Nile Valley pass though her streets.

From the bridge of the *Akrep*, Roos placed a Viber call to Quincy Thibauddeau. Reaching the hedge fund manager in his London office,

Roos greeted his friend whom he had met many years ago at an analyst meeting in New York City: "Morning, Quincy, Christian here. How are you, my friend?"

"Horrible," Thibauddeau responded. "My assets under management are continuing to plummet. Performance has picked up of late, but, as you know, it is so hard to reverse course. Clients are just so fickle."

"Sorry to hear the news." Almost afraid to ask, Roos continued, "How is Samantha doing?" Roos was referring to the movie and television star Samantha Rocket, a Marilyn Monroe doppelganger, if there ever was one. Quincy and Samantha were not married, but the couple had a child together.

Thibauddeau, "Have not a clue. She hasn't spoken to me in months. Ever since that dreadful paparazzi rag, *Pic Me*, published those nude photos of me and Kissy Lumpkins."

Roos laughed to himself about his playboy friend who lives in a constant state of female flux. "I know of her, but I missed the photos. Text me the pics after we hang up."

Kissy was notorious, a socialite stalking flax-wench, who worked the global money circuit from Palm Beach to Monaco and who was known for her relentless tenacity with a "john" in her gun sights. Lumpkins could lick the varnish off of a mega yacht's teak vanity as easily as she could claw her way through an eastern European doorman at the Ibiza uber nightclub Amensia. Like a three-month hibernating grizzly bear pulling up at a seat at Anchorage's Club Paris steakhouse's buffet table, the voracious strumpet consumed her prey without reservation.

"Ha-ha," Thibauddeau laughed. "What can you do? What's up with you, Roos? I read about the bet you have with Charles McCormack in the *World Times*. Is the story true?"

"Yes, it is accurate and the reason for my call. I was wondering if you could arrange for a captain to pick up a boat in Jeddah and reposition her to the Port of Hercules?"

Besides owning a two-hundred-foot yacht with a large crew who kept the *Haute Jinx* at the Port of Hercules, Roos knew that Quincy was extremely close friends with Aleco Kuesseoglou, the Chairman of Société d'Exploitation des Ports de Monaco, the manager of the Port of Hercules. Aleco and Quincy both attended the prestigious Swiss boarding school Le Rosey. Quincy was born in Paris, an important feeding ground for the elite Swiss school located in Rolle that has been educating students on the beautiful shores of Lake Geneva for over one hundred and thirty years. Roos thought that between Quincy's crew and Aleco, surely they could find a captain to reposition the *Akrep*. The Port of Hercules, which sits at the foot of the ancient rock of the Princess of Monaco, has taken on expansion plans under Aleco's leadership. A new seawall now extends the range of the port to accommodate large cruise ships. The naturally protected marina has been expanded to fit an additional twenty yachts bringing the capacity to seven hundred. If it floats, it can visit the Port of Hercules, a town that has been used by the Greeks and Romans for centuries. Julius Caesar stopped in on his war-waging ways through Europe.

Thibauddeau exclaimed, "Jeddah? Where are you now?"

"The Red Sea, about thirty nautical miles north of Jeddah. Not sure if you have been on these waters, but, Quincy, it is a spectacular scene." Roos began to describe the view through his high-powered binoculars from *Akrep's* bridge. "On the starboard side is the southeastern tip of Egypt, just before the Sudan. Up until this point, all desert on the Egyptian coast. Then suddenly this mist-filled oasis called the Elba National Park appeared. Home to Mount Elba, which gets a tremendous amount of rain creating illusory tropical jungle effect." Roos, spotting a mushroom-looking tree continued, "The place is also home to the rare and endangered Nubian Dragon Tree. The park looks like a movie set, it is just so out of synch with the surroundings. On the port side sits the mesmerizing Arabian red desert. Simply breathtaking."

"Jesus, Roos, be careful. I will make some calls on your captain situation. What kind of boat is it?"

Roos explained the specifics of the *Akrep* and also the fact that time was not of the essence.

"I imagine two of my crew could fly into Jeddah and bring her up," said Thibauddeau. "I will call Aleco and make sure you get a favorable berthing spot as well. I assume you will be visiting during the upcoming season. It will be nice to catch up. Been too long, my friend."

"Looking forward to seeing you as well. I will leave the keys with the harbormaster." Roos hung up.

Suddenly Roos noticed Kat's head pop up like an African ostrich. She had been sun-tanning topless for most of this leg of the journey on *Akrep's* bow area, occasionally on her iPad or iPhone, but mostly just taking in the brilliant Arabian sun. She positioned her head in a two o'clock direction, which lasted only for a brief moment. Exploding to a standing position, wearing just the bottom half of her La Perla black Glitter Rock Bandeau bikini and a pair of black original Wayfarer Ray Bans sunglasses, Kat jumped off of the bow's cushioned seating area down onto the starboard side walkway. From there she began running barefoot toward the aft deck. As Kat rounded the stern and made her way to the bridge, Roos aimed his binoculars in the same two o'clock direction. Seeing nothing at first, he began darting back and forth until he saw a small boat on the horizon approaching the *Akrep* from the southwest. Roos guessed the horizon was around thirty miles off in the distance; therefore he put the unknown vessel slightly closer at twenty-five miles off the *Akrep's* bow.

Without saying a word, Kat grabbed the binoculars out of Roos' hands and focused on the skiff that was making a beeline toward the *Akrep*. Kat could see that it was defiantly flying the notorious Somali pirate flag.

"Christian, we have unwelcome company coming. My guess is at forty knots. Put the boat on a direct course toward them, at maximum speed. Don't waiver. Make James Dean proud."

"Are you referring to the guy who said 'Live fast, die young, leave a good-looking corpse'? I think I have the first two covered," joked Roos, who was able to keep his head, while Kat was close to losing hers. Apparently he had yet to fully appreciate the severity of the situation.

And with that the topless retired Naval Officer went below only to return within minutes, wearing her bikini top this time, and handed Roos the Glock G30S pistol and Beneli shotgun. With the AK47 in her right hand and two extra clips in her left, Kat scampered up the port-side walkway to the bow.

As she was departing the bridge, Roos quipped, "Thanks for keeping me abreast of the situation from up on the bow."

Kat's glare conveyed a sense of concern and seriousness. "Christian, these are pirates."

Roos was now clearly distracted and extremely concerned, but he was still able to maintain his faculties and calculate the impending collision if both boats stayed the present course. He figured that the distance between the boats was fifteen miles. If the pirates were traveling at forty knots, a reasonable top speed for an outboard small-sized skiff, and the *Akrep* was topping out at thirty-four, then the time elapsed before meeting in the middle of the Red Sea was approximately twelve minutes.

Kat positioned herself lying down at the tip of the bow. The teak walkway, which circled the ship, was approximately four feet wide and sat below the exterior of the hull by two feet. On her stomach, she spread her legs in order to fit between the front and the raised bow's sun deck. Kat aimed the AK47 over the railing and waited. The weapon is capable of firing six hundred deadly rounds per minute. The standard thirty-round clip can be emptied with a light pull of the shooter's finger in just three seconds. While bullets can travel for miles, the effective range of Mikhail Kalashnikov's widowmaker is approximately thirteen hundred feet.

Mooge Abdikarim, a man quite aware of the intricate and vast network of the world of pirates, had been tipped off about the travel itinerary of the *Akrep* by a dockworker on the Hurghada Marina. Ransom money touches most of life in Somalia. It is a fairly good assumption that the actual pirates have no money. If they did, most likely they would not attempt the illegal and highly dangerous act of boarding cargo ships and other boats with Kalashnikovs and vests of ammunition. Starting with the informants, gang leaders, crew members and translators, the dirty money finds its way to a whole host of other characters who provide goods and services on credit in the criminalized daisy-chain including: station owners who provide the boat fuel, grocery stores who make food available and landlords who house the pirates and gun runners. In order to operate effectively bribes must be paid to local policeman, government officials and coast guard members. The cash gushes in the same way a private equity or hedge fund waterfall distributes profits to limited and general partners. Like an organized crime syndicate, the pirates operate a well run profitable business organization. The profits have attracted competition and the waters in the Gulf of Aden are seeing pirate "turf" battles, as pirate syndicates fight to maintain their market share in the lucrative growth business of hijacking ships.

As a marked man, Mooge made the correct decision to avoid the over-fished waters off of his country's coast and instead opted to target smaller private boats up in the virgin Red Sea. Ransoms reaching high seven figures with the large container ships, while extremely enticing from a cash perspective, attracted too much competition for a small time player like Mooge. They also were risky. The world's top shipping companies were starting to fight back with weapons of their own.

At full tilt the *Akrep* was pushing thirty-five knots. At this speed the bow was slightly elevated out of the calm waters, producing an excellent vantage point and natural protection for Kat, who was motionless at the tip of the bow. Sunken down, all Roos could see was her wind-blown long blonde hair looking like a golden Tibetan prayer flag on Mount Everest.

Mooge was facing forward at the stern of the *Milak* with his right hand firmly on the Mercury outboard engine's tiller handle with the hand grip, controlling the speed, turned all of the way to the right. His motley crew of young inexperienced pirates numbered six. All of them were wearing brightly colored facial scarves leaving only their dark and scared eyes exposed. Wrapped in various combinations of red and white checkerboard shirts, camouflage pants, dark green cargo gear and sandals on their feet, the *Milak* and its clay-brained roguish crew appeared as a lost Halloween party. Four of Mooge's crew were carrying AK47s with M43 cartridges containing 7.62 X 39 millimeter caliber bullets. The pirate positioned closest to the bow was clutching a hand-held Soviet Chi-Com RPG 7, a deadly weapon capable of propelling a grenade over a thousand feet, powerful enough to take out a helicopter or tank. The fifteen-pound weapon has an effective range of six hundred and fifty feet. From this distance the hit probability is a fifty-fifty proposition. From thirteen hundred feet the odds of hitting a target drop below ten percent. These odds are based upon ground firing. From a skiff traveling at forty knots, the odds lengthen dramatically. After three thousand feet the explosive self-detonates.

The buzz of *Milak's* outboard engine cutting through the Red Sea could now be heard aboard the *Akrep* as the two boats continued toward a head-on collision. Roos estimated the distance between the pirates and the tip of Kat's machine gun to be less than five miles, a separation which would be eliminated in less than five minutes. After several minutes, she could identify the members of the *Milak*.

As the two boats came within three thousand feet, Kat raised herself up slightly on the bow. With an ever so slight twitch of her right hand forefinger, she fired a fifteen-round warning shot into the air above the oncoming *Malik*. Mooge stayed on his course. The distance was now down to fifteen hundred feet, almost within range of an AK47, Kat thought out loud. Her index finger sent off another fifteen-round warning shot, after which she reloaded another thirty-round clip.

Mooge realized that the high seas game of chicken that he found himself engaged in was one that he was going to certainly lose given the relative size of the boats. A head-on collision would unquestionably be fatal for his entire crew. From a distance of seven hundred and fifty feet, seconds from impact, Mooge pulled his right hand, which was gripping the tiller handle, backwards sending the *Malik* into a hard right-hand turn. As the pirate skiff passed the *Akrep*, Kat repositioned herself over one railing stem to the left and was now aiming her weapon at the *Malik*, which was off her port side at a forty-five-degree angle. Taking dead aim at the crew—an angle which unfortunately would be required in order for the shooter to hit her intended target, the Mercury outboard engine, Kat exhaled and pulled the trigger with her rock-steady index finger. The first round severed Mooge's right hand from his wrist instantaneously. The subsequent rounds peppered the engine, causing it to catch fire and cut out.

As the engineless *Malik* bobbed helplessly in the water, Mooge, who was witnessing the *Akrep* escaping, shouted out the order to fire the RPG. By this time, the *Akrep,* continuing on the same course, was approximately fifteen hundred feet past the pirate skiff. Upon hearing Mooge's instructions, which traveled eerily across the water like a jury's verdict, Kat stood up, turned to face Roos on the bridge and furiously pointed right. In an instant Roos spun the wheel counterclockwise. The powerful *Akrep* entered a hard-banking left turn, which cast a fan-tailed water spray twenty-five feet off her stern towards the starboard side.

The *Malik* was now motionless and parallel with the *Akrep*, which was moving right to left at thirty-four knots from a distance of two thousand feet. Mooge's gang began unloading their AK47s in the direction of the *Akrep*. Out of effective range, the bullets flew in futility. A Navy SEAL would be challenged by these circumstances. Mooge's nineteen-year-old top lieutenant, who was no Navy SEAL, stood up and raised the Russian-made RPG to a resting position on his right shoulder. Peering through his red and gold keffiyeh, the pirate took aim and pulled the trigger, propelling an eighty-five-millimeter caliber rocket with the explosive capability of destroying a boat the size of the *Akrep* in a flash. A burst of fire and a cloud of smoke were followed by a deafening noise. The force of the blast propelled the shooter backwards over the gunwales of the skiff and he splashed into the Red Sea. He was unable to observe the rocket flying at eight feet over the water at a velocity of one hundred fifteen meters per second, like an aquaphobic torpedo. The remaining parties on each respective boat froze for three seconds as the rocket advanced. Kat and Roos both turned their heads to the left and watched the rocket miss the *Akrep's* stern by fifteen feet, a distance which only felt comfortable in considerable hindsight. Pivoting farther counterclockwise, Kat and Christian watched in amazement as the rocket self-detonated one thousand feet downsea. The fifteen-foot-diameter fireball lit the sky briefly before turning into a ghostly black cloud that rose slowly over the Red Sea like the devil's hot-air balloon.

Kat rejoined Roos on the bridge. A simple yet powerful embrace was all that was required. No words were spoken as the *Akrep* churned toward Jeddah.

From the aft deck, Roos sent Harrison an update. Still visibly shaken from the previous encounter — one unlike anything he had ever come close to before, the captain of the *Akrep* was unable to describe the events to Harrison. Instead he simply said everything was on schedule on Day 12.

Checking his messages, he was pleased to read one incoming from Quincy Thibauddeau. Sure enough, his friend had arranged for some of his crew to reposition the *Akrep* up the South of France. Roos wondered if he should disclose the unfortunate happenings earlier in the day. After consulting with Kat he decided to not do so. The pair slept on the boat in the safely guarded harbor of the Park Hyatt Jeddah Marina Club.

The Catholic and the Buddhist embarked on the sixty-five-mile drive to Mecca, a route that is almost exclusively through the Jeddah desert. The first part of the drive heads south on the outskirts of booming Jeddah. The skyline, bursting with modern skyscrapers, and three and half million people, appears like a mirage positioned between the Red Sea and the hilly red sand Jeddah Desert. After passing Jeddah, the route turns due east cutting directly through the desert.

Kat, staring into the blinding desert, asked, "What is the schedule in Mecca?"

Christian responded, "First stop is Mount Hira, located on the outskirts of Mecca. Need to change those shoes, baby. The hike up to the top is two thousand five hundred feet with serious rocky terrain in some parts."

Roos was referring to the one of most historically significant sites in the entire Muslim world. It was in the cave, Jabal Al-Nur, in the year six hundred thirty-two A.D. where a humble merchant while meditating was startled by Gabriel the Angel of Revelation, whose command was *Iqra* (read), became the first known recitation of the Quran: "Read in the name of your Lord who created—created man from a clot. Read: for your Lord is Most Bountiful, who teaches by the pen, teaches man that which he knew not" (Quran 96:1–5).

Almost one thousand four hundred years later, over one and a half billion people, twenty percent of the world's population, would end up following the religion founded by Prophet Muhammad—quite a few more than the estimated two hundred followers which Muhammad could lay claim to in the seventh century A.D.

Kat, listening intently, commented, "I did not realize that the Muslim religion was founded almost seven hundred years after the time of Christ."

Roos, "Indeed."

She inquired about the burial site of the founder of the Muslim religion, Prophet Muhammad.

Roos answered, "He is buried in the Al-Masjid al-Nabawi, also known as the Mosque of Prophet, up in Medina."

"I am surprised he is not buried in Mecca. Wasn't that his home sand?" she asked.

"Initially, but he became sideways with the local powers that be," Roos replied. "In the seventh century, Mecca was a center of trade for western Arabia, an economy controlled by the local Quraysh tribes with an iron fist. Understandable how these people, who followed a polytheism religion, naturally felt threatened by the new kid on the block preaching a one-god option. So, fearful that the new prophet would be bad for business, they kicked him out of town."

"Where did he go?" she asked.

"Medina. Where he methodically built his following."

"And?" she asked next.

"Well, as I indicated to Mac at the inception of this whole crazy trip and wager at Winged Foot, diplomacy has come a long way, but power still changes hands through bloodshed in most places on the planet. The dispute between Muhammad and the Quraysh was certainly no exception. After much bloodshed and thousands of battlefield deaths, the Prophet ultimately prevailed."

After hiking Mount Hira, the pair made their way toward the center of the town of Mecca where the Al Haram Mosque was located, the epicenter of Islam. The Mosque was constructed in the seventh century around the Kaaba, the holiest of all structures in the Muslim world. Taking a spin, a formal move known in religious parlance as a circumambulation, counterclockwise of course, around the house that Abraham built in the square with a capacity of almost a million people, Kat made a few observations. "I knew it was a large structure, but after now experiencing the venue firsthand, I must admit to being slack-jawed at the sheer enormity of the Al Haram Mosque. Equally as surprised by the Kaaba though. The house looks way smaller than I imagined."

Roos chimed in, "Concur. Looks slightly disproportional, but extremely impressive nonetheless."

Kat continued with some first-time thoughts, "Christian, I have not seen one American since we entered the Mosque."

"That is because there are none."

Some of the tens of thousands of people were walking, others praying, to which Roos added, "No need for a smartphone Qiblah app here."

Roos was referring to the directional finders that tell Muslims which way to face during their five daily prayer sessions, anywhere in the world. All roads face the Kaaba.

Back in the rental jeep, the couple headed back toward Jeddah's airport. On the way, Roos sent Frank his daily update via WhatsApp: "Day 13 and the Al Haram Mosque completed. CR"

On the tarmac, seated on a commercial flight from Jeddah, Saudi Arabia, heading for Tehran's Imam Khomeini International Airport, Christian Roos was buried in *Global Today*. Katherine Mandu was asleep. The article consuming his attention was entitled, *Iranian President Babak to Receive Buryian President Mussan in Tehran—Western World Outraged.*

Roos read from the article: "Ahman Mussan, leader of rebel nation Buryia, is scheduled to meet tomorrow with Persian President

Bambad Babak at the Sadabad Presidential Palace in Tehran. In light of Mussan's recent defiant admission of deploying weapons of mass destruction on his own people, killing thousands, including women and children, the Western world has expressed indignation and outrage at the reception."

Another article caught Roos' attention, this one appearing in the publication *Around Arabia* with the title, *The Saharan Sands of Time Running Out on America?* From the article he read, "The relationship between the United States and its strongest ally in the Arab world, Saudi Arabia, is becoming strained in a fashion not seen since 9/11. The strong alliance, formed in the 1930's, has been tested over the years. Relations became strained in 2001 when it was disclosed that many of the 9/11 attackers came from Saudi Arabia. At the core of the current disagreement is the United States' inability to deal with Buryian leader Ahman Mussan. Quite simply, the Saudis want Mussan gone and quickly. Buryia represents a significant threat to the stability of not only the Arab world, but to the entire Middle East and the rest of civilization, according to Saudi officials. The spokesman elaborated that the Buryian nuclear program must be stopped before the rebel nation can develop deployable weapons of mass destruction."

Roos, becoming increasingly focused on the situation, turned the newspaper page to the article with the title *Iranian Revolutionary Guard has its Guard Up.* Roos read from the piece about the increased security measures the Iranian government was implementing in anticipation of demonstrations, potential violence in the streets of Tehran and of course possible danger to the Buryian President Mussan. A man generally disliked by the Iranian people in stark contrast to views held by their leaders—a pervasive and poisonous dichotomy, unfortunately deeply rooted in the country. All units of the military and police will be deployed throughout the Persian capital, including the newly formed Cyber Police. The government warned of airport and train delays due to increased security involving unprecedented screening of passengers. In light of the recent experience aboard the *Akrep*, Roos was already on edge. The thought of Tehran, virgin territory for the world traveler, in a heightened state of alert only added to his anxiety.

Sitting on the tarmac, Roos reached for his iPhone and sent a text to Colin Murphy in Havana. "About to take off from Jeddah en route to Tehran. Sounds like the city is bracing for trouble on account of Mussan's visit. Please send me the contact information for the head of the U.S. Embassy in Iran."

Within two minutes Colin's response hit Roos' phone, "We don't have one. FYI word on the street is that Yousef Maaloof the leader of Hezbollah's paramilitary wing is vowing to stop the meeting. My advice, keep your head down and don't stray too far from the kabobs. Good luck, buddy."

With the plane breaking through twenty thousand feet on a north-easterly heading, Roos gazed out of his window seat onto the vast Arabian Desert—a no-man's land too busy imitating a maroon-colored raging ocean—to notice. As his thoughts drifted back to the Somali pirate attack, he glanced toward Kat who was sleeping like an angel—an illusory one, but an angel nonetheless. With an Ambien-induced sleep setting in, Roos' last conscious thoughts percolating through his mind just before he knocked off were of Kat's stunning performance aboard the *Akrep*. So unexpected and out of character for the life of the party yoga instructor he thought he knew so well—but obviously didn't. Such ignorance may be unfamiliar to many, but commonplace to the man who had fashioned a career out of misreading women. Roos muttered aloud, "Never really know someone until co-habitation. How about traveling around the world together?"

Ranier Roos was working on Saturday—as usual—a tradition never understood by his two sons, Christian and Ranier Jr. Their friends' fathers were always hanging around their houses on the weekends—reading, watching televised sporting events, napping and occasionally performing chores. But today was different. Dad promised to come home early and take the brothers to Washington, D.C.'s National Zoo.

But dad was late and the excited boys were left to be placated by their mother, Bridget, who did her best to calm their anxiousness.

As the yellow 1975 Dodge Coronet 440 convertible pulled into the driveway, Christian and Ranier Jr. were waiting on the front step. The boys jumped in the backseat, while their father entered the house for what they hoped would be an expeditious visit. After what felt like an eternity to the boys with an overabundance of testosterone, Ranier and Bridget emerged from the house. The parents joined their overheating offspring in the car, which backed down the driveway embarking on the forty-minute ride crosstown to the menagerie, assuming no unplanned unnecessary stops, which were a trademark of the older Ranier.

Bridget innocuously stoked the fire. "Boys, what animals do you want to see today?"

Ranier Jr. remained silent in deep contemplative thought, while Christian unequivocally answered, "Tigers and cheetahs."

Ever since he was a young child, Christian was fascinated by the powerful, lightning-fast big cats.

Cries of "hurry, dad, hurry" and "go faster" could be heard pleading from the backseat. "Are we there yet?" Suddenly the zealous encouragement went silent as a lifting sensation overwhelmed the passengers. The palpable excitement building from within magically lifted the car into the air. Looking out of the window, Christian saw the ground fading from sight. As the convertible became airborne, the tires — rubber no longer in contact with the road — ceased spinning. Flying over trees and rooftops, the car was quickly making up for lost time. Bridget's obvious displeasure with her husband's technique was evident in her pleas for an immediate return to the ground. Her request was met with grumbling from Ranier, who picked up the pace and altitude, to the delight of the boys.

When pressed, Ranier bristled. "Oh, Bridget, relax, everything will be fine. Would you prefer riding on the road, listening to the deafening commentary from the backseat?"

Within five minutes, the car was hovering over the entrance gate to the National Zoo. Christian looked in amazement as his father hand rolled the driver's side window down, and threw a twenty-dollar bill folded into an airplane—winglets included—into the dense air filled with the aroma of earthy smells. Pressing his nose to the rear window, still up to minimize the wind, Christian watched in wonder as the paper airplane performed a series of fighter pilot aerodynamic maneuvers. The unpiloted plane's sole passenger, Andrew Jackson, remained motionless as the plane banked into a lazy eight followed by a series of barrel rolls. By this point the plane, just two hundred feet above the ground, flew into an English bunt half outside level loop, converting into a zoom climb before culminating in a leaf fall—engine off. Like an autumn oak leaf, the plane rotated as it orbited to the ground for several minutes, ultimately landing like a surreal snowflake into the outstretched hand of a nonplussed zoo employee. After confirming the number of five-dollar tickets as four, the gatekeeper reluctantly yet instinctively waved the Roos car though the zoo's entrance gate airspace.

After cruising around the aviary, over the seal pool and past the bamboo-forested panda home, the Dodge was now positioned over the big cat exhibitions. The hovering car slowly descended like a helicopter approaching a tight landing zone, kicking up dirt and debris along with some popcorn and snow cones. Once on the ground, Ranier nonchalantly parked, cut the engine and motioned for everyone to exit the vehicle.

Immediately catching Christian's attention out of the corner of his eye was an oversized elevated glass thimble. Inside were two black, red and green dragons chasing each other in a rhythmic circle—each creature smacking the other with a long pointed tail dotted with shark-teeth formations pointing upward. Noticing his young son's attention drifting, Ranier lightly cracked Christian on the back of the head, grabbed his arm and led him back on the right path.

Christian bypassed the lions, pumas and even the cheetahs as he eagerly made a beeline for the Caspian tiger cage. Protected by a fifteen-foot steel fence forming a semicircle, the tiger's home away from home was inviting. An eggplant-shaped pool surrounded by lush vegetation, boulders and low-lying trees reminded inhabitants of their counterpart's natural environment. But this particular tiger would definitely not trade places—the last Caspian tiger living in the wild was shot in Iran north of Tehran in the Elburz Mountains. Being gawked at beat being shot at.

While waiting for the tiger to emerge, Christian heard a familiar voice—two actually—one so soft and sweet it sounded like angels singing, the other deep and bold, the type you would hear in a corporate boardroom during significant merger and acquisition deliberations. Christian approached the man and woman, who were stationed by the exhibit fence.

Charles MacCormick turned and faced the oncoming boy. "Let me be frank, you are never going to make it, Roos. You might as well give up."

Sakura Nagasawa stood in a traditional Japanese bow, dressed in an ancient-style brown kimono with bamboo, pine and Japanese apricot flowers. Mimicking a time-released video of a blossoming cherry tree, Sakura slowly unfolded and whispered in a spine-tingling tone, "Christian Roos will be safe. The Japanese Koshin Gods have already spoken by blessing him on his voyage. Any attempts at vengeance will be foiled by the deities. Visit the monkey cage and you will see the future."

Mac, clearly baffled by the beautifully exquisite talking porcelain doll, shook his head and simply replied, "Strange."

At this moment, emerging dramatically from a concealed side door was a zoo employee dressed in circus trainer gear. The stout man adorned a typical top hat and coat while holding a chair and whip. "Welcome to the Greatest Show on Earth" were his opening words. His second introduced the star, Vyaghrahasana, a female Caspian tiger named after the Indian word for the tiger yoga pose, a move she could perform on command. Vyaghra, the shortened, easier-to-pronounce version of her name rhyming with the erectile dysfunction drug Viagra, appeared from her faux mountainous lair and proudly stalked the inner fence line only occasionally gazing into the audience, which was fifteen deep by now. With a body length of five and a half feet and weighing over three hundred and fifty pounds, Vyaghra was hard to miss. The beautiful creature's reddish-orange fur, sporting prodigious black vertical stripes, glowed like a smoldering blood-stained Red Deer's carcass shimmering sunlight off a snow-capped Persian mountain.

As the tiger reached the spot on the fence where Christian was standing, the two made eye contact. Vyaghra's animal magnetism, fueled by her kaleidoscope eyes twisting and turning like mystical marbles, hypnotized the young boy, drawing him closer and closer to the fence. Without warning, Survivor's just-released song *Eye of the Tiger*, sitting comfortably at number one on the 1982 U.S. Billboard charts, began blaring from rock speakers.

In short order, the female Caspian tiger was retrieving balls out of the pool, literally jumping through hoops and doing the moonwalk. Emboldened by the crowd's enthusiastic reaction expressed through uproarious applause, the zookeeper channeling P.T. Barnum prepared for his *pièce de résistance*. With a whip he positioned the tiger onto a stepladder, front paws on the top step, hind legs still on the ground. The majestic animal, facing the audience, looked proud, almost as if she knew her species was extinct and that she was performing for posterity.

The pair played patty-cake, shook hands and even kissed. He then gave a command, which caused Vyaghra to let out a big roar. With her front paws planted and her hind left leg bent at the knee, she placed her tibia flat to the ground. Vyaghra then extended her right leg straight back and slowly raised it into a fake tail. Vyaghra winked, signaling the lack of awareness of her magnificent autological self-representation—a tiger posing in the shape of a tiger. With Vyaghra still striking the pose, the crowd stiffened as the trainer grabbed the tiger's upper and lower jaws. After prying them open, he deftly placed his head in the tiger's gaping mouth—barely sneaking through Vyaghra's eight-centimeter upper canines.

The sight of the man's head in the tiger's mouth startled young Christian, who abruptly turned his head away from the cage. Looking through the crowd he saw a strange-looking man walking methodically in his direction. Wearing a black logo-less baseball cap, black jeans and a gray trench coat, the middle-aged Caucasian, with his eyes hidden behind a pair of oversized Ray-Ban black Aviators, stood out in the weekend family zoo crowd like John Hinckley Jr. at a Ronald Reagan Presidential Library reception. Forcing his way through the crowd, the man was approaching the tiger cage on a course to rendezvous with Christian. He started to speak in a loud monotone voice. "Caged animals are defenseless against humans unless humans fight back on their behalf. Humans who commit crimes are put in cages. I ask you, what crimes did these animals commit?"

As the man cut through the crowd like a water skier carving a serene lake, he opened his coat, exposing himself to be a suicide bomber wearing a body vest chockablock with explosives. Clutching a detonator in his right hand, the man raised his arm slowly and sounded off. "These crimes against nature will not go unpunished."

People fled in all directions, knocking each other over, trampling small children. Panic set in with the flash of lightning. Christian stood still and watched the man's right thumb begin to descend on the detonator's red button. He heard the shot at the same time he saw Katherine Mandu positioned in one of the trees located within the tiger's cage. She was dressed in military fatigues and holding a rifle. As the bullet struck the man in the left side of his head, blood spattered out his right side onto Christian. The victim's trigger thumb twitched—then froze as he hit the deck. After firing, Katherine lowered her weapon, gave a thumbs up and shimmied down the flowering acacia tree.

The scene left Christian frozen and drenched in blood. He saw one person who remained as well. Calmly seated in a purple beanbag chair, North Korean Supreme Leader Kim Jong-un could be heard discussing the hard-and-fast rules of the all-important number eighty-one in the Chinese Ying and Yang philosophy.

Roos sat bolt upright in his airplane seat, his scream awakening Kat instantly. As she put her arms around her partner, she could feel Christian's racing pulse, pounding heart and perspiring skin. She squeezed tightly, trying to control his refractory quivering. "What's wrong, Christian?" Kat asked in the most concerned and confused manner.

"I. ...I had. ...I had a horrific nightmare."

"About what?'

Still in shock from what he saw in his dream, Roos deadpanned, "Blood and death."

Staring into Roos' vacant welled-up eyes, Kat inquired, "What happened?"

Roos, gazing downward at his hands wiping his shirt, the man with a near-photographic memory answered Kat's question. "I can't remember. Splattered blood is all I see and feel."

Kat, trying to calm Roos down, said, "Lie back down. Get some sleep. Everything is okay, baby."

# 11

## Caspian Sea of Darkness

*"The day which we fear as our last is but the birthday of eternity."*
—LUCIUS ANNAEUS SENECA

Zigzagging toward the enduring sunlight poking over the Elburz Mountains, Roos awakened early and in an anxious state of mind. His itinerary for the day included a visit to the Treasury of National Jewels, lunch with Maryam Tehrani, one of his Persian friends whom he met in Washington, D.C. while she was on a work assignment, followed by an AirJets flight to Amritsar in the early afternoon. Kat, understandably exhausted and not particularly interested in meeting one of Christian's ex-girlfriends, opted to stay behind at the hotel. The most visited site in Tehran, the museum holding one of the world's greatest collections of jewels, sounded intriguing, but sleep carried the day. Besides, she admitted that Iran scared her.

The private car and driver hired by Roos for the day was waiting in front of the hotel as he popped out.

Roos entered the vehicle and requested, "First stop, the Treasury of National Jewels."

Housed in the Central Bank of the Islamic Republic of Iran, the jewels worn by rulers for centuries are assembled into the greatest and most valuable collection that exists today. Exceeding England's Crown Jewels by a wide margin, the sparkle factor in the exhibit is blinding. Roos, never a fan of jewelry but a reluctant buyer over the years, found himself at the epicenter of the world's natural precious metals, which had been tortured by artists into vaingloriousness on a herculean scale. This level of ostentatiousness had driven many a man over the millennium to bear arms and storm the castle walls, overthrowing European empires in the process. Defiantly and proudly, the Persian baubles are on an "in your face" full display of vulgarity in a country with less than satisfactory human rights. Born from the blood, sweat and silent tears of oppressed people, the jewels represented strength and power to the outside world, but pain and suffering on the inside. Roos curiously read from the Treasury of National Jewels brochure: "Our intention in presenting these jewels is to get you more acquainted with the rich culture and civilization of Persia. And to learn from history the fate of those who pursue power and hoard wealth."

Roos gnarled out loud, "This place pales in comparison to the Museum of Islamic Art (MIA) in Doha, Qatar."

Christian googled the Neyab Restaurant, the place he was scheduled to meet Maryam for lunch. The restaurant was founded in 1875, when Nayeb-Gholamhossein moved his family to Tehran. After acquiring a public bath in the Bazar-e Shahhaf-ha, known today as the Bookbinders Market, Nayeb filled the bath's reservoirs, decorated the space with antique furniture, prints from the Shahnameh (Book of Kings) and beautiful Persian carpets. The finished product was the perfect setting for the budding chef to test his new innovative dish composed of rice, butter and kabob (beef, lamb or chicken). Five generations later, Chelo-Kabob is known unequivocally as the national cuisine of Iran and Neyab is one of the leading food brands in the country.

As Carl Strange passed through the front entrance to the Neyab Restaurant he was instantly greeted by a smiling Pooria Namdar, his old college roommate from Oxford University. The pair walked past a marble statute of the "Kabob King," Nayeb-Gholamhossein, the man who turned Persia's world of cuisine on its turban over a century ago. Strange and Namdar approached the front desk of the restaurant where three very serious looking Persian women were seated between two Iranian flags. The women, dressed identically in all-black roosaris, which covered everything but the brows of their modelesque faces from the forehead to just below their chiseled chins, looked all business. Despite being draped in traditional Persian clothing, the women's beauty was self-evident and showed through magnificently. Behind the desk their black manteaus were only visible from the shoulders down to the waist. The formal signs, Operator, Receptionist and Cashier were placed in front of the elegant and exquisite women, who Strange estimated were in their late twenties. Namdar, noticing that his old friend's insatiable lust for the female sex was still intact, requested a quiet table near the back of the intricate and ornate restaurant. Per custom, Namdar motioned for Strange to take the seat with the wall to his back, so as to afford the guest a sweeping view of the room.

Strange started off the conversation. "Namdar, it is so great to see you after all of these years. Quite frankly I was surprised to find you here in Tehran, given your father's role as a prominent cleric and friend under the Shah's regime."

Namdar's demeanor portended his response. "As you know, when Ayatollah Khomeini came to power, all of the Shah's inner circle fled the country. This exodus included many of the previously independent Shiite clerics. But sadly, my father stayed behind and became swept up in Ayatollah Khomeini's power play, which brought the clergy under the government's control."

Strange asked, "Where is he now?"

Namdar replied, "In the early 1980's, for his 'crimes' against the Islamic Republic, he faced a public execution by firing squad in the streets of Tehran."

Strange, remembering the multiple times he had met Mr. Namdar during his college visits to Tehran with his roommate, said, "Pooria, I am so deeply sorry for your loss. Your father was a great man." He continued, "Did you and your family stay in Tehran?"

Pooria sadly responded, "No, my mother moved my brothers and me down to the southern Iranian city of Isfahan. The ancient capital of Persia is beautiful, but my heart is in Tehran. My dream is a truly free Iran and that is why I returned."

Strange noticed Christian Roos walking through the center section of the restaurant.

Abruptly, Strange asked his friend, "Pooria, would you mind if we switched seats?"

Normally this was the type of request that would be met with curiosity; however, Strange's old roommate, who had spent four years living with the man, knew better than to ask why. "Not at all. Nice to see you haven't changed a bit, Carl. Mercurial as ever, my old friend."

When Roos arrived, Maryam was already seated at the table. After hugs and kisses and some perfunctory pleasantries, Roos proceeded to launch into a series of questions for the Iranian ophthalmologist. Clearly, Roos was anxious to learn more about Iran from an insider, on his first visit to the country.

"Looking around, everyone appears so young. What are the demographics of the Iranian population?" Roos asked.

Maryam replied, "The current population of Iran is seventy million, half of whom are under the age of thirty-five. The Iranian Revolution in 1979 kicked off a massive fertility boom. The Shah's family-planning centers and his regime's strict birth-control policies were terminated. The population at the time of the change in policy was just thirty-five million. Afterwards, fertility jumped to six per woman and the population growth rate hit six point four percent, and the government reversed course again in the early 1990's. Iran instituted a ten-billion-dollar family-planning program and opened a state-owned condom manufacturing plant. That program would be equally successful, producing a population growth of just over one percent that according to the United Nations was the greatest drop in the world since 1980. Now flip-flopping again, just last year the Health Ministry announced that Iran's supreme leader, Ayatollah Ali Khamenei, was ending the two-decades-old policy of controlled growth. The goal now is to double the population to one hundred and fifty million."

"Get it on or just get it on, sounds like quite a conundrum?" Roos remarked.

"Exactly," replied Maryam. "But, I guess men's desire to control female genitalia is not a new concept. Well, maybe it is in America. I guess one of the advantages of being such a new country is that you skip the social training wheels."

"Wow, and I thought the Catholic Church was the world's leading Peeping Tom?" responded Roos. "From the moment I walked off the plane, I sensed economic weakness. How are the Iranian people coping?"

"Terribly. Western economic sanctions imposed in response to Iran's continuing nuclear program are taking a devastating toll on the economy. The embargo on oil exports is the largest problem, but a close second is the fact that we have been blocked from the global banking community. Restricted money flows have created scarcities, which have led to hyperinflation, which now stands at forty percent. All of this is hurting business and causing layoffs. The unemployment rate is thirteen percent and rising."

"What is the word on the street about the new Iranian President, Bambad Babak?" asked Roos.

"People are tired of this government and generally distrustful of Babak or anyone else who would be elected president under Ayatollah Ali Khamenei. Until he leaves, the general view is one of bad business as usual."

"Are human rights improving?" he asked.

"Not really," said Maryam. "One of the famous coffee shops, Café Prague, closed last month over its refusal to install video cameras in the restaurant. Eighty-seven other coffee shops have been raided recently to ensure proper compliance with the camera policy. The government is scared that Western values are creeping into the country, threatening traditional Islamic values. Even suntans are being discouraged. The government just jailed eight individuals for their activity on the social media site Facebook, which in their eyes is nothing but a vehicle for subversive political messaging. The director of the YouTube video of an Iranian version of Pharrell Williams' smash hit *Happy* has been incarcerated. It is really quite ridiculous if you think about it."

Without so much as raising an eyebrow, the Sikorsky S-92 twin turbine helicopter touched down on the helideck of the oilrig. Workers on Wotherspoon Industries' offshore platform in the Caspian Sea were long ago anesthetized to the constant droning sound of helicopters, which were incoming and outgoing during all hours of the day and night. The Azeri-Chirag-Guneshli oil field, the largest under development in the Azerbaijan sector of the Caspian basin, located approximately one hundred kilometers east of Baku, Azerbaijan, was aflame in "Black Gold" and "Texas Tea."

The passengers on the helicopter were two stoic men in their early thirties wearing a distinct look of all business. They grabbed their gear and exited the helicopter, with the bird's propellers still cycling. With a duffel bag over his right shoulder and an oversized briefcase in his left hand, one of the men was unable to wave to the pilot as the copter lifted off into the Caspian Sea's darkness. A simple nod with his chiseled chin and shaved head was all the man offered. The pilot could see his passenger's steely look of determination and focus, which was illuminated by the bird's undercarriage lighting. It was more than enough. The other man produced a perfunctory wave as he focused on what was below.

Peering over the edge with night-vision goggles, the men were able to quickly locate the boat, which had been left for them, bobbing up and down in the unusually rough seas. The oilrig, a virtual floating city, was noticeably swaying more than usual. After securing climbing ropes to the railing circling the helideck with a climbing carabiner, the first man wrapped his waist with the line, clipped himself in and turned his back to the edge. Stepping over the two-piece steel railing, he calmly jumped backwards and outwardly into the night. The time to repel the elevation of one thousand five hundred feet was less than thirty seconds. Like toothpaste going back into the tube, the man lowered himself into the twin-engine inboard craft. Before he could start the engines, he heard the sizzling sound of his rope being pulled upwards into the darkness. Once his partner was securely positioned in the boat, the second man secured his line and jumped backwards, repelling into the darkness.

After securing his gear, the man started the twin two hundred fifty horsepower engines, one at a time. Before he turned the wheel and headed due south toward the Iranian border, at the bottom of the Caspian Sea, his partner methodically inventoried the four tanks of reserve fuel. The distance to their destination, Chalus, Mazandaran, Iran, was approximately three hundred nautical miles. If nothing went wrong, the trip would take ten hours. The pair decided to alternate between captaining and guard watch in two-hour increments.

The Caspian Sea, surrounded by the "stans," shared shores with Kazakhstan to the north, moving clockwise followed by, Uzbekistan, Turkmenistan, Iran, Azerbaijan and Russia. With a surface area of three hundred seventy-one thousand square kilometers, the Caspian Sea is the largest enclosed body of water on earth as measured by area. Large oil and natural gas reserves have been discovered in the Caspian Sea, which have lit the torch of a major water rush, as the bordering countries scramble to claim drilling rights. Wotherspoon Industries, an Aberdeen, Scotland, oil powerhouse, owned and operated by Padruig Wotherspoon IV, one of the wealthiest men in Europe, was leading the charge in the new oil riches of the Caspian Sea.

As the thirty-five-foot fiberglass center console vessel slalomed through the oilrigs, which looked like floating Christmas trees, the man with his hands on the twin screws motioned to his partner to check the contents in the oversized briefcase. The man nodded affirmatively, indicating that the contents were secure, and was met with a steely grin by his partner. To his expectation, the L115A3 Long Range Sniper Rifle, was undamaged by the transport. Part of the British Sniper System Improvement Programme (SSIP), the large-caliber weapon, which provides state-of-the-art telescopic day and night, all-weather sights, increasing a sniper's effective range considerably, is a groundbreaking long-range killing machine. Equipped with the new X3-X12-X50 sight and sporting scope, the rifle is capable of firing five 8.59 millimeter bullets, with an astonishing range of one thousand four hundred meters, plus. The lethal weapon fires the largest round made, the .338 Lapua Magnum Lockbase, a 3.681-inch, thirteen-gram bullet, traveling at three thousand three hundred and forty feet per second with five thousand foot pounds of thrust. Numerous confirmed kills with the weapon in excess of a mile have been recorded, the longest being an earth-shattering eight thousand one hundred twenty foot death shot. With a price tag of thirty-five thousand dollars, the L115A3 is the most expensive individually issued weapon in history.

The man of Middle Eastern descent, fluent in Farsi, closed the case and checked in, "Cheetahs in the water."

The voice on the other end of the secure line responded, "Vehicle with the license plate PBX 2384 will be waiting in the parking lot of the Noshahr Seaport. Make next contact from the ground en route to rendezvous."

The Cheetahs arrived in the Noshahr Seaport at 8 A.M., docked, grabbed the duffel bag and briefcase and made their way to the parking lot. Scanning the dated, salt-encrusted cars in the parking lot, one of the men quickly located the 2002 silver Peugeot Pars, carrying the license plate PBX 2384. Then he checked in, "Cheetahs moving on the ground."

Their contact responded, "Confirmed for Siyahbisheh. Rendezvous with the Tiger at 12:00. Ateshgah Park. Contact again en route to Shodhada Hospital."

Standing between the men and their destination were the breathtaking Elburz Mountains, which separated the Caspian Sea from the Iranian capital. The range extends in an arc eastward from the Turkmenistan border to Khorasan, the northeast region of Iran.

The Chalus Road, connecting Chalus to Tehran, twists and turns for one hundred and seventy-five kilometers through the snow-capped mountains with elevations exceeding ten thousand feet. As the Cheetahs reached the remote mountain town of Siyahbiseh, they scouted for the ideal setting for a staged car crash.

Driving slowly they approached a bend in the road, which had a steep thirty-foot drop off to the right. The landing area was eighty feet wide and predominately flat, more than enough space for a skilled helicopter pilot to drop in a bird. The driver parked by the edge, exited the car with his backpack and briefcase carrying the L115A3 and proceeded to climb down to the landing. He scouted out a hiding spot behind a rock formation that protruded out from the cliff. Leaving the gear behind, he began climbing back up. From the Chalus Road, the Cheetah pulled his cell phone and dialed the medevac flight support division of the Iranian Health Ministry.

In proper Farsi, the Cheetah called in an emergency, "Requesting medevac services on the Chalus Road at mile sixty-five in Siyahbisheh. Two injured. Please confirm."

Radio dispatch, "Please reconfirm location."

The Cheetah confirmed, "Mile sixty-five on the Chalus Road."

Radio dispatch, "What is the condition of the patients?"

The Cheetah responded, "Middle-aged males, both stable but non-ambulatory and non-responsive. Significant head injuries and compound fractures to the legs and arms."

Radio dispatch, "Confirmed. Medevac incoming in twenty minutes."

Reaching the vehicle, the Cheetah released the parking brake, shifted gears from parking to neutral and with the help of his partner pushed the car over the cliff. The car started slowly and picked up speed as it nosedived onto the rocky ledge before finally landing upside-down. They proceeded to climb back down the hill and position themselves behind the rock formation, where they waited for the incoming medevac helicopter.

They heard the helicopter before it was visible. Once in sight, both men were impressed to see the Mi 38, the latest civilian transport helicopter to come off the Russian Helicopter Company production line. Powered by twin TV7-117V Kilmov JSC engines, the bird can fly at two hundred eight-five kilometers per hour with a range of six hundred sixty kilometers. A virtual flying hospital, the Mi 38 can hold thirty passengers in a low-grade trauma environment. The Mi 38 touched down on the LZ, twenty yards from the car crash. Cutting the engine, the paramedic and two pilots rushed out and surrounded the abandoned vehicle. Sensing their moment, the men charged out from their hiding place and attacked the first pilot. Displaying his well-honed skills in the ancient martial arts, one of the men quickly overpowered the man. With tremendous force, the Cheetah's straight right hand to his opponent's jaw dropped the unsuspecting man. A catatonic glaze from his motionless eyes indicated a temporary paralysis, which was quickly followed by a collapse as he buckled and helplessly fell to the ground. The second pilot circled the car and confronted the other Middle Eastern fighting machine. Charging the man, the Cheetah launched into a roundhouse kick, which caught the man flush on the right temple. The energy knocked the man out cold. With two strikes, the skilled fighters disabled the overwhelmed Mi 38 pilots. The medic, a man in his early twenties, stood quivering at the sight before him. Holding his hands up, the man began frantically begging for his life in Farsi. One of the men calmly raised his SIG Sauer P226 handgun and fired a nine-millimeter round, which blew through the forehead of the medevac. Immediately the shooter dragged the dead body behind the rock formation.

His partner positioned the injured pilots onto two litters, each consisting of two wooden poles connecting a canvas sheet. His next move was to inject both men with a fractional dose of Etorphine, a synthetic opioid possessing knockout potency thousands of times more powerful than morphine. Approved for veterinary purposes, a modest dose of the drug can easily immobilize an adult elephant.

Quickly, the men literally sized up the two medevac pilots and began stripping them of their uniforms down to their underwear. Upon completion, the attackers disrobed, changed into the medevac uniforms, then dressed the unconscious pilots in their clothing. With the thread swap completed, the men paused, glanced at each other and proceeded with the gruesome plan drawn up in a faraway place.

In cold blood with complete premeditation, the Cheetahs bludgeoned the incapacitated bodies, breaking arms and legs in the process. After simulating injuries consistent with a catastrophic car crash, he and his partner lifted the litters with the bodies into the rear of the helicopter. The men jumped into the left and right seats of the Mi 38, turned on the engine and dusted off.

One of them checked in, "Cheetahs in the air bearing south."

The voice at the other end responded, "Tiger incoming to rendezvous LZ."

The helicopter was several feet from touching down on the remote northern corner of Ateshgah Park, located thirty miles northwest of downtown Tehran, exactly at 12:00. Kicking up an unexpected haboob, the Tiger, engulfed in sand, was unable to advance toward the helicopter, waved off the bird. Sensing the whiteout conditions, the pilot repositioned several hundred yards to the west in a grassy area. Sprinting, the Tiger jumped into the hovering helicopter. As the bird lifted, banking left, the new passenger, dressed in medical scrubs, assumed the role of the flight medic in the cabin with the injured men.

The co-pilot, leaning in, asked, "Captain, the Tiger is a woman?"

Laughing, the man answered, "Well it certainly appears that way."

From the cockpit of the medevac helicopter the Cheetah was piloting en route to downtown Tehran, he radioed Shodhada Hospital located adjacent to Tajrish Square, less than a mile south of the Sadabad Palace, and in proper Farsi reported, "Sierra Hotel, this is Delta Echo 28, incoming in five minutes with Code Red 2 X, males in their mid-thirties, severe trauma, request permission to land. Over."

The operator responded, "Delta Echo, please advise as to the condition of the patients. Over."

After receiving hand signal updates from the Tiger, the Cheetah radioed, "IVs started, blood pressure 160/100 and 145/90. Both patients breathing but non-responsive."

The operator gave Delta Echo 28 permission to land. "Northern approach coordinates 35°41'46"N 51°25'23"E Latitude °N, Longitude °E, repeat northern approach only. Winds five miles per hour out of the north. Trauma team will be waiting on deck. Over."

Approaching the helipad atop of the Shodhada Hospital, the pilots could see the trauma team, six individuals with two gurneys, assembled outside of the landing circle. From two hundred feet, the pilot could see the expressions on the medical professionals' faces. The pilots felt a bizarre kinship to Martian invaders as the bird lowered onto the helipad with the precision of a plumb bob.

Seconds after touchdown, the hospital trauma team repositioned the two injured men from the helicopter onto the waiting gurneys and hotfooted, to the open elevator. As per normal procedure, the Tiger accompanied the trauma team into the hospital, where an update was provided as to the treatment administered to date. The Tiger replenished supplies, which were used in treating the patients and executed the continuity of care paperwork officially transferring the patients from their authority to the hospital.

Afterwards, the Tiger returned to the helideck where she grabbed the oversized briefcase and dashed to the door leading to a small observation tower overlooking the helipad. The bird dusted off and disappeared to the south and the Cheetahs were gone for good. After climbing two short flights of stairs, the Tiger was now at the apex of the tallest building within a two-mile radius. The tower, covered with a bunker-style roof, had openings on all sides. The time was 1:00 P.M. The world-class sniper, positioned in the perfect spot, wasted little time in opening the case and removing the rifle. After attaching the nine and a half inch ACC Titan-QD Suppressor made of titanium alloy, the shooter positioned the L115A3 in the direction of the Iranian Presidential Palace. From the ultraprecision German-crafted Schmidt & Bender scope, camouflaged by a platinum gray tarp, the distance to the front steps measured out at three thousand four hundred feet. A kill from this distance, approximately two thirds of a mile, would have been challenging a decade ago. Unfortunately for unsuspecting targets, technology had changed. Intelligence sources placed Buryian President Ahman Mussan's arrival at the palace at 2:00 P.M.

The midday sun was shining brightly over the Iranian capital on a typical hot and clear summer day, which saw temperatures approach 100 degrees. The air was dead calm with high humidity yielding just average visibility—important data points considered carefully by the shooter.

Heat affects Point of Impact (POI) in two critical ways. Higher ambient temperatures cause a flatter trajectory due to lower air density. Rounds traveling through hotter temperatures experience fewer collisions with air particles per unit of flight path. Ammunition temperatures cause the nitro-cellulose-based powder inside the cartridge to burn at a higher rate. Through extensive testing Accuracy International concluded that the latter had four times the impact on POI in achieving the all-important First Shot Hit (FSH).

At exactly 1:50 P.M, the noise of the presidential motorcade's sirens could be heard from the right side of the tower. While still not visible, the sniper knew the target was approaching. The six-car motorcade traveled up Shariati, took a left on Vali Asr, eerily passed by the hospital, entered Tajrish Square, which is actually a circle, and exited at ten o'clock onto Maleki, before finally turning into the Sadabad Compound.

The sniper removed five 8.59-millimeter bullets from a container of dry ice, abundantly found in the medevac helicopter, and loaded them into the chamber, adjusted the telescope to the correct trajectory based upon her analysis of the conditions and readied for her mark to approach the kill zone.

Displaying skills that distinguished the assassin as a world-class sniper, the Tiger's entire body went into a complete state of relaxation—a condition similar to the fifth stage of the human sleep pattern, rapid eye movement (REM), also referred to as paradoxical sleep, because while the brain and other body systems become more active, muscles become more relaxed. Heightened mental capacity combined with an extremely still physical condition is the "perfect storm" for long-range sniper shooting accuracy.

As the motorcade approached, Iranian President Bambad Babak commenced the long walk down the marble steps of the Presidential Palace. Flush with dignitaries, soldiers and members of the Iranian government, against a backdrop of music and flags waving, the scene was the embodiment of nationalism.

When the third car carrying President Mussan reached the bottom of the steps, a security officer jumped out of the front seat, pivoted and opened the rear passenger side door with the grace and deft of a Spanish matador allowing a Toro Bravo to pass by. The president stepped out of the car and shook Babak's hand, while exchanging some pleasantries. The pair walked up ten steps to the first landing and turned back to the crowd, like Olympic Gold–winning synchronized swimmers.

The sniper focused the rifle telescope on the still target, exhaled and pulled the trigger, sending a death-token traveling at three thousand feet per second over three thousand five hundred feet. In less than two seconds, Mussan's head exploded, sending the Buryian president crashing to the ground, his blood and brain splattering the uninjured but horrified Iranian president.

Pandemonium ensued, as Tehran abruptly sank into chaos.

The sniper calmly lowered the rifle, pushed it to the side of the tower and proceeded at a modest pace down the stairs. Bypassing the rooftop elevator, the shooter, already dressed in scrubs, entered the sixth floor of the hospital from the stairwell. Passing signs for the maternity ward, the Tiger pushed the elevator button and entered as the wide doors opened. The sniper walked onto the street, instantly assimilating with the hospital staff, most of whom by this time had collected outside. Dematerializing with each step the Tiger turned right onto Vali Asr and vanished into the fog of confusion.

As the news of the assassination spread among the diners in the Neyab restaurant, a sense of concern, which started slowly, quickly plunged into panic. Was it an invasion? A terrorist attack? Unsure of the developments, most patrons fled the restaurant and poured onto the streets of Tehran that were quickly disintegrating into havoc. Roos grabbed his cell phone and called Kat using Viber. Her phone rang and rang. After the tenth ring, Roos hung up, waited two minutes and tried again. This time Kat's calm voice could be heard.

"Christian, have you heard the news of the shooting?"

"Yes. Where are you?" Roos asked in a rushed voice.

Kat's reply calmed Roos, "In the hotel room."

"Please pack our gear and meet me out front of the hotel in twenty minutes. I will pick you up on the way to the airport."

As Roos and Maryam walked out of Neyab, the driver was parked directly in front of the restaurant. The pair jumped in and made their way toward the hotel, which was less than ten blocks away. As the car pulled up, Roos could see Kat waiting in the lobby, with the luggage neatly in tow.

Roos, astutely sensing the potential value in having his Iranian friend travel to the airport, asked Maryam, "Would you mind accompanying us to Qaleh Morgi Airport?'

"Not at all," she responded.

The Qaleh Morgi Private Airport was located less than three miles from downtown Tehran. The route called for a short drive out of the city west on Azadi Avenue followed by a south heading on the Wawab Highway. With a six-thousand-foot runway, the main runway at Qaleh Morgi could handle virtually all private jet aircraft, including the Citation X, which only needed five thousand one hundred forty feet to blast off into the sky.

Traffic by this time was at a standstill, with people running through the streets, screaming and wildly waving the Iranian flag. The driver cut through the side streets, heading in a southwest direction, hoping to catch the Wawab Highway. The radio broadcast blaring in the car sounded to Roos like trouble, notwithstanding his complete lack of understanding of the Farsi language. He asked Maryam to interpret.

She obliged. "The Buryian president, Ahman Mussan, has been assassinated. No other injuries. President Babak was unharmed. A city-wide manhunt is underway. All airports, train stations and bus stations have been closed. Authorities are requesting that all citizens return to their homes immediately. A 5 P.M. curfew has been instituted."

Kat asked, "Roos, does that include the private airports?"

Roos responded, "I don't know, but we will find out soon enough."

As the vehicle approached the intersection with the Wawab Highway, the driver turned left and headed south toward the airport. Off in the distance, approximately half a mile, the flash of lights from police and emergency vehicles illuminated the four-lane highway. The roadblock brought traffic to an abrupt halt. Up ahead, Roos could see the police and military frisking civilians on the side of the road as their cars were being searched. It took over an hour for the vehicle containing Roos, Katherine and Maryam to reach the front of the roadblock. The intensity of the scene unfolding at a dizzying pace was palpable. An Iranian police officer, sporting an AK47, approached the driver-side window of Roos' car and began asking questions in abrupt, aggressive Farsi. With Maryam affirmatively nodding her head, the driver continued answering the young police officer's questions. The driver turned to the back seat where the three passengers were anxiously seated and in English asked for everyone's identification.

Roos wondered just how long it would take for the officer to notice the Israeli stamp that was still drying on his and Kat's passports. Had Roos and Kat flown into the Tel Aviv airport their passports would not have been stamped, per Israeli policy. The government is acutely aware of the difficulties that an Israeli stamp can cause for travelers who plan on visiting some of Israel's neighbors. But instead the couple had arrived by water aboard the *Akrep* and were caught with illegal weapons. The government loses interest in accommodating such travelers.

Oversized, with bright green ink, the Tel Aviv–Israel stamp stood out like a turban in St. Peter's Basilica. A seasoned traveler such as Roos understood the counterintuitive dynamic potentially developing here at the Iranian checkpoint. On the one hand, he and Kat had nothing to fear about the assassination. However, Americans in Iran lose many rights relative to local citizens, especially during times of crisis. The government needs to find someone to blame for the shooting and who better than someone from America, a country coined the "Great Satan" by the Iranian leaders.

By this time the officers had surrounded the car and demanded that all passengers exit the vehicle. A four-man team of search specialists descended on the car on their hands and knees, and the men scoured the front and back seats, the roof, trunk, undercarriage and front engine. They pulled Roos and Kat's luggage onto the roadside and began to rummage through the three bags in a very detailed manner. Examining pill vials, toothpaste tubes, contact lens containers, iPads and iPhones, where they studied recent Google searches, emails, texts and phone calls. Meanwhile, one of the more senior officers was questioning Maryam Tehrani about her relationship with Roos and Mandu, how long she had known them, how long were they in town. Maryam knew most of the answers, but asked Roos, "What is your next destination?"

Roos answered, "Amritsar, India."

Translating additional questions, Maryam asked, "Where were you when the shooting took place?"

Roos replied, "I was at the Neyab Restaurant with you, Maryam."
Katherine answered, "I was in my hotel room."

A lab technician appeared from a crime scene van with two In-stant Shooter Identification Kits. The technician took several cotton swabs of both Roos and Mandu's right and left hands. The experience, like an impending myocardial infarction, constricted Roos, reducing him to such a tightened state an ice pick would not fit up his rear. Disappearing back into the lab vehicle, the technician reduced the swabs with water, which would separate any materials present. After waiting ten minutes, the technician examined the results. Returning to the scene, he informed the officer in charge of the need to retest Kat. Roos watched helplessly while Kat acquiesced to a second examina-tion. When someone fires a gun, metal residue is detectable on the shooter's hands for hours afterwards, unless gloves are worn. Roos' results along with both of Kat's tests came back negative. The officer in charge motioned for Roos, Kat and Maryam to enter the car. They were free to pass through the roadblock.

Qaleh Morgi Private Airport, an uncontrolled field, had no in-house air traffic control tower. All instructions for landings and takeoffs were established by the air traffic controllers at Tehran's Imam Khome-nei International Airport.

Exiting the car, Roos' heartfelt appreciation for his friend's pivotal assistance was expressed both verbally and physically with a warm em-brace, which included the traditional double-cheek kiss. Her response was the epitome of class and style, "Salaam."

The G3 flight crew was anxiously awaiting Roos' arrival. The chief pilot indicated that the main airport in Tehran had been closed but no official word on the operational status of Qaleh Morgi had been issued. His recommendation was to get on the runway and take off as soon as possible. Roos inquired about the risk associated with such a move. Worst case, the pilot said they would scramble fighter jets and shoot them down. The seasoned retired F-18 jet fighter pilot smiled and told Roos that the odds of that happening were remote. Roos concurred with an enthusiastic, "Wheels up it is."

While the ground crew rushed to fill the airplane with the necessary fuel to reach Amritsar, India. Roos took the opportunity to reach out to his partner, Frank, with a WhatsApp text message: "Frank, Not sure if you have seen the news, but there has been an assassination here in the Persian capital. Needless to say, the city has gone horn-mad, hastening an early exit on our part, but not before I visited the Treasury of National Jewels. Such a shame, I was just starting to like this place. Tehran is quite different from the stereotypical western press description. They have the distempered leaders pegged correctly; the people are wonderful, but in desperate need of an unmuzzling. Heading to India at the moment. CR"

Frank responded, "Yeah saw the news. Thank God someone took out that roguish ruffian. I heard the airports are closed. How are you getting out?"

"Private field, I hope. If you don't hear back from me within thirty minutes, you will know I made it out. BTW remind me to tell you the Persian condom story. It is quite the stretch. CR"

Without contacting air traffic control in Tehran, the G3 took advantage of the confusion caused by multiple commercial flights circling the city waiting to land, positioned at the end of the runway and took off. Through thirty-nine thousand feet, the G3 had yet to hear a peep.

Occupying the first chair in the front section of the twelve-seat G3, Roos studied the flight route map appearing on the monitor. Tehran, Iran, to Amritsar, India. Distance—one thousand four hundred miles. Time—three and one-half hours. Heading—east-southeast. The route, which primarily flew over desolate land, connected, Tehran, Iran—Birjand, Iran—Kandahar, Afghanistan—Lahore, Pakistan—Amritsar, India.

As the plane reached cruising altitude, Roos unbuckled his seat belt and approached the cockpit.

"Any NOTAM?"

Roos' question referred to "notice to airmen" from the aviation authorities. The right seat pilot responded, "No, sir. Clear skies above twenty-four thousand feet."

His wingman chimed in, "Don't get all beaded up on us, Mr. Roos. Trust me, we will not be gaffing off the FAA gods' instructions and doing any flathatting below the hard deck. By the way, what is your profession, Mr. Roos?"

Roos, musing to himself about the macho inflight pilot talk — swashbuckling bravado exponentially synchronized with the altimeter — answered, "Investment management."

"What is the difference between pilots and fund managers?" asked the left seat pilot.

Roos, unable to muster a response, simply said, "Do tell."

With the Persian capital disappearing in his contrail, the seasoned aviator delivered the punchline. "No pilots hanging around with bad track records."

# 12

## Pashtun Peril

*"The only time you have too much fuel on board is
when you are on fire."*
—Unknown

Positioned from the right side of his airplane's rear seat window,
Roos was curiously observing the Registan Desert, an extremely
arid plateau in southern Afghanistan, which encompasses the
Helmand and Kandahar Provinces. Like a red-tailed hawk searching for
his next prey, Roos' eyes were darting back and forth as he studied the
unusual and unfamiliar barren landscape. It is an ecoregion, defined as a
relatively large unit of land or water that contains a geographically distinct
assemblage of natural communities with boundaries that approximate the
original extent of natural communities prior to major land usage changes.
The world's ecoregions share the same environmental conditions, species
and ecological dynamics. The Registan Desert ecoregion is bounded by
the extreme eastern part of Iran, southern Afghanistan and a small part
of western Pakistan. Living conditions are brutally challenging in every
inch of the desert's one hundred and seven square miles, and is considered vulnerable by world environmental standards, which cite overgraz-
ing, warfare and water extraction as the primary threats. Most indigenous
living organisms are classified as either endangered or near extinction.
Reptiles such as the point sprout racerunner, dark-headed dwarf racer
and toad-headed agama are struggling to survive in the arid conditions,
as are mammals including the Asiatic black bear and marbled polecat,
and birds such as the Egyptian vulture, spotted eagle and pale backed pigeon. Human life dates back fifty thousand years in the Registan Desert.
The opening of the Silk Road's southern east-west trading route, which

passes through the region, brought strategic significance to the desert in the first millennium B.C. Darius I of Persia fought here in the year five hundred fifty B.C. Alexander the Great, leading his massive Macedonian army, defeated Darius III in the year three hundred thirty B.C.

Keeping locals alive is the poppy trade. Afghanistan, which grows poppy on six hundred thousand acres throughout the country, derives an estimated fifteen percent of gross national product from the sale of paste made from the seeds. One byproduct of the natural medicinal alkaloid is morphine; another more lucrative one is opium. Convinced that poppy and the insurgency were inextricably linked, United States President George W. Bush instituted a policy of eradicating the poppy fields. The United States military attacked the most prolific growing areas located in the Kandahar and Helmand Provinces, in the heart of the Registan Desert. Destroying poppy fields, then sitting down with the local farmers to discuss the benefits of planting wheat or rice in lieu of the poppy plants, the trained American soldiers sounded more like economists attempting a strange form of agricultural diplomacy. A fully armed United States Marine would stand in a torched poppy field explaining to the local family farmer why growing wheat, which yields a price of forty-three cents per kilogram, or rice fetching one dollar and twenty-five cents per kilogram, is far better than sticking with the poppy, which sells for two dollars and three cents per kilogram on the open market. In a country where twenty-five cents buys bread for an entire day, the response always was a blank stare. Even if the farmer agreed with the recommendation, in all likelihood he wasn't the owner of the land—rather just a hired hand working for the feudal owners that claimed title to the properties dating back centuries. The challenges with this patently absurd voodoo economics, was most likely understood by the locals in the English tongue. Opium production surged in response to the poppy war. President Obama has since made peace with the poppies.

Colombia, Burma and Tasmania kick in the notorious psychedelic flowers, but it is Afghanistan that accounts for over ninety percent of the world's production of poppy, half of which comes from the Helmand Province. Official reports, which are understated, put the annual revenues of the Afghan poppy north of one billion U.S. dollars, a figure up fifty percent since American involvement twelve years ago. With production costs virtually zero, gross margins exceed ninety percent, making the poppy business uniquely profitable and valuable for the Afghani farmers and landowners.

As Roos imagined all of the horrific battlefield deaths buried below in the sand, his heart sank as his eyes were suddenly drawn to the top of the right wing of the airplane, where he saw something troubling, something that he had seen before. The G3 has an over-wing fueling capability through a cap located on the wing on each side of the plane. The cap is attached to the wing by four screws, which are countersunk, creating a polished aerodynamic environment. Ten years ago climbing through twenty thousand feet, after taking off from Dulles International Airport en route to Toronto, Roos vividly remembered the over wing cap on his G3 popping up like an ostrich. The fuel spilling out had a distinctly black look that day, convincing Roos that the wing was on fire. In the heat of moment, clearly distracted, Roos was unable to remember the physics of the prism of light, which changes the color of matter depending on the angle of view through the earth's atmosphere. From the ground a jet smoke trail looks white, whereas from eye level at altitude it is pitch black. He immediately began making phone calls to loved ones. The left seat captain emerged from the cockpit entering the cabin and gave a serious yet short look at the right wing. Without saying so much as a word, the pilot rushed back into the cockpit. The plane entered a steep left bank turn, proceeding on a very steep approach back to Dulles Airport. Coming in hot and spilling fuel over northern Virginia residential areas, the Gulfstream's pending landing was of concern to many different constituencies at the airport. Fortunately Dulles was prepared. The landing, surrounded by police vehicles, ambulances, and fire trucks, looked like a Steven Spielberg–directed movie shoot. The chief pilot, after bringing the airplane to a successful stop on the field, indicated that the range was around thirty minutes with that type of oil spill.

The situation in the G3 over Afghanistan was spooky in its similarity. The chief pilot came back in the cabin to get a look at the fuel cap. He glanced for five seconds and hustled back in into the cockpit without saying a word. The fuel was pouring out of the over-wing refueling cap, positioned like a submarine hatch in the up position, at an alarming rate. Within seconds the plane entered a dramatic nosedive, dropping the plane's altitude from forty thousand feet to ten thousand within minutes. The near weightless drop in altitude created a sensation, not quite unlike the Tower of Terror ride in Disneyland. From ten thousand feet the plane continued a steep descent. Roos was anxiously looking out of the window, searching for something on the ground, anything. From the inflight map, Roos could see that the plane was heading down west of Kandahar by approximately seventy miles. Laconic Kat remained exceedingly calm, without so much as saying a word. The captain came on the over air sound system, with the announcement to prepare for landing.

Within minutes the G3 touched down on the newly paved seven-thousand-five-hundred-foot main runway at Bost Airport in Lashkar Gah, Afghanistan, the capital of the Helmand Province, affectionately referred to by the United States Marine Corps as Hell Man Province. Originally constructed in 1957, Bost Airport was completely renovated in 2008 at a cost of fifty-two million dollars, a project that constructed a modern terminal, seven thousand five hundred foot asphalt runway and an agricultural center. Receiving fifteen flights a day, mostly turboprop passenger aircraft operated by Ariana Afghan Airlines, Safi Airline, Kam Air and Pamir Airways, Bost is the only complete civilian airport in southern Afghanistan. Serving as the gateway to the Helmand Province, nothing gets in or out without going through Bost.

Unlike Roos' previous unscheduled landing, this time there were no emergency vehicles in sight. The only thing visible for miles, in all directions, was sand. This may not be the end of the earth, Roos thought, but you could likely see it from atop a large boulder. The pilots opened the G3's door, instantly exposing the cabin to the chilling ten-degree Fahrenheit temperatures on the ground. In the climate-controlled cabin, with nothing but desert around, the frigid air created an antithetical sensation. With the assistance of a stepladder the chief pilot stepped up onto the wing and began examining the damaged fuel hatch. Members of the Bost line crew, who spoke only Pashto, the leading language of Afghanistan, joined the pilots under the wing for a valueless conversation. Eventually an English-speaking official of Bost Airport surfaced from the

FBO, promptly informing the pilots that the maintenance crew had left for the day but would be returning first thing in the morning. The pilots, who ended up sleeping in the plane, instructed Roos to return at noon.

Having the first significant negative development occur, while unwelcomed, was not unexpected. Roos believed his itinerary afforded several days of a margin of safety—five to be exact. In his mind, the first delay striking on day fourteen was infinitely manageable.

Jumping into an FBO crew car, Roos and Kat headed into the city of Lashkar Gah, which was located north of the airport by a quarter of a mile on an eight-foot-wide dirt access road. The circa 2000 Toyota Corolla had a "Total Loss" decal on the lower right corner of the windshield as well as a California registration sticker. Afghanistan is a country with a paltry car ownership of twenty cars per thousand, as compared to the United States, whose extravagance boasts eight hundred per every thousand citizens. Many accident-totaled U.S. cars find their way onto the dirt roads of Afghanistan.

Lashkar Gah, with a population of fifty thousand, is situated on the east bank of Afghanistan's longest and most important river, the Helmand. Originating in the Baba Range in east-central Afghanistan, the Helmand flows over seven hundred miles before finally emptying into swamps on the Iranian border. Five miles south of the city, the Arghandab River flows into the Helmand. Lashkar Gah, sitting at the junction of and in between the two rivers, appears to be figuratively trapped in the forked tongue of the region's indigenous De Witte's gecko lizard. The town, once dubbed "Little America" as a result of thousands of United States contractors coming to build an irrigation facility in the 1950s, became the most dangerous venue in all of Afghanistan during the war, which continues. Defending against Taliban insurgents, a different side of America's work force, namely the United States Marines, moved in as Lashkar Gah descended into chaos. More than seven hundred foreign fighters have been killed in the area over the past ten years, approximately a third of all allied fatalities in the country.

The United States Marines Helmand headquarters, Camp Leatherneck, home to seven thousand United States Marines, down from a peak of over thirty thousand, is located twenty miles north of Lashkar Gah. The base is conjoined by Camp Bastion, England's largest operation in the country. A pair of two-star generals in charge of the Helmand Province were recently fired for their failure to protect Camp Leatherneck during a 2012 Taliban attack of the base. Dressed as United States Army personnel, a team of Taliban fighters snuck past sleeping Pacific Tonga guards and attacked the allied stronghold with horrific success. The attack left fourteen dead and damaged six Harrier attack jets, with a twenty-four-million-dollar price tag, the largest aviation loss since the Vietnam War in the 1960's.

Traveling north paralleling the Helmand River, Roos, peering out of the rear left-side window could see locals bathing in the murky water. Others were washing bicycles and clothing. The Bost hotel was described in the airport's informational brochure as a ten-room hotel with twenty beds, food is fair, facility is fairly clean and considered a third-class hotel. Surrounded by a concrete eight-foot white wall, the building looked more like a low security prison facility than a hotel. An empty circular fountain was centered in the courtyard, surrounded by struggling parched grass and plastic outdoor furniture. The couple was greeted by a receptionist wearing a traditional *partoog-korteh*, loose fitting pants and long sleeve shirt made of light linen cloth. His long braided hair was covered by a turban. His skin was dark and leathered, a product of generations of exposure to the brutal conditions inherent in the Helmand Province. He greeted Roos and Kat, "Pakheyr, maakhaam mo pa kheyr." ("Welcome, good evening.")

Roos, flashing his credit card with one finger pointing into the air, was able to communicate with the man. After signing for two thousand Afghan Afghanis, approximately thirty-five U.S. dollars, the man escorted the couple down the hall to a stark double room. Facing west across the Helmand River with the setting sun was reflecting light off of the Afghan red painted cinder block walls, the guests were left with the trapped sensation of being inside of a scary Halloween jack-o'-lantern.

Before turning in for the night, Roos typed out his daily text for Day 14 to Harrison. Without access to a telecommunication service, the message never left his iPhone. A problem, for sure, thought Roos.

Carl Strange's connecting flight from Delhi landed in Amritsar, India, in the early afternoon. Based on Roos' credit card information, Strange proceeded to the chic modern Golden Tulip Hotel, an affiliate of Group du Louvre, owned by the Starwood Capital Group, a U.S.-based private equity firm. After checking in, Strange headed to the bar.

Word of the emergency landing spread like wildfire through the small war-torn town of Lashkar Gah. The news reached Basir Kazim before the G3's engines were turned off. The thirty-five-year-old Afghan was on the construction site of his latest residential real estate project. In the shadows of the newly christened Helmand Police Command Center, the leading commercial and residential real estate developer in the region was building luxury homes. His signature property in the development was the ten-thousand-square-foot home of the retired mayor. Boasting an indoor swimming pool, wine cellar and movie theater, the eight-bedroom property was the grandest private residence ever to be built in the city. The city, finally beginning to transition from war to a sense of normalcy, was experiencing a real estate boom of sorts. Properties that literally could not be given away as recently as three years ago were trading above one hundred thousand US dollars. Kazim's properties in the heavily protected neighborhood adjacent to the police headquarters started at two hundred fifty thousand and went up to a million. Kazim's company, Registan Realty, built everything in Lashkar Gah. The ten-thousand-seat football stadium, new terminal and agricultural center at the airport, Helmand Police Command Center and the Courthouse, the new home to the Chief Justice of Helmand Province, were all built by Registan Realty. The idea of awarding construction contracts under dodgy circumstances was certainly not unknown to the local authorities. Kazim wielded ultimate power throughout the profoundly corrupt police department and government. An old Afghan saying, "You join the Afghan army for prestige, and the Afghan police for money,"

precisely describes the state of corruption among Lashkar Gah's finest. Through his "make it rain" bribes, handed out to members of the police department on a scale similar to the United States Mint printing Treasury notes, Kazim became a man of supreme importance in the ancient capital of the Helmand Province.

Kazim was anxiously waiting for the "baton" to be handed off by the United States to the Afghanistan Army and police. This was a development that could only enhance Kazim's already strong position within the region.

Athletically fit and standing at six foot two with atypical Afghani bronze skin, Kazim, with his strong chin, Greek-shaped nose and cobalt blue eyes, was an extremely handsome man, and a likeable one at that. Brimming with self-esteem, he strode through bullet-ridden Lashkar Gah, a town surrounded by thirty thousand United States Marines for much of the past decade, like Alexander the Great on a Segway. Acting like a man who knew where all of the landmines and roadside bombs were hidden, Kazim displayed supreme assuredness and self-confidence.

Shunning typical Afghani garb, the real estate mogul could be seen around town in Gucci jeans, Forzieri shoes, Luigi Borrelli shirts and custom-made Hugo Boss suits. On runs through the desert, Kazim only wore Under Armour. In the winter months, which sent temperatures below zero, Kazim protected himself from the cold with the finest North Face gear. He was a man with style and sophistication, gleaned and honed through high-speed Internet access and money. Kazim, a lady's man extraordinaire, would walk on water, if there were any in the Registan Desert.

Basir Kazim did not have a religious extremist bone in his body; he was all about money, proud of it and made no attempt to disguise his greed. He was born in Kandahar on December 24, 1979, the exact day the Soviet Union invaded Afghanistan. The Soviet Union attacked in response to a coup that ousted Noor Muhammed Taraki, Afghanistan's pro-Soviet Communist President. Taraki rose to power as a consequence of the 1973 assassination of Afghan President Sardar Muhammad Daud Khan, who had come to power by ousting the king in 1973.

Under the pretense of coming to the aid of their Communist comrades in arms, thirty thousand Soviet troops poured through the Korengal

Valley, like lava running down a volcano. The military force would ultimately reach one hundred thousand before leaving fourteen years later in
defeat, licking their wounds with fifteen thousand dead and thirty-seven
thousand injured. The real objective was access to a warm-water port on
the Indian Ocean. In the eyes of the Soviet leaders, Afghanistan presented
an important stepping stone to an accommodative India.

Initially the Soviets installed Barak Karmal as president. He had
led the Afghan National Army teamed with the Soviets against the anti-
Communist Muslim Afghan guerrillas, commonly known as the Mujahidin. Assisted by the United States, China and Saudi Arabia, who
staged their military forces through Pakistan, a country who feared being the next domino to fall, the Mujahidin dug in their sandals and
fought to the death for fourteen horrific bloodshed-filled years. Over a
million Afghans died during the war, many more injured and another
five million became refugees in neighboring countries. The casualties exceeded the cumulative number of Americans lost in battle in the entire
history of the United States.

Basir's father, Farrukh, was a captain in the Mujahidin guerrilla
army. In 1982 when Basir was just three, Farrukh's unit, positioned in
the steep mountainside of the Korengal Valley, was overrun by Soviet
forces. Farrukh was killed in the attack.

Basir Kazim had lived in Afghanistan for thirty-five chaotic years,
only nine of which were war-free. For the first fourteen years of his life,
the United States was his ally, the last twelve, his ally and his enemy.
All he knew was pain and suffering, cold-blooded savagery, conflict and
horror. By the age of ten, Kazim had witnessed more killings than most
people would see in five lifetimes. His life was filled with mistrust, dishonesty and treachery, played on a chessboard before his young eyes by
the world's superpowers. Afghanistan, a poor country with insignificant
strategic value and virtually no resources, became a red herring during
the Cold War waged by the Soviet Union and the United States. The
result was a country torn apart from the inside out, drenched in the blood,
sweat and tears of her people, millenniums in the making. Despite defeat-
ing the Soviets the Mujahidin were unable to unite the hopelessly divided

people of Afghanistan. These political divisions resulted in a vacuum that would eventually be filled by the Taliban—a vacuum that Kazim knew would pale in comparison to the one coming as the Americans prepared for complete withdrawal.

Basir's childhood experiences left him determined to honor his father's anti-Communist commitment to freedom and capitalism. He set his sights on business and promised himself that he would become wealthy beyond his imagination. Basir did not see people as Pashtuns, Talibans, Afghan Nationals, Muslims, Christians or Mujahidins; rather, he viewed everyone as customers whom he could exploit and leverage to aggrandize his bank account.

Persistent rumors of poppy trafficking swirled around Kazim but never matriculated. People were simply too distracted by the daily struggle for food, shelter and clothing to worry about such issues. Others in positions of power, with less unfortunate circumstances, found themselves on the receiving end of Kazim's monetary generosity. In either case, his stock continued to rise as he stood his ground and worked tirelessly to improve life in Lashkar Gah.

Through his contacts at the airport and Bost Hotel, it did not take long for Kazim to learn Christian Roos' identity. A Google search of Christian Roos produced over one hundred results recorded in the past two weeks alone. Kazim clicked on one, a recent article from the *Bond Street Journal* with the title *Roos is Loose Around the World*, and began to read from the piece:

> *Retired CEO of Springer and Waldron and Wall Street maven Charles MacCormick has bet Christian Roos twenty-five million dollars on a twenty-five-day trip around the world. Roos, an accomplished value investor, left the country over a week ago on a daunting itinerary which has the Washington native traveling through Central America, South America, Europe, the Middle East, India, across the entire country of China, through North Korea and Japan before ending up back in New York. BSJ sources indicate that James Hawker, the head of derivative trading at MacCormick's old firm, has created a contract based on the wager, which has attracted enormous interest from the hedge fund community.*

# 13

## Shanghaied

Christian Roos pulled out of the hotel parking lot in search of breakfast with plenty on his mind. Before exiting the room, he left the following note:

*Morning Kat,*

*Heading to the airport to check on the status of the plane repair. Will return to pick you up by 11:30. Do not leave the room. Christian.*

Kazim placed a call to the interim chief of police, Tawaab Gahfoor. The previous two chiefs, Nigar and Islam, both of whom were women, were assassinated on the town's streets in broad daylight within the past twenty-four months. Kazim's call caught Chief Gahfoor in his corner office of the new Police Command Center.

"Morning, Tawaab," began Kazim. "What do you hear about the American who had the emergency landing yesterday at Bost?"

Gahfoor responded, "Morning, Basir. He was en route to Amritsar from Tehran when his plane suffered a mechanical failure. Plane is being repaired as we speak. The crew has filed for a 1 P.M. departure slot, which should not be an issue given the basic nature of the repair. The two passengers, a man and a woman, stayed at the Bost Hotel last night."

"I need a favor. Please have your force on the lookout for the American. Please notify me of his whereabouts."

"Already ahead of you," said Gahfoor. "He is having breakfast at Momand Kabuli Pulao."

Kazim, "Thank you."

"Of course," answered Gahfoor. "By the way, the hot water in my office shower is not working properly. Could you have a plumber take a look?"

Kazim replied that he'd send someone within the hour.

Seated on Momand's floor drinking chai tea, Roos was shoveling Kabuli Pulao into his mouth like a week-long-starved yak. Afghanistan's national dish is a creation of fluffed basmati rice mixed with chicken, beef or lamb, slivers of almonds and carrots, raisins and pistachios. Roos ordered the chicken Kabuli Pulao, which was served with fried eggs and biscuits. After paying the two-dollar breakfast tab, Roos ventured out of the restaurant where he was temporarily blinded by the sunrise. Rising over the eleven-thousand-foot Suleiman mountain range in Pakistan, the blazing sun cast unobstructed brilliant light across the Registan Desert, through Kandahar, across the Arghandab River, before ultimately illuminating Lashkar Gah. As he made his way to the crew car located in the parking lot in the back of the restaurant, a Santorini black LR4 HSE Range Rover with tinted windows slowly pulled into the parking lot's entrance on the south side of the restaurant.

As the door opened, the Arabica interior produced three men wearing white robes, sandals and a black *shemage*—an Arabian scarf, tied in such a way that only the eyes and part of the forehead were exposed. The men charged Roos from behind. Upon hearing the approaching footwork on the loosely graveled parking lot, he wheeled to find himself facing three menacing-looking locals. The man in the middle raised a four-by-seven-inch black gun aimed the barrel at Roos' chest and fired from a distance of less than twelve feet. Compressed nitrogen forced two probes, with one-inch needles connected to the gun by electrical wires, through Roos' orange North Face ski coat and Under Armour tee shirt, into his chest. The electrical charge from the Taser X26P, the latest smart product from the leading worldwide manufacturer of Taser equipment, knocked Roos to the ground instantaneously. The men quickly handcuffed Roos, gagged him, pulled a burlap bag over his head and threw him into the back of the Range Rover. With Roos now in a state of incapacitation, one of the men pulled out a syringe and injected a fractional dose of the powerful sedative Etorphine into Roos' left arm. The vehicle headed toward the southern part of the small town.

"Mac, Strange here. Calling you from the Golden Tulip Hotel in Amritsar, India. Roos was booked here last night, but he was a no-show check in. Just called the front desk and still no Roos. The assassination of the Buryian president in Tehran closed the airports for most of yesterday, but it was my understanding that all transportation venues were reopened by early evening. It is possible that he ended up staying another night in Tehran. I am waiting for my contact at the bank to give me the latest download on the Roos' credit card. As soon as I hear anything, I will call you, naturally."

Mac, concurring with his partner's assessment, said, "Sounds to me like he is still in Tehran."

As the time reached 11 A.M., Kat became concerned. Lacking cell service, she was unable to reach Christian. She walked down to the hotel's front desk where she found the same gentleman who had checked the couple in the previous night. Channeling her youth, Kat performed an excellent performance of charades by first acting out a phone call, which she followed up with an arm-stretched airplane flight around the lobby. The man reached below the counter, pulled out a telephone and began dialing one rotary turn at a time. After speaking to the person on the other end, he handed the receiver to Kat, who was relieved to hear the English language.

"This is Registan FBO. How may I help you?" asked the operator.

"Good morning. My name is Katherine Mandu. Christian Roos and I are passengers on the G3 that had the emergency landing yesterday. Not sure of the entire tail number, but being a AirJets plane, it ends with Quebec Sierra."

"Yes. I remember you. How may I help?"

"May I speak to one of the pilots?" asked Kat.

"Stand by."

The pilot came on. "Good morning, Ms. Mandu. The repair has been completed. We are confirmed for 1 P.M. wheels up to Amritsar, India. I trust your accommodations were satisfactory. Again on behalf of the company, I would like to express our sincere apologies for the emergency yesterday. What is your estimated time of arrival?"

"Let me ask Mr. Roos," said Kat. "Would you please put him on the line?"

"I have not seen Mr. Roos this morning."

"That is odd. He left the hotel this morning at 7 A.M., four hours ago. His note indicated that he was going to the airport to check on the status of the airplane repair. Neither of us have cell service, so I am unable to reach him."

"Give him another hour," the pilot advised. "Call me at noon."

She hung up the phone and returned to her room where her mind began racing.

Despite being in the middle of the night in New York City, Strange felt the necessity to call his partner.

"Mac, Strange here. Following up on our previous conversation, I checked in with my contact at the bank. You are not going to believe this. Roos' credit card is showing a thirty-five dollar charge at the Bost Hotel in Lashkar Gah, Afghanistan, last night. And an ATM machine withdrawal of three hundred U.S. dollars, paid out in Afghanis, the local currency in Afghanistan, today. I have researched the city. Besides being the gateway to the Helmand Province, the damn place is just twenty miles south of Camp Leatherneck, home to thousands of United States

Marines. A quick Google search indicates Lashkar Gah, a hotbed of Taliban activity, is one of the most dangerous places on the planet."

Yawning, Mac replied, "Must be credit card fraud. Check with the FBO in Amritsar."

"Already have," said Strange. "No record of a flight from Tehran landing in Amritsar. Oddly, my sources up in Iran indicate no record of a flight yesterday heading to Amritsar."

"Well call the hotel in Afghanistan," Mac said.

Strange said he'd try and let Mac know what he learned. Finding no information on the hotel online, Strange tried the airport at Lashkar Gah. "Do you have the phone number for the Bost Hotel?"

Strange's heart began beating at an increased rate to the ringing line of the Bost Hotel.

"Sahr pikheyr." (Good morning.)

Hearing a foreign language, Strange proceeded in English. "Trying to reach a hotel guest. His name is Christian Roos."

"Za na poheegum." (I do not understand.)

Strange spoke clearly, "I am trying to reach Mr. Roos."

"Karaar karaar khabaree kawa." (Please speak more slowly.)

Strange barked, "Roos. Roos. Roos. Roos."

The phone went on hold, and then began to ring. For the first time, Carl Strange heard Katherine Mandu's voice. "Hello."

"I am trying to reach Christian Roos," Strange said.

"Are you one of the pilots?" asked Katherine.

"Yes," Strange answered. "Captain Leacock here. Who, may I ask, is this?"

"Katherine Mandu. I spoke with the other pilot just a few minutes ago."

"Yes he told me. That is why I am calling. What appears to be the problem?"

"Like I told your partner," said Kat, "Mr. Roos left the hotel this morning at 7 A.M., indicating that he was heading to the airport to check on the status of the repair. I have not seen him since. By chance have you?"

Strange, "No."

"Wheels up at 1 P.M. still?" she asked.

"Yes, keep us updated." After hanging up, Strange was scratching his head as he began analyzing the phone conversation. His logical mind working like a computer, he thought the chances of the woman he spoke with not being Katherine Mandu were infinitesimal. How would anyone else in Lashkar Gah know about Christian Roos? What possible motive would anyone have to impersonate Katherine Mandu? Why didn't she know the pilot's names? Well, Strange thought, it was a one-off charter from Tehran. He knew that one of the two pilots was usually assigned passenger duty. Hanging coats, fetching coffee, coordinating luggage and transportation on the ground were the menial tasks loathed by so many pilots of high-performance jet aircraft. So what happened? Plane was being repaired, indicating an in-flight mechanical, requiring an emergency landing at Bost Airport in Lashkar Gah, Afghanistan. Plane is ready for a 1 P.M. takeoff. Roos left the hotel at 7 A.M., heading to the airport. He never shows and is now missing for almost five hours.

Strange decided to call Mac again with the update. "Mac, listen, sorry to bother you again, but I think we have a situation."

Mac listened carefully as he always did when news of this magnitude struck.

"Okay, keep me updated. I have several hours before I need to call the Hawk. Let's talk before then."

In lieu of the scheduled noon call with the pilots, Kat decided to drive the one mile down to the airport. Flashing some cash to the gentleman at the front desk, she was able to arrange for a car ride. The two AirJets pilots greeted her at the curb of the FBO. Glancing for the first time at the gentlemen's name tags fastened to their crisp flight shirts, Kat saw the names Captain Larson and Captain McCarthy. She inquired, "Where is Captain Leacock?"

Captain Larson answered, "Don't know anyone by that name. Captain McCarthy and I flew you and Mr. Roos yesterday out of Tehran. Speaking of Mr. Roos, any sign of him?"

"Negative."

"I have notified the police of the situation," said McCarthy. "Not surprisingly, the response I received was rather ho-hum. Essentially the police officer indicated that we are in a war zone and that people go missing here by the hour. They took his description and promised to let me know of any new developments associated with Mr. Roos' whereabouts. An abandoned crew car was spotted this afternoon by a local restaurant owner. He called the FBO a little while ago. Apparently Mr. Roos ate breakfast in the restaurant and left alone shortly before 8 A.M. this morning."

"Ms. Mandu," said Captain Larson, "needless to say this is an extremely unusual situation, one that we have certainly never encountered before. We have received instructions from headquarters to take off no later than 5 P.M. today, with or without Mr. Roos. We simply cannot risk another night here. I hope you understand."

Kat shrugged her shoulders and stepped back off the curb and into the hotel car. Leaning out of the window, she instructed the pilots, "I will be in my hotel room. Call me the instant you hear from Mr. Roos. I will do likewise."

The black Range Rover pulled left off the main road. After traveling one mile into the desert, the vehicle approached a large complex, which was surrounded on three sides by an uneven fifteen-foot craggy rock wall. The rear southern-most side of the property backed to a rock-ribbed hill with an apex rising one thousand feet above the desert. Stretching east-west for three quarters of a mile and half a mile south, the small mountainous formation encompassed over two hundred acres, the size of a spacious golf course. The sole entrance was demarcated by a copper-plated thirty-foot steel gate, which opened in halves inward toward the property. The walls, five hundred feet on each side, formed a perfect two hundred and fifty foot square, an area equal to slightly less than six acres. A gravel road led up to a one-story structure, which blended into the landscape like a mirage in the desert. Constructed completely of indigenous rocks, the house was virtually indistinguish-able from the surrounding landscape. The Range Rover pulled up to the left side of the house and entered through the garage. With the Taser shock faded, Roos—still under the affects of the sleeping agent—was semi-conscious in the back area of the vehicle where he felt the distinct sensation of downhill circular motion.

At 4 P.M. the phone in Kat's hotel room rang.

"Ms. Mandu, Captain Larson here. Any word from Mr. Roos?"

"Unfortunately no."

Captain Larson, "Ms. Mandu we are wheels up in exactly one hour. Will you be boarding the plane?"

As she paused, Kat puzzled over her early call from Captain Leacock. Had she misheard the pilot when he introduced himself? Possibly, but doubtful. Recalling the conversation, she acknowledged that she asked first if he was one of the pilots. If someone planned premeditated harm to Christian, surely they would have picked a safer venue than Lashkar Gah. Who was the gentleman that introduced himself as Captain Leacock? She did recognize both Larson and McCarthy as the pilots who flew them from Tehran. She was sure of that. Obviously someone had either taken Christian or killed him. Kat could think of absolutely no scenario that would have Roos abandoning her in the middle of a war zone in the Afghanistan desert. None.

"Ms. Mandu, are you still there?" asked Captain Larson.

"Yes, sorry," she said. "Just thinking through my decision. Would it be possible to fly me to Kathmandu, Nepal, instead of Amritsar?"

Captain Larson placed her on hold and rejoined the call after several minutes. "Ms. Mandu. Yes. Kathmandu is serviced by Tribhuvan International Airport, which has a nice ten-thousand-foot runway. The distance is just a little over one thousand nautical miles. The flight time should be a little over three hours, depending upon the winds. I assume we can charge the additional amount of this trip on Mr. Roos' account with our company?"

Kat quipped, "As long as you reimburse me for the thirty-five-dollar hotel charge from last night, which was caused by your frickin' fuel flap failure."

"See you soon, Ms. Mandu."

Kat packed her bag, as well as Christian's. Inside his kelly green Swiss Army oversized duffel bag, Katmandu placed the following note:

*Christian,*
*My heart knows only of hope, while my mind is bursting with fear.*
*No more painful decision have I ever made than the one to leave you.*
*Wherever you are, please know that, as perversely sounding as humanly*
*possible, I believed the course of action to be right thing to do given the*
*nightmarish circumstances that befell us. I am en route to Kathmandu,*
*Nepal, on the G3 and will be waiting for you at the Dwarika's Hotel,*
*forever. Love, Kat*

She left Christian's bag at the front desk, along with some cash and a look that only a female in a desperate situation could give. It was a look the gentleman had seen more than once before in his life, a look that he acknowledged with a comforting affirmation.

Precisely at 5 P.M., the G3 lifted off from Bost Airport with Katherine Mandu in the rear port seat. Kat placed her right hand on the eye-shaped window, gazed out upon the bleak Registan Desert and said out loud, "Good luck, my love."

After hearing the latest update from Strange, which provided no illumination on the situation, Mac sent the following agreed-upon emergency text to James Hawker, "Train Derailed." Within minutes Mac received a call from the Hawk over at Springer and Waldron and the two discussed news about Christian Roos' disappearance.

With the markets scheduled to open in thirty minutes, the Hawk braced himself for all hell breaking loose with the Caboose.

# 14

## The Hedgehog and the Fox

*"Revenge is a dish best served cold."*
—DOROTHY PARKER

Gradually regaining consciousness, Christian Roos found himself handcuffed to a wooden desk chair alone in the dark. After several minutes, he heard several men talking in Pashto outside of the room. As the lights were turned on, the first person Roos saw was Basir Kazim, dressed in Under Armour gear from his head to his toes, which were covered by New Balance running shoes.

Kazim asked, "What are you Americans doing here?"

"I am Swiss!" replied Roos.

"Not according to your passport. Your country has been fighting in Afghanistan for over twelve years, memorializing the military contest as the longest in America's brief history. I read a report from *National Geographic* recently that showed only one in ten, eighteen to twenty-four-year-old Americans, just ten percent, can identify Afghanistan on a map of Asia. Sounds like the only people who can identify my country are the ones fighting here. To me that is the most unbelievable statistic I have ever heard. What do you think of that, Christian Robinson Roos?"

"Obviously the situation is complicated," replied Roos. "From time to time the United States government tends to take a very reactionary position to events that directly affect her sovereignty. When the Twin Towers of the World Trade Center fell on 9/11, someone had to pay the price. The people demanded retribution, plain and simple. I think that is understandable."

Kazim's surprising response was, "Fair enough. So what brings you to Lashkar Gah?"

"Well, a man of your import surely has figured that out by now. I am traveling with a female companion. Is she here as well?"

"True," said Kazim. "What do you think of AirJets? The company's salespersons solicit me all of the time. Oh, your female friend. No she took off today out of Bost around 5 P.M. You know women, just so unreliable. Gone like a Rumi-inspired Whirling Dervish at the first sign of trouble."

Roos thought to himself, wow! But then again he could not really blame her.

"Excuse me, I do not believe you have introduced yourself."

"Apologies. Basir Kazim here."

"Well, Mr. Kazim, do you think you could remove these handcuffs?"

Kazim motioned to one of his guards to remove Roos' handcuffs.

Roos, shaking his hands in order to get the blood flowing again, thanked him.

"So, Mr. Roos, please tell me about the RoosCaboose derivative contract I read about in the *World Times* online version."

"It is a quite simple and straightforward financial concept," replied Roos. "I am embarked on a twenty-five-day trip around the world during which I am visiting thirty of the most sacred sites, in twenty-two cities, in fifteen countries located on five continents. My four partners and I have each bet five million on a successful circumnavigation. A gentleman named Charles MacCormick has bet twenty-five million that I will fail. While these are large sums of money, they pale in comparison to the trading that has erupted in the derivative contract, which is being run out of Springer and Waldron by the firm's head derivatives trader, James Hawker. A derivative contract is a financial instrument, which derives its value from another security. The total notional amount outstanding in the contract is approaching a billion dollars, from what I have heard through my partner. The price of the contract fluctuates constantly depending upon news of my travels. It will not take long for the Street to ascertain the fact that I have been kidnapped here in

Lashkar Gah. As one of the most dangerous places on planet earth, I don't think the news will be viewed positively by the people who are long on my success. The shorts, people who are betting against me, will be rejoicing and most likely increasing their positions, to the extent possible."

"Why don't I do that?" asked Kazim.

"Do what?"

Kazim answered, "Short the contract and detain you here past the twenty-five-day deadline."

"Well for starters," said Roos, "for you to be able to short a position in the contract, there must be a willing buyer on the other side of the trade. Given the situation that has developed, with you as the captor making the bet, I doubt any serious person would step up to that trade. Do you?"

"How would they know it was me?"

"Do you have an existing trading account with Springer and Waldron?" Roos asked.

"No, but I have multiple accounts with Swiss banks."

Roos changed the subject. "Before I departed on this trip, I secured twenty-five-million dollars of kidnap and ransom insurance. The company providing the coverage is extremely sophisticated. They are stocked with ex-CIA, Special Forces types, who have quite a good track record of successfully negotiating with people like yourself."

Kazim, flashing his temper, said, "Listen, Roos, don't compare me to street thug kidnappers. You don't know anything about me. I am a savvy businessman, who operates a successful real estate development company."

Roos backpedalled. "Of course, I have seen some of your work, including the airport. Very nice. Is it a family business?"

"No, just me. My father was an officer in the Mujahidin and was killed by the Soviets. I never knew my mother. Now let's talk more about the derivative contract. I am confident that my Swiss banks have relationships with Springer and Waldron."

"Wall Street is a very close-knit community," began Roos. "A large short position coming from an unknown client who is trading through

a Swiss Bank is not going to fly. I am in daily contact with my investment syndicate partners. Yesterday was the first day I was unable to make
contact. Today is the second. I can only assume word of my kidnapping
is already spreading throughout the Street. My guess is the contract will
go bidless when it opens for trading, which may have already happened.
Please forgive me; I don't know what time it is.

"It is 4 P.M. here, 7:30 A.M. in New York."

Roos' mind was scrambling. Kazim was turning out to be as far
as humanly possible from the man he thought would kidnap him in
Lashkar Gah. He needed to come up with a plan and fast. Roos quickly
deduced that the insurance angle was not going to work. Kazim was
thinking in bigger terms, much bigger. Feed the beast, he calculated.
He is focused on his ability to manipulate the trading in the derivative
contract through his control of me, thought Roos.

Scanning the room as he contemplated his predicament, Roos noticed a life-size bronze sculpture mysteriously looming off to his left.
The bearded man with shoulder-length flowing curly hair was dressed
in a robe wrapped at his waist exposing his strapping torso. The statue's
hollowed-eyed stare vanquished everything in sight. His right hand was
clutching a scroll while his left arm was cradling a helmet-like mask,
the tragedian's iconic calling card. Recalling his Brown University days,
Roos' thoughts freewheeled to Professor Allessandra Bugiardini's class-
room, where the magisterial teacher unveiled the beauty of the Greek
classics, one lovely page at a time. A business major, Roos had only
enrolled in the class as a fraternity rush requirement. His acceptance to
Sigma Chi was dependant upon convincing the Florentine native to join
him in a reenactment on the College Green of the scene where Orpheus
and Eurydice, the individuals involved in the ultimate tragic Greek love
story, flee Aristaeus and fall into a nest of live snakes.

Snapping him out of his transfixation was Kazim, who asked im-
petuously, "Well?"

Roos answered with a question, "Is that Euripides?"

Proudly Kazim answered in the affirmative, explaining that he had
always admired the fifth-century B.C. tragedian considered the father

of the deus ex machina, translated "God out of a machine," a plot trick utilized by playwrights when they had written themselves into a figurative corner. At the opportune moment, a god, magically lowered onto the stage by a crane, would save the day. What better role model for Kazim than the third tragedian, thought Roos.

And then suddenly a flash bomb went off in Roos' offbeat but spot-on mind. Calling on Mercury, the Roman god of profit, in a classic "God out of a machine," Roos made a shameless appeal to the snollygoster's propensity for avarice. He announced, "Mr. Kazim, I have an idea."

"Let's hear it."

Roos responded in a placating tone. "I appreciate and respect your desire to shun the modest spoils associated with kidnapping insurance. It takes time, and quite frankly is not without risk. I am sure you are aware of some instances, especially recently, where extraction teams have rescued clients without paying a penny of ransom money. Kidnappers have been taken out by skilled military operatives in the process."

Kazim, again angered, answered, "Yes I know, hence my complete lack of interest in the concept. Now what is your idea?"

Hatching a plan to fillip his new friend, Roos ventured forth, "Think the opposite of your initial idea, which was to short the contract and detain me, ensuring a profit. For reasons I detailed, that is simply not possible. And even if you were able to wrangle a buyer, the stakes would be too small to bother with. I have a scheme that will allow you to make a fortune."

With his interest piqued, Kazim asked him to go on.

"What if you produce a video showing me held in captivity? You know, like one of those unfortunate scenes which appear all too often on Al Jazeera television. A captured individual, who may be a member of the military or a civilian, sits quivering at a nondescript steel-top desk, while members of a gang, wielding weapons, stand at attention against a backdrop of bizarre flags. The image will crush the value of the derivative contract. What fool would bet on my ability to extricate myself from those circumstances, let alone complete the stipulated itinerary within the allotted timeframe? The answer is nobody but you, Basir Kazim."

Kazim, intrigued but slightly confused, asked, "So why would I take a long position?"

"Because you are going to let me go free on my merry way tomorrow. Please keep in mind that this is certainly not my first choice and definitely not my style. But let's face reality, which I have, you have me in a very compromised position, leaving me little choice. As we say in America, desperate times call for desperate measures. With the price virtually zero, the ability for you to take a huge position would be as easy as picking poppies and making heroin, ruining young people's lives along the way. After making the bet through your Swiss banks, I would complete my journey through India, Nepal, Tibet, China, North Korea and Japan, before flying back to New York City."

"How do I know you will make it?" asked Kazim.

"You don't. But I will. Trust me. After you place your trade, I will inform my partners, who will increase their positions, as will I. Our interests will be perfectly aligned. We will all be on the same team."

Roos tried to suck those last words back in, but it was too late. Everyone on the same team is a foreign concept to a man like Kazim, who has only known deceit and treachery his whole life.

Kazim excused himself from the room. As he reached the door, he turned to face Roos and in a low despotic voice cautioned, "You better not be using any Piketty math on me, Christian Robinson Roos." His heavily armed associates remained behind, along with a nervous Christian Roos, who was digging deep within himself in order to keep it all together. But the captive did manage to crack a smile conveying an imprimatur of Kazim's reference to economist Thomas Piketty, the French toady who bungled his income concentration calculations en route to gratifying the zeitgeist — the ninety-nine percent.

Behind his trading desk in Springer and Waldron's Wall Street headquarters, the Hawk was pacing. As the hour approached 9 A.M., his phone started to light up with calls from players in the RoosCaboose contract. The previous night's close was one ten, ten percent over par, indicating that as of yesterday, the majority view among investors was for Roos to complete the trip successfully, within twenty-five days. That opinion would change quickly.

Within hours the price dropped to fifty on light volume. The Hawk, who had traded principal positions successfully, managed to get flat the position and was no longer committing capital to facilitate trading in the contract. Despite his "inside" knowledge of a possible kidnapping, the Hawk did not feel comfortable acting on the information that, he acknowledged to himself, may or may not be true. At this point he was strictly matching up buyers and sellers from an agency position, receiving commissions for his troubles.

After several hours, Kazim returned to the room where Roos was being held. He quickly gave instructions in Pashto to his associates, which caused the men to grab Roos and usher him out of the cave-like space. They traveled down a long medieval corridor defined by rocks, illuminated by a light every ten feet or so. At the end of the passageway stood a twenty-foot horseshoe arch, sometimes referred to as a keyhole arch, a traditional design used in Islamic architecture. Supported from the ground by two stone columns, the arch widened above the entrance in a semicircle before ending in a point. The keystone was a black rock. Once through, a magnificent large square room was exposed, which Roos quickly understood to be the command center of Kazim's lair. Each wall contained three keystone arches, with the same ominous looking black keystone, all of which Roos could see from the dim lighting led down a separate passageway. In the center of the enormous one hundred by one hundred foot room, was a symmetrical Roman bath with steps leading into the warm bubbling water all on sides. Scantily clad women were lounging around drinking wine and eating fruit being served out of large silver-plated bowls by a very deferential wait staff.

Off to the left was a war room looking area, but upon closer examination the only maps on the walls and tables were of Helmand Province poppy fields. In one section were tables filled with flat-screen Bloomberg terminals being operated by team of a dozen or so individuals, none of who looked over the age of thirty. Glancing upward, Roos marveled at the cone-shaped ceiling structure, which ascended up several stories to a small opening, shining sunlight from God's flashlight. The appearance was very similar, Roos thought, to the Champagne caves in Reims, France. In order to keep the interior walls dry, the Romans tunneled down and outwards, while excavating the rich limestone from the mines. Not as critical in Lashkar Gah, a city which receives a stingy annual rainfall of less that one hundred millimeters, almost of all which falls from the vast Registan sky during December, January and February. The rest of the year, the land is blanketed by drought conditions. The opening contained a retractable glass roof, obviously for the winter rainy season. Not much escaped the owner of the house, who appeared to have an unlimited budget, which clearly did not come from real estate alone. Roos surmised that Kazim's wealth derived from the infamous Afghani poppy trade.

The cone-shaped walls, which started above the keyhole arches, were filled with murals that went beyond pastiches. The images affixed to the walls were exclusively of ancient battle scenes, many of which took place in Kazim's home country. On one massive triangle, which worked its way to the small roof opening, was an enormous mural depicting what Roos recognized as the Battle of Gaugamela (Arbela). On October 1st in the year 331 B.C. at the young age of twenty, Alexander the Great marched his army from Macedonia in search of the Persian leader Darius III, whom he found in modern-day Mosul, Iraq. His forty-thousand-man army was outnumbered five to one by the two hundred thousand Persian force. Displaying brilliant military leadership and his legendary crushing phalanx fighting formation, Alexander defeated Darius III, officially ending the Persian Empire and opening the way to India and all her treasures. In the lower right-hand corner, an image resembling a map cartouche, showed a thirty-three-year-old Alexander the Great on his deathbed, surrounded by his top generals, who asked, "Which amongst us will replace you?" One of the greatest warriors of all time responded, "The strongest."

Scanning the other walls Roos stood in amazement at the sights of the Battles of Ipsus, Constantinople, Thymbra and Alesia.

Kazim, taking note of Roos' fascination, said, "I can see you are a Renaissance man. Are you aware that scientists have recently discovered examples of oil painted murals in the famous Barnian Caves high in the mountains near Kabul, which date back to the fifth century? A good four hundred years before the Europeans started using oils and resins in their artwork."

Roos, nearly speechless, replied, "No."

Kazim continued, "Scientists talk of the opposable thumb as the characteristic which distinguishes human being from animals. As far as I can tell the only thing separating the two species is the fact that humans can kill from a distance. Animals can't, but would if they could."

Roos was flat out dumbstruck by the scene, which looked more like a full-blown Hollywood movie set than the inside of a private home in the middle of Afghanistan's Registan Desert. Kazim motioned to his associates, who immediately brought Roos over to his private open office area.

Kazim stared deep into Roos' eyes and asked, "Can I trust you?"

Roos' poker-faced response was, "Yes." Roos aggressively continued with the theory that states that a good offense is a good defense, "Here is how this will go down. There is a man named Alexei Romanov who runs Vengeance Capital, one of the largest and most successful hedge funds in the world, out of New York City. He is a heartless and ruthless ex-mobster, entirely lacking a conscience, who has reportedly killed dozens of people. My sources tell me that Romanov has shorted over a quarter of a billion dollars of the RoosCaboose. A big number for sure, but only about one percent of his assets under management. When he sees our video, which he will, he will become your pigeon. I am not sure of your financial situation, but judging from these surroundings, it appears to be quite robust." Roos paused and glanced upwards through the tiny sunlit opening and said, "But the sky is the limit for you. Romanov will take as much as you want."

The scene became quiet. Before Kazim could respond, Roos seized the moment and set the hook already swimming in the Afghani's mouth. "Romanov is Russian. The country that invaded Afghanistan and killed your father."

A solemn look unfurled over Kazim's face. "Alright. I agree, subject to two conditions. My identity must remain confidential. As I can assume you appreciate, I am surrounded by tens of thousands of United States Marines. Your president has waved the white flag and made peace with the poppies, but I do not want to unnecessarily provoke anyone. Secondly, you must contact me immediately if you encounter difficulties."

"Agreed to both, I have two conditions myself as well. First, you need to help me get to Amritsar, India. I assume that was your G650 I saw the other day, with the tail number 348BK *(Bravo Kilo)*, sitting in the hangar at Registan FBO?"

"Yes, beauty, isn't she? You said Beijing was on your itinerary, correct."

Roos acknowledged that it was.

"You can use the plane through Beijing," said Kazim. "That way I can keep tabs on you. What is your second condition?"

"After this is over you get the hell out of the heroin business."

"Why do you care?" Kazim asked.

"Through my charity work over the years with inner-city disadvantaged kids and hospitals, I have seen the devastating effects that heroin has on humanity. A pain and suffering that disproportionately affects the young. Two years ago, after one of our board meetings, the Medical Director, Dr. Kensington gave the hospital trustees a tour of the new intensive care unit. As the group strolled through the antiseptic facility with sparkling Formica floors, so clean you could eat off them, I was drawn to a patient in the infectious disease wing. Breaking from the pack, I walked into the room. Against the hand motioning by an attending doctor to stay away, I mentioned my board status and approached the bed, which was encapsulated by a clear plastic bubble. The young man, an African American was laying on his back with chest tubes protruding from his emaciated body, one which, doubtfully exceeded one hundred pounds. His collapsed cheekbones, sunken vapid eyes and exposed ribcage smelled of doom and signaled an impending death. I asked the doctor the nature of the patient's illness. His answer—human immunodeficiency virus—that unfortunately had progressed into AIDS and ultimately led to a double acute pneumonia infection. His prognosis—weeks to live at best. He added that a quicker expiration would be heaven sent based upon the agonizing pain associated with dying in such a manner. A healthy person's CD4 or T-Cell count is between 500 and 2,000 per cubic millimeter of blood. Treatment begins at 350 and AIDS is defined below 200. The doctor indicated that the twenty-three-year-old's count was just 175, and dropping by the minute leaving his body defenseless against bacteria, viruses and other germs—all of which lead to deadly infections. The doctor explained that in this exposed condition his organs would begin shutting down soon, one by one, creating intense pain. When I asked the cause of the disease, I heard the patient contracted HIV from a contaminated needle, which he used injecting heroin. Mr. Kazim, surely you are aware of the cost savings realized by junkies from shooting versus smoking?"

Kazim refrained answering the question and from making the promise.

"Maybe not now," said Roos, "but you will before it is over. I can see goodness in you. Now let's make the video and call Zurich."

Seated behind an antique Persian wooden desk, Roos adorned a red-checkered hood, which matched those of Kazim's three henchmen who were standing behind him. With arms folded and an ornate Persian sword called a Shamshir in each hand, the men looked like a cross between the Power Rangers and angry sushi chefs. Earlier Kazim had dispatched one of his employees to buy some Taliban flags in the local Lashkar Gah convenience store. All four flags were displayed on the wall behind the men. With Kazim's iPhone video in play mode, to the sound of strange music, one of the men ripped off the hood, exposing a disheveled Christian Roos. Looking desperate, Roos simply shrugged his shoulders and looked upward through the opening of Kazim's secret lair and into the clear blue skies that appeared to zoom heavenly.

As he brandished his Shamshir upward, one of the men cried, "Death to the infidels."

The camera went dark.

# 15

## Fool's Gold

*"Gossip is charming. History is merely gossip.*
*But scandal is gossip made tedious by morality."*
—OSCAR WILDE

Within hours, the video and accompanying photographs went viral on social media sites, such as YouTube, Facebook, Instagram, Vimeo and Twitter.

After a crash course in derivative trading taught by Roos, Kazim called his private banker in Zurich with the instructions to bid five cents for five hundred million dollars face value of the Roos contract. If executed, the trade would cost twenty-five million and pay twenty to one odds, a jackpot of five hundred million dollars.

A devilish grin surfaced on the chiseled face of Alexei Romanov as the hedge fund maven stood his ground on the mighty Vengeance Capital coliseum styled trading floor. The twelve-foot plasma high-definition monitor on the wall behind him was tuned to Al Jazeera, which was showing the footage of Roos in an "undisclosed" location somewhere in the Middle East.

"Get the Hawk on the line, immediately," were the standing orders to his longtime assistant.

Normally unflappable, James Hawker was visibly shaken as he took the call from Romanov. "Hi, Alexei. What can I do for you?"

"Have you seen the footage of Roos?" Romanov asked.

Hawker, "Yes. Simply terrible."

Romanov callously fired back with a rhetorical question, "Yes simply tragic. What is happening in the contract?"

"Bidless," was Hawker's comeback. "Last offer was a dime. No trades since the news broke, needless to say." The Hawk thought Romanov's pathetic hollow-heartedness and humbuggery had sunk to a new level, one so low it would most certainly cause a United States Congressional member's cheeks to turn red.

Romanov's insatiable greed surged. "Let me know if any buyers surface. I have more appetite on the short side."

Hawker, "Of course. Just to confirm you are short three hundred twenty million at the moment."

Romanov just laughed as he hung up the phone.

With women storming the pool, music playing and copious amounts of food and drink being consumed in all corners of Kazim's lair, the master of the house's cell phone rang.

With a nod and a glance back at Roos, Kazim said, "Trade has been executed."

"Congratulations," said Roos. "If you wouldn't mind, I would like to turn in for the night. I have a big day ahead of me tomorrow. I assume there is room in the inn?"

"Of course. Wheels up at 8 A.M. tomorrow."

"Perfect. Do you think someone could check the Bost Hotel for my luggage?" Roos asked.

"Already taken care of. Hassan, please escort our guest to his room. Good night, Christian Robinson Roos. Get some rest, I have a feeling you are going to need it."

Roos thought that of all the crazy days he had experienced in his life, without question, this one was the capper. Finding himself as the point person who would ultimately decide the outcome of the *Mete on the Street—Russian Versus Afghani Part Deux*, was surrealism of the highest order. The drug dealer and the mobster, battling for money on Wall Street in the crazy world of derivatives, who were both "deriving" value out of the transaction from another source—vengeance. Kazim's flavor was retaliation for his father's death, while Romanov's was simply Vengeance Capital.

Roos pondered who would get the last hurrah—in Lashkar Gah.

But not for long, as his mood seesawed from curiosity to a display of raw emotion as he read Kat's handwritten note, which she had left for him in his duffel bag.

Driving to the Bost Airport with his destination on the forefront of his mind, Roos thought of a quote from one of America's greatest writers and thinkers, Mark Twain. "India is the cradle of the human race, the birthplace of human speech, the mother of history, the grandmother of legend, and the great-grandmother of tradition. Our most valuable and most astrictive materials in the history of man are treasured up in India only!" Having never been to India before, Roos was most anxious to see the place.

Well beyond planes, Roos embarrassingly admitted to himself that he was curious and quite frankly hyped-up about his first spin in the General Dynamics new Gulfstream 650. Powered by twin Rolls Royce BR 725 engines, the flagship of the Gulfstream fleet tops out at a maximum operating mach of .925 with a range of seven thousand nautical miles. By connecting New York City to Dubai and London to Buenos Aires, the G650 has unrivaled range. Owners can select from twelve different interior configurations, with the maximum capacity being eighteen passengers. The wing is just five inches shy of one hundred feet. Billed as the fastest, largest, longest-range, most advanced business jet, the G650 is the unquestionable beast of the skies.

The total distance from Jumma—Amritsar—Varanasi—Bodhgaya—Katmandu—Lasha—Beijing was just shy of three thousand nautical miles. Deploying a G650 on this mission was akin to bringing a surface-to-air missile to a knife fight. But Kazim offered and Roos was certainly not going to decline such hospitality. Besides the man had laid down some serious coin on the outcome of the trip. What was a little more jet fuel at this point? In addition, it was a perfect way for Kazim to keep tabs on Roos' progress.

As the plane broke through fifteen thousand feet, Roos was pleased to see his iPhone light up with five bars. He needed desperately to make some phone calls to Kat, family members and Frank Harrison to let them know that he was as sound as the pound. First up was his dear mother, Bridget. The time on the East Coast of the United States was 3:30 P.M.

"Hello, Christian. How are you?"

"Sorry for not calling sooner, but I was in an area without cell service. I am fine, currently on a flight to India. I will explain the video the next time we visit."

Roos' mother, Bridget, just laughed and inquired, "What video?"

His next call was to Kat. Without ringing the call went straight to voicemail.

Next he placed a Viber call to Frank Harrison who yelled, "CR! Are you alright?"

Roos responded, "Couldn't be better, my friend. My AirJets plane had a mechanical over southern Afghanistan of all places. Same exact problem I had years ago on a flight from Washington Dulles to Toronto. Had to put down in a town called Lashkar Gah. Google it. I think it is the most dangerous place on the planet. After two nights and three days, I'm afraid that I must agree with the consensus."

Harrison asked, "Where are you now?"

"On a flight to Amritsar, India. But making a stop on the way in Jammu. Need to pop up to see the Vaishnodevi Temple, which is located thirty-five miles north of the airport. Then heading south to Amritsar, home to the Golden Temple. Tomorrow I am taking a dip in the Ganges River in Varanasi before visiting the Bodi Tree in Bodhgaya. The remaining schedule has me visiting, Kathmandu, Nepal; Lhasa, Tibet; Beijing, China; Pyongyang, North Korea and Tokyo, Japan before catching the overnight flight across the Pacific to New York."

"How in the hell did you get out of Lashkar Gah?" asked Harrison.

"I deployed the Reverse Stockholm Syndrome," responded Roos. "Are you familiar with that one? Without question the move of my life, if I may be so bold. It is a phenomenon where captors sympathize with their kidnapping victims. Let's just say that I played to my captor's net worth and stayed clear from an emotion that he was completely devoid of — religious extremism. How is the Caboose trading?"

"Not very well," said Harrison. "After the video hit, the contract went bidless. But later in the day rumors starting swirling about a massive trade taking place between Romanov over at Vengeance Capital, on the short side, and an Arab sheikh, on the long side, who was represented by a Swiss bank."

"Five hundred million face traded at five cents on the dollar. Can you believe Romanov? Or how about his clients at Vengeance? Do they have any idea what he is doing with their money?"

"Correct. How in the world did you know that?" asked Harrison. "As to your question, the Vengeance investors neither know nor care what the fund is investing in as long as Romanov keeps posting eye popping returns."

"The guy is an Afghani heroin dealer, not an Arab sheikh," Roos replied, "but he isn't hurting for cash. I am in his G650 at the moment. Amazing plane. Have you been on one yet?"

Harrison, spitting out his tequila, said, "Only you, CR, only you, my friend."

Roos got back to business. "I plan on calling the Hawk and getting long more of the Caboose. Need to scratch my value itch. My suggestion would be for you to do the same."

"But this has cost you three days. Will you be able to complete the journey within the allotted twenty-five days?"

"Out of my allotted twenty-five nights, I have ten nights left but only eight nights scheduled," Roos responded, "Two in India, one in Kathmandu and Lhasa, two in Beijing, one each in Pyongyang and Tokyo. I built in a five-day cushion, remember? I still have two left. In a pinch, I can do Beijing in one night and opt for a day trip to one of the other destinations."

"Okay. But, CR, be careful," was Harrison's warning to his friend. "You know the kind of man Romanov is, don't you? If the rumors are true, which I believe they are, he is now short eight hundred and twenty million of the Caboose contract. Romanov is going to go crazy when he hears the news of the staged video. And you know he will find out."

Roos answered confidently, "Yeah, yeah. Don't worry, Frank. I have this."

"Please," said Harrison, "allow me to make a suggestion, or phrased a better way, help me help you. I don't think you should call the Hawk to make a personal trade. Let me do it for you. If Romanov got wind of that, he may just split your head open with another bottle of Smirnoff. What is your appetite?"

"At five cents, I would do as much as possible up to five million cash, for a face value of one hundred million."

"Got it," Harrison said, "I will set up a new account at Springer and Waldron, with you and me as equal partners. I will go in for another five million as well. Not sure how much we will get, but whatever the amount we will split it fifty-fifty. I will front the cash and you can reimburse me on your return. CR, you have five million liquid, correct? Deal?"

Roos confirmed he had.

"I hear the G650 has a stateroom large enough to squeeze in a double bed. Are you and your girl members of the mile-high club yet?" asked Harrison.

"Negative! Get a load of this. While I was in captivity she bolted. And took the AirJets G3 with her!"

"For God's sake," said Harrison. "Can you believe that move? Women!"

Roos signed off with "Adiós, mio!"

"Hi, Strange. Mac here. Are you still in Amritsar?"

"Yes," was Strange's response. "I am still booked at the Golden Tulip Hotel. What have you heard from Roos?"

"Nothing directly. However, I just got off the phone with the Hawk who tells me that Roos' investment partner, Frank Harrison, is actively buying the Caboose contract on the long side. I can't think of any reason he would be doing this other than having direct knowledge that Roos has escaped from Afghanistan and back on course. Can you? Is there something we are missing here? Come on, Strange, get that big brain of yours cranking into high gear."

Strange asked incredulously, "Isn't Hawk our partner? He would never tell you the identity of the buyer if he wasn't, now would he, Mac? Of course he was signaling that Roos is back on the loose. Don't need to crank the Strange brain to figure that out."

Mac grumbled, "Agreed."

"He is booked here tonight at the Golden Tulip Hotel. As soon as I gather some intelligence, I will pass along immediately."

As soon as Mac and Strange received confirmation that Roos was back on the rails, they would be in a strong position to increase their exposure in the Caboose.

The G650 landed at Jammu Airport located in the northern section of India just fifteen miles from the Pakistani border. From here the pilots had arranged for a helicopter to take Roos up the mountainous route to the Vaishnodevi Temple. The Sanjhichatt Helipad provided an excellent staging ground for travelers to visit the Temple.

But before Roos could get started he had to wait while Central Industrial Security Force, (CISF) the organization in charge of all airport security within the country of India, boarded Kazim's G650. The military personal were accompanied by two specialized detection dogs trained in the art of smelling for gold. Smuggling gold into India from Southeast Asia and Arabia, specifically the Philippines and Dubai, had surged of late. The love affair which India and gold shared for thousands of years showed no signs of abating. If anything, the obsession was intensifying. Indians are the world's biggest "gold bugs," purchasing over two and one-half tons of gold per day. With little production capability within her borders, India was forced to import over eight-hundred tons of gold last year. As the Rupee continues to fall against worldwide currencies, the Indian economy faces challenges, exacerbated by their people's insatiable demand for gold.

Gold transcends beauty within the Indian civilization by playing a critical role in the Hindu religion. Quite simply gold is religion in India, gold is life in India. Ever since the Creator dropped some liquid gold out of which Brahim was born, Indians associate gold with Hinduism and think of the metal as sacred.

Roos was laughing as the dogs were alerting all over Kazim's gold-laden G650 interior. The plane was equipped with gold faucets, vanities, kitchen counters and even glasses made of gold. After an extended review, the CISF personnel, assuming that the plane's gold-plated interior would not be melted into bars and sold throughout the country, decided to deplane and let the passenger into the state.

Roos made a quick trip to the Vaishnodevi Temple, making the trek up eight miles to an elevation over five thousand feet. He stood in awe of the great view from the top but was expecting a more elaborate and ornate structure. He loved the visit nonetheless, clearly a most sacred site in the Hindu religion.

After the visit to the Temple, Roos then headed back to the Jammu Kashmir Airport and boarded the G650 for the short flight to Amritsar, a major northwestern city of one million.

As Roos entered the lobby of the Golden Tulip Hotel in Amritsar, he was greeted by his old friend from business school, Vipreet Ramroot. After graduation Ramroot returned to his native India, where he joined his father's jewelry company, Ramroot Gold. Through a combination of hard work and determination, and the assistance a strong Indian economy, Vipreet was able to grow Ramroot Gold, which at the time of his joining was a small successful family business operating out of Amritsar. The company sold gold and jewelry, which would be considered in the middle of the market to the lower end on both quality and price. Vipreet's knowledge of the capital markets, which he acquired in business school, proved valuable as it allowed the company to raise capital expanding Ramroot's manufacturing capacity substantially. But it was Vipreet's two-year internship post graduation at American jewelry powerhouse Tiffany that would help launch Ramroot into the major leagues of the Indian jewelry industry.

After exchanging pleasantries, the pair of old B school buddies started discussing business.

"How is it going at Ramroot?" Roos asked.

"Quite well," said Vipreet. "Sales are booming along with the Indian economy. And our move into the higher end of the jewelry market is rocking. We are becoming the Tiffany of India."

"What did you learn while working at Tiffany that was so significant?"

"The power of marketing," said Vipreet. "I mean look at those robin egg light blue boxes. The jewelry needs to be beautiful, of the highest quality and expensive but the infamous blue box says it all. It reminds me of that case study you and I worked on in Dr. Goose's marketing class."

"You mean the one where the struggling vodka company raised prices by thirty percent and sales doubled?" asked Roos.

"Exactly," said Vipreet.

"What color did you select for your packaging?"

"Saffron, one of the three colors in our National Flag. In Indian culture the color stands for courage, sacrifice and spirit of renunciation. I am sure you are aware of the significance that jewelry, specifically gold, plays in the Indian wedding ceremony."

"Actually not really. Please elaborate."

"Well to put the metal in perspective," said Vipreet, "India consumes approximately one-third of the world's production of gold. With virtually no in-country production capability, quickly you can see the large impact this has on the Indian economy. Of the one-third of the world's production, which we are forced to import, approximately fifty percent is given as presents to the ten million brides who get married each year here in the country."

"Wow, that is amazing. Almost three thousand United States dollars per bride."

"I worked with my father and his team to create an entirely new marketing and business strategy for Ramroot. Seeing the economy improving, I believed that a market existed for higher-end products, such as jewelry with a strong branding campaign behind them. It took some serious convincing over quite a long period of time, but my vision of the company prevailed. Ramroot rebranded itself as a high-end manufacturer of exclusive wedding jewelry, which only came in the saffron box."

"How has the strategy played out?" Roos asked.

"Brilliantly! Sales have increased tenfold over the past five years and profits are up over a thousand percent. We have opened thirty stores all over India and just recently hired Santos out of Argentina to handle our new social media advertising campaign for Ramroot Gold. You remember our old classmate Gabriel Santos?"

"Absolutely," said Roos. "As a matter of fact I was just visiting with him on his boat anchored off Ipanema Beach in Rio de Janeiro. Great guy. Tell me about the campaign."

Ramroot excitedly began telling Roos of the latest advertising work. "Picture the sun rising behind the Taj Mahal signifying the start of a new day. A handsome couple dressed in traditional Indian clothing is riding an elephant toward the entrance of the Taj. The beautiful creature's image is shown in the reflecting pool. The woman is Vainavi Chatterjee, winner of the Ms. India beauty contest several years ago, after which she would go on to finish up as the first runner-up in the Miss Universe Pageant. She now is a famous actress and model here in India."

Bursting with pride, Ramroot continued, "In the advertisement, Vainavi is wearing a product from Chennai Silks, a textile unit in south India, which has created a signature saree just for Ramroot. The piece is an exceptionally stunning saree, meticulously woven with twelve precious stones and metals to depict eleven of Raja Ravi Verma's popular paintings. Explicitly projected is 'Lady Musicians,' one of the painter's very famous works that displays women belonging to diverse cultural backgrounds. The best part of the saree is that the women in the paintings are intricately hand-woven and beautified with jewels of gold, diamond, platinum, silver, ruby, emerald, yellow sapphire, sapphire, cat's eye, topaz, pearl and corals. It is made from pure silk with textures from the most precious stones and metals. The theme is designed with the intention to pay tribute to the historical culture of the saree in South Asia. Already in the Limca Book of Records, this forty-lakh-worth saree will be the first silk saree that required the use of over seven thousand jacquard hooks and sixty-five thousand cards during the weaving process. The precise design was created using CAD Software. Moreover, a group of consummate workers took nearly five thousand hours, and a team of thirty skilled weavers, using a double warp, for seven months were involved. This is the first time gems and art have been put together to make a sari and interestingly this saree is up for sale. It is a creation, which is truly art in itself, that can be worn by a bride and is not meant for only creating a record."

Roos asked, "How much is the saree?"

Ramroot announced, "One hundred thousand United States dollars. We are just renting the outfit for the first shoot. But if the campaign works, we have an option to purchase it."

Roos laughed. "Christ! So let's hear the ad."

Ramroot was only too happy to oblige. "The man is simply dressed in an Armani dark blue suit with an open collar white dress shirt. He commands the elephant to stop, bend down and pick up a package with his trunk. He opens the saffron-colored box, removes the ring and proposes to his girl seated behind him on the animal. She smiles and kisses him deeply with a nodding head. The tag line pops up: *Marriage takes courage, requires sacrifice and a spirit of renuncification, all of which are challenging, but made a little less so by a diamond in a Saffron Box, only from Ramroot Gold.* He then places the ring on her finger, after which he drapes gold chains over her neck."

Roos clapped. "Bravo. Bravo Vipreet."

"Thanks, my friend. The early reviews have been nothing short of astounding. Hop into my car, I will take you by the Golden Temple and also show you one our manufacturing centers. Afterwards we can grab some dinner."

The Golden Temple, located just ten minutes from the hotel, is the most sacred shrine of the Sikhs. Built on a small lake thousands of years ago, now filled with holy water, the Temple has been home to the Buddha. After the Buddha, another famous religious meditator, Guru Nanek, continued to frequent the site over the sixteenth and fifteenth centuries.

"Well it is the right color for sure. Gold!" remarked Roos.

The pair jumped back into Vipreet's custom-saffron-painted Aston Martin Vanquish and headed for the Ramroot factory.

The car was heading west toward the Pakistani border, in the general direction to the FBO where the CISF bordered the plane looking for gold. The Aston Martin pulled off the main road and traveled a mile or so down to the Ravi River, which serves as an official border between northwest Pakistan and India. Roos filled in Vipreet on the plane inspection.

"Did they find any gold?" Vipreet asked.

"Only affixed to faucets. But I can imagine smuggling is a huge problem along the Pakistan-Indian border here in the north."

"Forget the north, gold smuggling is exploding all over India," said Vipreet. "Through boats, trains, cars, planes, parachutes, on persons. You name it and it is being done. Just last week gold valued at over one million U.S. dollars was found in the bathroom of a commercial airplane. The government is raising the import tax in an attempt to slow demand but the situation is worsening by the day."

"What is Ramroot's policy with illegal labor which must pour over the Ravi River daily looking for work?"

"Most laborers who have approached us are not qualified to produce luxury jewelry especially in high-security settings. But occasionally we find the right people and absolutely hire them. India is a country going through unprecedented transformation, some that is good and some not so good. This is a moment for minimal analysis and maximum action."

Walking through the manufacturing facilities showed thousands of technical skill workers operating under extremely close quarters producing high-end gold and jewelry, which will undoubtedly be hanging from beautiful brides in the near future. Conditions in the plant were clean and safe but not desirous.

Vipreet continued, "The situation is getting crazy. Just last week, Holy Man Swami Shoban Sarkar told government officials that he had a dream where he was approached by the nineteenth-century ruler Rao

Ram Bux Singh, who told him about one thousand tons of gold worth forty billion buried at Daundia Khera in Uttar Pradesh. The dig is on!"

"Do you use smuggled gold here at Ramroot Gold?" Roos asked.

Vipreet, after a long pause, said yes. He justified the usage as a way to stay competitive with pricing. "Lower cost of goods sold allows for higher profit margins, which generate greater cash flow for reinvestment into new property plant and equipment, enabling the company to increase production, expand its store base and ultimately hire more employees at better wages. At the end of the day, it is better for India."

The conversation quickly turned to food, drink, women and Roos' schedule for tomorrow. Roos was learning quickly that his old friend knew a lot about the subjects.

"I plan on taking a dip in the Ganges River at Varanasi and visiting the Bodhi Tree before catching a flight to Kathmandu," said Roos.

"Should not be a problem considering you have access to Kazim's G650, Roos. More commercial flights have been added of late, but travel around India is still challenging. I would have to strongly recommend against your swimming in the Ganges River, especially at Varanasi. Without a doubt it is the most sacred site for worshipers to swim in the holy waters. But these are worshipers who have been doing this for hundreds of generations and people whose bodies have painstakingly built up a strong resistance to the extreme pollution in the Ganges River, one slow death at a time. Toxic chemicals and human waste flow freely through the magical waters. On any given day four hundred cremations and nine thousand animal carcasses float through the waters. Roos, you can't go in that water, period. Your bet was to visit, which you will. The river covers over four hundred square miles and passes through over one hundred and fifty towns and villages and cities, which combined have a population in excess of thirty million. The overall rate of water-borne disease incidence, including acute gastrointestinal disease, cholera, dysentery, hepatitis A and typhoid exceeds two-thirds."

"Understand," said Roos. "How about we go out after dinner tonight and have some fun? I am sure you know the places to go, my friend."

Before going out, Roos sent a text via WhatsApp to Frank, hoping it would go through: "Greetings from Amritsar at the close of Day 16. On the way to Varasani in the morning. Recovered from the unexpected and frightening Afghanistan detour. CR"

"Hi, Mac. Strange here. Confirming that Roos has checked into the hotel here in Amritsar."

"Thanks for the update, partner. Let's increase our position in the Caboose. Please jump on this opportunity with as much of our capital as you please. Safe travels and stay out of trouble and in touch."

The scene at Varasani the next morning was intoxicating and nauseating—a menagerie with both animals and people appearing in all shapes and sizes. A unique painting that upon first look conveyed unimaginable impoverishment, but upon a closer examination revealed a lovely richness—a magisterial juxtaposition. Individuals barely clothed who appeared so frail, so helpless enjoyed a look of complete contentment as they waded into the dirty polluted waters of the Ganges River to pay respect to their beloved deity, Buddha. By the thousands, shirtless pilgrims with arms flailing were praying knee deep in the dark muddied waters of the holy Ganges River. Dipping their heads, their babies, their entire bodies, the masses were liquefied with spirituality. Against a backdrop of brightly colored buildings atop a series of cement steps, which numbered in the hundreds, Indians were reveling in one of Hinduism's most sacred of all venues. Boats of all shapes and sizes were slowly bobbing up and down along the confused and convoluted Ganges shoreline. Strange smells were wafting through the still air like smoke clouds through marmalade skies. Odd-looking birds were cruising the waters for a midday snack, an occasional fish popped up on a makeshift fishing line cast by a shirtless and shoeless shoreline angler and the enticing smell of quintessential Indian street food of Chaat doused in lemon, pomegranate, kala namak, tamarind and various chutneys permeated the air.

Catching Roos' attention among the mass of humanity was a regal-looking boat gently cruising down the river, captained by a dark-skinned shirtless man with a salt-and-pepper beard, which flowed like a horse's tail down to his bellybutton. His hair was wrapped in a red and yellow scarf. With his right hand in command of the tiller, the captain steered the boat like an Olympic downhiller through swimmers, boats, floating objects such as boxes, dead animals, tree limbs and bottles. Sitting under a white cloth canopy towards the center of the wooden V hull boat were four individuals: three beautiful Indian women surrounded an English-looking gentleman. The distance from Roos' vantage point, halfway up the stairs that led to the main river landing, was too far for an identification. But instinctively Roos knew the man, who clearly stood out in the crowd like a whale in a goldfish bowl, was a player. The women were laughing as they sipped on wine, nibbled on grapes and chatted with their dashing host. Roos thought to himself, the Ganges River was unquestionably a place that had a little something for everyone.

"Hey, Mac, Strange here. Roos made it down to Varasani."

"Are you sure?"

"Absolutely," said Strange. "I am on a boat in the Ganges as we speak. I can see him gawking at me from the shoreline."

Ever since the figurative fig fell on Buddha's head sending him into an enlightened state of mind, the ostiole of the world's most famous ficus tree has been watching over Buddhism for over two thousand years. They may say that the fig doesn't fall far from the tree, but the one that coco bopped Siddhartha Gautama traveled far and wide. Ultimately, shedding its leaf, the fig would end up spreading the word of Buddhism to over one billion people around the globe.

Roos approached a man under the famous tree who looked like Bob Marley standing on his head after a weeklong rasta bender.

Tongue in cheek, Roos inquired of the man, "Is this the original Bodhi Tree?"

The disheveled yet strangely distinguished-looking elderly gentleman, fighting back laughter, categorically answered Roos, "No. The original tree dates back to the third century B.C. Legend has it that King Puspyamitra chopped it down in the second century B.C. during his persecution of Buddhism. King Sassanka took an axe to the tree during the seventh century A.D. This one, which you are witnessing, was planted by an English archaeologist in 1881. It is anyone's guess as to how many trees have lived in this holiest of soil over the millennium."

Clearly an extremely religious man, he continued, "But you see, sir, the tree is really just a symbol of spiritual teachings of the 'awakened one,' Siddhartha Gautama. The ultimate metaphor for true happiness, if you will."

"Thank you very much for the enlightenment." And with that, Christian Roos made his way to the Hotel Bodhgaya Regency in Gaya. In the morning he would head to the Gaya Airport for his short flight to Kathmandu, Nepal, where he desperately hoped to be reunited with Kat.

Pulling out his iPhone, Roos texted Harrison on WhatsApp: "Day 17 update, Frank. Down here in Gaya. On to Kathmandu, the footsteps of the Himalayas, in the morning, where purportedly Kat is waiting for me. Any bets on that happening? CR"

# 16

## Himalayan Rendezvous

*"What we obtain too cheap, we esteem too lightly; it is dearness only that gives every thing its value."*

—THOMAS PAINE

V exed and bursting with vengeance, Alexei Romanov stepped onto the platform, which lowered into his private office located on the floor beneath Vengeance Capital's elliptical trading floor, a theater scrupulously modeled by the founder after the famed Coliseum in Rome. The hedge fund leased the top three floors of the eighty-story building located on Park Avenue in midtown New York City. Occupying the entire eighteen-thousand-square feet of the top floor, the trading room enjoyed sweeping three-hundred-sixty-degree views of the Manhattan skyline. The floor to ceiling, twenty-foot windows were arch shaped in a room which was a perfect square measured by four sides of one hundred and thirty-four feet each. In the space in between each window, every eleven feet, stood a bronze or marble statue. A total of forty-four figures, mostly Greek gods, philosophers, Caesars, military mavens and of course gladiators, were visible from the every vantage point on the trading floor. Romanov's obsession with gladiators and the Coliseum began at an early age and only increased with the advancing years. Of particular interest to him was the elaborate mechanical system, which controlled numerous lifts capable of transporting, gladiators, animals, trees, circus apparatus and a whole host of other extensive props, from an area below the floor of the Coliseum into full view of the spectators. In eighty A.D., with the elite of the Roman Empire in attendance, within minutes the equivalent of a Broadway production could be choreographed on the floor of the mighty Coliseum. A widely held misconception about the ancient structure, which experts like Romanov were quick to dispel, was the notion that the Coliseum was all about violence. Plenty of gory deaths took place on the blood-stained dirt floor, but the venue was about so much more than gratuitous violence.

Romanov designed the hedge fund's headquarters in a similar fashion. Anyone with a position of analyst, client service, marketing representative, portfolio manager or administrative worked in offices located on either of the first two floors. Each floor had platforms resembling an open elevator, which could in a moments notice transport anyone up to the trading room on the top floor. Vengeance Capital employees quickly learned that this exciting joyride was rarely ordered to bestow commendations upon them. Rather the "ride to hell" most always meant one of two unwanted things about to be forthcoming, either condemnation or decimation. Most of the backslapping and congratulatory salutations were reserved for the traders, who already worked on the floor. The savvy and ruthless modern-day gladiators, fashioned and molded by and after their founder, ruled the firm with clenched iron fists. Everyone else in the firm was subordinated to the top floor, which was stocked with individuals who wielded superlative intelligence, intestinal fortitude and cunning, as they charged into financial battle.

Six tiered rows of seats circle the trading floor providing a total capacity of four hundred. Clients, interns, non-trading personal of the firm and potential clients all were invited to sit in the observation seating around the trading desk. From this vantage point spectators could take in the view resembling a cauldron of boiling testosterone. The floor itself contained only one piece of furniture, a one-hundred-and-twenty-foot long and fifteen-foot-wide table made of travertine limestone, the material that was used in the original construction of the Coliseum's floor, pillars and exterior walls. Mined in the hot springs of Tivoli, just twenty miles from Rome, the stone is distinguishable by holes caused by carbon dioxide evasion and the natural common colors of cappuccino, chocolate and cream. The firm's trading table has sixty seats, which are spread out five feet apart, each complete with a Bloomberg flat-screen terminal and an Apple twenty-seven-inch iMac.

Alexei Romanov rolled up his sleeves and sat at the head of the table in his five-foot space, just like all of the other traders. Vengeance Capital deploys a global investment strategy, which requires a twenty-four hour around-the-clock trading operation. The lights never go out on the top floor. The room is magnificent; however, one aspect has created bit of controversy with the female employees. In the Roman Coliseum the first section was reserved for members of the Roman Senate. Not interested in missing any action by leaving their seats to urinate, a drain system was developed, affording the dignitaries the ease of essentially peeing from their seats. The waste traveled around the ring before it poured through openings to underground latrines. Romanov, violating multiple city ordinances, went ahead with Vengeance's modern concept of the traders public urinal system. As one of the largest taxpayers in the city, Vengeance's transgressions went "unnoticed" by the authorities. Two feet deep and three feet wide, the trench, which circled the inside of the first row of amphitheater seating, resembled a small stream. Chemicals kept the water clean and at the same time allowed for changing of the colors. If the water is blue, it must be Monday. The fear masquerading as a joke among the traders was that if the water ever looked yellow, triumphant Vengeance Capital had been conquered.

Word of Roos' escape from Lashkar Gah had reached the fierce head of Vengeance Capital and the revelation hit Romanov with the force of a jackhammer. Romanov was a man unaccustomed to being deceived out of large sums of money. But this was exactly what he believed was happening to him and his clients. He wasn't sure how deep the scheme went, but he was sure of one fact: Roos was in on the ruse and he would pay dearly for his actions.

As the platform continued descending to his private office, Romanov raised his arms in the air, clenched his fists and growled, "Christian Roos!" And with that Romanov lowered his right arm parallel to the platform. He pointed his thumb outwards and assumed the downward *Pollice verso*, Latin for turned thumb position. Now eye level with the trading floor, Romanov rotated in a 360-degree direction sneering at the sight of his entire trading team standing in *Pollice verso* unison.

Determined to even the score, Romanov's mind was bubbling with machinations as he scrolled through his iPhone contacts until he reached Hard Yang. Hitting send, his Viber call traveled seven thousand miles through a fiber optic network before it reached Beijing. As the phone was ringing Romanov could be heard muttering one of his favorite quotes by Proximo in the movie *Gladiator*, "I did not pay good money for you for your company. I paid it so I could profit from your death."

Romanov greeted his former college classmate, "Hello, Hard. Romanov here. I have a job for you."

Hard Yang was born in Beijing in 1975. Her parents were loyal Communist Party members. Hard's father worked as a doctor, practicing the ancient art of Traditional Chinese Medicine (TCM). Based in Taoism, TCM utilizes herbal remedies and acupuncture to treat a variety of illnesses. Her mother was a civil engineer, working most of her career on the construction of dams and bridges, which were springing up all over China like dandelions. Hard, after excelling in academic studies through high school, enrolled at Tsinghua University, located prominently in her hometown of Beijing. She joined the university's international famous Department of Pharmacology and Pharmaceutical Sciences, where she became an expert in toxicology, defined by the university in their literature as the study of the adverse effects of chemicals on living organisms. It is the study of symptoms, mechanisms, treatments and detection of poisoning, especially the poisoning of people. Yang's field of expertise was in thallium, an odorless and tasteless metal of bluish-white color found in trace amounts in the earth's crust. Thallium is widely used in insecticides and rat poisons, and in the manufacture of components for the semiconductor industry. Highly lethal and difficult to detect, consumption of one gram is all that is required to induce thallium poisoning, a condition which begins with flu like symptoms, progresses to neurological weakness and ultimate cardiac arrest. Larger doses of thallium result in death almost instantly.

Standing at five feet ten, Hard Yang was unusually tall for a Chinese woman. At one hundred and thirty pounds, sporting long toned legs, a tight stomach from years of yoga and magnificent B cup size natural breasts, Yang cut a stunning pose. Despite being buried in a Chinese drug company's research division, Yang's Rooney Mara bangs and knife-cut face would have redefined the international marketing "it" girl look, if the Mad Men of Madison Avenue ever saw her. Her long black hair, which nearly reached the top of her beautifully shaped rear, was of a quality befitting the finest wig makers in the world. Seductive and alluring, Hard could make a Beijing local delay his drag on an unfiltered cigarette, as he watched her walk past—in the smog-infested Chinese capital, the ultimate compliment. Her facial features, befitting a Ford Agency model, were simply exquisite. Yang's uniquely Asian shaped eyes looked like two heaven sent teardrops, which could fall sideways onto her high cheekbones at any moment. Her pale pink lips contrasted perfectly with her dark black hair and blended marvelously with her light skin tone. Hard Yang was a woman whose extreme beauty was only surpassed by her mysteriousness, foreshadowed by her impenetrable kaleidoscope hazel eyes, born from millenniums. Exuding sex and intelligence, Hard set the libido of men ablaze, who lustfully desired to ravish her.

The femme fatale straight out of central casting responded to hearing her old friend, "Alexei, so great to hear from you, it has been too long. How are you my dear friend? I trust the Big Apple is treating you with the proper respect that you have earned. As to your request, of course I would love to help you out, but, as you know, I have retired from the business. My days of hanging out with the wrong crowd are over. I have a new life now. You may have read that I am a pharmaceutical research scientist working at the Xicheng Medical Company here in Beijing."

Romanov, a man unaccustomed to hearing the word no, implored, "It has been too long indeed. Over three years, I believe. Everything is good here in America. Congratulations on the position at Xicheng. I remember when the company went public in the 1990's, with the launch of Xichpro, their novel cholesterol drug. Listen Hard, I understand where you are coming from, but this is a most important assignment, one which will pay an enormous multiple of the standard rate."

"What is involved?" she asked.

Romanov explained delicately, "A man named Christian Roos will be arriving in Beijing tomorrow. You need to make sure he never leaves the city. Importantly, it must look like an accident or natural causes. An open murder case is simply not a possibility."

Yang exclaimed, "Tomorrow! Alexei do you think a little more notice would be appropriate? If I were to accept the job, it would have to be somewhere besides Beijing. My past is exactly that, here in my home city. I cannot risk another poison death investigation here. I am sure you read that the authorities have reopened the 1995 murder case at Tsinghua University. If someone at the People's Armed Police ever connects the dots, I will be spending the rest of my life in a hard labor prison camp, a place where I definitely do not want to live."

Unfazed Romanov fired back, "The target will be in Pyongyang, North Korea, in two days. I do not think there could be a more discrete venue, a country without a free press. Roos is an American, someone who would not cause any consternation if he turned up dead. Can you get into the country? The fee is two million U.S. dollars."

Hard Yang quipped, "Of course I can get into North Korea. My father's brother lives in Pyongyang, where he works for the government, aka the Democratic People's Republic of Korea. What a name? Two million dollars? How would you get that kind of cash to me on such short notice? Please give me the background on the target."

"You will have half tomorrow, hand delivered, with the balance delivered after the job is completed. Roos is a forty-two-year-old Caucasian and businessman, with no military background and no evidence of any advanced fighting skills. He is traveling with a female companion, who is not to be harmed unless the situation is unavoidable. Roos will be staying at the Koryo Hotel in downtown Pyongyang."

Yang asked, "How much time do I have to decide?"

"One hour. Call me on this number," was the response from the founder of Vengeance Capital.

Yang took less than ten minutes to return Romanov's phone call, with the response, "I will take the job. No more communication until I contact you upon completion."

Before taking off from Gaya Airport for Kathmandu, Roos called Kat and for the umpteenth time received her voice mail. Ever since he left Lashkar Gah, Roos had been trying to reach her with the news of his extrication from Afghanistan. At this point he could only hope she was waiting for him at the Dwarika's Hotel "forever" as she wrote in her letter. He would find out soon enough.

The iconic summit of Mount Everest, climaxing over twenty-nine thousand feet above sea level, pierces the jet stream without apology. Looming just one hundred and ninety miles to the northeast of Varanasio, Mount Everest came into view from the G650 shortly after takeoff. Roos walked into the cockpit as the plane was still climbing to get a better look at St. George's Hill, a sight he had never seen before. The world's tallest mountain appeared as an optical illusion. With thick clouds covering the first third of the mountain range, Everest looked like a dolphin breaching the water's surface exposing the powerful dorsal fin. Mimicking a rookie, Roos pulled down the jump seat and strapped himself in, where he remained for the entire forty-minute flight. With each advancement towards Kathmandu, Mount Everest increased in size through the panoramic seven-foot wide cockpit window, which was mimicking the zoom lens on a high tech camera. The landing at Tribhuvan International Airport was epic, a field sitting at four thousand feet above sea level and twenty-five thousand feet below the peak of Everest.

The Dwarika's Hotel was only ten minutes from the airport. Covering just twenty square miles, nothing was too far away in the relatively small city of Kathmandu. Roos could feel his heart starting to palpitate as the cab drew closer to the hotel.

Built in the 1970's by Dwarika Das Shrestha, the hotel is a wonderful tribute to the heritage of Nepal and the indigenous population of Newars. Civilization dates to the time of Christ in the Nepalese Valley, but it was not until the twelfth century under the reign of the first Malla King, an empire that lasted over six hundred years, that the place took off. Using original wood windows with intricate carvings, terracotta roofing and wood held together by mud, the Dwarika's Hotel is a throwback to the vertically oriented structures that dominated the architecture of

Kathmandu for centuries. Emphasizing courtyards, known as chowks, and exterior artwork including abundant statues and animal imagery, the hotel feels like a museum of Newarian history. The Newars are a deeply religious people who worship both Hindu and Buddhist deities on a daily basis. A culture rich in ceremony, the Newars host countless festivals throughout the year in order to pay proper respect and homage to their spiritual leaders in the sky.

The receptionist greeted Roos, who quickly inquired about Katherine Mandu's status as a hotel guest. She politely informed him that it was the hotel's policy not to divulge information about guests to unrelated parties who have not been registered by the occupant.

Roos implored, "I can assure you that Ms. Mandu would not have an issue with you informing me of her status here at the Dwarika's Hotel. We have been traveling together for two weeks."

The receptionist asked for a moment to alert the front desk manager of Roos' request. After a few minutes, the manager appeared and informed Roos that in fact Katherine Mandu was a guest of the hotel, but that she was off heli-skiing today and not expected back until later tonight. Roos complained that he had been calling the hotel for several days asking to be connected to Ms. Mandu's room, and repeatedly being told that no guest under that name had registered.

After three years of aggressive lobbying and negotiations with Nepal's Ministry of Tourism, the country finally acquiesced and agreed to allow heli-skiing in the Himalayans. A French company, Heli-Ski Nepal, was granted the original contract. Owned by Francois Archambault, a member of the French Ski Team in the 1990's, the company started service in 2012. Operating out of Pokhara, one hundred miles west of Kathmandu, skiers are taken to camps at the foot of the Annapurnas Mountains, the second highest section of the Himalayans. From there they catch rides in the company's B2 and B3 Ecureuil helicopters up to ridges anywhere from eighteen thousand to twenty-six thousand feet. Hopping out, skiers cut virgin tracks down five- to ten-thousand-foot lines. On a good day, the company pitches expert skiers on the ability to ride over forty thousand feet of fresh tracks.

Roos thanked the manager, dropped his gear and headed for the Pashupatinath Temple, located a mere stone's throw from the hotel. Brahma may be the creator and Vishnu the preserver, but it is Lord Shiva, the destroyer, who is the most powerful and fascinating deity of the Hindu trinity. While known by many names, Pashupatinath is Shiva's moniker of choice among his followers. *Pashu* means "living beings" and *pati* means "master." Pashupatinath, the most famous of all Shiva Temples in the Hindu world, literally is translated as the "Master of all living beings." Shiva dissolves in order to create since death is the medium for rebirth into a Hindu new life. Dating back to four hundred A.D., the pagoda-styled temple sits on the banks of the Panchakanya River, named for one of the five virgins. Millions of Hindus make the trek every year to pay homage to Lord Shiva. It is one of the most important pilgrimages for his devotees. It was important to Roos as well given the fact that it was most certainly on his list of required visits to the world's most important sacred sites.

From the Fusion bar in the Dwarika's Hotel, Roos could see Kat entering the hotel. Sporting North Face gear, a Prussian blue Cheakamus triclimate ski jacket with black Apex mountain pants and khaki Verbera boots, the local strode through the lobby with confidence. With her beautiful long blonde hair disheveled, her face wind-burned rosy red and her lips chapped from exposure to the blistering sun at thousands of feet of elevation, Kat looked to the hotel guests and employees milling around the lobby like a cross between a model and an Olympic downhill skier. But to Christian, she simply appeared as a goddess, a vision, which he was hoping to witness ever since the couple became separated in Lashkar Gah, Afghanistan.

Kat's face lit even brighter as she saw Christian making a beeline for her. The couple embraced each other, maintaining a bear hug for several minutes without saying a word. Roos felt the warmth of her heart. But he could also feel an icy chill, the kind of glacial condition resulting from a long day of heli-skiing, which freezes one's bone marrow in an illusory sense. The chill deepened as Roos exclaimed, "I have been calling your cell phone for three days now!"

"Christian, I was so worried about you. Thank God you are safe. What happened?"

Roos first asked what happened to her phone.

"The AirJets pilots were instructed to takeoff no later than 5 P.M. I waited as long as possible for you. I just didn't know what to do. It wasn't until 4 P.M. that I made the executive decision to depart with the plane. I was in such a disoriented, panicked state of mind that I left my cell phone in the hotel room."

"Where did they drop you?" Roos asked.

Kat answered, "Here in Kathmandu."

"Did it occur to you to buy a phone or call me?"

"Christian, I don't know your cell number. As a matter of fact, I don't know anyone's phone number. Don't we all just scroll through contacts and hit send? I saw the video on Al Jazeera, which was beyond sickening and frankly I just assumed the worst. How did you survive that situation?"

Roos incredulously griped, "What about the cloud?"

"In the Himalayan Mountains?" Kat implored.

"Why did you register here at the hotel under an assumed name?"

"I just felt more comfortable going stealth," she said. "In case the press tried to contact me, or possibly disgruntled and or ecstatic investors. Blame it on my DNA. Both of my parents fled to Kathmandu to deal with their demons. Funny how I never thought I could come home again, even after you first called. I just never believed it would actually happen. Trauma plays strange tricks on the human mind."

"For Christ's sake, Kat!" Roos changed the subject, "How was the skiing?"

Kat welcomed the shift and tone of the conversation. "Honestly, it was the best day of skiing in my life. When I was a kid, my parents would take me to these bunny hills in nearby Kathmandu, which were neither very interesting nor challenging. The government made a smart decision to opening heli-skiing here in the Himalayas. I hear next year that parts of the Everest range will be opening as well. From the helicopter and the runs on the Annapurnas Mountains, I could see the Dhorpatan Hunting Reserve. Christian, the scene brought back so many memories."

At this point, Roos ordered some drinks, sat Kat down and explained what transpired in Lashkar Gah with Basir Kazim.

"Christian, that is really a crazy story. Congratulations. Let's hit the sack, I am beyond exhausted."

Vacillating between anger, exhaustion and blistering erotic thoughts, Roos acquiesced by choosing the latter. In the elevator he sent a Day 18 update to Frank. "Circumstances dictated taking a page from Oscar Wilde's book tonight. He may have been a gay man married to a woman, but he sure was on mark when he said that a woman is to be loved and not understood."

Next morning in the hotel restaurant, the couple dined on traditional Nepalese cuisine of Dal Bhat, steamed rice and cooked lentil soup, momos, a delectable fried dumpling filled with chicken, roti, fried unleavened bread, fruit salad and chai tea. In the city synonymous with adventure, a hearty breakfast is par for the course. Kat asked Christian if there was time to stop by and visit one of her father's close friends.

"Sure. Who is it?" he asked.

She began describing Ranulph Fiennes, one of her father's best friends, in excruciating detail: "In 1998 a Carnegie Mellon student named Michael Kobold founded the Kobold Company, an organization committed to horology, the science of timekeeping, as part of his entrepreneurship class. His vision was to create the world's most advanced expedition watches. After a year or so of struggling, unable to manufacturer watches and effectively market them, Kobold had the common sense and foresight to get some help. He hired Ranulph Fiennes to become the company's first brand ambassador in chief, an amazing man who is described by *The Guinness Book of World Records* as the 'world's greatest living explorer.' He was born in the United Kingdom in 1944, just months after his father was killed in the war. Fiennes was raised in South Africa. He would travel back to the U.K. for college, where he studied at the prestigious Eton. Joining the British military after graduation, Fiennes would go on to be a tank commander in the Royal Grey Scots and then join the Special Air Service (SAS), the sister organization to the Special Boat Service (SBS). This is where he met my father.

As you will recall, Christian, my dad was in the SBS. Both units are the equivalent of the Navy SEALs in the United States military."

"Yes, interesting. I think I met him at a dinner in London years ago," Roos replied. "He is an accomplished climber, if it is the same person I am thinking of. Is that what makes Fiennes the 'world's greatest living explorer'?"

Kat proudly explained, "Kind of, but that is not what has distinguished him among his fellow outdoor extremists. Fiennes has a long list of being the first to accomplish extraordinary feats. He was the first man to reach both poles, cross the Arctic Ocean and Antarctic Ocean, and circumnavigate the world along its polar axis, an expedition that took three years to travel the fifty-two-thousand miles. More people have been on the moon than have accomplished these feats. He was the first person to Hovercraft the Nile River. He led an expedition that discovered Uban, the lost city of Yemen. In what I think was his greatest achievement, in 2003 just four months after a massive heart attack, Ranulph achieved the 777 by completing seven marathons on the seven continents in seven consecutive days!"

"If Mac bet me twenty-five million that I could not make it around the world in twenty-five days, he surely should stay a long way from Mr. Fiennes."

She continued, "He has climbed Everest from the Tibetan and Nepalese side, K2 and the north face of the Eiger Mountain. In 2009 he became the oldest Briton to summit Everest. My dad climbed with him on numerous occasions. As a kid, I can remember Mr. Fiennes joining us on hunting trips. He is a fantastic human being."

"Are you familiar with the watches?" asked Roos.

Kat rolled up her the right sleeve of her pink Coldgear Infrared Under Armour fleece storm hoodie and showed Christian her watch, a Kobold Phantom Black Ops chronograph. With a black canvas strap, a black steel domed face covered with anti-reflective sapphire crystal and green luminous hands and hour markers, the timepiece is sleek and full of intrigue. "In anticipation of Michael Kobold's trip to summit Everest in 2009 in order to raise money for the Navy SEAL Warrior Fund, he was invited to train with the SEALs at their Coronado, California, base. He took the opportunity to discuss with the SEALs what the characteristics would be for the ideal rugged military watch. This was the result."

"I have been meaning to ask you about that watch. Great looking. What does one of those set a person back?"

"Three thousand four hundred fifty dollars, but Ranulph gave this to me as a Christmas present in 2011," said Kat. "Apparently the SEALs love the watch, but are not issued one per budgetary constraints. Out of respect for their selfless and noble sacrifice to their country, Kobold gives generous discounts to the members of the elite fighting unit who choose to own one individually."

"So does Fiennes live here in Kathmandu?"

"Yes, part of the year when he is working with Kobold, but his primary residence is in England. But get a load of this. Kobold would make two climbs of the mighty Everest. The first summit was in 2009 when he was joined by his wife, Anita, and Fiennes. The second expedition in 2010 was only with Anita. During both climbs, the couple was accompanied by two local Kathmandu climbing experts, Namgel Sherpa and Thundu Sherpa, with seven and nine successful summits respectfully. Not once, not twice but three times, Namgel and Thundu saved Kobold's and his wife's lives during the second climb, which turned out to be the couple's second successful summit of the world's tallest mountain. The first occurred in the death zone when Michael's oxygen supply became interrupted. The second near-death experience occurred when an ascending climber inadvertently unhooked Michael's carabiner at the edge of a ten-thousand-foot drop. The last on the descent, Anita collapsed at the South Col camp. She was oxygen deprived causing her to throw up the lining of her lung, which became lodged in her throat. On the mountain she was declared dead for over four and a half minutes. Namgel and Thundu injected steroids and epinephrine into her arm bringing her back to life. Apparently, Michael is a man possessing extreme integrity, one who knows how to return an important favor. In 2011, he brought the pair of high altitude mountain guides in the Himalayan Range to Kobold's Pittsburgh, Pennsylvania, headquarters in the

U.S., where Dale Poindexter, Kobold's head watchmaker trained them for ten months in the art of watchmaking."

"Brilliant story, please go on!" said Roos. "What is the death zone?"

Kat choked up. "It is the corpse-strewn one mile stretch, which separates climbers from the Sol Col and the Summit. The air is so thin it can take up to twelve hours to complete the ascent, a speed of less than a tenth of a mile per hour. Sadly, my dad perished in the death zone."

She composed herself and continued, "With their calm hands, steady nerves and low heart rate, formed from countless Nepalese generations who have lived over the millennia at high altitudes, Namgel and Thundu quickly mastered the requisite skills to become horologists, manufacturing high performance expedition and adventure timepieces. But initially, living for the first time ever outside of Nepal, at sea level to boot, the men were discombobulated in Pennsylvania. At lower altitudes the human body is exposed to higher levels of pressure. This acute acclimatization, which does indeed happen in reverse even though you always hear about the opposite, low to high altitude adjustment, has the effect of bombarding the body's blood stream with oxygen. In their first several weeks in the United States, the pair acted like kids who consumed too much sugared candy for dessert. The dynamic was akin to sufferers of the common condition, Attention Deficit Hyperactivity Disorder (ADHD) who need to be put on either Adderal or Riddlin in order to help a person calm down and focus."

Roos by this time had googled the company. "Check this out."

Ross handed Kat his iPhone, which was displaying a Kobold advertisement featuring the late actor James Gondolfini flipping the bird to the tag line, *Even James Gondolfini thinks Kobold is No. 1.*

A fan of the timepieces, Gondolfini expressed disappointment that they were too small for his outsized wrist. Unsolicited, the famous actor who played Mafia crime boss Tony Soprano in the award winning television series *The Sopranos*, scribbled out a design and ordered the watch. While initially thinking the design was too ugly to produce, in just a few years the toughest diver watch made by Kobold has outsold every other timepiece offered by the company. With an edgy advertising campaign, the silver stainless steel manly looking watch, with a performance to over three thousand feet underwater, has achieved cult status among collectors all over the world. Gondolfini and Michael would go on to develop a strong friendship, which sadly ended with Gondolfini's untimely death.

On the way to the airport, the couple anxiously stopped into the recently opened Kobold store in Kathmandu, which is located in a renovated horse stable of the one of the residences of Nepal's Royal Family. The two-story structure has a showroom on the first floor. The watchmaking happens upstairs. After a long overdue embrace, Fiennes asked Kat, "How is your mother, Aoibheann?"

"She is doing okay. Of course she still misses dad terribly. Mentions him every time I see or talk to her. How are you doing?"

"I miss your father as well," said Fiennes. "He was a man of tremendous character and integrity, not to mention intelligence, and he wasn't a bad climber or hunter either. He suffered a horrible pinch of hard cheese on Everest that night when the weather conditions changed so suddenly." Fiennes continued answering Kat's question, "I am okay. As you probably read, I was forced to drop out of my planned expedition to cross Antarctica in the winter. I have been training for over five years to be the first to make the world's coldest journey across two thousand miles of ice in temperatures which hit seventy degrees below zero."

"Wow, yes, I saw the news," she said.

Fiennes said, "I told the *Guardian* newspaper, I am not good at crying over spilt milk or split fingers, but it is extremely frustrating."

Most people with a deformity develop a sixth sense, which allows them to observe individuals struggling with trying not to notice. A highly intelligent man, Ranulph Fiennes was surely no exception to this rule. Observing Roos staring at his stubby fingers, the world's greatest explorer said, "In 2000, as I was traveling across the Arctic my bloody sled with all of my provisions fell through the ice. The development left with me with no choice but to remove my gloves and reach in to rescue my gear. The water was hovering around just below freezing."

Roos interrupted, "How did you decide who would put their hands in the ice?"

"Well, seeing that I was by myself," said Fiennes, "the decision was quite an easy one. My fingers were ramrod stiff and ivory white. They might as well have been wood. I had seen enough frostbite in others to realize I was in serious trouble. I had to turn back. They evacuated me the next day. The doctor told me that the top third of all of my fingers and half of my thumb would have to be amputated at a cost more than nine thousand dollars. Crikey, I was not going to pay that. I did ask the doctor if I would be able to play the piano after the surgery. His response was absolutely yes, to which I replied, that is great because I was unable to play the piano before."

Almost afraid to ask, Roos inquired, "What did you do?"

"I purchased a set of fretsaw blades at the village shop, put the little finger in my Black & Decker folding table's vice, and gently sawed through the dead skin and bone just above the live skin line. The moment I felt pain or spotted blood, I moved further into the dead zone. I also turned the finger around several times and cut into it from different sides. This worked well, and the little finger's knuckle finally dropped off after some two hours of work."

"That is awful, I am so sorry to hear," offered Roos.

"Thanks for the sympathies, but it really is not a bother. The finger shavings have not affected my life in any material way. But missing one thumb puts me in a pickle every now and then. What do they say? Our opposable thumbs separate us from the rest of the food chain?"

Roos changed the subject. "Mr. Fiennes, it such a pleasure to see you again. Over breakfast, Kat filled me in on your background. Quite an extraordinary life you have lived so far. Congratulations on your charity fundraising work on behalf of the British Heart Association, Marie Curie Cancer Care and Seeing is Believing, along with many others I am sure. Bravo."

"Why thank you. Did you say see me again?" he asked.

"Yes, I wouldn't expect you to remember me," said Roos, "but who could forget you. We met at a dinner party hosted by James Smith from Putney Partners at Mosimann's Restaurant in Westminster, London. I believe it was June of 2005. You had just returned from climbing Mount

Everest from the Tibetan side in March. After dinner you gave a lovely presentation, which included an awesome slideshow of your ascent. I believe you made it within three hundred meters of the summit, raising two million pound sterling and a new MRI scanner for the British Heart Association in the process."

Fiennes, obviously impressed by Roos' recollection, responded, "Excellent evening, I remember it well. As you probably heard me say during the presentation, James Smith is one of my closest friends. He just retired from Putney and is devoting his full energy to charity work."

Roos, "You finished the presentation, which covered the entire ascent, with photographs of your expedition near the summit. After which the lights in the room were brought back up. You asked if anyone had any questions. Do you recall the first one?"

"I do indeed," Fiennes replied. "An English bloke asked me how I got down! To which I responded, that is an excellent question. More people die on the descent than do on the ascent. Fatigue and complacency is a dangerous combination, especially when added to the precarious footing on the downslope, where one's natural body weight works against, unlike for on the ascent."

"The gentleman who asked the question was Carl Strange," Roos said. "He worked with James Smith in the London office of Springer and Waldron in the 1980's. James of course went on to found the hedge fund Putney Partners, while Strange worked his way up to the position of Global Chief Investment Strategist at Springer and Waldron. If you knew Strange the way I do, the brilliant question would not surprise you in the slightest. He is an unusually intelligent man. As coincidence would have it, both Strange and I were staying at the Caledonian Club located just on the other side of Belgrave Square from Mosimman's. The top Scottish Club in London boasts one of the best Scotch bars in all of England. Strange and I spent the better part of the night draining Lagavulin twenty-five-year-aged single malt, neat of course. The bartender kept chastising us with his admonishment, one should never drink Scotch without water and never ever drink water without Scotch."

"Interesting. What is he doing now?" asked Fiennes.

"Retired from Springer and Waldron a few years ago. He is a partner with Charles MacCormick, the retired CEO of the investment bank, in an investment company. Mac was at the dinner as well."

Fiennes replied, "Well normally this is the part of the conversation where most people would say it is a small world. But I have spent too much of my life circumnavigating the damn globe to say something stupid like that. The earth is a big place. What brings you to Kathmandu?"

Roos was embarrassed, but nonetheless told Ranulph the story of the bet with Mac. Fiennes just chuckled.

"Does anyone need a watch?" asked someone moving toward them.

Fiennes responded, "Hi, Michael. I thought your flight arrived later today? Katherine and Christian, please meet my business partner and the founder of Kobold Watch Company, Michael Kobold."

"Flight was early, imagine that. Thanks for the introduction, Ran (Michael referred to Sir Ranulph Fiennes as simply Ran). It is a pleasure to finally meet you, Katherine. Ran has told me so many nice things about your father. Please allow me to pass along my condolences as well."

Quietly Katherine said, "Thank you."

Roos, a man who never wore a watch quipped, "Well I think the answer to that question about needing a chronometer is definitely yes."

"Splendid!" said Kobald. "When Ran and I climbed Mount Everest in 2009, we brought back some limestone from the summit, which we used to construct the dial in twenty-five of our signature Himalayan Everest Edition watches. At a price of sixteen thousand five hundred dollars, the unique timepieces sold out within hours during our opening night party here in Kathmandu, but I do have a special one left. Please allow me to show you."

At this point, Michael motioned to Kat and Christian to follow him. Walking past the counter, flush with watches, the threesome entered a door leading to a staircase that took them to the second floor. An open area with several custom-made wooden benches and a few business desks were all that existed in the workroom. Namgel Sherpa, age twenty-eight, and Thundu Sherpa, age thirty-nine, equity owners in

Kobold's new Nepalese subsidiary, were diligently pursuing their newly learned craft. The ex-high altitude mountain guides were expected to earn twenty times the average Nepalese annual salary of five hundred dollars in their infinitely safer new career.

Roos and Kat met the two deferential and gracious gentlemen, who slowly rose from their desks, without making full eye contact. Kobold reached into one of the desk drawers and pulled out the last of the summit of Everest limestone timepieces. The face may have been buffed, but the watch's intoxicating luster camouflaged millions of years of nature's fury, a juxtaposition almost incomprehensible.

With trepidation Roos ventured a controversial question, "How have the locals reacted to the new store here in Kathmandu?"

Michael grinned. "Interesting question. The grand opening party was held right here on May 26, 2012. In attendance were Nepal's Royal Family, political leaders, and the U.K. and U.S. both sent their highest State Department officials involved with Nepal. Of course the press and local business leaders were in the audience as well. Ran gave a brilliant speech on Nepal's history, adventure exploring and naturally Kobold Watch Company."

He continued, "We were hailed in the local newspapers as visionaries who would stimulate the Nepalese economy, create jobs, increase tax revenues and boost tourism."

"Excellent," Roos said.

Michael, "But, two days later someone wrote a very negative article in the paper calling Ran and me the Everest Rock Mafia. The writer went on to claim that our actions would encourage many more foreigners to come steal our natural resources which are so important to our history."

"What happened?" asked Kat.

Michael answered, "Well Ran had left Nepal for the U.K. the day after his speech. I on the other hand was still in the country attempting to calm down the masses. After several weeks, an arrest warrant was issued and I was to be sent to jail, a place nobody ever wants to be but certainly not desirable in Kathmandu where cell conditions are prehistoric."

"What did you do?" Kat asked.

"My friends in the Royal Family arranged for a military pick up in the dead of night. I caught a private flight to Hong Kong."

"But obviously you are standing in Kathmandu today," observed Roos.

"Thankfully," said Michael, "the Royal Family worked out an arrangement with the officials. Let's just say that you should buy this last Everest watch because neither we nor anyone else will be removing rocks from the summit of Everest and building anymore watches with them."

Roos plunked down his black card with enthusiasm to acquire the unique timepiece with the black-and-gray rock face, stainless steel casing and brown leather strap and asked, "Kat, do you like this one?"

Before she could answer yes, Michael interrupted and said, "I wanted to name our two-year-old daughter Kathmandu. I love the name. But some of the grandparents had other 'better' ideas."

In the taxi on the way to the airport Roos followed up with Kat about his late night drinking session with Carl Strange. But not before he commented on Ranulph Fiennes and Michael Kobold. "Fiennes has to be one of the most beguiling and unique persons I have ever had the pleasure to meet. And believe me, I have met many of the world's power players. He was just so real, so honest, so extraordinairy, I was just blown away by his persona. And I found Michael to be a genuinely good person, honest and extremely dedicated to his craft.

She agreed. "I would throw in sexy as well for both men."

Roos switching gears, said, "Baby, you will not believe the story Strange told me in the Caledonian Club's bar that night. Apparently back when Strange was working at Springer and Waldron, he would travel quite extensively to meet with the firm's most important clients. In the early 1980's he met with one such client, Padruig Wotherspoon III, a Scotsman from Aberdeen. Padruig's grandfather founded the oil company Wotherspoon Industries in the 1920's. The company plodded along up until the early 1960's, when the United Kingdom Continental Shelf Act came into force. The rush was on as companies scrambled to construct rigs in the oil rich North Sea off the coast of Aberdeen. Wotherspoon's business took off. Strange's first encounter with the one of the

United Kingdom's richest men was at the Caledonian Club, where they dined along with two associates. After a serious in-depth conversation about the current investment landscape, talk turned to Wotherspoon's true love, the Scottish Highlands, which are so abundant with his passions of golf, whisky and fly fishing."

Roos knew that Kat's interest was piqued by the story as she asked, "How old was he?"

Roos continued, "Padruig would have been in his forties when Strange met him."

"Go on," she said.

"I could see Strange's entire demeanor morphing as he continued telling me about Wotherspoon III between snorts of wee drams of Lagavulin Twenty-Five, which were going down like water despite the fact that we both were drinking it neat. After dinner Padruig and Strange repaired to the bar. At this point in my conversation with him, Strange pivoted and pointed to the table in the corner of the room where he and Wotherspoon III enjoyed after-dinner drinks. So get this. Strange charmed the man, as he is capable of doing to just about anyone. The two men became fast friends that evening. After several hours of comparing notes about women, swapping sex stories and naturally discussing Scotch and hunting in exhaustive detail, Padruig invited Strange up to his castle on the Isle-of-Skye in the northwestern Highlands of Scotland."

"Did he go?" asked Kat.

"Yes, the very next day. Strange had client meetings in the morning, which he was able to attend on account of Padruig's business schedule. Wheels up on his G3 were scheduled for 2 P.M."

Kat asked, "G3?"

"Kat, it was 1982, The G4 did not start production until 1983 and the G5 and G6 were still sleeping like babies in the mother of all aerospace wombs."

The Scottish Highlands were one of Roos' favorite destinations in Europe. The beauty of the mountains are breathtaking, the Scotch intoxicating and the golf world class. One of Roos' favorite courses, Royal Dornoch Golf Club, sitting majestically on the Firth of Dornoch, a short distance from the town of Inverness, the gateway to the Highlands, is ranked number thirteen in the world. The landscape is spellbinding. The roar of William Wallace can be heard echoing through the lush green fields populated with gorse and alpine wild flowers. The remote Inner and Outer Hebrides comprise a diverse and widespread archipelago off the northwest coast of Scotland. Isle-of-Skye is in the Inner Hebrides and the largest island in the entire archipelago. A popular joke on the weather-torn islands goes like this: "If the wind ever stopped blowing, the entire population would fall over."

Roos continued with the story being told to him by Carl Strange in the Caledonian bar in 1995. "Padruig and Strange fly into Aberdeen, where they hop into one of the Wotherspoon Industries helicopters for the short trip to the Isle-of-Skye located directly across northern Scotland from east to west. Helicopters buzz around the European oil capital city like bumble bees. The birds ferry workers out to the hundreds of oilrigs in the North Sea around the clock three hundred and sixty-five days a year. Padruig's castle was named *Uisge-Beatha*, Scottish Gaelic for 'Water of Life,' an obvious reference to the owner's beloved liquid, whisky. The estate was located on the southwestern side of Isle-of-Skye, two miles east of the world famous Loch Coruisk, home to an enormous seal colony. The castle was situated in the heart of the spectacular Cuillin Mountains, a massively rugged and jagged confusion of granite and grabbo, which straddled the Isle-of-Skye like a noose. Soaring to heights of three thousand two hundred feet, the range sports peaks with names like Am Bastier (The Executioner), Sgurr A Ghreadaich (The Peak of Torment) and An Garbh-Choir (The Wild Cauldron). The helicopter crossed the Bay of Raasay and landed on a field adjacent to *Usige-Beatha* where it was met by one of the employees in a campus green Range Rover."

"What was the castle like?" asked Kat.

"Strange said it was the most impressive one he had ever seen. After an elaborate dinner consisting of haggis, a dish of sheep's lungs, liver and heart, all wrapped in the animal's stomach and wild Scottish salmon, Padruig and Strange played a game of flap-dragon in front of a roaring fire."

Kat inquired, "Flap-dragon?"

"I had to ask as well. It was the tradition at the *Usige-Beatha*. Participants attempted to snatch plums out of a snifter full of burning brandy, Remy Martin, X.O. cognac in this particular case." Roos continued, "The men discussed the next day's activities. The day would begin with a boat tour of the Loch Coruisk for some seal, otter, puffin and golden eagle watching. The tour would continue by water southward out of the Loch through the Scavaig River for some salmon fly-fishing. In the afternoon the cruise would continue south out of the Scavaig River into the Loch na Cuilce, around the small island of Soay, before emptying into the North Atlantic Ocean on a due west heading for some migrating whale watching. "

As the taxi pulled up to the airport, Kat asked, "Where is this story going?"

Roos grabbed the luggage, paid the driver and continued telling her the tale he heard from Strange. "The weather in Scotland is notorious for sudden and violent changes in atmospheric patterns. Locals, all one hundred thousand of them, are weathermen charlatans who at the drop of a hat will opine on the state of air and atmospheric conditions over the Hebrides. Without question it is the number one topic of conversation everywhere on the islands."

He continued. "The weather is brutal in the Hebrides. The wind blows at fifteen knots on average all year with gusts kicking up over fifty knots. Exposed to the strong westerly winds, rainfall hits the northwest region the hardest where annual amounts average over seventy-five inches and over one hundred and fifty in the wettest regions. The winter months average snow or sleet every other day."

After meeting one of Kazim's pilots in the lobby of the Kathmandu Airport's FBO, Christian and Kat were escorted onto to the tarmac where the G650's Rolls Royce engines were purring like a Himalayan snow leopard. After boarding the aircraft, Roos continued, "The boat had four people on board, Padruig Wotherspoon III, Padruig's son Padruig IV, Carl Strange and the captain, a man Padruig called Mal. Besides captaining the boat, Mal was Wotherspoon's right hand man at the castle, where he served as the head of security for Uisge-Beatha, fly-fishing and hunting guide, oversaw a staff of twenty, and was essentially a jack of all trades."

"How old was the son?"

"Strange indicated the boy was around twelve. Wotherspoon's boat was a 55 MKII, the ultimate Hinckley power yacht. She was the queen of the fleet, according to the luxury mid-size yacht builder. The vessel was aptly named the *Uisge-Beatha Da*, the Water of Life Two. As planned, in the afternoon after a successful day of wildlife watching and salmon fly-fishing, the *Uisge-Beatha Da* completed the trip around the southwest coast of the tiny Soay Island, providing the boat an obstructed view westward. The winds began picking up, the sky darkened immediately, rain began to fall heavily and the surf kicked up ten-foot swells. The ominous looking weather worsened within minutes, as visibility from the boat's bridge evaporated. Wotherspoon III discussed the situation with Mal and the decision was logically made to abort the whale watching expedition and head back to home to Loch Coruisk pronto. Instructing everyone to don life jackets, Mal maneuvered the boat up the western side of Soay Island, named for the Norse word meaning sheep island, and headed east through a narrow and dangerous channel separating Soay from the Isle-of-Skye's southern coast. Racing the storm proved futile. The *Uisge-Beatha Da* was rocked and rolled by the winds, heavy rain and swells now exceeding twenty-five feet. With steep rocky cliffs and no anchorage, Soay Island offered limited access and a foreboding coastline."

The G650 had lifted off from the runway en route for the trip to Gonggar Airport, positioned forty miles southwest of Lhasa, Tibet. Located just over the mighty Himalayan Mountain range, in the equally as powerful G650, the flight would take less than an hour. But the time elapsed was closer to three hours on account of the different time zones between the two countries despite their close proximity. Breaking with tradition followed by most of the world, the countries of Afghanistan, Nepal and Tibet divided time zones in increments other than sixty minutes. Lhasa was two hours and fifteen minutes ahead of its neighbor on the southern side of Mount Everest. Roos proudly showed Kat his newly acquired Kobold watch, one of the few in the world that has un-usual increments displayed on their dials, which includes two time zones.

On a commercial flight, passengers would be scrambling to secure port side window seats in order to maximize the view of Mount Ever-est and the other magnificent peaks that grace the Himalayan Moun-tains. On Basir Kazim's spacious G650, Kat and Christian had their pick from any of the eight twenty-eight-by-twenty-inch windows, which lined each side of the forty-six-foot cabin tucked into the one-hundred-foot-length, high-performance aircraft.

She encouraged Christian to continue with the Strange story.

"At this point I could see Strange becoming quite emotional as he described what happened next in the channel. Over a third of boats, which sink during usage, do so from water breaching the gunwales. Half-way through the four-thousand-foot-wide channel, a rogue wave bar-reled down upon the fifty-five-foot *Uisge-Beatha Da* already in retreat. Mal, who had mentioned earlier to Strange that he was an ex-member of the Special Boat Service, an elite branch of the special forces of the United Kingdom's military, was clearly an expert captain. But the situ-ation was way out of his capable hands. Fearing a stern swampage, Mal frantically spun the bow around in an attempt to crest the forty-foot wave head on. Unable to maneuver the boat in time, the wave struck the *Uisge-Beatha Da* smack on the starboard side. The boat heaved at first as she rose up the side of the wave, like a paddling surfer preparing to ride the gnarly groundswell's green house. About three quarters of the way up the honker, the boat fell victim to the laws of physics. Simply unable to crest the wave, the *Uisge-Beatha Da* tilted at a ninety degree angle before capsizing into the cold raging North Atlantic Ocean."

Almost breathless, she asked, "What happened next?"

Roos described Strange, who took a two-finger snort of his Laga-vulin, stared off into space and said, "I came to in a field, on my back, shivering and drenched. As my eyes opened, I saw a half a dozen or so of the famous Soay Island sheep staring down at me. Feeling like George Clooney in the movie *The Men Who Stared at Goats*, I began spitting out Neptune cocktails of the cold salty Atlantic Ocean water.

Padruig IV was laying next to me, his father was nowhere to be seen. Nor was Mal, for that matter. But he would appear shortly and tell us the horrible news that Padruig Wotherspoon III was missing and that the *Uisge-Beatha Da* had sunk in the channel."

Roos continued, "Mal described how he rescued Padruig and Strange and dragged them through the water to the safety of the shore. Apparently there was an inlet, which was cut through the rocky cliffs. A fortunate occurrence for sure."

Kat asked, "Did they ever find Wotherspoon's body?"

"Strange said no. Of course forever grateful, Strange asked for Mal's contact information. His full name was Malcolm Manders."

A curious look enveloped Roos' face. Acting as if the lights had just been turned on, he asked Kat, "Oh my God, it has just occurred to me, wasn't that your father's name before he changed it to Mandu?"

Staring in disbelief, she said, "Yes, it was."

Roos asked her, "Where did he go after the Falkland Islands military campaign?"

"I assumed he went to Kathmandu, Nepal, after a brief time spent back in England. I will call mother from Tibet and ask if she knows anything about the story in Scotland."

Roos began furiously pounding away on his iPad, which was connected to Kazim's Wi-Fi in the sky. After sending Harrison an update of his progress on Day 19 that he was leaving Kathmandu on his way to Lhasa, Roos scanned his favorite news sites, *Financial Times*, Bloomberg, ESPN and BBC News, along with social sites of Twitter and Facebook. Clearly the "cyber powers that be" had picked up on his travels and were bombarding his URL by pushing pop-up advertisements on everything from camel tours through the Sahara desert to Sherpa-guided mountaineering expeditions to the summit of Everest. The latter prompted him to comment to Kat, "Baby, want to hear a great line? I recently attended a Media Summit in Abu Dhabi on behalf of our venture capital firm, Fiber Capital. A speaker who was head of agency strategy at Buzzfeed had this to say about online advertising, 'You are more likely to summit Mount Everest than click on a banner ad.' I think he is correct."

She laughed then glanced outward toward the snow-capped Himalayans and waved to her father as the plane passed by the summit of Mount Everest. She wondered out loud if the man who saved Carl Strange and Padruig Wotherspoon IV from certain death in the treacherous waters off the coast of the Isle-of-Skye was in fact her father. She would find out soon enough.

After landing in Lhasa, Roos and Kat headed straight for the Polata Palace. Observing the empty vestment on the throne symbolizing His Holiness the Fourteenth Dalai Lama of Tibet, Tenzin Gyatso, in the Temple sent off an eerie vibe. Having been exiled to Dharamshala, India, in 1959 during the Tibetan uprising, the Dalai Lama had not slept in the coffin-like rectangle bed for over fifty years. The people of Lhasa, meaning "Place of Gods" in Tibetan, have not seen their spiritual leader roaming the streets here in almost six decades.

Citing previous Mongol control of the high mountain plateau, the Chinese military, to the extreme displeasure of Tibetans, have controlled Tibet since the early 1950's. The past five years have seen a re-escalation of tensions between Tibet and China. In response to mass protests staged during the Beijing 2008 Olympics that visibly embarrassed the government, China has come down hard on the land of the monks by imposing severe legal and religious restrictions.

Built in the year six hundred forty-one, the Polata Palace is one of the more visually impressive structures on planet earth. Sitting atop Red Hill, the three hundred and sixty thousand square foot structure, sporting thirteen stories and a height of four hundred feet, rises up one thousand feet from the valley floor. The fortress-type compound contains a thousand rooms, two thousand shrines and over two hundred thousand Buddhist statues.

Kat asked Roos, "If the Gelugpa School was founded in the late fifteenth century by Tsongkhapa, as this statue states, how could the current Dalai Lama only be the fourteenth throughout the entire history of the School of Tibetan Buddhism?"

"Must be the lack of booze combined with meditation leading to the ultimate state of happiness. The math works out to an average of just under forty years per Dalai Lama. My Church has had sixty-one Popes over the same five hundred and twenty-five years. With the stresses of Rome, the average Pope didn't last ten years in office."

Back in town the couple checked into the St. Regis Hotel located in the famed Barkhor area of Lhasa. Avoiding the tourist-laden restaurants like the Crazy Yak Saloon where diners arriving in tour buses are entertained by traditional Tibetan dancers, Roos and Kat headed for the Sichuan Dragon. After gorging on the likes of fungus with hot and sour sauce, ma po bean curd and Sichuan shredded beef, the couple took in some local flavor at Makye Amye, a nightclub named after the famed Tibetan beauty who captured Tsangyang Gyatso's heart over three hundred years ago. An avid writer and poet, the lascivious Sixth Dalai Lama would go on to write a poem about his love interest. Born in 1682, the young Dalai Lama would tragically die in Mongolia en route to Beijing, China, in the year 1706. The playboy, who led a life of debauchery outside of Hindu teachings, never blew out the candles on his twenty-fifth birthday cake.

Roos read the last stanza from one of Tsangyang's love poems, which was printed on the back of the drink menu, titled *See or Not*. "Come into my arms. Or let me live in your heart. In silence, in love. In stillness, in joy."

Always the hopeless romantic, Roos threw in his two cents. "Unconditional love is a topic that has been around for quite some time, possibly since the beginning of time. The notion of unrequited love is something I have mused about endlessly." Roos asked her, "Baby, do you think a person's true love of another is contingent upon receiving love in return?"

She responded, "You are asking the wrong person. Romantic love is a concept that has evaded me."

Roos, clearly surprised, asked, "Really?"

Kat without hesitation replied, "Yes. Growing up without a father figure shaped my views on relationships in a very negative way. Every time I feel myself getting close to someone, I instinctively back away. Maybe I am afraid of catching a bad case of daddy issues. Surely you agree with my innate fear of this disease, Christian."

Roos, a man who had seen so many twists and turns of love's kaleidoscope and witnessed other's audacious and foolhardy relationships with eye-popping age differentials, begrudgingly agreed. He thought to himself that old sayings become old through the aging process of truth.

As the couple exited the Makye Amye Bar they turned left onto Dongzisu Road. Kat, slightly perplexed, asked Christian, "Isn't the hotel in the other direction?"

Roos responded, "Yes, but it is such a lovely night, I thought we could take a stroll up through the old section of town. It is only ten minutes or so from here. I am very curious to see the status of the Jokhang Temple. As you will recall, the venue is one of the thirty sites on our itinerary."

"Is it being built?" she asked.

Roos came back with, "No. Razed, by the Chinese government, along with many other historic structures. All part of the Beijing crackdown."

After hitting Balang Street, Roos headed in a northern direction that cut through some of the historic homes and buildings of Lhasa's old town.

Within minutes they were in an open square staring at the ruins of the once majestic Jokhang Temple, the scene of much significant Tibetan history. Flush with people, the place was brimming with excitement. Street food vendors were busy selling spicy cold noodles and beef momas. Traditional music played by monks provided the inspiration for locals performing the cham dance. Wearing colorful masks and lively costumes, the dancers lit the street afire with rhythmic movements of meditation symbolizing an offering to the gods.

Roos opined, "Well the Chinese may have leveled the place, but the memories, the feelings of spirituality, here are so thick one could cut them with a single-bladed steel-forged Tibetan sword."

Kat heard the screams first, causing her to wheel hard right, where she saw a bright light moving in her direction. Maybe fifty feet away, the scene was both foreign and indescribable, but nonetheless, one that imparted universal danger.

Roos observed the crowd approaching. Now from less than twenty feet, he could see a monk dressed in full Tibetan clothing, ablaze in a spiritual act of self-immolation—the ultimate act of defiance toward the Chinese government. The man, unable to run farther, ceased screaming as he collapsed to the ground. Locals, who had seen this before—hundreds of times—covered the monk in clothing, blankets and everything else of a fabric composition at their disposal. The music stopped, the dancers stood motionless as the people expressed horror. But the look on the oppressed locals eerily expressed a sense of respect, understanding and enduring pride.

From a distance of less than ten feet, the rancid smell of burning skin and hair wafting through the air engulfed Kat. Staring directly into the vapid monk's eyes, the sight of a smoldering body draped in cloth on the street, caused her knees to buckle as she fainted. Kat's collapse was in the direction of Roos, who was able to break her fall. As Roos caught Kathmandu like an Olympic pairs figure-skating partner, he thought to himself, the ex–Naval Officer who knows her way around a weapon—or two—had a tilt button after all. A notion that he had held true from the moment he met her years ago, one changed in the last three weeks never to be thought of again. But it resurfaced, in the flash of a suicide by burning—a truly horrific sight.

Sensing some business, a local teenage boy peddled his rickshaw up to Roos who by this time had laid Kat on the ground. By the time the human-propelled taxi arrived, Roos had resuscitated her and was pouring cold water down her still trembling throat.

"St. Regis Hotel" were the only words Roos said as he assisted Kat into the rickshaw's bench seat underneath a green and red canopy. Driving off, she stared at the bouncing gold tassels hanging from all sides of the three-wheeled bicycle's roof.

Walking through the lobby, Roos pulled out his iPhone and sent a message to Frank, "Checking in again on Day 19 from Lhasa, Tibet. Heading to Beijing in the morning, but need to make a stop in Hong

Kong along the way. Each day brings increasingly bizarre revelations. Can only imagine what craziness awaits us in Asia. And I say us, because in fact Kat was waiting for me in Kathmandu, as promised."

Harrison's tense text came back within less than a minute, "Hong Kong!"

Scrambling through the Roos itinerary the Wall Street trader saw no mention of the British territory which had been turned over to the Chinese when the ninety-nine-year ground lease expired at the turn of the century.

Roos attempted to calm his partner down. "My partner at Fiber Capital, Anand Narayan, called me today. He has been working with a Hong Kong–based billionaire tech maven who is extremely close to committing substantial capital to our second tech telecom venture capital fund. He wants me to meet with him tomorrow afternoon at the Hong Kong Peninsula Hotel and close the investment."

Frank, not understanding the logistics, questioned the timing, "How can you make it from Lhasa to Hong Kong and end up in Beijing in one day? And will this affect the schedule in Beijing already planned?"

"Frank, I have it under control. Day 20 is only a travel day. No visits to sacred sites are planned. I will put Kat on a commercial flight from Lhasa to Beijing. Remember I still have the use of our Afghani friend Basir Kazim's G650, which I have dubbed the flying Four Seasons. I will fly from Lhasa to Hong Kong in less than four hours, have my meeting and will then proceed to make the three-hour trek up the eastern coast of China to Beijing, arriving later in the evening. Easy peazy lemon squeezy."

Frank persisted. "But what about the time change traveling across China?"

Roos explained that the Chinese had decided long ago not to fool with the complexities of time zones. When the billion plus Chinese look at their watches, the time is always the same regardless of location within China's borders.

As the couple made its way through the lobby, Roos inquired if the Iridium Spa was still open, specifically the pool. Hearing an affirmative, Roos insisted that Kat take a dip in the 32-degree Celsius, two-thousand five-hundred-square foot roof top pool. Besides views of the property's lakes and the Himalayan Place, if one looked closely on a clear night the magisterial Mount Everest was also visible to bathers. The entire pool bottom and sides are made of pure gold, which when lit up by underwater lights, illuminates the water into a wet gold. Swimmers feel a sensation of emersion in a white wine from Bordeaux such as the Haut Brion Blanc, which looks like gold but tastes like heaven. Perennially ranked in the top fifteen most beautiful pools in the all of the world, the Iridium Pool at the St. Regis Lhasa is pure majesty, which leaves guests feeling contemplative, relaxed and free. Roos and Kat quickly made their way to the pool.

Snapping Roos from his Fudarakusen state of mind was the personalized ringtone on his iPhone. The sound of Japanese star Nakajima Miyuki singing incoming.

Roos hopped out of the wet gold, toweled off and began to read the message from Sakura, "Hi, Christian. Dinner at Jiro sounds lovely. I return from Hong Kong in two days, so assuming no change in plans, I should be able to make the dinner in Tokyo. Sakura"

"Nice to hear from you. Looking forward to dinner in Tokyo. Coincidentally my schedule has me in Hong Kong tomorrow. If you are free, please meet me at the restaurant Felix in the Peninsula Hotel in Kowloon at 6 P.M. Flying to Beijing after dinner."

"I am staying at the Peninsula. Hope the world hasn't changed you. See you at six."

Even though her words were sent in a text, Roos could hear them, their sweetness, beauty and dignity. Like Cherry Blossom Trees flowering timelessly through an ancient proud land, one deeply steeped in respect and honor Sakura lived up to her namesake. Despite Roos' general obtuseness when it came to females, he sensed something truly special about his new Japanese friend, Sakura. The girl named after the gentile yet powerful national treasure of Japan—the Cherry Blossom Tree—had piqued his instincts like never before.

# 17

## Peking Duck

*"Every Communist must grasp the truth,*
*political power grows out of the barrel of a gun."*
—MAO TSE-TUNG

Kat's flight from Lhasa, Tibet, to Beijing crossed almost the entire length of the China. In a Tibetan Air Boeing 777, the trip covering almost fifteen hundred nautical miles would take a little over four hours. Most of the flight would be over the rugged mountainous terrain of central China. The flight path called for crossing the Yangtze River about a third of the way to Beijing. Starting as melting ice from the glaciers in northwestern China's Qinghai—Tibet Plateau, water runs four thousand miles across the country before emptying into the South China Sea. The Yangtze is the world's third-longest river and the longest in Asia. Unfortunately, the plane crossed the mighty river too far to the west to afford a view of the Three Gorges Dam built on the Yangtze in the Hubei Province. Opened in 2003 at a cost of twenty-three billion dollars, the hydroelectric project, with generation capability of twenty-two thousand, five hundred megawatts, equal to fifteen nuclear reactors, is the world's most powerful dam. It is a brilliant engineering feat displaying man harnessing nature's raw power on an unimaginable scale.

The flight landed at Beijing Capital International Airport at 1 P.M. local time. On final approach, Kat looked up from her iPad and asked her seatmate, "What is happening on the ground in Beijing? Looks like a massive fire is engulfing the city."

The Chinese man, who spoke perfect English, responded, "Not fire, just typical Beijing smog. I have been reading that the levels are extremely high of late causing school and factory closures. It really is quite remarkable."

"What is responsible for such extreme conditions?" she asked.

"China's economy is growing rapidly," replied the man. "The country is attempting to urbanize hundreds of millions of rural citizens. Managing these large tasks in a short period of time has led to rushed urban planning, inefficient energy systems, poor transportation and horrendous factory conditions. Layer on top extraordinary cigarette smoking rates by the Chinese, twenty million people crammed into a relatively small city area, cars without proper pollution controls and the insatiable demand for coal-powered electricity and the result is what you see out of the window at the moment. One way to measure pollution is through Fine Particulate Matter (PM2.5). The Chinese government recently announced emergency measures if the PM2.5 exceeds three hundred micrograms per cubic metric for three continuous days. No other city in the world comes close to these levels. The PM2.5 has routinely exceeded seven hundred, a level which surpasses the machines calculation ability."

"Will they be running the Great Wall Marathon the tomorrow with this smog?" she asked.

"The air quality improves dramatically outside of Beijing. The race is several hours away by car and also at a favorable increased altitude."

With visibility in the taxi down to a matter of feet, Kat was in no mood for sightseeing, especially by herself in a strange city. She instructed the driver to take her to the Sofitel Wanda where she hunkered down for the night with a few pay per view movies and Chinese takeout in Beijing.

Roos slept in one of two staterooms equipped with queen size beds on Kazim's G650 for most of the four hour flight from Lhasa to Hong Kong. The little time that he was awake was judiciously used to study the information that Anand had provided him on his meeting with Lee Wong the son of Cheng Ka Wong. At the age of eighty-five, with an estimated fortune of forty billion dollars, the elder Wong is considered the richest man in Hong Kong and one of the wealthiest in the world. Known as the Hong Kong White Tiger, without question he is the most powerful person in city. His rags-to-riches story is one of legend. Growing up poor in the west Jiangxi town of Pingxiang was difficult. Centuries of war had ravaged the region and essentially left the inhabitants for dead. Pingxiang's location caused the city to become the choke point for the warring ancient Chu and Wu Empires. Thousands of years of years later the region became a shining example of Chinese manufacturing. This renaissance, led by the young Wong, is where the White Tiger began to build his fortune. Starting at the early age of twelve in a small clothing factory in Pingxipang, he rose to become the largest manufacturer of goods in all of China. He intelligently diversified his holdings into banking, real estate, casinos and telecommunications.

Billionaires in Hong Kong are not a dime a dozen, but they are not too hard to find. A tidy net worth of one billion dollars gets you the number fifty spot on *Forbes* Magazines Hong Kong's richest list.

The White Tiger's son, Lee Wong, at age forty-seven was running his father's telecommunications operations and was on the *Forbes* list himself, squarely in the middle of the pack. Through a series of acquisitions, Lee Wong had built Safe Harbor Telecom into the dominant provider of Internet, landline and wireless services to the approximate seven million residents of Hong Kong. Boasting a market share north of forty percent, Safe Harbor was a cash machine. As one of the most densely populated areas in the world, profit margins at Safe Harbor were extraordinarily attractive. Ringing skyscrapers with fiber was easy and there was no need to build out the networks to less profitable lower traffic rural areas. All in all, the conditions were ideal for a telecom operator.

Roos read further and learned of the connection between his partner and Lee Wong. During the 1990's Anand Narayan ran Ring Laboratories, the most prestigious research institute in the world, a subsidiary of the American telecom giant Ring Corp. A man in this position instantly becomes the most important telecom person in the world—period.

With both a research budget and a venture capital fund in the billions of dollars, Ring Laboratories was the go-to place for funding of new research projects and investment capital for start up business ventures. Narayan held the invaluable purse strings for over two decades like Buffalo Bob Smith on the *Howdy Doody Show*, during which time he built an unrivaled Rolodex while earning a few favors along the way. The highway to Ring's New Jersey global headquarters was littered with the road kill of aspiring men with dashed hopes and the essence of torch lit dreams of the victors.

After graduating from Princeton, Lee Wong was hired as an analyst by Narayan at Ring where he learned the ropes for several years before returning to Hong Kong to work for his father's empire.

On final approach into Hong Kong International Airport, Roos stared out of the right side of the airplane at the Chinese "Las Vegas," Macau. Roos thought to himself that the much talked about casino haven look rather underwhelming. But possibly at night the venue was more impressive. The magnificent Hong Kong Harbor, looming just twenty miles across the Zhujiang, provided a tough comparison for Macau. A product of the nineteenth-century Opium Wars, which erupted between England and China when the latter would no longer accept Chinese molasses in exchange for green tea, modern day Hong Kong was born from the beguiling scent of brewing tea—and the nefarious redolence of burning opium. Quite a nose full for the city deriving its name from the English phrase *Fragrant Harbour.*

As the plane taxied toward the Hong Kong Business Aviation Center, Roos saw one of the Peninsula Hotel's storied Rolls Royces waiting by the hangar. Built in 1928, the iconic flagship property of Hong Kong Island based Peninsula Hotel Group, is Hong Kong's oldest and most prestigious hotel. The "Grande Dame of the Far East" as the place is known, is furnished with antiques and historical artifacts, allowing travelers to re-live a bygone era through the property's timeless elegance—not to mention opulence. An Asian gentleman, standing on the driver's side of the Peninsula green Phantom Wraithe, was holding a sign in his white-gloved hands, with the name Christian Roos printed in both English and Cantonese. The latter symbolized the pride—deeply embedded—in Hong Kong's heritage by her seven million plus residents. The Special Administrative Region of the People's Republic of China remains fiercely independent from its billion plus populated neighbor—and equally as leery.

Living in just four hundred and twenty-six square miles, the citizens of Hong Kong are stuffed tighter than a shrimp in a steamed Har Gow dumpling. With seventeen thousand Hong Kongers living per square mile, the territory ranks fourth in the world for population density. Excluding the interesting but extremely small anomalies of Macau and Monaco, only Singapore ranks higher in density than Hong Kong—and barely at that. An old saying amongst the skyscrapers dotting the Victoria Harbor is that if every Hongkonger went to sleep at the same there simply would not be enough beds to accommodate everyone.

Lee Wong remained seated in the vehicle as Roos entered the spacious rear seat. The surprisingly youngish and handsome billionaire spoke in perfect English. "Welcome to Hong Kong, Christian. You must be starved. We will grab some food on the way to the Happy Valley Racecourse. We are lucky, the horses only run on Wednesday afternoons. By the way, nice plane. I have been trying to buy one for over a year now. Gulfstream is so backed up with orders for the G650 that the company tells me that an order placed today won't be filled until late 2017."

Roos politely responded, "Pleased to be here. My partner speaks so highly of you and your father. The plane is not mine. A business partner loaned it to me for a bit of traveling. Can't you buy someone's production slot?"

Lee continued, "No. The last bubble in general aviation was in the late 1990's during the launch of the G5. Things got a little crazy. General Dynamics, the owner of Gulfstream, is trying to dampen speculation, which they believe is disruptive in the secondary market and ultimately deleterious to the value of their new aircraft. Ideally they prefer a linear pricing, so that when the G750 is on the market, the price will be more than a used G650. Think of an IPO that prices at twenty dollars per share and the first trade is at fifty dollars, a dynamic, which leaves a sour taste in many a greedy mouth. Nice problem to have, I guess?"

Roos curiously asked, "But how can GD stop someone from selling a plane in the production queue?"

"Good question," Lee responded. "Their contracts have a non-assignability clause, which admittedly is difficult to enforce. People are creating shell corporations to purchase planes, then selling their interest in the company at a premium to an anxious G650 buyer. You can imagine that people with sixty million dollars laying around to purchase an aircraft are not used to being told no, or to wait."

Roos smiled. "Understand."

Clearly disgusted, Lee quipped, "Rumors are that a Russian oligarch just paid seventy-two-million dollars, an eight-million-dollar premium for a 2014 delivery. Ridiculous. Another example of dirty Russian money oozing into the developed world."

In Cantonese, Lee instructed the driver to make a stop at the Ladies' Market located on Kowloon, directly across the Victoria Harbor from their destination on Hong Kong Island. As the rolling living room steamed eastward across the Tsing Ma Bridge, at seven thousand feet one of the world's longest suspension bridges, the magnificent skyline of Hong Kong came into view. Lee explained to Roos that one of the first moves in the aftermath of the British 1997 cessation of control of Hong Kong was the construction of the new island based airport, west of the city.

"The old airport was located in downtown Kowloon, which created strict zoning height restrictions. Consequently, the real estate action was concentrated in Hong Kong Island. But that has all changed now and skyscrapers are popping up in Kowloon like Chinese Mainlanders shopping with their wheeled suitcases, loud voices and rude behavior."

Smiling, Lee added, "But they do bring the Mao Se-Tung's in bunches!"

Roos was almost too embarrassed to ask, but felt compelled nonetheless to hear the story about the British ground lease expiration.

Lee obliged, "The ownership transition from the Brits to the Chinese has to be one of the most misunderstood concepts in the history of Hong Kong, which dates back thousands of years. Might be some hyperbole on my part, but I didn't live in our previous era. One can really only know what they have experienced."

Roos agreed.

Lee continued, "Since the Opium Wars in the middle of the nineteenth century, the Brits owned Hong Kong. But the terms of the deal called for a ground lease that expired in 1997. Speculation was rampant about what the new 'owners'—the PRC—would do with their newfound capitalistic haven. Hindsight is twenty-twenty, but to us it was obvious that China was not going to mess with this golden goose, busy laying golden eggs—by the hour."

A skeptical Roos politely responded, "Very interesting."

Lee offered up some personal thoughts and experiences, "If you think about it, Hong Kong provides a perfect Trojan Horse allowing Chinese commerce with the world, while still maintaining a communistic regime. In either event, the turn of the century cyber Armageddon has turned out to be an epic yawner. But enough of that, let us eat."

The driver pulled over on Tung Choi Street located in central Kowloon. Lee and Roos exited and began walking down the one kilometer Ladies Market. An amalgamation of street venders, food purveyors and local entertainment acts, created a scene, which on the surface resembles a mare's nest. The only thing that keeps the market from descending into anarchy is the exchange of money—the universal catalyst transforming chaos into order.

Lee motioned for Roos to follow him. The pair approached a quintessential street food establishment, which was displaying a variety of animals, mostly birds—all upside down hanging from hooks—skin glistening. If it walks or flies, it is in danger of ending up in some dim sum or rolled in a plum sauce lathered, scallion nesting pancake here in Hong Kong. Out in front of the windowed stationary food truck were large bamboo baskets of steaming dumplings stuffed with pork, shrimp, vegetables and god knows what else. Smoke was billowing, casting the most unusual of smells—some good, some knee buckling noxious odors—conjuring unimaginable sources. Wafting vomit clouds emitting the strangest of smells would suddenly surface at the most random of times. Roos thought to himself, the derivation of the Hong Kong "fragrant harbor" held truer nearer the water.

Lee began arguing with the lady who was peering through the restaurant's small opening. After an awkward exchange, seemingly lasting for hours, the lady accepted Lee's offer of two hundred Hong Kong dollars, approximately twenty-five U.S. dollars. In short order, Lee and Roos were gorging on delectable soup dumplings, Peking duck and Cantonese beef fried rice.

The billionaire Lee, noticing Roos' curiosity about his exchange with the lady, volunteered, "Christian, I was negotiating the price of the meal. Trust me, it is not about the money. Rather it is part of our culture. Paying retail is just about the most rude and disrespectful thing one can do to their fellow Hong Kongers."

After a quick stand-up meal, Lee and Roos ventured to the Happy Valley Race Track via the Cross Harbor Tunnel, one of three tubes under Victoria Harbor, named for Queen Victoria. The underwater route, connecting Kowloon with Hong Kong Island, was typically a logjam of traffic moving at a snail's pace.

Set in the hills surrounded by skyscrapers, Happy Valley provides for a stunning contrast. The tight flat grass track resembles a Roman amphitheater, sans the actors. Built commensurate with British rule in the eighteenth century, the track would burn to the ground and lay dormant for decades only to be rebuilt by the Hong Kong Jockey Club into a preeminent racing facility, the only place for gambling in Hong Kong.

It didn't take long for Lee to improve his already robust financial position. The man who quibbled over ten U.S. dollars with a local dim sum proprietor, struck gold in the second race, a Class 4 contest. *King Derby* finished the twelve hundred meters a nose before *Hayhay*. At twelve to one odds to win, Lee's one million Hong Kong dollar wager paid off just over one and a half million U.S. dollars.

A seasoned veteran of the investment management business, Roos knew to keep his mouth shut. Business was over and without a doubt Lee would become a new client of his firm. The ultra superstitious

Chinese would never pass on a good luck charm, even if it materialized in the form of an American. Roos' mind drifted to 6:30 P.M., the time he would see Sakura Nagasawa — again.

Frenchman Philippe Starck has designed everything from coffee machines to SLS Hotels and even the late Steve Jobs' seventy-eight-meter super yacht, *Venus*. Starck shared a very important philosophy with the iconic Jobs, widely considered one of the greatest businessmen of the information age or any age for that matter — minimalism. The Peninsula Group tapped the eclectic Parisian during their recent renovation. His assignment was the Felix Restaurant prodigiously located on the twenty-eighth floor of the hotel, a venue providing jaw dropping one-hundred-and-eighty degree views of Victoria Harbor and neighboring Hong Kong Island. Besides his signature sleekly designed elegant restaurant, Starck threw in the Liquid Gold Alchemy room, a small circular bar serving exquisite cocktails and the finest French wines, the Crazy Box, a sound-proof dancing room complete with a footprint floor allowing revelers to track their progress and a wave elevator transporting guests to a pre-dining sensation of time traveling.

Roos found Sakura seated on the outdoor patio bar located on the hotel's top floor. As Roos approached her, the woman, engrossed in the view, instinctively turned, smiled and stood to meet him. Roos' eyes started low observing Sakura's silver and black Rorschach designed brocade Lanvin Pee Toe Pumps. Stimulation ensued as he work quickly upwards in approval of Sakura's knee length black silk dress. Beautiful multi-colored butterflies, the Japanese designer Hanae Mori's signature, were fluttering in defiance of common aerodynamic lore all over the traditionally Asian loose fitting dress. One of the gossamer aeronauts was positioned just below Sakura's left breast — wings stretched out — symbolically lifting her heart to the heavens.

After a warm embrace, Sakura asked, "Christian, this place is so beautiful but so formal and quite frankly a little over the top for me. What do you say we take a walk?"

"My thoughts exactly," were the words from the man who would unequivocally say yes to virtually anything the mesmerizing Japanese woman asked. Continuing, Roos ventured, "I know a great place where we can get some carryout. We can jump on a junk for a picturesque dinner in the Victoria Harbor."

Smiling, Sakura replied, "Sounds delightful, Christian, but it would be very unusual for a Japanese person to eat street food."

Winking Roos rebutted, "No worries, the place I have in mind is connected to a building."

Looking like a brown banana with ends in the air, The *Duckling* was effortlessly cruising Victoria Harbor by the Public Pier passing the legendary Star Ferry on her port side. Sporting the traditional Princeton orange battens, the *Duckling* exuded a mysterious dignity, echoing a life gone bye but strangely visible. What could be more perfect for Sakura Nagasawa, the epitome of mystification, thought Roos.

Fortunately she was returning empty from an afternoon cruise and the *Duckling's* crew couldn't resist a little moonlighting, an illumination Roos had nearly worked himself into an emotional frenzy imagining. Once aboard, the head steward introduced himself as Andy, but his real name was Gao. As is so common, he had adopted an English first name.

"Would you like some champagne?"

Sakura, not much of a drinker, politely declined. Roos, a consumer of alcohol, declined as well. The steep steps of the Beijing Marathon loomed just twelve hours in the distance.

At 8:00 P.M. sharp, the Symphony of Lights commenced, a synchronized light and music show utilizing forty-five buildings on both sides of Victoria Harbor. Not knowing which view was more desirable—the magnificent skyline of Hong Kong aflame in brightly colored lights twinkling off the blue water to music, or Sakura's endearing sincere expression of amazement—the irreformable man with an incorrigible obsession for beautiful women chose the latter, naturally.

Roos escorted Sakura on the short walk back to the Peninsula Hotel. Staring into her eyes, still glowing from the magical brilliance on the water, Roos held her close. Moving ever so slowly, he moved his lips closer to hers. Fearing a roadside bomb, Roos proceeded with unprecedented caution, an approach that was both well respected and rewarded by Sakura. She paid the heedful and considerate man with rich dividends.

Turning, Roos said, "See you at Jiro in Tokyo in four nights."

Sakura's broad smile crinkled her nose. "I will be dreaming of sushi, Christian Roos. Safe travels."

Looking backwards out of his taxi en route to the airport, Roos saw Sakura staring at him into the Hong Kong darkness.

As the taxi pulled into the Hong Kong FBO at 10:00 P.M., Roos fired off a text message to his partner.

"Evening from Hong Kong on Day 20, Frank. My business diversion is complete, but I am afraid my love life is spiraling out of control. Headed to Beijing momentarily. Twenty days in the books, still have one spare in my back pocket. Let's hope I don't have to use it. Miss you, buddy. CR"

Frank's response hit Roos' iPhone within minutes, "Pic please!"

Roos fired off a shot of Sakura on the *Duckling's* stern with the Symphony of Lights in the background.

Frank's one word response simply said, "Strong."

On just a few hours of sleep, Roos was having more than second thoughts shortly after the commencement of the Great Wall Marathon. Based upon the time provided, Roos was assigned to start the race in the third interval. Runners, full of hope and excitement, launched every ten minutes. The weather was cool and overcast, perfect conditions for running the world's most difficult marathon. In the bus out from the Beijing, which departed at 3:30 A.M. for the Ying Yang Square in the Huanyaguang section of the Great Wall in Tianjin Province, Roos sat next to two experienced marathoners. Each of them had completed over one hundred and fifty marathons in their careers, including the Great Wall Marathon last year, which they claimed to be the hardest in the world. When asked, neither gentleman could think of what would be second hardest. The course requires runners to scale grades exceeding ten percent up one thousand feet in less than a quarter of a mile. All totaled, there are five thousand one hundred and sixty-four steps, which must be ascended and descended on the Great Wall.

Shortly after the start, runners are faced with their first of many serious tests along the twenty-six-plus-mile route. A thousand-foot climb looms at mile one. The descent feels steeper — a pitch that runners would be forced to retrace on the return. Despite hydrating and taking salt pills for most of the past two days, Roos was already laboring in the high altitude conditions. His goal was simply to finish the race in the allotted time of eight hours. Race officials imposed a reentry to the Great Wall at mile twenty-one within six hours.

Kat slept until noon. After a quick shower, she headed to the Old Shanghai restaurant located on the lobby level of the Sofitel Wanda. Serving traditional Shanghainese and Sichuan dishes in a fine dining setting, the place sounded perfect to Kat. By the time she arrived the restaurant was packed with a decidedly local looking crowd. Always a good sign, thought Kat. The very formally dressed and acting Chinese maître d' escorted her to a two top table with both chairs backing against the wall and a broad view of the restaurant. Feeling like a glass of wine, Kat asked the waiter for Old Shanghai's list. She was by no means a wine connoisseur, but even Kat was surprised at the size of the book that the waiter presented to her. Never really thinking that wine, especially reds, could hold up to the spicy Chinese dishes, Kat usually ordered vodka sodas. As she was buried in the vino tomb, a distinguished looking gentleman appeared following the maître d' to the table adjacent to Kat's. Wearing khakis, a white linen dress shirt, brown loafers and a blue blazer, the man exuded confidence and style. His tan face contrasted strikingly with his jet black hair and crystal blue eyes. Kat could not help but take notice of her new neighbor, who she guessed was a weak six handle, an age that presented with a high standard deviation. But he could easily pass for a man in his late forties, she thought. Some sixty-year-old men looked hot to Kat, others looked dead. Unlike women who hit the wall at a much earlier age, according to her, the diamond anniversary is the male moment of truth.

Unlike Kat, the man had neither concerns nor cares about the age of the beautiful woman in his sights. She was wearing a Ralph Lauren light Lovett wool turtleneck tunic with black Hanni leather boots. Her hair was sleekly tied in a humble ponytail.

Sensing Kat's indecision about the wine list, the man spoke up, "With spice a little sugar always comes in handy."

Kat replied, "Excuse me?"

Her new friend responded, "I think a German Spatlese Riesling from the Moselle Valley would be a safe selection. Would you care to join me? Please allow me to introduce myself, my name is Carl Strange."

Kat, clearly stunned, asked, "Did you say Carl Strange?"

After hearing an affirmative answer, Kat introduced herself as she rose to join Mr. Strange at his table.

Strange returned the favor, "Did you say Katherine Mandu?"

Kat, now seated at Strange's table, responded, "Yes. By chance are you the Carl Strange who was the Chief Investment Strategist at Springer and Waldron?"

Strange, with his trademark wit and intelligence, retorted, "Never much liked the term CIO. In my mind it conjures up an image of a wrinkled old lady in an off the beaten path circus tent wearing a gypsy dress and a bandana staring into a crystal ball. Or a person moving a planchette around a Ouija board, or throwing tarot cards with her left hand while she reads your palm with her right. But indeed it is I. By chance are you the Katherine Mandu who is traveling around the world with Christian Roos?"

Clearly determined not to be outdone, Kat quipped, "Yes, you could say that. Are you the gentleman who was on the *Uisge-Beatha Da* when it sunk off of the coast of the Isle-of-Skye?"

Strange looked straight into her eyes and said, "Yes I was. Your father saved my life and for that I will always be grateful to your family. If there is ever anything I can do for you, please do not hesitate to ask. I am completely serious. I was so sad when I heard the news of his unfortunate experience on Mount Everest, which took his life way too young."

"That is very kind of you to offer your gratitude and your assistance. Both are very much appreciated. My father was quite an interesting man. How well did you know him?"

Instead of answering her question Strange asked another, "By the way, where is Christian Roos?"

"Christian is running in the Great Wall Marathon."

"Crikey! Marathon? What in the hell is he thinking?

"Sometimes, I just don't know," she said.

Strange laughed and continued answering Kat's question about her father, "I only met your father in person once, on that fateful day on the Isle-of-Skye in the Hebrides in the Scottish Highlands. After the accident, we were transported to the Raigmore Hospital in Inverness, where Padruig IV and I were treated for relatively minor injuries. Upon our release, your father had already departed Scotland. We communicated via email for years, but I never saw him again. He had moved to Kathmandu, Nepal, and changed his name from Manders to Mandu. I think the combination of the combat exposure in the Falkland Islands and the boat accident really had quite an affect on your father."

Kat's emotional response was, "Sadly yes."

Sensing the need for a change in conversation, Strange grabbed the wine list and starting reading through some of the selections. Seeing 2010, 2011 and 2012 vintages of the big powerful Bordeaux wines like Haut Brion, Mouton Rothschild, Lafitte, Latour, Margaux, La Mission Haut Brion, Ducru Beacaillou and Cos Estournal, Strange just shook his head in disgust. Also on the list were equally as young vintages of some of the top Italian wines like Solaia, Tignanello, Ornellaia and Sassicaia. "No wonder the French and Italians are so upset about the current state of the world wine market. Not one of these bottles is listed for less than six thousand Chinese yuan, which is one thousand United States dollars. These wines should not be consumed for at least ten years and preferably fifteen. This is wine infanticide!"

Kat chimed in on the subject, "I agree. Christian and I were just in Tuscany where we visited Piero Antinori's vineyard. We definitely heard some grumbling about the Chinese drinking a 2012 Solaia with Moo goo gai pan doused in hot chili sauce. Christian attended Vinexpo this year, where the talk was all about the Chinese wine market. After the French, the Chinese had the highest attendance of any country. During his visit to Latour, he was informed of the Chateau's decision to no longer sell into the future's market, a huge development that could have significant implications for the future value of Bordeaux wines. Let us face facts, people are not paying over one thousand dollars a bottle because of the taste, aging aside. The product has morphed into an investment. Like a game of musical chairs, nobody wants to be standing when the music stops playing. What brings you to Beijing, Carl Strange?"

Strange replied, "I am speaking at a conference tomorrow."

"Investment conference?" she asked.

"No. I have retired from the investment world. The conference I am attending is sponsored by the non-profit organization, Earth Wildlife. Their mission is to protect endangered animals from becoming extinct and to eradicate animal trafficking. The former is largely caused through hunting and the latter is unfortunately growing dramatically around the world as unscrupulous characters attempt to profit from animal bodies in the most horrific of ways."

Kat asked Strange what he was speaking about.

Strange answered confidently and proudly, "I traveled to the Galapagos Islands off of the coast of Peru in the 1980's. The islands are home to the Marine Iguana, the only ocean-going lizard. Listed as vulnerable, the species is facing threats from climate change and animals, like dogs, on the Galapagos. Tomorrow, I will be speaking about the Marine Iguana, a reptile described by Charles Darwin as 'Hideous looking and a most disgusting clumsy lizard.' Call me a contrarian, but I fell in love with the little guy sporting spikes reminiscent of the Sex Pistols lead bassist Sid Vicious' hairdo. I have devoted significant time, energy and personal resources to help the reptiles, which scientists believe are one of earth's oldest living residents. They have been kicking around for millions of years and my hope is that we will not see them become extinct. Do you know that the Marine Iguana can stay submerged for over an hour while hunting for food?"

"I did not. Bravo for your efforts, Carl!"

Strange offered her an invitation, "You should come listen to my presentation. I will also be speaking about another passion of mine, the Golden Poison Dart Frog. Despite the small size of just two inches, the frog has enough poison to kill ten adults, making it the most toxic animal in the world. I have quite a large collection of Golden Poison Dart Frogs. The animal needs to interact with natural surroundings in order to develop poisonous venom. Raised indoors on Park Avenue, my Golden Poison Dart Frogs are as harmless as a flea. Well, enough of that talk, let's order some food."

"Yes, food sounds good," she replied. "We have a very busy schedule tomorrow, which has us visiting the Forbidden City, Tiananmen Square, Lama Temple and the Temple of Heaven, all here in Beijing. But I am sure Christian would love to see you. Possibly we could all have lunch tomorrow. Are you staying here at the hotel? We depart Beijing in the afternoon."

Strange, while buried in the menu, responded, "Yes."

After lunch, which included several bottles of wine—the more expensive ones arriving after the spicy food had disappeared, Strange asked if she had plans for the afternoon. After hearing no, Strange invited Kat up to his room to meet some of his Golden Poison Dart Frogs. A clearly enamored Kat said, "Yes."

Roos returned to the hotel at 8 P.M, exhausted, dehydrated and in both mental and physical pain. He ordered some room service, sent Harrison a message on Day 21 via WhatsApp and went to bed in short order. But before he went to sleep, Kat inquired about the marathon.

Roos asked if they could discuss the event tomorrow at breakfast. But he did let her know that he finished the course. When told of her luncheon with Carl Strange, Roos asked Kat to check out the conference online.

From the hotel room Katherine googled Earth Wildlife's website. Sure enough, Carl Strange was listed as a speaker, scheduled for 11 A.M. tomorrow.

"Hey, Mac, Strange here."

Mac was happy to hear his partner's voice, "Evening, Carl."

Strange, "Here in Beijing. Roos and Mandu are here as well, safe and sound. As matter of fact I had lunch with Katherine today."

"How did that happen?"

Strange, "I saw this smoke show woman sitting by herself in the hotel restaurant. So I hit on her. What are the odds of that?"

Mac, "Strange busting a strange? I would say pretty short. Where was Roos?"

"Running the Great Wall Marathon, of all things. I think we are having lunch tomorrow," Strange replied.

"What did you tell Katherine you were doing in Beijing?"

"The truth," Strange said. "I am speaking at an animal conference tomorrow. My presentation is about the Marine Iguana and the Golden Poison Dart Frog."

Mac laughed out loud. "Oh, Carl. By the way, nice going on the trading in the RoosCaboose. According to a report I saw from Springer and Waldron, we are hedged out and already have inked a thirty-million-dollar profit. Touché. And you never know, another opportunity may surface between Beijing and New York City. Last time I checked, a significant amount of terra firma and ocean blue separated those two destinations."

Over breakfast, while eating a bowl of congee—a rice porridge with pickles, peanuts and chicken, youtiao—deep-fried dough sticks dipped in steaming soya milk and xiandoufu—a pickled fermented tofu, Roos began describing the Great Wall Marathon to a relatively uninterested Kat. Despite her lack of enthusiasm, she was able to eek out, "How was the race?"

Roos jumped in, "Brutal. I just had no idea of the elevation changes on the course. About a third of the race takes place on the Huanyaguang section of the Wall, which was built during the Northern Qi Dynasty in the year five hundred fifty A.D. At mile twenty-one, racers re-enter the wall after an extended run through the extremely hilly and lush countryside. The course winds through the thousand-plus-year-old villages of Xiaying, Qingshanling, Chedaoyu and Duanzhuang, which are lined with locals dressed in tattered dark clothing with incredulous looks pasted on their hardened faces. The final ascent on the Wall, which has over two-thousand steps, rises over eleven-hundred feet in less than a kilometer. A slightly steeper grade would almost challenge acrophobia sufferers, it is simply that severe. Walking is quickly replaced with climbing, as participants mimic Spiderman scaling a Manhattan office building up the Wall. With breathtaking wide views of the Tianjin Province on all sides, runners are transported back in time, imagining warriors in their Nikes patrolling the ancient Great Wall."

"How far from Beijing?" asked Kat.

"One hundred and thirty kilometers southeast. A two-hour bus ride."

Kat next asked, "What was your time?"

"Seven hours and thirty-three minutes, a pace equal to seventeen minutes per mile."

Roos continued, "But today's schedule could be more difficult— one of the most challenging of the entire trip. We need to knock off the four sites here in Beijing, catch a flight to Pyongyang arriving in time to make our 4 P.M. meeting with Hyun-woo Rhee. I get the sense that the North Koreans are not big fans of tardiness."

After breakfast the couple set out through the smog to the epicenter of Beijing, the Forbidden City. Developed during the Ming Dynasty, modern day Beijing, which flows out from the Forbidden City in concentric circles, still embodies the founder's blueprint. Consuming Buddhism from a fire hose, a stupefied Roos and Kat were left to marvel at the mass confusion that is Beijing, a virtual living and smog-breathing museum. A unique sea of humanity, looking like a chaotic combination of the Tour de France with cyclists wearing facial scarves, a car convention staged on parking lots which doubled as highways and a cigarette smoking contest. Throw in near blackout conditions and one gets the sense that they have been roofied and flown to the red planet of Mars. The pinball machine called Beijing has twenty million pinballs ricocheting somewhere, though exactly where is an uneasy question to answer by the first time visitor. The ancient city of Peking has a pinch of everything. If it exists on planet earth, it can be found in the Chinese capital city. High-end shopping, dim sum street vendors, beggars, Communist Party military personnel, sophisticated international businesspersons, People's Armed Police and high-performance athletes, all blend together like Peking duck wrapped with a scallion in a hoisin-sauce-soaked pancake.

Deep in the Forbidden City, officially known as the Palace Museum, Roos was counting out loud the number of brass stubs on an imperial entrance. The oversized red door leading to an ancient emperor's bedroom was framed by layers of brightly colored wood panels all containing a repetitive soothing design. Roos finished counting with, "Seventy-nine, eighty, eighty-one."

Kat asked, "What are you counting?"

Yin and Yang is the Chinese philosophy of how seemingly opposite or contrary forces are interconnected and interdependent. The harmonious principle of Yin and Yang is the key to Chinese architectural design. Yang represents the odd numbers—male which of course was preferred for emperors, while Yin was symbolic of the feminine world. Three, five and seven were important numbers, but it was the number nine that got things all stirred up under the emperor's silk dragon logo hanfu. It is believed that the Forbidden City contains nine thousand nine hundred and ninety-nine rooms.

"Door studs," replied Roos. "Apparently, eighty-one was the 'sixty-nine' of the Ming Dynasty."

Kat excitedly quipped, "I was born on August first, 8/1."

Roos, bursting out laughing, exclaimed, "Touché, Kat!" Catching himself, Roos continued, "My birthday is July twenty-ninth. 7/29. Seven hundred twenty-nine divided by nine equals eighty-one!"

She laughed and said, "Unbelievable. Why is it called the Forbidden City?"

"It was the sole residence of the power players of China for centuries, dating back to 1420 A.D. and through the 1920's. The place was finally opened to the public in 1949. I love the imperial architecture. So unique."

Unable to flag down a cab in the furious midday traffic, Roos and Katherine walked the two miles south to the Temple of Heaven. The quality of the air was ghastly. By the time the couple arrived, their clothes were darkened by soot floating through the streets like ashes from a college pep rally bonfire. China's emperors would make the same trek for centuries in order to pray to the God of Heaven and ask for a successful harvest. Looking like a large piece of white asparagus peeking through the rich soil of the Rhine River Valley or a missile preparing for launch from Dr. Evil's secret underground lair, the Temple of Heaven is unusual and foreboding. Surrounded by two hundred and seventy-three hectares, the facility is the largest place of heavenly worship in the world. Built in 1420, the simple yet powerful structure is round on the north side and square on the south. This contrast symbolizes a round heaven and square earth. The Chinese may have had a special line to the heavens, which from time to time would pay dividends by influencing weather patterns, but the shape of their backyard down on terra firma was still shrouded in mystery.

Next on the schedule was the Lama Temple, located two miles north of the Forbidden City. This time Roos was able to hail a taxi for the short in distance, but long in time, ride. This, the most renowned Tibetan Buddhist temple outside of Tibet, is known as the Palace of Peace and Harmony. After visiting the temple, on the way back to the hotel, Roos and Katherine jumped out of the taxi for a quick twirl through Tiananmen Square.

As the couple walked through the massive open square toward the Monument to the People's Heroes, Roos' attention was drawn to a large group of Japanese tourists, all of whom were sporting and firing their Nikon long lenses cameras. With professional quality photography made possible by Steve Jobs via iPhones, Roos wondered to himself why the Japanese still clung to their traditional bulky equipment. Catching himself, Roos could be heard softly saying, "Quintessential deeply engrained Japanese culture manifesting itself in yet another form of everyday life in the Land of the Rising Sun."

Kat curiously asked, "Come again, Christian?"

Before he could answer, Roos' mind was instantly transported to Hong Kong and aboard the antique junk *The Duckling* as she slipped her way through the calm deep waters of the harbor. The light show sent beams bouncing off of her sienna sails, the champagne poured, the soft melodic tones of traditional Chinese music oozing through the wood deck, all collided to create a scene worthy of a romanticist's wedding.

Roos pulled out his iPhone and fired off a WhatsApp to the Japanese woman who was suddenly dancing in his head—a crowded venue that had seen its share of women dancing on it as well over the years.

"Sakura, Christian here. Hong Kong was magical. Who would have thought that you could ride a 'Duckling' so heavenly. Jiro soon."

Roos thought there were multiple ways of swapping Sakura for Kat at dinner, but nailing down the tactic to deploy appeared a secondary consideration at this point.

Kat and Roos hopped back in a taxi, picked up their luggage at the hotel and made a beeline to the airport. Roos placed a call to his RoosCaboose partner, Frank Harrison. Catching him on the back nine at the Foot, Harrison ducked into the nearby woods off the fairway of the par-four fourteenth hole on the west course.

"Hey, Frank. Touching base with an update. Finished up here in Beijing on Day 22 and now on my way to the airport where we will catch an early afternoon flight to Pyongyang, North Korea."

Frank whispered, "How does the remaining schedule look?"

"One night in Pyongyang and one in Tokyo. On plan to arrive at The Foot by noon on day twenty-four. But to refresh your memory, North Korea is the toughest destination by a wide margin. We are traveling under aliases as representatives of a Swiss-based private bank."

Now in his trademark deep voice, Harrison boomed, "Jesus Christ, CR, be careful. Touch base with me asap if anything goes wrong."

"Will do if I have connectivity. Keep your phone on at all times."

Roos inquired as to how his friend was playing.

Hastened on by the rest of his group, Harrison by this time had repositioned from the trees and was standing over his Titleist Pro V1, which was sitting in a fried egg lie in the fourteenth hole's eponymous shamrock-shaped beguiling bunker guarding the left side of the fairway. Harrison, appearing as an oversized leprechaun burrowing into Ireland's national symbol, responded, "Not bad, had three pars and a kick-in birdie on number five, where I almost holed out for eagle from the left greenside bunker, four bogeys and doubled eight, just can't play 'Arena'. Finished with a forty-one on the front. Even on the back so far. Wait a second." Frank motioned to his caddie, "Hey, Bman, throw me my seven iron. Sorry CR. The good news, more importantly though, is my partner Jimmy's play. He shot three under on the front and we have Tommy and Drew down one on the back after winning the front three and one. Hold on."

Harrison's comments reminded Roos of the chatter he always heard from dumbfounded Lahinch and Ballybunion members, who were appalled at Americans walking off the green blabbing about their personal score. Tomfoolery laced with embellishment leading to delusional comments about how they could have shot par, if only they had not three putted four times, lipped out on two snake birdie putts, hit a ball O.B. and sent another swimming and lastly busted a "T.C. Chen," a double hit chip shot made famous by the Taiwanese golfer. This self-centered attitude has sentenced the U.S. to eight losses at the hands of the European squad in the last ten Ryder Cups, a team event considered the most treasured in the golf world. Europeans only care about one thing and that is who won the match.

As Harrison, a man who clearly understood the sanctity of a team effort, readied for a challenging bunker shot, Roos listened with childish anticipation.

Roos heard the requisite snap at impact, followed by a distinctive thud as the ball caught the lip of the bunker and ricocheted backwards over Harrison's head—landing back in the trap—followed by "Absolutely unbelievable! How could that damn ball hit the lip? I hit the shot perfectly. Bman, what the hell just happened? Pards, I am sorry, I thought seven was the right weight. Play hard, Jimmy, your hole."

Roos smiled as he hung up the phone.

# 18

## Vengeance Calling

*"Earth provides enough to satisfy every man's needs,
but not every man's greed."*

—MAHATMA GANDHI

Xing Air flight #9 from Beijing to the North Korean capital city of Pyongyang took less than ninety minutes to traverse the four hundred and thirty nautical miles, most of which are over the South China Sea. With the South Korean border to the south and the Chinese border to the north the self-imposed exiled communist North Korea is sandwiched between two powerhouses. Across the South China Sea to the west lies the Chinese mainland. Japan floats across the Sea of Japan to the east. North Korea is surrounded like a stone in the ancient Chinese game of Go. The collapse of communism during the later part of the twentieth century has continued into the twenty-first century. Just five countries remain who believe in a communistic philosophy: Vietnam, China, Laos, Cuba and North Korea. However, only Cuba can claim to be in the same communistic zip code as the North Korean regime headed by thirty-one-year-old fanatical ideologue Kim Jong-un, the third family member to lead North Korea. Jong-un's grandfather, Kim Il-sung started The Democratic People's Republic of Korea in 1948 and led North Korea until his death, at the age of eighty-two, in 1994. In 1950 Kim Il-sung invaded South Korea and nearly captured the country, however, the United Nations stepped in and turned back the North Korean army. Kim Il's son, Kim Jong-il, assumed control of North Korea, upon his father's passing, and ran the country with an iron fist for eighteen years, until he died of a heart attack while inspecting a power plant. Kim Jong-il became violently angry when told of leaks in a North Korean dam. Unable to recover from the rage built up inside, Kim Jong-il croaked right on the spot.

The Pyongyang Sunan International Airport lies fifteen miles to the north of Pyongyang, a distance from which the Ryugyong Hotel is grotesquely visible. Unlike the beautiful willow trees so plentiful in Pyongyang, which literally mean "Capital of Willows," the Ryugyong Hotel looms on the horizon like an unsightly deformity. The structure dominates the stage for all entrants to the police state's capital city. Dubbed the Hotel of Doom, the one hundred and five story structure sits eerily empty as a bone-chilling metaphor for the failed isolated communist country. Begun in 1987, the original completion date was scheduled for 1989. Twenty-five years and seven hundred and fifty million dollars later, the project, described by *Esquire* magazine in 2008 as "The worst building in the history of mankind," remains a shocking blight on the Pyongyang skyline. It is routinely airbrushed out of official Democratic People's Republic of Korea propaganda materials. Owning the undesirable distinction as the *Guinness Book of World Records* tallest unoccupied building, the three thousand room windowless, monolithic concrete shell casts hideous in a new light.

After being whisked through security and immigration by airport officials, Roos and Kat found their luggage and proceeded through the empty airport. Other than airport personnel the pair struggled to see anyone else. Escorted through the exit, they saw a driver, standing almost in a military salute, next to a circa 1980's black Lincoln Town Car, holding a sign with exquisitely printed English letters, which spelled Mr. Remy Zaugg and Ms. Zoe Zubriggen.

Kat, staring off in the distance, remarked, "Christian, this may be the most unusual thing I have ever seen. It looks like something Captain Kirk and Lieutenant Spock would see on the Vulcan planet Kronos."

With the luggage in the trunk and the "Swiss bankers" in the back seat, the car took off for the twenty-mile ride to Pyongyang, a city sitting one hundred and twenty miles north of the Demilitarized Zone, the ultimate binary demarcation that separates North Korea from South

Korea. Like a light switch, with the North in the off position and the South occupying on, the two countries could not be more different. Seoul, the South's capital, brimming with over twenty-three million people, more than the entire population of the North, is the world's third largest city. Rapper PSY's music video, Gangnam Style, describing the Beverly Hills of South Korea, has been viewed over two billion times. But not once by a North Korean citizen living in a country denying Internet access to its people.

The back of the car was stuffed with propaganda. One passage from a brochure entitled *Welcome to the DPRK, the Juche-oriented socialist state which embodies the idea and leadership of Comrade Kim Il-sung, the founder of the Republic and the father of socialist Korea,* which caught Roos' eye, stated:

> "The Democratic People's Republic of Korea is a genuine worker's
> state, where all the people are completely liberated from exploitation
> and oppression. The workers, peasants, soldiers and intellectuals are
> the true masters of their destiny and are in a unique position to defend
> their interests."

The driver made quick progress traveling down the roughly paved Pyongyang—Kaesong Highway that has five lanes on each side. After ten minutes, only a few cars could be seen on the highway.

Roos leaned in toward Kat and whispered, "So far I have seen more machine guns and North Koreans picking through trash on the side of the highway than cars up until this point. This place makes Havana look like Paris."

After passing through Pyongyang, the highway leads down to Kaesong, the capital of Korea during the Koryo Dynasty, which ruled the country from the tenth until the fourteenth centuries.

The entrance to Pyongyang is heavily guarded. Quickly one gets the sense that there are those on the "inside" and those on the "outside" of the capital city's gates. As the car progressed toward the government city center, impeccably dressed female military personnel began popping up at each intersection, directing "carless" traffic. Looking like Leonard Bernstein flailing his genius arms at an empty

New York Philharmonic Symphony, the Korean traffic guards waved through invisible vehicles.

The driver stopped in front of a non-descript circa 1970's government building. A huge North Korean flag dominated the top floors, along with a painting of the founder of People's Democratic Republic of Korea, Kim Il-sung.

After passing through a metal detector and being hand searched, Mr. Remy Zaugg and Ms. Zoe Zubriggen were escorted to a stairwell by three Korean guards wearing full military uniforms, complete with Russian made AK47 machine guns. Reaching the fourteenth floor on foot, one of the guards opened the grey metal steel door and motioned to enter. The ensuing hallway was unusually wide and lined with framed life-size paintings and photographs of Kim Il-sung, Kim Jong-il and Kim Jong-un, images of military weaponry such as tanks and rockets, and the Korean army marching in formation through the main square of Pyongyang to waving throngs. Approximately halfway down the hall the Swiss bankers were escorted into a windowless conference room. Instructed to sit in the middle section on one side of the forty-foot conference table, Zaugg and Zubriggen waited for the newly appointed head of finance for the Democratic People's Republic of Korea, Hyun-woo Rhee, to arrive. A career military officer and confidant of the new Supreme Leader of the DPRK, Rhee was appointed to his new post upon Kim Jong-un's accession to power. Besides loyalty, Rhee, standing at just five feet four, was the correct height for the self-conscious dictator, who surrounds himself with subordinates who physically and emotionally must look up to him. Despite teasing his hair and wearing platform shoes, Kim Jong-un is unable to rise above sixty-five inches. For over thirty minutes they waited, as the three military guards stood at attention directly behind them.

Preceded by the distinctive sound of hard-soled military style shoes stomping on Formica flooring, a middle-aged man, dressed in a black priest suit that exposed a two-inch horizontal strip of his fully buttoned gray shirt, marched into the room and introduced himself, in perfect English, as Hyun-woo Rhee. He was a man who possessed a presence of authority. Following him into the conference room were twelve individuals, all of them male and dressed in drab DPRK uniforms. Filing in behind their boss, like sober guests in a wedding reception conga line, the distinctively younger looking individuals seated themselves on the opposite side from Zaugg and Zubriggen, without saying a word. Rhee awkwardly assumed the seat at the head of the table, twenty feet away from the Swiss bankers.

Commencing the meeting, Rhee said, "Mr. Zaugg and Ms. Zubriggen, welcome to the People's Democratic Republic of Korea. We are scheduled to meet for one hour, after which you will be taken to the Koryo Hotel. I will be hosting you for dinner at Okryu Restaurant at 8:30 P.M. Thank you for making the effort to come meet with me today. Our comrades in Cuba, specifically Javier Castellanos, speak very highly of you and your financial institution, Aebi Bank and Trust Company. Why don't we start with an explanation of your institution's overall investment strategy?"

Zuagg began, "Ms. Zubriggan and I are honored to be here today. On behalf of Aebi Bank & Trust Company, please accept our sincere appreciation for the kind invitation. Dinner sounds lovely. The investment philosophy of Aebi is grounded in a value approach, utilizing fundamental analysis with a long-term investment horizon. We like to always remember Warren Buffett's rules of investing. Rule number one, do not lose money, rule number two reread rule number one."

Rhee asked, "Who is Warren Buffett?"

Zuagg continued, "Mr. Buffett is the Chairman and Chief Executive Officer of the American insurance company, Berkshire Hathaway. He is considered to be one of, if not the greatest, investor in the world. With a net worth in excess of fifty billion dollars, nearly all of which has been created through his ownership in Berkshire's publicly traded stock, he is one of the richest men in the world. Berkshire's annualized growth in book value per share, the defining performance metric according to Buffett, over the past forty eight years has been just under twenty percent, trouncing the Standard & Poor's 500 Index's total return of ten percent over the same period of time. Placing Berkshire's performance in proper perspective, dollars must be assigned. If one had the foresight and good fortune to invest one dollar in Berkshire forty-eight years ago on January 1, 1964, the value of the holding as of December 31, 2012, would be five thousand six hundred and eighty-six dollars."

Rhee asked, "Does he accept individual investment management accounts?"

"No," replied Zuagg, "but one can participate right along with the Oracle of Omaha by purchasing shares in Berkshire. Aebi is a one of the top shareholders of the company."

"Are you seeing any interesting investment opportunities in the commodity markets, like uranium or plutonium?" asked Rhee.

"Mr. Rhee, as to uranium, are you referring to U-235 or U-238 and is your interest in reactor grade or weapons grade plutonium?"

Zuagg, always prepared, had recently studied up on the world's most controversial and potentially valuable commodities. According to the World Nuclear Association, reactor grade plutonium is recovered as a by-product of typical used fuel from a nuclear reactor, after the fuel has been irradiated, (burned) for a period of about three years. Weapons grade plutonium is recovered from uranium fuel, which is at least ninety percent U-235 that has been irradiated for only two to three months in a plutonium reactor. After a lengthy spinning process in centrifuges, uranium, which is mostly U-238, magically becomes pure gold at U-235.

Rhee replied, "We have an interest in acquiring all types you have mentioned, assuming the price is right, of course."

Zubriggan was wearing a conservative knee-length black Armani Collezioni scoopneck sleeveless featherweight dress, with matching jacket and a pair of one hundred twenty millimeter black So Kate Patent Louboutins. Her flowing blonde hair was uncharacteristically furled in an Asian-themed do-it-yourself sock bun. On the fly, she was forced to substitute the sock with something available, which turned out to be a leopard mesh black Victoria Secret thong. Sans makeup and jewelry, the woman was the epitome of class, style and elegance. Cresting a Louboutin pumped height of six feet, Zubriggan illuminated the windowless, drab non-descript conference room, filled with elfish yes men, and made it brighter than a near-death experience.

To the palpable surprise of the North Korean contingent, Zubriggan entered the conversation with an answer to Rhee's question. "Gentlemen, as I am sure you are aware, Switzerland is a country which has prided herself on a longstanding tradition of global neutrality. Switzerland and neutrality are synonymous and, in general principle, the laws of the country preclude the joining of military alliances unless attacked. They must not take sides in international conflicts, which includes providing military passage through the country. Switzerland was never attacked during either of the World Wars. The country has not been involved in an outside conflict in over two hundred years. In keeping with tradition, Swiss authorities have identified uranium and plutonium, unquestionably the most controversial materials on planet earth, as literally 'too hot to handle.' And as such it has barred all Swiss based companies from dealing in the transuranic radioactive chemical elements. Please understand that the Swiss government is not taking sides here, as they never do, in the global debate about which of the residents of planet earth are allowed to have nuclear weapons. To the contrary, they are remaining neutral, as they always do."

Roos felt like a passenger in a sliding car, with locked brakes, suspended as he braced for the impending impact.

The gang of twelve seated across the table looked unsure which way they should face, and the three military guards still standing at attention, appeared as hopeful extras auditioning for a part in a Clint Eastwood western.

Rhee studied Zubriggan and asked incredulously, "Are you taller than Dennis Rodman?"

Not knowing what to make of Rhee's question, everyone in the room froze. The inquisitor broke the silence with another question. "I met Dennis Rodman during his recent visit here. He is so tall. Do you know him?"

Roos, incredulous at the direction the conversation was taking, was clearly caught off guard and mistakenly answered, "No, but I do know his old Chicago Bulls teammate, Michael Jordan."

Rhee's audible gasp billowed down the oversized, understated conference table like discharge from a Taepodong ballistic missile. Practically falling off his narcissistic elevated high backed chair, Rhee exclaimed, "You know MJ?"

Roos, feeling like he had made a terrible mistake, responded, "Yes, we are acquaintances, certainly by no means good friends. We have attended some of the same social events and played golf at Robert Trent Jones Golf Club in Washington, D.C. on several occasions. He joined the club when he was playing for the Washington Wizards. He has visited my home in Pebble Beach, California, as well."

Rhee composed himself and continued on the business at hand, "We have always respected Switzerland's independence and their detachment from the urge to involve themselves in the private affairs of independent countries."

Rhee, the lifelong military man, droned on, "Mr. Zaugg, is Aebi Bank and Trust Company investing in drones? Does your firm have access to shares in General Atomics?"

"Through its San Diego – based American subsidiary, General Atomics Aeronautical Systems," replied Zaugg, "General Atomics is a world leader in the design, manufacture and operation of Unmanned Aircraft Systems (Drones), Tactical Reconnaissance Radars and Surveillance Systems. The company's flagship Predator is the most battle-tested Unmanned Aircraft System in the world. Capable of flying at twenty-five thousand feet, for forty hours at one hundred twenty of Knots True Airspeed, carrying Hellfire missiles and lasers, the drone has truly changed the military world. Unfortunately the enormously profitable company is privately owned. Our private equity team and investment bankers cover the company, but we have not participated in any debt or equity financing rounds to date. Our view is that the commercial, non-military applications for drones will far exceed the military usage in the future. Until now, virtually one hundred percent of the applications have been of a military nature. But our analysts see all types of commercial usage burgeoning in the areas of private security, transportation, agriculture, weather and oceanography to name a few. It is our belief that General Atomics will need to access the public markets sooner, rather than later, in order to generate the capital necessary to expand into these growth markets. It is our hope that Aebi will partici-pate in future General Atomic financings."

Zubriggan mused to herself, giving two points to Christian for pull-ing off that response.

"Those drones are flying around us like worker bees at a virgin queen bee convention," Rhee said. "They are extremely difficult to hit and when our surface-to-air missiles do take a Predator out, another drone pops up faster than a stone crab claw. We would have a significant interest in acquiring drone technology. Sometimes when investments bomb, it can be a good thing."

Zaugg turned to his associate and said, "Ms. Zubriggan, I assume you are taking note of Mr. Rhee's requests?"

"Of course I am, Mr. Zaugg," she replied.

Rhee continued with his military investment theme, "Are you seeing any transactions in the new long-range sniper rifle made by the Brits?"

Zuagg stumped, "Mr. Rhee, forgive me, but I don't believe I am familiar with this weapon."

Zubriggan interjected, "Mr. Zaugg, if I may?"

"By all means, Ms. Zubriggan."

Zubriggan held forth, "Mr. Rhee, the British Sniper System Im-provement Program has developed the most technically advanced long-range sniper rifle in history. With a price tag of thirty-five thousand dollars, the weapon called the L115A3, is also the most expensive indi-vidually issued piece of military equipment. Modern day warfare has migrated from the battlefield to urban areas, with enemy targets increas-ingly mixed in with the civilian population. The British developed the L115A3 with Taliban insurgents, in the Iraq and Afghanistan wars, dead in their sights. The bolt action, five-round rifle checks in at just over fifteen pounds with a four-foot barrel firing the devastating .338 Lapua Magnum caliber. A Corporal of the Horse of the British Army has the longest recorded kill in history with the weapon. In November of 2009, Corporal Craig Harrison took out two Taliban with consecu-tive shots from his L115A3 at a distance of eight thousand one hundred and twenty feet, just over one and half miles. In a display of the most prodigious marksmanship in history, Harrison's third shot took out the Taliban machinegun."

Rhee replied, "We could certainly use a few of those down south on the Demilitarized Zone (DMZ). Who manufacturers the L115A3?"

"Accuracy International, based in Portsmouth, England," Zubriggan answered. "The company was founded in 1978 by Malcolm Cooper, the only consecutive Olympic Gold Medal winner in the fifty-meter rifle three positions event. You may recall he won Gold at the 1988 Summer Olympics held in Seoul, South Korea."

Rhee interrupted, "Never heard of him."

Zubriggan, "Well sadly he died after a battle with cancer in 2001 at the young age of fifty-four. But not before he was able to launch Accuracy International, which to this day is a privately held company selling the world's highest precision long-range sniper rifles to over sixty countries around the world. The weapons utilize the techniques learned from competitive shooting, combined with full military ruggedness, honed and refined over thirty years."

Rhee motioned to one of his assistants to approach. He whispered into one of the twelve elves' ear, and the man immediately left the room.

"Mr. Zaugg and Ms. Zubriggan, this has been most interesting. Thank you again for visiting with me. I will see you both at dinner." And with that Mr. Rhee left the room.

On the way back to the hotel, Roos inquired of the driver, with significant trepidation, if he would stop at the Ryugyong Hotel. After some consideration, elucidated by five Benjamins, the driver consented. Kat snapped a few pictures of Roos standing on the main steps to the freakish looking abandoned hotel. The video captured Roos doing his Captain Kirk imitation, "Mr. Spock. I just don't understand how people can live this way."

Toggling into Mr. Spock, Roos answered his own question, "Captain, it is really quite logical if you think about it. Man's state of equilibrium is the sum of his experiences. No more, no less. North Korea is earth's orbiting moon, so close to reality, yet so far, but a truism known only by Earthlings. Does reality exist in a vacuum? If an iPhone plays a song, but nobody is there to hear it, does it make sound? I think not, Captain."

Roos, morphing into Starfleet medical officer Leonard "Bones" McCoy, replied, "Damn you and your Vulcan logic, Spock!"

The North Korean driver just stared in a state of nervous confusion.

After being dropped back at their hotel and alone for the first time since the meeting, Roos turned to his partner, "Kat, can you believe that meeting? Rhee had absolutely no interest in discussing legitimate investments with us. He treated us as if we were two international arms dealers."

"Well, Christian, it wasn't like we were actually pitching legitimate investment strategies, were we? Last time I checked we were simply acting as imposters, for the sole purpose of being invited into Pyongyang. Sounds like the perfect red herring, double entendre to me."

"Or bad marriage, but either way, point well taken."

As they rode up the elevator, Kat asked, "Christian, do we have to attend this dinner tonight?"

"Only if we want to leave the country tomorrow. It will be fine. Dinners are completely social in this culture. Business rarely comes up, so I have been told. Besides, without question, the food will be outstanding. Speaking of business, how in the world did you know about the British long-range sniper rifle?"

"I read about it in the Financial Times last week," she replied. "Apparently the Iranians found a L115A3 on the rooftop of a Tehran hospital, a little less than a mile from the Presidential Palace. Unconfirmed reports claim that ballistic results show it was the weapon used to assassinate President Mussan. Sounds like quite a gun."

"From that distance, sounds like quite a shooter to me, technology notwithstanding."

Kat changed the subject, "What was the basketball conversation all about? Do you really know Michael Jordan?"

Roos explained the bizarre obsession possessed by the North Korean leader, Kim Jong-un, with American basketball, especially the Chicago Bulls and the team's past stars Dennis Rodman and Michael Jordan.

"Yes. I am friends with MJ's agent. Great guy, who handled everything for him, soup to nuts."

Carl Strange was on full alert as he walked through the lobby of the Koryo Hotel in downtown Pyongyang. A seasoned traveler who was intimately accustomed to some of the world's more precarious and treacherous destinations, Strange was visibly nervous in the North Korean capital. Having been interrogated at the airport for hours, Strange was concerned. Travelling under an assumed identity posing as an English Foreign Service officer, Strange listed his official purpose of the visit to North Korea as diplomatic. Only after a British Embassy official who was one of his old drinking buddies came to pick up Strange would the North Korean guards release him into the country. Passing by the thirty-foot jade dragon's mouth located in the center of the lobby, Strange veered left towards the registration desk and checked into a suite on the hotel's forty-third floor located in the left tower. The symmetrical twin tower structure resembled a tighter version of the Tower Bridge in London. The building, which pushes four hundred sixty-nine feet into the sky, was completed in 1985. Sadly, Kim Il-sung's pipe dream of showcasing the power and strength of the Democratic People's Republic of Korea, twenty-eight years later only averages nightly occupancy of just ten percent. On any given night, the number of American visitors can be counted on one hand.

Leaving the porter to drop off the luggage and close his hotel room door, Strange did what he always did and headed straight to the bar, which in this circumstance was a circular one located on the forty-fourth floor.

After pressing the elevator button, Strange stood silent and alone in a strange place, thinking to himself what a strange life he had lived. From sitting in a below ground bedroom in depressed Newcastle, England, to here in Pyongyang was indeed a bizarre cosmic leap. As the elevator door opened on the forty-third floor, Strange instantly looked down toward the ground and quickly stepped into the empty elevator and pressed number forty-four. As Christian and Kat walked out, Roos' double-take only showed Strange's back.

Approaching the entrance to the nearly empty venue, Strange pulled out his phone and called Mac. The time in Pyongyang was 7:00 P.M, which translated thirteen hours behind to 6 A.M. in New York.

"Morning, Mac, Strange here."

On his way to 6:30 A.M. mass, Mac replied, "Morning. Where are you?"

"Koryo Hotel in Pyongyang, North Korea." Strange continued, "Everything okay, Roos is booked here tonight, then tomorrow night in Tokyo, followed by an overnight flight to JFK. When trading opens in a few hours, I intend on extending our long position in the Caboose. Roos is definitely incoming on time."

"What is Pyongyang like?" asked Mac.

In typically strange Strange behavior he rattled off a strange sentence, "A dystopian world, where the laws of humanity have been hijacked through a controlled Pavlovian dehumanization process. I am afraid it has persisted for generations. But I must admit the people whom I have interacted with so far appear no worse for the wear. After all, it is quite difficult to be envious of the unknown. The Supreme Leaders have systematically kept the people in the dark, both literally and figuratively, for over sixty years. The food is brilliant though, nothing but enticing smells of bimibap mixed rice, bolgogi marinated beef and kimchi wafting through the desolate streets here."

"Are you sure Roos is in Pyongyang?" Mac asked.

"I just passed him on the elevator on the forty-third floor of the hotel. We must be staying on the same floor."

Mac, "Perfect. Keep me in the loop."

As he entered the bar, which boasted three hundred and sixty degree unobstructed views of downtown Pyongyang, something that Strange wasn't immediately sure added value to the scene, his libido exploded. The man with an insatiable desire for hot woman, an obsession with the female body and a proclivity for coitus with the world's most beautiful creations stood speechless and motionless. The source of his temporary petrification was an Asian woman seated at the bar drinking a martini.

Hard Yang was wearing one of fashion icon Roberto Cavalli's fall designs. The simple short dress spectacularly displayed an orange and black print, from the nipples above, of a Bengal tiger, complete with the magnificent creature's eyes. Below the breasts was a black and white herringbone pattern. The symbolism of an Asian femme fatale overcoming an Englishman, from her breasts, was more than prescient. The dress ended just below the rear of Hard Yang, almost as if the zigzag checks were sending sonar signals down her lovely light-skinned, toned legs to her one hundred twenty millimeter black Queue de Pie Veua Velours, which of course were displaying the signature Christian Louboutin red bottoms, visible only if one were to be lucky enough to view the shoes from that desirable angle. Yang lit the bar afire, drawing Strange towards her like a moth to a flame.

Sitting next to her, Carl Strange introduced himself, making use of his middle name, "Good evening my name is Carl Douglas."

Hard Yang responded, "Pleasure to make your acquaintance, my name is Wang Fang. What, may I ask, brings a Caucasian like yourself to Communist North Korea?"

Strange feeling like an Olympic Gold Medal winner, whose only remaining challenge was not tripping while ascending the podium, responded, "I am on an around-the-world voyage. Heading to Tokyo tomorrow, followed by a flight back home to New York City. By the way, is that a Vesper martini you are drinking?"

Yang, while rubbing her hand on Strange's thigh, in a steamy voice said, "Of course it is."

"Bartender, two more Vespers, if you please." And with that Strange excused himself to the restroom, where he washed his undercarriage, gargled with mouthwash and popped a twenty-milligram Cialis.

Yang made quick time of rummaging through Strange's blue blazer, which he left on the chair during his trip to the restroom. In short order she found a sixteen-gigabyte swivel USB high-speed metal flash memory pen thumb drive. Connecting through a plug to her iPhone, Yang downloaded the drive's content. When prompted for a password, Yang typed ChristianRoos. Imagine that, she thought, as she was ushered into the file's contents. Hard Yang quickly scanned the three files on the drive. The first, named Christian Roos Itinerary, contained all of Roos' travel plans. The second, named Bank Records, listed credit card purchases for Christian Roos and the last was a ledger showing what looked like securities transactions, named RoosCaboose. Convinced that she had located her target, Hard Yang replaced the drive back in the blue blazer, reached into her purse, opened a vile and dropped a crushed Rohypnol pill into Carl Strange's Vesper martini. The drug manufactured by Hoffman La Roche was a fast acting memory impairment pharmaceutical, defined visually by a distinctive split ridge down the center of the pill with Roche on one side and either a one or two encircled on the other side.

As Strange returned from the restroom, Yang toasted her new friend. After a few healthy gulps, she reached in, grabbed the man with both hands and whispered into his right ear, "Let's go to my place."

Strange quaffed his Vesper, paid the check and escorted Hard Yang to the elevator. The excitement exploding within Strange was almost too much for the experienced world traveler to disguise. As the elevator descended from the forty-fourth floor, Strange's fantasies began to build. His mind playfully wondered if had he ever seen a woman as beautiful as Yang, as sensual, as wonderful. His rhetorical mind kept answering no.

Hopping into a "Beijing Taxi," which in North Korea is quite an experience, Strange was exposed to the communist version of modern transportation. The government recently purchased eighty taxicabs from China in an effort to appease the burgeoning North Korean middle class's appetite for transportation convenience.

Hard Yang instructed the driver in Korean to her destination. The streets of downtown Pyongyang defy description. Dark, empty and lacking definition, the scene in downtown is surreal. The car took a left down a barren one-way street, straddled by a hodgepodge of convenience shops, laundromats and bars. Outside a few locals were milling about in the most useless and aimless of ways. As the car pulled up to number ten Pysong Street, Wang Fang motioned to the driver to pull over. As the couple exited the Beijing Taxi, Strange was overwhelmed by the smell of food. The restaurant, located adjacent to the car, was billowing steam out onto the street, spreading the most foreign fragrant bouquets.

Grabbing her new friend's hand, Hard Yang escorted Strange to the second floor apartment above the restaurant. As the couple entered the non-descript one-bedroom flat, Hard Yang grabbed Strange and pushed him up against the wall. Running her hands up his back and up to his neck, the woman pulled his face towards hers. Her plump pale lips massaged his mouth, as she used her hands to caress his upper body. Protruding her tongue in and out of his mouth, Hard Yang began to incapacitate her more than willing prey. Strange positioned his hands on Wang's thighs, which felt like living marble statues. He began to reciprocate with his tongue, which only emboldened the already heated Hard Yang. With both hands, Strange pulled her dress over her head exposing a body of perfection. Her spectacular natural breasts stood like lighthouse beacons, which both warned and welcomed foreigner visitors. Glancing downward, Strange witnessed a taught stomach anchored by a Victoria's Secret black dream angels cheekini thong. Strange began French kissing his female companion. Pushing her backwards towards a purple bean-bag chair, Strange lowered Fang onto the awaiting love bubble. Wasting no time, Strange started licking Yang's breasts. Sucking and teasing her taught nipples brought instant gratification to the woman, who quickly became lost in sexual thought—a blissful zone, grounded in a dirty base of survival instincts, stamped with a time code dating back to the beginning of life itself. Strange slowly lowered his tongue down Yang's torso, passing her bellybutton, until he reached her hairless moist vagina. To the intermittent flash of neon lights in the windows, with large gooey gelatinous bubbles endlessly rising and descending in the adjacent lava lamp and the smell of kimchi wafting in the air, Strange began tantalizing Yang's love muscle with his tongue. Using his fingers as accompaniments, Strange began to satisfy the beautiful Yang in the most erotic of ways. After forty minutes and multiple pulsating orgasms, Hard Yang performed a Mongolian reversal and flipped Strange. Sitting atop, she mounted him, her long black hair flowing like a merry-go-round gyroscope, and her powerful waist riding him in a slow controlled sensual way. Yang's technique was flawless. As she rose up, squeezing her pelvic muscles, waiting over thirty seconds, releasing and then sliding back down on Strange, the man's essence was expropriated by euphoria. Dismounting at the exact correct time, Yang slowly slid down Strange's body, stopping when her supple lips reached his zone, which she engulfed with passion and purpose. She would repeat this process for over an hour, sending Carl Strange into an exulted heaven on earth state. Finally pulling out, Strange at the request of Yang, showered her as he screamed and she moaned.

While Strange was collecting himself in the bathroom, the woman who called herself Wang Fang, repositioned herself into the kitchen. It was here where she prepared two glasses of Soju, the Korean vodka-like rice liquor with high alcohol potency. In one glass, the toxicology expert poured in a lethal dose of four grams of pure thallium. The pair drank the first round in a flash. Wang Fang quickly reloaded with another round.

Feeling dizzy, confused and unstable, Strange made a toast, "Wang Fang if you proposed marriage to me while we were having sex again, it would cause me to say yes I do, Miss Strange."

Before Yang could respond, Strange stared into her eyes and saw something pernicious, a look of darkness. The alluring Chinese woman's unforeseen morphing from breathtaking eroticism to pure evil, clearly shocked Strange. Barely able to stand the Englishman exclaimed, "Gordon Bennett!" before hitting the deck like a felled Pacific Northwest Douglas-fir tree. With Carl Strange passed out on the floor, Hard Yang, exited the apartment through a fog of steaming chicken and kimchi stew, reached for her iPhone and pressed send when Alexei Romanov's number surfaced.

"Romanov here."

If anyone was within earshot, which they were not, the coldblooded femme fatale's voice could be heard saying, "The job is done," as she walked through the empty unavailing streets of Pyongyang. "Absolutely positive, Alexei."

"Positive" was the word bringing a nefarious sneer to Romanov's face.

# 19

## Dreams of Sushi

*"I never think about the future, it comes soon enough."*
—ALBERT EINSTEIN

Hawk's cell phone lit up with Romanov's incoming afternoon call.

"Hello, James. Romanov here. Please give me a quote in the RoosCaboose."

The Hawk responded, "Last trade was at par."

Romanov, standing in the heart of Vengeance Capital's coliseum trading floor, boomed, "I want to short five hundred million dollars of the contract."

The Hawk incredulously responded, "Alexei, you are already short eight hundred and twenty million. Is that not enough exposure already? I would need some time to assemble my thoughts on the feasibility of such a trade. What is your price?"

"Herd those cats and get back to me," Romanov replied. "We can discuss price at that time, which I expect will be sooner rather than later."

Upon hanging up, the Hawk instantly called Mac.

"Mac, Hawk here. Vengeance wants to short another half a billion. What is he thinking? When is the last time you have spoken to Carl Strange?"

A surprised Mac said, "Today. Roos was in Pyongyang. Let me check in and get back to you. As far as I know, everything is okay."

When Roos and Kat arrived at Pyongyang Number One Boat they were escorted to a private room located in the aft of the floating restaurant moored on the Taedong River. Hyun-woo Rhee and his wife were already seated at a four top round table in a glass enclosed area providing two hundred seventy degree views of Kim Il-sung Square, the Taedong and the spooky skyline of Pyongyang. Rhee's elfish dozen were nowhere in sight, but his three military armed guards were standing at attention in positions surrounding the table, machine guns and all.

After introducing his wife who appeared as dutiful and deferential as she was beautiful, Rhee got right to business as he turned his head toward Roos and said, "Mr. Zaugg, I briefed the Supreme Leader on our meeting. He wants to meet you tomorrow."

Kat, remembering Christian's statement that "business" never takes place during North Korean dinners, simply gave him a look that each understood but neither liked.

Roos, summoning all of the poise and professionalism he had in his tank, ventured this response, "Mr. Rhee, that is a most kind and generous offer. Ms. Zubriggan and I would be honored to meet with Kim Jong-un, but we really must be departing North Korea tomorrow as originally planned." Instinctively knowing that more would be required, Roos continued, "We have important meetings scheduled for tomorrow afternoon in Tokyo. Additionally, I am delivering the dinner keynote speech at the Swiss Chocolate Makers Convention at the Mandarin Hotel in downtown Tokyo."

Rhee, looking more serious than at any moment to Roos in their short relationship, forcefully yet politely stated, "Mr. Zaugg, I must insist you agree to a meeting with our Supreme Leader Kim Jong-un. He would be most disappointed by your decision. Frankly a no-show would be an incomprehensible insult, which I am afraid to inform you will not be happening under any circumstances."

Rhee's henchmen, none of whom spoke English, a fact that was not confirmed but was simply known to all present, sensed their boss's important tone. All three of the uniform-wearing men noticeably clenched their AK47s while leaning ever so slightly forward. The tension engulfing the scene was temporarily cut as the floating restaurant eased from the dock.

Roos was a man who knew when to concede, when to throw in the towel and fight the fight another day. "Well, I suppose the candy makers should not be accepting any nuggets from strangers. Mr. Rhee, we are honored to attend tomorrow's meeting. Would you please excuse Ms. Zubbrigan so that she could make some phone calls advising of our change in plans?"

Rhee happily responded, "Of course. I am glad you have agreed."

After dinner, Christian Roos and Katherine Mandu returned to the Koryo Hotel at 10 P.M. Oblivious to his surroundings, Roos was begging for the bed. Exhausted, drained and confused, he was painfully trying to keep it together. Kat, sensing her partner's weakened condition, offered up some well needed support and encouragement.

"Christian, look at the bright side. How many people can say they have met the leader of communist North Korea, Kim Jong-un? My God, it is going to be the experience of a lifetime! Personally I am so excited, I may not be able to sleep tonight."

Roos laughed out loud as he dialed Harrison's number on the black rotary dial telephone sitting next to his hotel bed. "Hi, Frank. End of Day 22. I am in Pyongyang. Still alive, but naturally exhausted both physically and emotionally."

Harrison responded immediately, "CR, any chance you will not make it back by the twenty-fifth day?"

Roos responded promptly, "Well, since you asked, a minor issue has come up. I will be staying here in Pyongyang another night."

"Why? Will this affect your return date to NYC?" was Harrison's response.

"Don't ask why, just too exhausted to go into the details. But trust me when I say I have no choice in the matter. Relax, I will be arriving at The Foot on day twenty-five."

Harrison interrupted, "Wait. One more night in Pyongyang, one in Tokyo followed by a flight to JFK. I may have gone to public high school, but by my math, you wake up in Tokyo on Day 25 and catch a twelve-hour flight to JFK. There is no way you will make it to The Foot by noon."

Laughing, Roos spit out, "You sound like Phileas Fogg!"

"Who the fuck is Fogg?"

Roos explained that Phileas Fogg was the protagonist in Jules Verne's 1873 novel, *Around the World in Eighty Days*. Fogg, who traveled by steamship and train, returned to London after circumnavigating the globe, after eighty-one days. Fogg, who thought he had lost the wager that required the trip to take no more than eighty days, was happy to learn that he had crossed the International Date Line, giving him an extra day.

Roos replied, "Frank, I will be crossing the International Date Line on my flight from Tokyo to JKF, which will give me an extra day, basically offsetting the twelve-hour flight and thirteen-hour time change. The International Date Line sits on the 180-degree line of longitude, an imaginary line that demarcates two separate calendar days. All points east of the IDL are twenty-four hours ahead of locations west of the IDL. Crossing the line from the west adds twenty-four hours, while eastern travelers pick up a day."

Harrison shot back, "Are you sure? I have a huge amount of cash on the line here. As do you, need I remind you?"

Roos explained the timing, "Absolutely. After we hang up, I will email you my fight details. We depart Tokyo at 8 A.M. and arrive in JFK at 7:30 A.M. on the same day. Here is the math: 8 A.M. Tokyo time is 7:00 P.M. in NYC the previous night. The twelve and a half hour flight lands at JFK at 7:30 A.M. tomorrow which is 8:30 P.M. the same day in Japan. But since the flight crosses the IDL, you need to subtract the thirteen hours that I lost due to the time change traveling west. When you do this, it puts the landing at JFK back at 7:30 A.M. the same day as the takeoff. Got it big boy?"

"Who's on first; what's on second. Got it, I think. Godspeed, CR. By the way, the name IDL is perfect for you, my friend."

Kat proceeded down the forty-third-floor hallway and, to her surprise, emerging from an open door were three North Korean military police carrying luggage out of a hotel guest's room. Fearful to make eye contact, Kat put her head down and kept walking.

As the call with Harrison ended, Roos smiled as he saw Kat walk through the front door. Her explanation of what she saw on the floor fell on deaf ears to the man who had seen too much already over the past twenty-two days.

After hanging up the phone with Christian Roos, Frank Harrison called James Hawker. "Hawk, Harrison here. Give me some color in the Caboose."

"Hey Frank. The current outstanding volume is nine hundred million. Last trade was at par. I know you are long the position. If you are looking to increase your exposure, I should be able to accommodate your interest."

"What size are you talking?" Harrison asked.

"As much as you want."

"I will be back to you shortly," and as Harrison hung up, he sent a text to Christian Roos.

"CR, Do me a favor. Text me a photograph of yourself with two extended fingers on your right hand and three on your left, with the skyline of Pyongyang in the background. Make sure that hideous hotel is in the picture."

Normally a bizarre request such as this would elicit an equally unusual response, but Roos was not feeling like himself. "Of course, incoming within minutes" was CR's response.

Armed with irrefutable data on his friend's travel progress, Harrison called the Hawk over at Springer and Waldron. "Hawk, Harrison here. I have size interest on the long side in the Caboose. What can you show me?"

The Hawk responded, "Two fifty at fifty cents and half a bill at a quarter."

"Give me an hour," Harrison said as he hung up.

The Hawk again dialed Mac. "The Caboose is heating up. Romanov appears to be of the belief that the short side is the place to be. He has come in for another five hundred million. I am in touch with Frank Harrison, who is interested in increasing his long position. What do you hear from Strange? Is something going down here that we don't know about?"

Mac replied, "Let me check. Strange has gone crickets as of five hours ago."

The Hawk's cell phone rang on the Springer and Waldron trading desk, "Hey, Hawk, Harrison here. I will bid two hunds at a quarter."

"Done, you have more appetite?"

"No," Harrison said, "but please expect calls from Greg Powers from Net Neutrality Holdings LLC, Stone Baxter from Wolfram Global Partners and Mark Elliott from Sixty Two Thousand Capital."

Within the hour, the three hedge funds that Harrison brought in on the original deal and that sold out on the first day, each came back in for one hundred million on the long side of the Caboose. These trades combined with Harrison's two hundred, all shorted by Vengeance Capital, rounded out the hedge fund's additional five hundred million, putting the gladiator Romanov's net short position at one billion three hundred and twenty million dollars.

Roos was concerned about the time. Luncheon with Kim Jong-un was scheduled for 1 P.M. sharp. Rhee's car was picking the couple up at the Koryo Hotel at 9:30 A.M. The time was 9:15 A.M. Kat was in the bathroom of their hotel room, primping for an uncharacteristically longer period than usual. Waiting in his boring rumpled blue Hugo Boss suit and white wrinkled dress shirt, Roos was pacing the room. His Hermès tie with cannons and muskets muzzled his nervousness. Why such an early pickup for a 1 P.M. luncheon was a question that percolated throughout Roos' inquisitive mind. He mused to himself that nothing in this crazy country appeared to make sense, so why should something as simple as luncheon logistics?

As Roos began preparing an assault on the bathroom, Kat calmly opened the door and strode out cool as a cucumber. Channeling illusionist David Blaine, she managed to pull together yet another sharp outfit on Day 23. She had miraculously donned a crisp Ralph Lauren Black Label flared turtleneck long sleeve red dress. Adding to the conservative communist look, Kat was wearing red stockings and blue Louboutin Canassone

Botta tall one hundred millimeter boots. Rounding out the outfit was a Roberto Cavalli matching blue lamb shearling Russian flat domed hat.

"You look fantastic," Roos told her. "If I didn't know better I would think you were dressed as the North Korean flag, which has blue stripes at the top and bottom and a large red swath in the middle area. But you are sans the red star set in a white circle located in the red center section of the flag."

Kat quipped, "Not so fast, Mr. Zaugg," as she crossed her arms with hands extending downward grabbing the bottom of her red sweater dress. For affect, she slowly pulled it over her head exposing her breasts, which were snug as a bug in a rug tucked in a Victoria's Secret El Color Rojo Carioca bra and a silk and satin red Maison thong. But most interestingly, in plain view now was a hand-painted North Korean Five Point Red Star floating in a white circle on Kat's stomach.

Roos literally fell on the floor in hysterics. Rolling on his back he shot his right leg straight up in the air simulating a flagpole. "Hoist that puppy comrade."

Without skipping a beat, the yoga star threw the dress off and placed her right hand on the top of Roos' right leg, her left secured a grip just above his right knee. With a quick kick, Kat extended her legs and torso horizontal to the ground, holding the position still, before she started creating waving images by sending pulsating rhythms from her head to toe and back again. It was all Roos could do to maintain his leg position and hold his iPhone steady as he filmed the North Korean flag in the form of a beautiful woman waving over him. "Communism has never looked better!"

Kat dismounted in style to a full standing position where she popped her dress back on, extended a hand and pulled Christian from the VIP seat in the champagne lounge.

"Are you planning on showing our host?" Roos inquired with trepidation.

"Not sure, but you just never know when something like this may come in handy. Now let's get this show on the road."

This time Rhee was in the car as it sat outside of the Koryo Hotel precisely at 9:30 A.M. As Roos and Kat approached the car, Mr. Rhee stepped out from the rear right door and met the oncoming couple on the curb. Rhee motioned for Roos to join him in a private conversation out of earshot from Kat.

"Mr. Zaugg, there is a misunderstanding. My invitation, which I extended on behalf of the Supreme Leader, was for you alone, not Ms. Zubriggan."

Roos occasionally reacted poorly in response to these types of circumstances, especially ones that cut out the girls. "Well, I clearly heard you invite us to lunch, as a matter-of-fact you insisted that we attend."

"I insisted that you attend, Mr. Zaugg."

Venturing into a dangerous zone, Roos snorted, "Mr. Rhee, I changed my schedule in order to accommodate your request. At this point, either Ms. Zubriggan joins me, or I am not going. It is as simple as that."

Rhee's three-man army had now joined the scene as they exited the car.

This time it was Rhee who knew when to throw in the towel. Surely he could explain to his boss why Ms. Zubriggan was in attendance far easier than showing up empty handed.

The group boarded the car and headed to the center of town. Passing the foreboding government building where Zaugg and Zubriggan visited with Rhee yesterday, the car continued around the square before turning down a tree-lined side street leading down to the water. A series of smaller housing structures began popping up, each with a pond, front porch and ample views of the Taedong River. A small train station appeared off to the right. Rhee's car pulled up within feet of the tracks where a train was waiting. A coal-fired steam engine and a passenger car sat waiting, surrounded by armed military personnel, who were swarming the train station along with dogs. A quick glance at the scene displayed tanks, surface to air missiles, lookout towers and bunkers.

Exiting the car, Kat asked Christian, "Are we really going to board this train, which appears to be heading north?"

"Sure looks that way. Don't forget the flag!"

Rhee, his body guards, Kat and Roos boarded the circa 1950's passenger car and walked down the aisle of wooden floors. Rhee motioned for the couple to sit on the south side, facing forward, of a four top Formica table. The thinly cushioned seats were made of gray vinyl. The guards, who were already on the train, stood at attention during the entire one-hundred-and-fifty-mile ride. They headed north for the first sixty miles where the train turned in a northwesterly direction towards Sinuiji, a northern town sharing a border with China. The Yalu River, meaning boundary between two countries in Manchurian, flows from tributaries in the north into the East China Sea and is all that stands between North Korea and its powerful neighbor. The East China Sea was never out of sight from the left side of the train car.

Roos asked Mr. Rhee what their final destination was.

Rhee peered from his daily edition of the Minju Choson, the state-run North Korean government newspaper considered to be the publication of choice for Cabinet Members, and replied, "Sinuiji. Our Supreme Leader has a palace there."

Having studied up on the region, Roos paused when he heard the final destination. Satellite images, sadly the major source of information about North Korea, showed one of the country's infamous prison camps located within the city limits of Sinuiji.

"How is the Wihwa Island and Hwannggumpyeong Island Free Trade Zones Development Plan with the Chinese progressing?"

Roos was referring to a deal cut in June of 2011 between Kim Jong-un's father and the Chinese government to develop two islands into free trade zones. Sitting downriver from Sinuiji, the islands of Wihwa and Hwannggumpyeong will be turned into the DPRK's version of Hong Kong, according to the plan, which several years later appears to be off to a slow start. The attractive tax benefits, lifting of tariffs, visa free status and one hundred year lease offered up as incentives, apparently have failed to offset the concerns held by development companies, largely based in China, about the complete lack of existing infrastructure, systematic risk and of course the periodic flooding of the Yalu River. A rising tide may lift all boats, but the relatively flat islands, which currently afford little protection from the Yalu, never fair too well during the rainy season.

"Wonderful and on plan," retorted Rhee as he sank back into the delusional world depicted by the *Minju Choson*."

Despite Rhee's stated view, Roos saw absolutely nothing along the route indicating a whiff of economic activity associated with the island project or any other projects. Dominating the countryside were scenes of poverty, desperation and gloominess. Emaciated animals, makeshift housing and malnourished people scraping and scrounging the landscape were the only sights afforded.

The literal choo-choo train pulled into Kim Yong-un's private station in Sinuiji. After a short drive in a black SUV with tinted windows, Roos and Katherine were escorted into a drab looking windowless structure, where they soon found themselves facing each other while seated at a long dining room table. After a period, which felt like time spent in the high school principal's office while waiting to be picked up by an embarrassed and angry mother — a bad combination indeed — there was a loud commotion heard.

Strutting into the room like a one-legged bull infused peacock, Kim Jong-un, in a dumbfoundingly quiet voice given the man's bodacious demeanor, before he even reached his seat asked, "Mr. Zaugg, Mr. Rhee tells me that you know Michael Jordon. Where did you meet him?"

"Mr. Supreme Leader, first on behalf of Ms. Zubriggan, the Aebi Bank and Trust and the entire country of Switzerland, I thank you for your kind hospitality." Glancing across the table, Roos saw Kat biting her lower lip as she slightly tilted her head down towards the ornate table setting.

Interrupting, Kim Jong-un stated in perfect Swiss German, "I have and always will have a strong affection for Switzerland and the lovely Swiss people. I attended a school just outside of Bern up until university, where I have many fond memories."

Roos froze. The only part of his body showing any movement was his heart, which was sinking through his stomach on the way to becoming a bowel movement.

After a prolonged pregnant pause, Kat spoke up. In equally impressive Swiss German, she responded, "Thank you for your kind words about our country and our people. It warms my heart that your experience was so profoundly positive."

Roos, not knowing what was being said, continued on about Michael Jordon in English, a subject he hoped would transcend language, "It was in Lake Como, Italy, at the wedding rehearsal dinner for my friends, James Knox and Sarah Childress, who were getting married at Villa d'Este. I was seated at one of the ten tops. MJ was standing behind me, when I heard, 'Michael meet Remy.' I turned in my seat, looked up and saw what looked like a foot-long lit cigar, one which extended over my head for sure. No ashes were falling, though, on account of the skilled smoker. His downward extended hand met mine with his fingers reaching halfway to my elbow. As I began to stand up MJ said, 'Hey don't get up.' I continued to a full standing position and said, 'Hello, very nice to meet you.' The six-foot-six-inch bull of a man simply said, 'You are still not up.'"

The five-footish Supreme Leader's face contorted into a confused frown wanting to scowl. "I don't like short jokes."

"Well he is quite tall," Roos scrambled.

Recovered now, Kim Jong-un asked, "Did you ever meet him again?"

"Sure, later that night a group of the wedding guests were sitting out on the veranda of the hotel Villa d'Este overlooking Lake Como, one of the most beautiful inland scenes in the world in my opinion. Michael pulled out his iPod docking station and started playing Motown songs. As *My Girl* came on the rotation, an African-American woman at the table stood up and starting singing along to the famous Temptations song, in a spectacular professional voice. Only latter did I come to learn that the singer was the famous Gaffney Brown. Mr. Supreme Leader, the scene was really quite magical. Unfortunately, the hotel night manager walked out and explained to one of the individuals at the table that a hotel guest was complaining about the noise. Noise? A Grammy Award–winning performer serenading the bride and groom on the eve of their wedding with starlight and moonlight twinkling off of the deep clear waters of Lake Como is hardly noise. MJ laughed and said, 'What is wrong with those people? With this scene, they should be making love, not listening to us!'"

Kim Jong-un cracked a smile, which degenerated quickly into giggles collapsing into full on laughter. Roos looked over at Kat and, with a wink, conveyed a message of complete lunacy.

Kim Jong-un excitedly continued with his hero-worshipping. "How was the wedding?"

"Best one I have ever attended. The event was classy, exquisite and small, but extremely luxurious in a very thoughtful style. If the event were a song it could be only played by an ensemble of drop-dead gorgeous women," was Roos' candid response.

Kat's look of incredulity was visibly noticeable as she worried, almost overtly, that Kim Jong-un would pick up on Roos' ridiculous tongue-in-cheek reference to Hyon Song-wol, a member of the group Pochonbo Electric Ensemble. Unconfirmed reports indicate that Kim Jong-un recently had his ex-girlfriend executed for a failure to launch.

The Supreme Leader's English was thankfully not the best, but Roos knew that, naturally.

Unable to contain his man crush on MJ, Kim Yong-un all goo-goo eyed, asked, "Mr. Zaugg, what is MJ like?"

"Mr. Supreme Leader, Michael is a great guy. A real guys guy. MJ appreciates his friends and believes in the lost art of chivalry. He is not a complicated man. MJ likes basketball, golf, drinking, cigars and gambling. Oh and motorcycles. He loves motorcycles."

Almost squeaking, Kim Yong-un asked in a high-pitched voice, "Motorcycles?"

Roos then proceeded to tell the Supreme Leader the story of the time when Michael Jordan visited him in Pebble Beach, California, in 2005. The year earlier MJ realized a lifelong dream by formalizing his love affair with motorcycles by establishing Michael Jordan Motorsports. The company teamed up with Suzuki Motor Corporation of Japan and sponsored a three-man racing team. Riders Jason Pridmore, Steve Rapp and Montez Stewart proudly wore the MJ logo and competed in the Superstock and Superbike Class on the United States motorcycle Grand Prix. In 2005, the pinnacle of the world motorcycle circuit, the MotoGP held one of their races at the iconic Laguna Seca Racetrack set up in the golden hills on the Monterey Peninsula. Overlooking the breathtaking Northern California coastline, Laguna Seca, home to the famous corkscrew turn, is a storied racing venue.

Roos continued to describe the events to the salivating dictator who was reduced to a wide-eyed kid on Christmas Eve listening to stories of sugarplums dancing. "Knox, Childress and MJ were in town over the weekend in order to attend the MotoGP event. The night before the main Sunday race they attended dinner at my place. The entrance to our house was draped by a beautiful California oak tree, which formed a magisterial archway over the wooded gate wedged between a wall made of the indigenous Carmel Valley sienna-colored stone. Panicked about a possible head collision, I tied balloons around the branch directly above the entrance. The color was Carolina Blue, of course."

The Supreme Leader asked about the color choice.

"The colors of MJ's alma mater, the University of North Carolina, are Carolina Blue and white. As they say in Chapel Hill, 'If God was not a Tar Heel why would the sky be Carolina Blue?'"

The atheist just stared at Roos. "Please continue, Mr. Zaugg."

"The next day MJ invited us to join him in his box to watch the races. Of course we accepted, arriving at Laguna Seca by 10 A.M. Passing through security at the box's entrance, we were escorted to a large circular table overlooking the track. The zinging sound of high-performance motorcycles was piercing through the crisp and crystal-clear Northern California air like North Korean surface-to-air missiles."

Kim Jong-un smiled.

"MJ's longtime best friend, Big Mike, the only person on planet earth granted permission to call Michael Jordan Little Mike, rounded out the group of seven, in an outdoor box which could comfortably hold a hundred people. A bartender and two servers were handling the food and beverage. The parents of some of MJ's team riders popped in for some pre-race well wishes. The paparazzi were swarming the scene, furiously snapping their long lens cameras. MJ never blinked—not even once—despite one aggressive cameraman hanging upside down on an adjacent box in order to get a close-up shot of the world's most famous and recognizable star in any sport."

Roos continued. "A commotion ensued at the entrance. The head bouncer glanced over to the host, MJ, for a decision. Looking like Mafia boss Vito Corleone played by Oscar winner Marlon Brando for his performance in the epic film *The Godfather*, MJ just nodded, the cigar protruding from his mouth. And with that, a dashing man with long flowing blondish-brown hair, tight jeans, Italian loafers, a white collared shirt unbuttoned to his bellybutton and the most beautiful searing blue deep-set eyes, strode into the box. He appeared as Jesus Christ on a people mover as he approached the table where we were all seated."

"Who was the man?" Kim Jong-un's question sounded more like a command.

"Fabio."

"Who?"

Roos explained who Fabio was to the man who apparently was not a fan of trashy romance novels. "Fabio Lanzoni is an Italian fashion model, actor and spokesman. But he is best known for gracing the covers of hundreds of romance novels."

Kim Jong-un inquired as to why Fabio was attending the races.

"As he sat down that is the exact question I asked him. It turns out Fabio was the official race marshall. Fabio was seated next to MJ, a man he clearly possessed great affection for. It was very apparent to all seated at the table that meeting MJ was an important moment for Fabio. Unfortunately for the Italian sex symbol, the feeling was not mutual. Frustrated by receiving one- and two-syllable word responses, Fabio, an intellectual with a resolute demeanor, remained undaunted."

"Fabio asked MJ how he got involved with motorcycles. MJ responded, 'Can't remember. You?'"

"Fabio then went on, 'Well, I grew up in Milan where motorcycles are a way of life. But not the ones we are seeing here today on the racetrack. Mostly scooters; I believe Vespa is the common term that describes the vehicle here in the States. When I was eight years old, I borrowed my uncle's scooter and proceeded into town for some food.

When making a turn into Drogheria Suana, I was distracted by this beautiful girl and hit a taxi head on. The bike flipped onto the hood of the vehicle while I was still commanding the handlebars. As the car continued forward, the bike and I bounced off onto to the trunk, followed by a complete splatter onto the cobblestone street.'"

"MJ puffed on his cigar, took a sip of his Bloody Mary and didn't say a word. Breaking the silence I asked Fabio if he was hurt and did he go to hospital. Fabio laughed. 'Yes, I was hurt, but the taxi driver was a friend of my father's. I begged him to not tell him what had happened, fearing far worse injuries.'"

"MJ just smiled. At this point, the PA announcer gave a ten-minute warning to the race start. Fabio announced, 'Well I must be going now. It was a pleasure meeting everyone.' And with that, the romance novel uber coverboy slipped out of the box as gracefully as he had entered."

To the delight of the Supreme Leader, Roos went on, "Fabio was finishing his ceremonial lap as the official race marshal on a Ducati tipping out at one hundred and twenty-five miles per hour. His hair trailing behind his chiseled face looked like a Commonwealth Bay windsock. With scantily clad Red Bull girls on each side of the starting line, the National Anthem played, and heartthrob top-ranked Italian racer Valentin Raossi stood up on his bike and performed his trademark rearranging of his 'package' to the wild screams of the females in attendance, the green checkered flag was dropped and the race was on."

The dictator abruptly announced, "Let's launch, I mean lunch."

During the meal, conversation was non-existent. All individuals at the table traded blank stares with each other while consuming an inordinate amount of delicious Korean food, which was being served in waves. Suddenly the Supreme Leader stood up and without saying a word or making even the slightest of gestures, he limped from the room. Kat and Roos were escorted back to the choo-choo train and made their way back to Pyongyang and the Koryo Hotel.

Before retiring for the night, Roos texted Frank on WhatsApp: "Day 23 — Hard to convey but there was something charming about Kim Jong-un, almost childlike. I got the sense he would prefer to ditch the Supreme Leader pretense, turn in his detonator button and just be an NBA fan living in a suburban Chicago neighborhood. To Tokyo tomorrow. CR"

Frank's response hit within seconds, "CR, he is a vicious toad, a pariah who oppresses his people in the most horrible of ways. Didn't he feed his uncle to a pack of dogs and execute his girlfriend?"

Roos half joking texted back, "Well he was born into the job. It isn't like he invented tyranny. I am just saying that he appears to be quite uncomfortable in the position. One thing for sure, world fears of this guy going postal and launching a nuke are baseless. Madness in this zip code comes with the frequency of a Transit of Venus. In this case, I believe the kimchee fell too far from the barrel, a distance wide enough to void the evil eyes of his gene pool."

Hyun-woo Rhee's car and driver, sans Rhee this time, were waiting in front of the Koryo Hotel exactly at 9 A.M. Having slept until ten, Roos and Kat were feeling reasonably rested for the first time in days. Spirits were buoyed with the end of the trip in sight. Less than seven hundred nautical miles separated the respective capitals of North Korea and Japan, a distance that would take less than two hours by plane. They arrived safely just after noon. The last two sacred sites on the itinerary, the Sensoji Temple, one of Japan's greatest cultural and religious icons dating to the seventh century AD, and Meiji Shrine were both conveniently located within short distances from downtown Tokyo. After planned afternoon visits, Roos had a grand finale surprise planned, one that he thought about constantly since he made the arrangements ten days ago. Thankfully Roos' contact, Masafumi Yamagata, was able to change the plans on a day's notice.

The extra night in Pyongyang threatened the original dinner reservations. In the glitzy high-end Ginzo shopping district sits Sukiyabashi Jiro, one of the greatest sushi restaurants in the world, ruled with an iron fist by the iconic eighty-eight-year-old chef, Jiro Ono.

Located in the basement below the entrance to the Ginzo Metro, the painfully authentic Japanese restaurant with very ordinary furnishings gladly shares none of the glitz of the neighborhood. Anointed a Shokunin, the highest Japanese distinction for an artisan perfecting his craft and designated as a Japanese National Treasure by the government, Jiro Ono stands alone atop the sushi world. With only ten counter seats at the lone sushi bar, a reservation at Sukiyabashi Jiro is one of the hardest tickets to secure in the epicurean universe. Only Ferran Adria's restaurant north of Barcelona, El Bulli, which is now closed, was a more difficult reservation to secure. Making dinner at Sukiyabashi Jiro even more challenging is snarky chef Jiro Ono's unwritten rule of only serving groups containing at least one person fluent in Japanese. The prickly genius is prone to petulant behavior towards diners who don't act in the appropriate manner. Masafumi Yamagata, Roos' previous longstanding client was able to secure a reservation for four at 8 P.M. His wife, Koyuki, would be rounding out the foursome.

"Kat, are you up for some sushi in Tokyo tonight?"

"Sounds lovely but I am exhausted. Would you mind if skipped Jiro?"

Roos was expecting this response from Kat, who was never much for raw fish, nor mingling with his old clients. It wasn't that she was antisocial, rather just preferred to hobnob with people she knew socially. And since he had already invited Sakura who had accepted, a fact unknown to Kat, it might be a little crowded and awkward with five people sitting on four counter stools. Roos responded, "Of course not. I completely understand."

Roos and his friends over the years informally selected their favorite dish and ventured out around the world to find the finest example. Hearing exaggerated stories of the best bowl of French onion soup, cheesesteaks, paella or cassoulet always amused Roos. A sushi connoisseur, Roos was all about tuna, specifically toro, the fatty underbelly of the fish. Unlike cooked dishes, raw toro is all about the quality of the fish. Having only eaten sushi outside of Japan, considered an oxymoron by most, Roos was anxiously awaiting the visit to Sukiyabashi Jiro, a restaurant which Parisian critic Michelin has thrown three prestigious stars for years. Tokyo has fourteen three-star Michelin restaurants, twelve of which serve Japanese cuisine. Not even Paris, with ten, has more three star restaurants. With thirty-one three-star restaurants within her borders, Japan leads the world. Second is France with twenty-six, America and Germany each have ten, and Spain and Italy each have seven.

Roos' excitement about experiencing a meal at Sukiyabashi Jiro stemmed from the two unique types of toro served by Jiro. Toro is sold around the world, but the choicest parts of fatty tuna, otoro and kama, are rarely seen outside of Japan. Chef Jiro, who instructs his apprentices to massage fish before serving, is known to prepare both with perfection. Change comes slowly at Sukiyabashi Jiro. A recent modification to the cooking technique instituted last year called for forty minutes of massaging of octopus, an increase of ten minutes from the previous half hour exercise. Apprentices must serve a minimum of ten years before they are permitted to serve sushi to customers.

The most sacred religious site in Tokyo, the Sensoji Temple is located sixteen miles north of the airport. A modest distance but in the brutal afternoon rush-hour traffic, the trip could take several hours each way. Roos arranged for the driver to drop the luggage off at the Peninsula Hotel on Yurakucho Street in the swank Chiyoda section of downtown Tokyo. He and Katmandu hopped on the underground Tokyo Metro for the forty-minute ride to the Asakusa stop, home of what is popularly referred to as the Asakusa Kannon.

Named for the Buddhist goddess of mercy, Kannon personifies compassion and is one of the most worshipped and revered divinities in the modern and ancient Asian world. Beginning in India in the first century A.D., Kannon devotion spread through Nepal, Tibet and across China before making her way to the shores of Japan. Kannon's paradise is known as Fudarakusen, literally translated as Mount Futuraka—the Japanese transliteration of Sanskrit Potalaka, the Holy Lands in Tibet. The Fudarakusen, Buddhist's Holy Land, is thought to have originated on a mountaintop in the southern tip of India.

Upon entering the Kaminarimon Gates leading to a series of buildings, shrines and pagodas, Kat commented, "Christian, this does not look like it was built in the seventh century."

"Most of the structures were burned to the ground during Allied bombings in 1945," he replied. "Perverse poetic justice for the goddess of compassion, wouldn't you say?"

Ancient lore describes two fisherman in the year six hundred twenty-eight A.D. pulling a small golden statue of Kannon out of a river. Out of this treasure grew the magnificent Temple of Sensoji, but the genesis of this holiest of sites in Japan is sequestered out of the public's sight.

Back on the Tokyo Metro the couple headed for the Yoyogi Station, a thirty-minute ride that could take three hours by car to travel the eleven miles separating the Sensoji Temple from the Meiji Shrine.

The Meiji Shrine brilliantly stands in remembrance of the end of Japan's Feudalism and official xenophobia. In 1868 Japan's borders were closed to the outside world. Nobody was allowed in and nobody was permitted to leave. Trade was limited to the Dutch East India Company, who could only dock at the small island of Deshima in Nagasaki Harbor. Emperors had long since lost power in Japan, but the fifteen-year-old new kid on the block, Meiji, translated as the Enlightened Ruler, became synonymous with the new age for Japan. Millions of Japanese descend upon the Meiji Shrine during the New Year holiday. Tradition calls for the purchase of lucky charms, which will bring good fortune in the New Year. Katmandu picked out a pink-and-green Omamori, which protects the holder and brings good luck. Roos went for the Red Dragon.

Walking out, Roos' attention was instantly drawn to a unique structure displaying straw containers of sake. Reading the inscription, Roos learned that the sake is offered as a gift annually to the enshrined deities, Emperor Jingu and Empress Shoken, by the Meiji Jingu Nationwide Sake Brewers Association. After a quick scan, Roos counted out two hundred and eight of the brightly adorned symmetrical containers, each over two feet in height.

After making the short six-block walk from his hotel, Roos arrived at the Ginzo Metro stop at 8:15 P.M. Sakura was already waiting at the top of the escalator. Dressed in a full traditional plum-colored silk kimono sporting pink Japanese Cherry Blossoms, her beauty was breathtaking. Sakura in all her dignity stood as a guidebook chronicling the history of Japan—a poem—whose stanzas weave the fabric of a society bookmarked by exquisiteness and elegance—pain and suffering—like silk threads through her kimono.

As Roos stood silent in her presence, his mind was running like a computer program trying to isolate an instance that had rendered him speechless before. Like a broken slot machine, the reels just kept spinning. Breaking the silence were Masafumi and Koyuki Yamagata who arrived at 8:25 P.M. just in time for the group's 8:30 P.M. reservation.

Punctuality is critically important in Japanese culture, especially to old school purists like Jiro Ono. Unsuspecting customers who rudely show up late for their dinner reservation at Sukiyabashi Jiro, usually find themselves eating somewhere else. The chef has no predetermined response to tardiness, which could get you bounced; rather, the master makes a game time decision, which incorporates factors beyond just the time of arrival. An apology spoken in Japanese probably is a good place to start. But a move that will almost assuredly get you ejected from one of the ten counter seats is photography. Glam photo bombing shots with the chef and his team or the interior of the restaurant are strictly prohibited. The Yamagatas arrived exactly on time. As the foursome was walking down the stairs to the basement-level restaurant, Masafumi quickly advised Roos and Sakura about the unwritten code that should be followed in order to maximize the pleasure of their dining experience.

"I recommend that Koyuki and I sit on the ends, with Christian next to me on the inside and Sakura next to Koyuki. The meal is quick, possibly lasting thirty minutes or less. Jiro will be placing approximately twenty pieces of sushi on our plates, one at a time. Each piece is seasoned to taste and requires no work on our part, leaving us to pick up with chopsticks, if you please, but fingers are the accepted tools of choice here at Jiro. My recommendation is to let Koyuki, Sakura and me handle all communications with the staff in Japanese. Christian, you just sit back and enjoy the show. I presume you are a connoisseur of sushi and that you eat everything. Unless you have an allergy, I would pop every piece in your mouth with a smile. Lastly, don't ask for any soy sauce. It is a pet peeve of Jiro."

"Thanks, Masafumi, how about the bill? Of course, dinner is my treat. Do you want to pay and I will reimburse you?"

Masafumi confirmed Roos' instincts. "Yes, that would be ideal."

And with that rather unusual pregame meal meeting, the four diners entered the restaurant and were greeted by the Japanese word for welcome, *Irasshaimase*. Seated in their prearranged formation, the group received hot towels and menus. Roos noticed the cover inscription:

> Sushi is a very simple, unique Japanese cuisine.
> But it is no use trying to skimp—only a genuine
> professional sushi chef can reach your heart. You will
> appreciate the excellence of the professional
> sushi chefs at Sukiyabashi Jiro. Enjoy fresh seafood of
> the season direct from Tsukiji to your table at Sukiyabashi Jiro.

Regardless of what is served on a given night at Jiro, one thing is for sure: it came from the Tsukiji Fish Market, located in downtown Tokyo. Handling over four hundred different types of seafood, over seven hundred metric tons per year with a monetary value equal to eight billion U.S. dollars makes Tsukiji the largest seafood market in the world. Frenetically paced, wholesalers take an average of only thirty seconds to analyze factors such as oxidation levels, firmness of the meat, eye color and whether the fish was caught in a net or a line, before they make multi-million-dollar bids.

Jiro Ono has identified three techniques, which he follows religiously: firstly, sushi rice must be served at body temperature, secondly, the rice should have a salty vinegar taste and lastly, the different types of fish placed on top of the rice all have different optimal serving temperatures, which are all known to within several decimal points by the master.

Recently in an interview read by Roos, Jiro Ono was asked the secret to life. He responded, "Once you decide on your occupation you must immerse yourself in your work. You have to fall in love with your work. Never complain about your job. You must dedicate your life to mastering your skill. That's the secret of success and the key to being regarded honorably. I've never once hated my job, I fell in love with my work and gave my life to it."

The menus are an unnecessary conventional formality. All patrons must order the chef's daily prix fixe dinner that includes twenty, give or take, pieces of sushi served in blistering fashion. Exceptions are not permitted and certainly no California rolls are served, as a matter of fact no rolls of any kind are served. Just sushi. The drink options are beer or Japanese sake. Tea is served at the end of the meal along with honeydew melon.

A distinguished man with a countenance of accomplishment, Jiro Ono was proudly positioned behind the sushi bar, which surprisingly only had two of the ten counter stools filled. The Roos group brought capacity to six, leaving four prized seats open. When Roos left the restaurant they were still empty, despite several unannounced diners appearing at the front door. Showing up without a reservation is rudeness on an unimaginable scale in the eyes of the sushi master who instructed his maître d' to send them away in a terse manner.

Jiro's eighty-eight-year-old eyes and face lit up when he saw Roos' party pull up to his "operating table." Happy to see Japanese-speaking patrons, of course, but the honor and respect shown by Sakura to appear in her kimono clearly made a demonstrable impact on Jiro. He instantly engaged in a direct conversation with her—language that clearly surprised, evidenced by the look of disbelief emblazoned on her face. Japan is still a man's world. For a man of Jiro's status to shower so much attention onto Sakura was quite a tribute. Roos thought to himself, octogenarian status notwithstanding, the man clearly still had his virile faculties in full working order.

With military precision, the master, along with his fifty-year-old son and his apprentices, prepared to belt out the following twenty-one pieces of sushi in less than thirty minutes:

## Menu

| | |
|---|---|
| Hirame — Halibut | Kuruma Ebi — Boiled Prawns |
| Sumi-ika — White Squid | Sayori — Needlefish |
| Buri — Yellow Tail | Hamaguri — Boiled Clams |
| Akami — Lean Tuna | Saba — Mackerel |
| Chu-Toro — Fatty Tuna | Uni — Sea Urchin |
| O-Toro — Extra Fatty Tuna | Kobashira — Baby Scallops |
| Kama-Toro — Rare Fatty Tuna | Ikura — Salmon Roe |
| Kohada — Gizzard Shad | Anago — Sea Eel |
| Take — Salmon | Tako — Boiled Octopus |
| Akagai — Ark Shell | Tamago — Egg |
| Aji — Jack Mackerel | |

Before Jiro Ono served the first course of his famed toro trilogy, the sushi master, with a wink and a wry smile, which twisted his taut facial skin around the corners of his mouth and fierce eyes, launched into an impassioned discourse. Diminutive size and age notwithstanding, Jiro commanded strict attention from his staff and patrons alike. His countenance may have been more imperious while addressing his apprentices than the paying customers, but both constituencies knew that important information was being conveyed and froze accordingly, as they stood at attention, hanging on every syllable. As his last native language word traversed the prodigious but strangely stark counter, Sakura, observing Christian's look of wonder, leaned in closely to him and said, "Jiro was describing the three underbelly toro cuts he will be serving: chu-toro located near the tail, o-toro, dead center and kama-toro up by the collar bone. Deeper the water, the colder the temperature, therefore he said the fat content is greater on the underbelly and increases from the tail up to the head for maximum brain warmth."

Roos, nodding affirmatively, whispered, "I have always thought that a frigid mind was no good, in a sense, the ultimate turnoff. Nothing like a fire in one's belly to meet new friends and make things happen. Was that all he said?"

Laughing under her breath, Sakura responded, "He said judging from your physique, your intelligence must only be surpassed by your toasty thermal reading."

The indomitable Jiro, who effortlessly shrugged off a cigarette-induced heart attack at age seventy, despite lacking English language skills, looked at the couple and gave a nod of understanding. The glance was a smart one, accompanied by an enlightened demeanor, crafted and honed from cumulative observations gleaned betwixt a golden and diamond jubilee. Only apparent in person, if he chose to show you, one could witness the playful child trying to emerge from the nethermost part of his stone-faced persona.

Roos was quite familiar with the quality of chu-toro served in American-based Japanese restaurants, the latest craze in the food-obsessed nation, which were opening at a rate approaching smartphone app growth. He marveled at the difference in what lay before him. The fish shined in a brilliant rose color with a slinky texture and bodacious marbling resembling the finest rocks from a Rosa quarry in Alentejo, Portugal. Or did the fatty crevices look more like foamy sea water runoff cutting through the twinkling pink sand on Bermuda's mile-long Elbow Beach? Roos wasn't sure, nor did he care as he placed the oversized piece of sushi, nestled on painfully and religiously worked rice, into his mouth. The indigenous sticky rice was harvested from the bountiful paddies abundant in Nara Prefecture, delivered by an exclusive Jiro supplier and ultimately cooked by apprentices who toil with the unique short translucent grains — exclusively for ten years — before they matriculate to preparing fish, but only if they make the cut. Becoming an artisan or craftsman, referred to as a *shokunin* in Japan, transcends mere technical skills. The essence delves far deeper, requiring an attitude and social consciousness on the part of the practitioner, which is both spiritual and material in nature resulting in a life dedicated to the pursuit of perfection.

As he consumed the rich taste of the chu-toro, Roos could not help but draw the correlation between maguro, the lean tuna cut, and filet mignon. Possessing deceptively impeccable attractiveness, each cut sorely lacked a profound taste, in a manner similar to a premier wine consumed before its time. A 2010 Latour will be magisterial in 2030, but today an impatient drinker of the vintage will be left feeling decidedly vacuous. Toro, the bone-in ribeye of the sea, has a funky appearance, which at first glance appears sinewy, completely belying its heavenly flavor. Regardless of the cut, Roos' internal thoughts confirmed that the aquadynamic torpedo-shaped bluefin tuna with its retractable fins, had indeed come a long way from the days when it was deemed unworthy for human consumption. Just several decades ago, toro was considered too disgusting to be eaten. Prior to the twentieth century no self-respecting Japanese person would consume any part of the fish at all, earning tuna the disparaging name *gezakana*, which literally translates as "inferior fish." Quite a migration indeed for the tenacious predator. Recently a bluefin sold for a record one million eight hundred thousand dollars, a staggering price, which works out to just over three thousand per pound, or twenty bucks a bite. Spurred on by the flavor and his thoughts of the tuna's rise to epicurean prominence, Roos turned to Sakura and said, "One man's trash is another's treasure."

Shiori responded, "If present trends continue, bluefin tuna will soon be neither, it will be reduced to man's memory."

Jiro's next course presented with a paler cameo-pink color and accordion-shaped vibrant white oily lines, cut so deep the sushi appeared as if it may fall apart upon touch. As Roos' anxious fingers cupped the serving, as if holding an injured chickadee, and popped the o-toro sushi into his mouth, he instantly experienced the unique sirloin feel of the tuna, which fused with the fatty tissue generating a delectably rich and creamy sensation. The significance of the derivation of the Japanese word for the cut, *torori* meaning "melts in your mouth," hit home with the toro aficionado—instantaneously. A Houdinish feeling of evaporating flesh going down his throat left only the chef's signature extra-vinegar-marinated rice remaining as the food raced toward his stomach.

The Holy Ghost of Jiro's trinity, kama-toro, an extremely rare cut representing well less than one percent of the fish, looked like a magnificent piece of Kobe beef from the Tajima strain of Wagyu cattle grazing the lush grass fields of the Hyogo Prefecture. Relishing in the higher blood flow to the area of the body, which is closer to the gills, the darker and firmer cut produced an intensely concentrated taste. Hints of raw meat permeated throughout the luscious and velvety savor, creating a culinary juxtaposition leaving Roos in a bewildering satiated state. The texture, significantly less dematerializing, allowed for a longer and more constant flavor. The saltiness from the pinch of soy sauce and rice vinegar combined with the buttery tuna flesh to create a complex semi-sweet finish, which dillydallied in Roos' palate for a seemingly never-ending glorious fifteen seconds.

Sakura, sensing Roos' state of euphoria, solicited a review of the kama-toro. Roos responded ever so quietly, "A brilliant and equally unusual example of the mysterious taste known as *umami.* The rice would give it away, but a blindfolded taste test with kama-toro sashimi would unquestionably yield interesting observations from perplexed, but happy participants who would be, figuratively and quite possibly literally, begging for more."

Sakura acknowledged but added, "Blindfolds wouldn't work here in Tokyo. And by the way, most Japanese have rejected the attempt by the world to label *umami* as the fifth taste after sweet, sour, bitter and salty. The true meaning of the word transcends the baseness of physical parameters, such as taste no matter how sophisticated the pallet, and takes on a cultural and philosophical significance here in Japan, firmly rooted in Zen Buddhism and the Shinto religion."

Roos asked for elaboration.

Sakura obliged, "Manufacturers of monosodium glutamate, or what is commonly referred to as MSG, would love to usurp the flavor enhancing properties of glutamic acids. After all what does meat taste like? The Western world needs to be told and MSG marketers would love to tell you. We here believe in the kangi, the equivalent of Latin roots, which tells us that umami means 'beautiful taste.' It is hard to translate the totality of the essence of the meaning into English. But food is considered umami when it reaches its peak of quality and fulfillment. Representing the best which nature can offer; the food touches most of our senses, sight, smell, touch and taste, awakens positive emotions and augurs positive outcomes. Christian, toro is a supreme example of happiness."

With the epic tasting flight complete, it took all he could muster, combined with an authoritarian look from Sakura, to resist the urge to ask for a round-trip. Instead he bowed to Jiro from his low-back counter chair and said, "I'd like to buy the world a toro."

Jiro smiled and said, "Food is subsistence, it shouldn't take long to consume."

The best sushi experience of his life lasted less than five minutes—but felt like a hedonistic eternity.

The bill for four came to one hundred thirty thousand Japanese yen, or approximately one thousand three hundred U.S. dollars. Four Sapporo beers and four glasses of sake came to ten thousand Japanese yen, leaving the food at one hundred twenty thousand. Roos' mathematic focused mind quickly calculated the cost per piece of sushi to be fourteen U.S. dollars and forty dollars per minute. Roos thought it would be difficult to burn through that kind of cash that quickly even at Jiggles in New York City. The entire meal cost three hundred thirty-six dollars per person, tip included, of course. There are possibly worse things you could do in a high end restaurant like Sukiyabashi Jiro than leave a tip, but it would take a creative mind to come up with what that would be.

The foursome bowed to Jiro and walked into the Tokyo night. Roos peeled off thirteen Benjamins and forced them into his reluctant friend's Marlboro Red–busy hands. "Well, Christian, what did you think?"

"Jiro touched my heart. Best toro I have ever tasted. Especially enjoyed the extremely rare kama pieces, which are located near the head. The marbling was tremendous. Every piece on the menu, pleasurably but painfully, set a new quality bar, which unfortunately has now ruined me for life from a sushi perspective. The greats in every field are defined by simplicity and focus. Steve Jobs preached this concept building Apple into the largest company in the world. Distilling complicated concepts into understandable products, which scream ease of use, is the formula for mega success in business and life. Imagine Jiro's people walking through the massive Tsukiji fish market everyday. Focused like a laser beam, Jiro's buyers are able to compartmentalize and block out the mania, allowing them to accomplish their mission of securing the absolute best quality seafood for their specific menu. The chaos to order transition, which takes a whole tuna on an auction floor from the fish market to the ten-seat counter proudly sitting atop Jiro's magnificent rice, is a magisterial beauty. Jiro is a genius. Best sushi meal I have ever had, bar none. Thank you for arranging the reservation. My flight is quite early tomorrow, so I must be heading back to the hotel."

Roos walked Sakura to a nearby taxi stand. As the car door opened, Roos released her hand from his, looked into her eyes and gave her a hug and a kiss on the cheek. It was all he felt was appropriate—for the first time in his life – it was all he wanted. Roos was mesmerized by the foreign woman in a kimono, whose dignity trumped his lust—something he had never experienced before—but wished he had. She smiled, thanked him and delivered a transfixing abracadabra: "Will I see you again?"

Roos, composed himself, held her tightly in his arms and softly spoke, "If I can make it to Winged Foot Golf Club by noon tomorrow, the answer is yes."

There existed enough of a language barrier for his fairy-tale comment to fascinate her into a peaceful state of mind, body and spirit. As the cab drove off through the Tokyo streets brimming with cars and people, Roos stood motionless and watched until she was out of sight—just as she had done in New York City. In the back of the cab a spellbound Sakura googled the Winged Foot Golf Club. The first image to appear on her iPhone was the Club's logo, displaying a pair of feet with wings attached at the ankles.

Grounded in ancient mythology from Greece and Rome, the Winged Foot logo represents Mercury, the Roman god of commerce adopted from the Greek god Hermes, born into cult status in southern Italy circa 500 B.C. Described as possessing fleet feet, grace, wisdom and happy guise, Mercury would also become the god of science, eloquence, the arts and the patron of travelers. Upon his appointment as the messenger of gods on account of his quickness, Mercury was presented with his defining attribute, winged sandals called *talaria*, which endowed him with great speed of motion. Along with his *petasus*, a winged hat, wherever called upon by his fellow gods, Mercury would arrive in a flash.

A broad, satisfied smile engulfed Sakura's face. What better person to send me this message than Mercury the messenger god and patron of travelers himself, she thought. The cab driver could hear a faint sound in the back of his vehicle—a beautifully sweet sound, "Fly, Christian Roos, fly."

Back at the hotel, Roos sent his final text to Frank: "Day 24 about over. Arrive tomorrow at JFK and then on to The Foot and journey's end."

An enraged Alexei Romanov was barreling down the FDR Expressway toward the Brooklyn Bridge in his black Mercedes S550. With his over-sized hands gripping the vehicle's steering wheel, the driver could see and feel his pulse surging though his body. His mind was abuzz as to the possibilities concerning his enterprising nemesis who was turning out to be extremely difficult to eliminate. Romanov's suspicions were proved correct when his contact in Japan confirmed that Roos had in fact checked into the Tokyo Peninsula Hotel. Still in need of absolute proof, Romanov demanded his associate secure a photograph of Roos. When the image hit his phone, Romanov knew he had been foiled again by the elusive Roos. At this point, Romanov was hellbent on making sure the third time was a charm for the clients of Vengeance Capital—and of course himself.

The early morning sun was glistening off the East River as the hedge fund maven crossed the iconic bridge. He continued south onto Clinton Avenue in the heart of the Carroll Gardens section of Brooklyn. His destination was the restaurant Sicilian Slice for an impromptu meeting with the owner Baldassario "Boom" Bamonte. Once a mob stronghold brimming with social clubs, Carroll Gardens had experienced a life-changing transformation. Led by the yuppies, Carroll Gardens has become a bedroom community for the high finance players on Wall Street. But there were a few holdouts, as there always are, and Bamonte was one of them and proud of it.

Nicknamed "Boom" on account of his skill in designing and deploying bombs, Bamonte's expertise was in IEDs, an acronym for Improvised Exploding Devices.

Romanov found Boom in the back kitchen making Sicilian Slice's homemade pasta of the day, ravioli, which with the help of his female sous chefs, he was planning to stuff with a mixture of veal, spinach and parmigiano-reggiano.

After asking Boom to excuse the staff, Romanov skipped any perfunctory chitchat and got right down to business, "Boom, I need you to arrange a hit."

Boom's response was unconditional. "You know I will do anything for you. What are the details?"

Ever since Romanov used his deep connections with the mayor of New York City to have Boom's sentence for murder commuted, Bamonte was forever indebted to his friend.

Romanov explained, "The target's name is Christian Roos. He is landing at JFK tomorrow morning at 7:30 A.M. on a flight from Tokyo. From the airport he will be driving immediately to the Winged Foot Golf Club in Mamaroneck. I need you to take his vehicle out before it reaches the club."

As he clapped his flour-covered hands producing a gust of white powder, Boom replied, "Consider it done."

Romanov handed Boom a brown paper bag containing a quarter of a million dollars and said, "The other half will be hand delivered by me upon successful completion of the job. I will be personally witnessing the burn."

Boom matter-of-factly asked, "Any spot along the route from JFK to Winged Foot that you would suggest?"

"Yes," answered Romanov. "But first the key is to have one of your associates identify Roos' vehicle as it departs JFK."

Boom shot back, "Of course. I have just the man for the job. My cousin Romero works as a skycap in Terminal 7, you know, the international one. Come to think of it, the IED could be placed in Roos' luggage at the carousel."

"Too risky." Romanov's answer came in the midst of a whirlwind of mental calculations. Continuing, he said, "Airport security would most likely detect the presence of an exploding device, and if not, the canines surely would. The route will take Roos north on the Van Wyck Expressway, which turns into the Hutchinson River Parkway after crossing the East River on the Bronx-Whitestone Bridge."

Placing his large hands flat onto the flour-covered table, Romanov leaned in closely and said, "Listen carefully, Boom. This whack has to occur between the bridge and the intersection of the Hutch and Interstate 95. This half-mile stretch extends the length of Ferry Point Park. Depending upon traffic, drivers heading to The Foot either stay on the Hutch leading to the club's north gate on Old Plain White Road or exit onto 195 North to the Fenimore Road south gate. Essentially, it is a coin toss as to which road Roos will take. I have too much money at stake to risk such a gamble."

Busy pinching freshly stuffed ravioli squares, Boom offered an interesting scheme, "How about the bridge? Surely through your relationship with the mayor you can refer me to contacts within the MTA Bridges and Tunnels. As you know, the suspension bridge has tollbooths for traffic heading in each direction on the north side. I can place someone who will be able to affix an IED on the underbelly of the car when they go through the tolls. A planned distraction, caused by another plant, will serve as the opportunity."

Romanov grinned. "I can't take the chance of relying on someone else. You need to plant the IED. You are the best in the business."

Uncharacteristically Boom launched into a personal line of questioning. "Alexei, this is not really any of my business, but this is quite an aggressive plan with clear risks for you. What did this Roos guy do to you?"

Romanov fired back, "It is just about money."

Boom responded, "Don't you have enough of that by now?"

The Russian, becoming agitated at his longtime enforcer, said, "He cheated me, and I need to settle the score."

Boom acquiesced. "So be it. Sorry for the questions. I will use an ammonium nitrate and fuel (ANFO) bomb with a rapid controlled IED (RCIED) rigged up to a cell phone. You might recall that an ANFO was the type used in the Oklahoma City terrorist attack."

Signaling the tipping point, Romanov replied, "I will be the one to make the cell phone call. What is the range?"

Without looking up from his ravioli, Boom answered, "Well, this is not an exact science, especially on twenty-four hours' notice. But the short answer is the closer the better. Approximately three hundred yards past the tollbooths there is a truck pull-off station. You should park there and the trigger point will be when the target vehicle has passed your location by fifty yards."

Romanov nodded his head in approval, turned and walked out of Sicilian Slice. Pulling out his phone, the deep-pocketed hedge fund star with indebted friends in high places called New York City's most powerful government official and one of the most popular politicians in America, Mayor Georgio Giordano.

Romanov, uncharacteristically deferential and pleased to hear his close friend's voice, said, "Mr. Mayor. How does this beautiful morning find the Big Apple's favorite son?"

The mayor, laughing, responded, "That depends upon the purpose of this call."

Romanov cut to the chase. "I need access for one of my associates on the Bronx-Whitestone tomorrow from 8:00 A.M. until noon. His name is Baldassario Bamonte."

The mayor grumbled, "How could I forget Boom, your buddy I sprung from Rikers."

"Thank you again, Mr. Mayor. He is a reformed citizen because of your generosity."

Snapping, the mayor barked, "Cut the bullshit, Alexei. Boom will have access. But I can't afford any PR nightmares from traffic delays. My friend over in New Jersey, Governor Sotheby, is still being skewered over the lane closings on I95. They are simply crushing him in the press and the Dems aren't exactly keeping quiet either. Understand?"

Romanov, with a straight face, commented, "You have my word."

Hanging up the phone, the mayor simply grumbled at the disingenuous honor proffered by the earth-vexing crook-pated figure he had come to know so well. "I am starting to not like the types of people I must deal with in my business."

# 20

## Homecoming

*"Every traveler has a home of his own, and he learns to appreciate it the more from his wandering."*

—CHARLES DICKENS

On day twenty-five of the trip, Roos and Kat were booked on Asian Airlines flight nine seventy scheduled to depart from Tokyo's Narita Airport at 8 A.M. and to arrive at New York's John F. Kennedy Airport, the same day at 7:30 A.M.

At 3 A.M. in Tokyo, after just several hours of sleep, Roos hurriedly typed out his final daily WhatsApp update: "Frank, Love Japan. Clicked off the last two sites here in Tokyo last night. I have all thirty on Instagram and Vimeo. Departing for Narita Airport in fifteen minutes. If everything goes as planned, we will land at JFK at 7:30 A.M. today. Of course you can check online with the airline for status updates. Should be at The Foot by 10 A.M., two hours before the noon deadline. Tell Mac and the Judge that you and I will challenge them to a four-ball match. Lunch first, followed by pegs in the ground at 1 P.M. CR"

Roos' mind was racing through time calculations. He knew from memory that the distance from JFK to The Foot, via the Van Wyck Expressway and either the Hutch or I95 depending on the traffic, was exactly twenty-eight and a half miles. Either portion would be favorably against the regular morning commute into the city, but the ten-mile stretch on the Van Wyck, crossing Queens, would hit smack into the heart of traffic headed into the city from Long Island. With no traffic the trip is forty-five minutes, maximum. Roos thought that in tomorrow's morning rush hour the trip would likely average ninety minutes. Continuing his backward calculation, Roos estimated that a departure from JFK no later than 10:15 A.M. by car would be mandatory.

The non-stop trans-Pacific flight covers the 5,843 nautical miles in twelve hours and thirty-five minutes, at an average speed of four hundred and sixty-four nautical miles per hour. Flying against the Jet Stream, the return flight from JFK to Tokyo takes fourteen hours and ten minutes, roughly twelve and a half percent longer. Roos thought this math all made sense, based upon the Jet Stream's fifty-mile-per-hour average speed, which equated to approximately twelve percent of the average aircraft speed. However, he knew the Jet Stream, which circled the globe from west to east in virtually a straight line, could kick her heels up and generate speeds upwards of two hundred and fifty miles per hour. Recalling an interview with Dr. Jennifer Francis of Rutgers University, Roos knew that global warming was wrecking havoc with the Jet Stream. Dr. Francis blamed Hurricane Sandy, May snowstorms, June temperatures in McGrath, Alaska, swinging from ninety four to fifteen degrees Fahrenheit in days and the dust bowl drought in the North Great Plains on the changing Jet Stream. As he explained this dynamic to Kat, who was buried in Japanese tea and miso soup, she asked, "Christian, does that explain why the timing of east to west air travel is more variable than the west to east?"

Roos answered, "Regardless of which way you are circling the globe, airplanes and their passengers are vulnerable to the vagaries of the Jet Stream."

"Yes, yes. However, if you are going east to west the Jet Stream kicking up to two hundred and fifty miles per hour is going to have a disproportionally larger impact on average speed than if the wind speed drops to zero on an easterly heading. The Jet Stream is not going to reverse, is it, Christian?" Kat was sounding like a high school student who just caught the mathematic teacher with his pants down, figuratively speaking.

Roos grinned. "Never thought of the concept in those terms, beauty and brains, touché!"

Riding the moment, Kat usurped Roos' mental HP12C. "If the Jet Stream takes the day off today, it will slow our average speed by roughly twelve percent, adding ninety minutes to our flight. Worst case, assuming the pilot doesn't try to make up lost time by pressing on the throttle, we will land at Kennedy at 9 A.M. instead of 7:30 A.M. Going through customs and waiting for luggage should take an hour maximum, which puts us in the car by 10 A.M., a fifteen-minute 'margin of safety' as measured against your 10:15 A.M. deadline. Isn't that what your hero, Warren Buffett, always talks about?"

Roos laughed hysterically at her mental jumping jacks in the middle of the Tokyo night. "What if the flight is delayed?"

"There's always AirJets. But at this point, Christian, our fate is in someone else's hands." Finishing her tea, Kat commanded, "Let's get moving."

Roos' knew there were only four aircraft in the AirJets fleet that could complete a non-stop flight from Tokyo to New York: the Gulfstream G550 and G650, and the Bombardier 6000 and 7000 Global Express, all of which would not make the trip for less than a quarter of a million dollars, before the fruit and cheese plate. Juicing on Ambien, Roos wholeheartedly preferred his seven hundred fifty dollar coach seat, complete with bottled water, a toothbrush, slippers, and two hundred forty-nine thousand two hundred fifty in savings.

Fractional aircraft ownership was a concept that always puzzled him. After years of listening to socialite babble on the subject at cocktail parties, he concluded that the AirJets of the world were the poster child for a long-held principle he followed in his investment career. Business margins are inversely related to the intelligence of the customers. How else can one explain consumers paying a premium for fractional aircraft ownership, which exceeds both of the other options, chartering and outright ownership? The premium can exceed twice the charter rate and three times the cost of ownership. Sure there is a convenience factor, but Roos could neither quantify nor justify it.

"Kat, too late for AirJets, besides this trip has already cost enough, and the thought of dropping another quarter of a million is, well, just too nauseating."

"Arguably the stupidest words ever to come out of your mouth." Kat was in no mood to mince words. "Don't forget I stand to earn two million dollars."

Roos knew that it could be the single most glaring example of being "penny wise and pound foolish" since British Petroleum, running weeks behind schedule and tens of millions of dollars over budget in trying to complete its troubled Macondo well in the Gulf of Mexico, took many financial shortcuts which contributed to spilling five million barrels of oil into the Gulf of Mexico, the largest pollution disaster in United States history.

The Boeing 777, carrying the passengers on Asian Airlines flight nine seventy, touched down at JFK thirty minutes late on runway 13R-31L—at ten thousand feet it was one of the longest in North America.

"Wake up, Christian." Kat was shaking her travel partner.

His blue eyes opening like a chickadee's on a spring morning, Roos still felt the effects of twenty-five milligrams of Ambien. With a yawn he exclaimed, "Have not slept that well since my colonoscopy was administered with the heaven on earth anesthetic, Propofol. I can see how the King of Pop became hooked on the stuff. How was the jet stream blowing, baby?"

Kat, despite being up all night, still could spit out a logical answer, "Given the fact that we were thirty minutes or four percent late, I would say forty-eight miles per hour."

As the pair inched forward in the immigration line, Roos noticed four individuals, three men and a woman, dressed in official uniforms and sporting handcuffs and Glock pistols. The foursome, accompanied by two Belgian Malinios detection canines, appeared to be focusing intently on Roos and Mandu. As the pair approached the green light at booth number thirteen, one of the officials, in an authoritarian manner, stated, "My name is Agent Tim Bell. I am with Homeland Security. Are you Christian Roos? Is your traveling partner Katherine Mandu?"

"Yes" was Roos' clearly concerned response.

"You will need to come with us," instructed Agent Bell.

The four agents, two dogs, Kat and Roos all proceeded through a side door, down a long corridor, which had a door on the right side only, about every fifteen feet. Finally stopping at one, the female agent, along with one of the male agents and a dog, escorted Kat into the room. As Agent Bell motioned for Roos to keep walking, Roos peered into the room and saw three blank walls, a steel-top desk with one chair on the side facing the door and two chairs on the opposite side.

Agent Bell led Roos into the next room and seated him facing the door.

Peeling through Roos' passport, looking like Agatha Christie's fictional detective Hercule Poirot, Homeland Security Agent Tim Bell read off, "Mexico, Cuba, Peru, Brazil, Italy, Turkey, Iran, Israel, Saudi Arabia, Afghanistan, India, Nepal, Hong Kong, China, North Korea and Japan. All in twenty-five days. My oh my, Mr. Roos, would you care to explain the nature of your rather extraordinary travels?"

Roos just could not resist. "How did you know I was in Afghanistan? My passport was not stamped in that lovely country on account of our emergency landing."

Agent Bell, "We know everything, it is our job. Now answer the question, Mr. Roos."

Roos, clearly irritated, played with fire. "Well, if you know everything, why the questions?"

At this moment, Agent Bell had to be restrained by his partner from approaching Roos, who was seated on the other side of the steel-top desk.

"Okay calm down," said Roos. "Obviously I am exhausted. Please accept my apology for the facetious remark. The nature of my travels is easily explainable—it was a wager. Please do not take this the wrong way, as I, with total respect, state that surely you must have read about my bet with Charles MacCormick. The story has been reported in the media, quite extensively." Glancing at his iPhone, which indicated the time to be 8:30 A.M., Roos continued, "How long do you anticipate this is going to take, and by the way, what exactly is this?"

"We need to ask you some questions," said Bell.

"Well let's get on with it."

"Who is Katherine Mandu?" asked Bell.

"A very close friend of mine from Washington, D.C."

Agent Bell, "A romantic friend?"

Roos, "On a trip around the world, is there another kind?"

Agent Bell, "How long have you known her?"

Roos, "A few years."

"Where did she live before D.C.?" Bell asked.

Roos, "Kathmandu, Nepal."

Agent Bell, "How do you know that information?"

Roos, "She told me."

Agent Bell then asked, "During the past twenty-five days, was Ms. Mandu ever out of your physical presence?"

"We were certainly not handcuffed together," Roos said. "Well at least not for long. We were apart on a daily basis, similar to any other normal opposite sex couple traveling together."

"Mr. Roos, we know about your capture in Afghanistan," Bell told him.

"Oh yes, please forgive me, your omnipotence provisionally escaped me," Roos shot back. "Yes, of course we were apart for a period of approximately three days while I was being held captive by some rather inhospitable characters in Lashkar Gah, Afghanistan. A little head's up in case you find yourself in that position, refrain from referring to Afghanistan. It is a meaningless term, which, to date, has eluded the Pushtan's lexicon. The hierarchy in that part of the world dictated for thousands of years by the Pashtunwali is tribe, honor and then family. Hence no passport stamps."

"Are you surprised she stayed behind for you?" asked Bell.

"I may not be the dumbest guy in the world when it comes to understanding the female mind, but I am certainly in the top one hundred. However, even I can answer that question with virtual certitude. She stands to earn a two-million-dollar fee if we make it together to Winged Foot," Roos, looking at his iPhone, continued, "by noon.

Gentlemen, it all about the Benjamins, and don't ever forget it. Can I go now?"

Agent Bell, "We have reason to believe that Ms. Mandu is an international enemy spy."

"Oh for God's sake, I have had enough of this bullshit. I want a lawyer. Can I make a phone call?"

"Who do you want to call?" Bell asked.

At this point, a third agent entered the room, announcing that Roos' luggage was clean.

Roos answered, "My lawyer, Kevin Kinsale. I think I am entitled."

Agent Bell, "Not exactly. The Homeland Security Act of 2002 allows for the detention of persons of interest, like you, ungoverned and unprotected by the United States Constitution. But you can call your lawyer, if you wish."

Before Roos could hit Kinsale's number on his speed dial, a fourth gentleman entered the room. Looking infinitely more sophisticated and important than the two Homeland Security Agents, the man handed a note to Bell and announced, "Agent Bell, please let Mr. Roos leave immediately. Mr. Roos, welcome back to the United States. Please accept our apologies for any inconvenience which we have caused."

"What about my travel companion, Ms. Mandu?" Roos asked.

The stone-jawed man, dressed in a three-piece dark suit, with a white shirt and blood red tie, said, "She has been released as well."

Joining Kat outside of U.S. Customs, Roos let out a huge sigh of relief that turned into one of the biggest smiles of his life as they approached the luggage carousel. The cause for his emotion was the sight of his friend Ryan O'Dowd.

"Can't tell you how great it is to see you, Ryan. Obviously you got my message."

Ryan gave his friend Roos a bear hug and laughed. "Why yes, I did. So glad you were able to extricate yourself from Afghanistan. Another day and the insurance company was going to send us in. I understand you are in quite a hurry to get to Winged Foot. But please when we have some time together, I want to hear the boopdiddley."

Since Ryan retired as the leader of SEAL Team Six he spent his time between giving motivational speeches and working as an extraction expert for a major insurance company. As one of the most highly decorated combat veterans of all time, O'Dowd was deployed over ten times on more than three hundred combat missions — in the most dangerous theaters in the darkest corners of the globe — without ever losing a team member. "It would be my pleasure. I can't thank you enough for the secure ride up to the Foot. A whole bunch of cash is hanging in the balance on whether we can make it to Mamaroneck by noon." O'Dowd's partner, Mark Jackson, loaded the luggage into the back of the black Suburban with tinted bulletproof windows, then jumped into the shotgun seat. Kat and Roos sat in the middle seat. O'Dowd grabbed the wheel, turned the ignition key and sped off.

"Don't sweat the load, Christian, in my world this is leave. If anyone decides to mess with us, they will experience Alpha Mike Foxtrot. Right, Mark? In case you were concerned, you will be pleased to learn this vehicle is equipped with the DOD's latest safety gizmos."

As O'Dowd raised the four-inch-thick steel partition between the middle seat and the rear of the vehicle, he began to explain the installed features. "The undercarriage, roof and all sides of the vehicle have an interior layer composed of four-inch-thick Kevlar, a powerful lightweight material able to withstand quite a blast. Not to say the vehicle is impenetrable, but an IED or RPG will have to work hard to get inside. Too bad this technology is so expensive and costly to transport. It would have saved many lives and limbs over in Iraq and Afghanistan. I am sure you are unfortunately aware that roadside IEDs are the leading cause of casualties in these two campaigns. Over three thousand American men and woman have lost their lives to the villainous contraption, while thousands more have been disabled. The windows are laced with bulletproof glass strong enough to deflect an AK47 firing from close range. Other features include oxygen tanks, food and water supply and even a life raft. The bloody thing can even be submerged in up to a hundred feet of water, completely airtight."

O'Dowd's words fell silent on Roos, a man who had spent the majority of his career battling equity valuations and artless performance benchmarks. His eyes were fixated on the Colt M4A1 carbine—barrel skyward—sitting between O'Dowd and Jackson in the front seat. Weighing just under six pounds, the thirty-three-inch truncated version of the M16A2 was the weapon of choice for Navy SEALs in close quarter battle.

"I have no doubt in you. By the way, please say hello to Katherine Mandu."

"Pleased to meet you, miss."

From the car, which departed JFK at the stroke of 10:00 A.M., Roos called Harrison. "Frank, did you make the 1 P.M. tee time?"

Harrison, clearly perturbed, said, "Don't joke with me, where are you?"

Roos screamed, "On the Wyck! See you in less than an hour. How did we end up our trading in the RoosCaboose?"

Harrison, toggling into his trader mode, boomed in his New York Italian accent, "Crushed it. Started small, then went long size, when the shit hit the fan in, er, what was that country again, Pashitan? Our joint account at Springer and Waldron ended up with a forty million profit. The three funds I brought into the syndicate all sold up fifty percent on the first day and then came back in for size. Too funny. Word on the Street is that Vengeance Capital lost over a bil. The Hawk played Romanov badly, just toyed with him like road kill. Talk is that your Afghani poppy pal inked over five hundred million on you, CR! Good news, though, Mac flipped his position as well and made off with a nice profit. Speaking of Mac, rumor has it that he had his old partner at Springer and Waldron, Carl Strange, tailing you around the world. Strange has gone crickets since North Korea. Need to debrief on that as well. A win-win, my friend, well done. I spoke with the Hawk today, the contract is settling tomorrow. We need to go deep into some serious Frenchie and Italian reds at dinner tomorrow at Ruby's Bar and

Grille. Can't wait to hear the stories. I am sure you met some new female friends along the way." Harrison always held a keen interest in CR's love interests.

"So much to discuss," Roos replied.

Kat's obvious indifference to the proceedings at the airport intrigued Roos. He knew what a cool cat she was but her reaction was abnormal to say the least, especially after an all night twelve-hour flight on the heels of circumnavigating the world in twenty-five days. Most average women would not have lasted a week. Laughing, Roos envisioned his lovely ex-wife and her predictable flummoxed reaction to such an asinine adventure. But then again, Roos knew Kat was far from average, a "fat tail" so and certainly no ex-wife.

"Kat, you will love this. The gentleman questioning me from Homeland Security, Agent Bell, clearly a man who has been reading too many espionage books, thought you were an international enemy spy!"

Kat's demeanor spontaneously changed with the speed and intensity of Mount Everest weather. The woman he had spent most of the last month with suddenly looked mysterious to Roos, as he continued, "Well, what do you think of that?"

The woman who was born in the foothills of the Himalayan Mountains, an expert in the ancient art of yoga, and who possessed uncanny coordination and physical skills, an immense intelligence and strong discipline, not to mention stunning beauty, simply responded, "Christian, if it is okay with you, I will skip the victory lunch. I don't want to distract from your moment in the sun. I will forward my bank wiring instructions for the two million dollars. Please feel free to deduct travel expenses."

Understanding, but naturally disappointed, Roos begrudgingly acquiesced to his dear Kat's request. "Of course, baby. When will I see you again?"

With tears dripping from her endearing eyes, vaulting off her high cheekbones like liquid Norwegian ski jumpers, Kat, uncharacteristically vulnerable, in a solemn voice, one foreign to Roos, said, "I think I am finally ready to go see my father."

Leaning in, she tilted her head and kissed Christian with meaning and passion unfamiliar to the man who had just had the time of his crazy life.

Pulling away she whispered into his right ear, "Ma Tapailai Maya Garchu."

As planned, Romanov's Mercedes S550 was parked in the truck stop located through the north tollbooth on the Bronx-Whitestone Bridge. An anxious yet confident Romanov was sitting behind the wheel with a look of resoluteness as he surveyed the scene. Clear skies and calm would be soon supplanted by billowing smoke and chaotic gridlock.

Dressed in an official MTA supervisor uniform, Boom was positioned in the sixth tollbooth from the right in a row that totaled twelve lanes, a strategic vantage point that would allow easy and quick access to any lane chosen by O'Dowd.

As O'Dowd steered the Suburban across the Bronx-Whitestone Bridge, traffic was noticeably light. The delay at JFK customs had caused the travelers to miss the peak rush-hour traffic. O'Dowd eased forward toward the eighth E-ZPass lane from the right side of the road, just two down from where Boom sat inside a booth.

Ensconced in the MTA office, one of Boom's assistants cut the power to the computer system for all twelve of the northbound toll lanes. With all of the tollbooths and E-ZPass lanes inactivated, the modest lines waiting to cross the bridge began increasing, as did tensions—especially inside of Roos' vehicle. O'Dowd instructed Jackson, "Mark, this feels off to me. Keep your eyes peeled. If this is a body snatch we need to be prepared to E and E."

"Roger that, buddy." Mark continued, "Let me take a quick look around."

O'Dowd, "Good idea. While you are out, make sure we are not carrying any limpets."

Jackson circled the vehicle—twice—looking under both the front and back sections of the Suburban. Afterwards he made his way down the row of toll lanes inspecting the cars waiting in line for suspicious-looking individuals, ones he had developed a skill for detecting during his multiple tours of duty.

Seeing Jackson two lanes down, Boom burst into action. Deploying a textbook commando move, Boom exited the booth, hit the deck and proceeded to barrel roll underneath the Suburban, with his hands about his head clutching his homemade IED. Boom's last turn landed the bomb specialist on his back.

As he hopped back into the vehicle, Jackson reported, "All clear."

Seeing Boom in position, Romanov signaled to his accomplice stationed inside of the MTA offices to reboot the toll computer systems. Suddenly, and just as quickly as the system had closed down, the toll lanes and E-ZPass gates came back online. O'Dowd, seeing instantly that everything was back in working order and unaccustomed to and made nervous by unanticipated delays, barked to no one in particular, "Let's go."

With the Suburban on the move, Boom flipped the IED's activation switch and placed the magnetic death ball on the Suburban's undercarriage, slightly missing his intended target—the vehicle's center. Boom was forced to settle for the rear axle.

Romanov watched Boom duck into a tollbooth and the Suburban starting to roll. As the vehicle proceeded northbound on the Wyck Expressway, O'Dowd's suspicious and highly trained military mind, honed through decades of experience in dangerous situations around the globe, locked in on Romanov's vehicle.

"What do you make of that black Mercedes parked up a quarter of a click on our right side?"

Jackson laughed. "Most likely waiting for his mistress."

As the Suburban passed, the Russian mobster turned hedge fund superstar initiated his first billion-dollar phone call. After Romanov hit the last 0, the signal made its way to the activated IED—by now located less than four hundred feet away—in two seconds.

The explosion lifted the read end of the Suburban almost straight into the air. Airborne, the vehicle split into two at the rear axle. The remaining two tires separated from the expressway's asphalt surface as the vehicle entered an aerial forward roll. Continuing up and onward, the car ultimately landed on its hood and began sliding across the northbound three lanes, causing sparks and fire to fly out of the back. Distracted by the commotion at the toll gates, Mark Jackson had failed to secure his seatbelt and was quickly knocked unconscious from the blunt force collision with the interior ceiling. The airbag prevented further damage to O'Dowd's wingman.

After the car had ricocheted off the interior Jersey wall and come to a resting stop, O'Dowd's face had pounded the driver's side airbag but thanks to his secure harness, he too was relatively injury free. O'Dowd quickly assessed the damage to the vehicle's passengers. Despite Mark's unconscious state, all in all safe was his immediate conclusion, but the experienced combat veteran felt far from out of the water. Whoever planted the IED was close by, for sure, thought O'Dowd. Looking out the front window, from an upside down position, he saw a large man making a beeline toward the upside-down car at a hell-for-leather pace.

A man who had seen his share of hand-to-hand combat knew he was in for one more. And judging from the size of Romanov, the undefeated Navy SEAL knew he was in for the fight of his life.

O'Dowd searched for his weapon in vain. Realizing that time was of the essence he released himself from the seat harness, opened the side door and rolled out onto the road. The retired Navy SEAL—in name only—immediately rose to his fighting stance. At six feet tall and weighing two hundred pounds O'Dowd was conceding a height and weight advantage, but not a significant one. Undaunted was his state of mind as he knew the tale of the tape was meant for professional boxing not military-style street brawls, which he excelled at through years of experience.

Kat and Roos, strapped in their military-style cockpit harnesses, found themselves virtually unscathed physically, but shaken to the bone mentally. Hanging upside down staring out of the front windshield, which was perversely providing an inverted rearview, all the couple could see were smoke and fire along the pavement. Fearful that the Suburban would burst into flames, or be hit by on-coming cars, they quickly unbuckled and leapt out of the vehicle and made for the small shoulder at the edge of the highway lanes. Cars, trucks and trailers piled up in long lines and many came over to assist them, but they waved off any help. Having come through twenty-five days of dangerous travel and encounters, Roos was intent on making sure all of them were alive and intact, and then making their way to Winged Foot.

Once he had gained his composure, Roos made his way back to the SUV and carefully extricated Jackson, who was slowly regaining consciousness. Kat was quickly with him and the two brought Mark over to the side of the road. There the three watched, gap-mouthed, the scene that was unfolding between O'Dowd and Romanov, while from off in the distance they began to hear the wail of firetruck sirens and police cars making their way through the now-heavy traffic to the smoldering vehicle. They knew they needed to quickly absent themselves from the scene before the police arrived and once O'Dowd was finished with his fierce battle with Romanov.

As the men squared off in lane two, each was assessing his opponent. Having no way of knowing O'Dowd was a SEAL and seeing no weapon, Romanov instantly liked his chances. But he would have to act quickly in order to take out Roos who he last saw hanging like a Jamaican fruit-eating bat in the back seat. O'Dowd appeared a technical fighter, one which Romanov felt he could overpower—like he had done to so many antagonists in his past.

O'Dowd, a man descended from a long line of cast-iron Belfast boxers, couldn't wait to get it on.

Romanov, making the first move, charged O'Dowd firing an overhand right intended for O'Dowd's left chin. The blocking upward thrust left hand thrown by O'Dowd nearly fractured Romanov's right arm at the elbow.

Observing Romanov recoiling from the pain, O'Dowd used the opening to land a stiff right hand to Romanov's left kidney. The strike sent the Russian buckling to the ground. As he rose to his feet helplessly exposed, O'Dowd unloaded with a right-left combination to the temples of Romanov.

The mighty Russian fighter, who had spent the better part of the past ten years engaging in fights over his Bloomberg, appeared rusty, but who wouldn't against O'Dowd, a fierce fighting machine? The force of O'Dowd's fists sent Romanov to the pavement—again.

Rising up again after another pummeling and realizing that his opponent was too quick with his punches, the more unconventional brawler decided to switch tactics. Returning to his Moscow street style—one that served him so well—Romanov put his head down and charged with reckless abandon. As his head hit just below the chest, Romanov wrapped his long arms around O'Dowd's waist. Continuing his momentum forward, the force lifted O'Dowd off the pavement as the pair of interlocked combatants careened to the ground. O'Dowd's back hit first, followed by his head jolting backwards with a force just short of knocking him unconscious, but not before the crafty fighter was able to deploy a brilliant tactical move. Upon the initial impact, O'Dowd was able to thrust a short burst kick with his right leg landing his foot squarely into Romanov's groin area. The force knocked the wind out of the cutthroat lout, rendering him motionless. O'Dowd seized the opportunity to stand and back away.

As Romanov made it to his knees, O'Dowd charged his prey and unloaded an uppercut kick from his right foot, sending Romanov flat on his back.

Romanov looked down and out, but he had one last trick up his sleeve. Strapped to the interior of his right leg was a Russian military knife, a Kizlyar Korshun with a serrated seven-inch steel blade. Romanov charged O'Dowd, who was focusing like never before. Quick swipes of the blade crisscrossing O'Dowd's face mere inches away had the SEAL's undivided attention, and for the first time in his life had created an eerie sense of impending doom. With the Russian's fury intensifying, O'Dowd thought, Of all the life-threatening, precarious situations he had experienced—is this how it is going to end?

Romanov's swiping turned to thrusts that provided an opening for O'Dowd. On the Russian's next thrust with his right hand, O'Dowd went low to his opponent's left side with a crushing leg whip to the kneecap. The force crumbled Romanov instantly—the knife released and landed several feet away.

O'Dowd lunged for the blade, but Romanov was able to roll, pounce from a crouched position with his hands extended and grab his opponent's legs at the knee. The interlocked men rolled toward the knife, creating a coin flip as to who would reach it first. As perverse luck would have it for O'Dowd, Queen Elizabeth II's regal profile metaphorically landed face up on the English pound, the most used coin in his home country of Northern Ireland. From his back, O'Dowd grabbed the knife and held the weapon in a cricket bat grip—with the blade facing Romanov, who by this time was directly on top of him. But Romanov had his considerably larger and stronger hands wrapped around the knife as well. For what seemed like an eternity to both men locked in a life-or-death struggle, the fighters deadlocked in an arm-wrestling contest of strength and will. Rebuffing the tip, Romanov was able to reverse the direction of the knife and was slowly but steadily inching the steel toward O'Dowd's chest. Shutting his eyes, O'Dowd summoned all of his might—but it was not enough. With certain death less than an inch away the loud crack of rifle shot whined through the air. With eyes wide open, O'Dowd saw two rounds hit Romanov's body—the first ripped through his right shoulder—the second caught the Russian's torso above the right pectoral muscle. The force of the blasts blew Romanov off O'Dowd and sent him flopping to the concrete pavement. O'Dowd's head pivoted right watching his opponent's dog-eared collapse—then left in the direction of the shooter where he saw Katherine Mandu standing next to the Suburban holding his gun.

With emergency vehicles approaching, Romanov stumbled toward the interior lane where Boom had just pulled up in his silver Chrysler 300C. Romanov slumped into the rear seat as Boom sped off.

O'Dowd's partner Jackson by this point had commandeered a vehicle, put Kat and Roos in the back seat, assisted his depleted partner into the front and headed for The Foot. As Jackson pressed on the accelerator pedal, O'Dowd heaving and slightly disoriented, from his shotgun seat turned toward the backseat where Kat was positioned and proudly complimented her. "Nice shot."

The time was 10:45 A.M.

Precisely at 11:30 A.M. Jackson drove through the Fenimore Road south gate and proceeded to the Clubhouse. Roos turned to Kat. "When I made this bet, I knew I needed a sidekick. My instincts told me you were the one, but honestly I didn't know why, it just felt right and still does. In hindsight, I could never have imagined how invaluable you would turn out to be. Without you, I would be dead broke, or just broke and most likely dead. Let me know if you need a partner on Everest. Check is in the mail."

Kat's vacant stare and silence confirmed Roos' belief, which had been building by the day, that his Nepalese good-luck charm would be vanishing from his life — once again.

As Roos exited the vehicle he thanked O'Dowd and Jackson and entered the Grille Room, which was packed, but the mood was non-celebratory, in a very gentlemanly Winged Foot kind of way. No jerks need apply, the membership of The Foot was class laced with civility, embodying a true chivalrous culture. Needless to say, a substantial amount of money was won on the wager and, of course, an equal amount was lost. The Honorable Henry A. Hebblethwaite took less than thirty minutes to study the passport and visa documentation, as well as the Instagram photos and Vimeo videos. Marveling at the technology available for free no less, the Judge announced, "The RoosCaboose winner is Christian Robinson Roos."

Asking Mark Jackson to pull over while exiting the Winged Foot driveway, Kat opened the car door, walked over to the third green and pulled out her satellite phone as she leaned up against a huge Fordham Gneiss boulder. The private phone rang in the director's corner office in Langley, Virginia, a phone with a number only known to a select few individuals.

"Jack, K2 here. Mission accomplished. I am ready to settle down now and have some kids. It has been an honor to work for you."

"K2, your excellent performance in Tehran demonstrated perfection," Jack responded. "Your service and dedication to the United States is exemplary, befitting of the highest awards this country has to offer. Unfortunately, given the nature of the assignment, you will be receiving none as your identity is forever secret."

"Yeah, yeah, of course. Make sure you keep it that way." Kat, never one for sappy bullshit, was overtly raining on the director's over-the-top accolades. "By the way, what was the story with the keystone cops at JFK Customs? I didn't know Homeland Security Agents were so ruthless! I assume they were not reading from the same playbook?"

"Don't worry," Jack replied, "I assure you, no one knows of your existence. Sorry about the scene at JFK. You know this was a POTUS, DOCIA and SECDEF Eyes-Only Top-Secret Mission. The Homeland Security gang are still the new kids on the block. Does Christian Roos have any insights that we should be aware of and or concerned about?"

Grinning, Kat confidently stated, "None. He doesn't have a clue," and with that, Katherine Mandu, the ex–Naval Officer, world-class sniper turned private assassin for hire, hung up her encrypted phone—for the last time.

As the foursome, comprised of the Judge, Mac, Harrison and Roos, made their way toward the first tee of the championship west course, Mac leaned toward Roos and asked, "Christian, do you think still the world is as safe and as good as you thought twenty-five days ago?"

With his ears still ringing, Christian Roos introspectively glanced down the majestic eighteenth fairway, then upwards toward the crystal blue sky. Soft spoken yet purposefully, Roos inquired, "Mac, why do you suppose Tillinghast designed Winged Foot's golf courses among these towering oak trees? And why do you think he built these menacing steep-faced deep sand traps? Why the lightning-fast greens and fairways lined with near-bottomless rough? Was it really necessary to design the putting surfaces with such severe undulations?"

Mac grumbled, "Absolutely. Otherwise it would be too easy. Not a true test of one's abilities. What would be the challenge? What would be the point? Anyone could play the game with ease. It is through adversity that one's game and, for that matter, character are fortified. A trait that makes us all stronger and better people more able to withstand life's inevitable curveballs."

Roos looked into Mac's steely blue eyes, which were busy glistening in the brilliant sunshine of the day, and responded, "My thoughts exactly. Tillie designed this place to make us better golfers. As to your question, I think whoever built the balance of this planet wanted to makes us better people, a stronger civilization, one filled with individuals trying to raise the curve. Despite the obvious issues, probably for the best, don't you think? After all, we wouldn't want to play the par-five sixteenth, 'Hells-Bells' eighteen times, now would we, Mac? Too easy."

Mac's grumbling intensified as he added, "Nor would we want to play 'Arena,' the par-four eighth all day. Too goddamn tough."

"So my adventure around the globe is similar to a loop on Tillie's masterpiece. Some easy stretches of wide fairways; others, like a short-sided downhill bunker shot or buried rough lie in the trees, so challenging you feel like picking up your Titleist and packing it in."

Roos ventured an impromptu observation, "I looked into the eyes of His Holiness, the leader of the Catholic Church, a man who wants salvation for all, and those of a desperate Somali pirate who wanted to kill me. I paid over one thousand dollars for raw fish, ten times the amount a young Mexican man voluntarily walked in front of a car for. I locked eyes with a plumb loco inflamed Tibetan monk from a distance so close the rancid smell of his burning skin seared my nose, and reveled in a magical fragrance of an otherworldly Japanese beauty. I witnessed poppy's dark side through a villainous charade perpetrated in a hell on earth landscape known as Afghanistan. I also experienced near unimaginable extravagance in Hong Kong, a city born from the spoils of the poppy trade. I broke bread and discussed the NBA with a currish communist tyrant. A billionaire tried to murder me with an IED over an amount of money that totaled less than five percent of his hedge fund. I saw terror manifest itself in the faces of thousands of Iranians as they took to the streets after a political assassination. I met a man who expressed magnanimous gratitude to two young Himalayan Sherpas for saving his life. He changed their lives and brought commerce to their hometown of Kathmandu as repayment for their ultimate act—the same town that later tried to incarcerate him."

Pausing for a moment, Roos continued, "But, Mac, all of this looked the same to me."

Mac quipped, "What did you see?"

Roos responded, "A red herring."

Scoffing, Mac asked, "For what?"

"Humanity. This is who we are and it is never going change," Roos retorted in a bold but matter-of-fact way. Continuing, "I think this is what Isaiah Berlin meant in his essay, *The Hedgehog and the Fox*. The hedgehog knows one big thing—man is imperfect. The DNA of humanity may embody imperfection, but its face of kindness is found in adversity. That doesn't mean that civilization is bad, despite evil in the world. Goodness still carries the day. But, Mac, I believe in the end, it is all about the journey. Integrity, honesty and maintaining humanity through goodness and kindness is how to keep score, not by the number of strokes, which can add up and make us look bad at times."

Roos continued, "As to your question about safety, I am confident that you are well acquainted with crisscrossing global trends of rising life expectancy and dramatically declining incidence of homicide. Mac, unquestionably the world is safer and healthier today on a relative basis than at any other time in history. A man walking the streets of medieval England had over ten times the chance of being killed than today and actuarially will live three times longer. I would have lost this bet five hundred years ago, even after adjusting for the modes of transportation of the day. But today, my friend, is a completely different story."

Mac composed himself. "Well I still think the world has gone mad."

Before teeing off, Roos clandestinely googled the phrase that Kat whispered to him in the car. A serene look of contentment unfurled over his face and an overpowering feeling of peace engulfed him. Gazing down the long lush fairway of the first hole, he turned to his longtime dear friend, Harrison, and proudly said, "Frank, the grass has never looked greener."

# Epilogue

*"Reality provides us with facts so romantic that imagination itself
could add nothing to them."*

—JULES VERNE

Six months later.

The weather conditions on Mount Everest were perfect, but
that can always change, thought Katherine Mandu, as her expedition, attempting to summit Everest from the Nepalese side, made its
way to the South Summit. Through 2012 there had been three thousand
eight hundred seventy-seven successful summits from the Nepalese side
and one hundred and thirty-four deaths. Attempting to conquer the
mighty Everest from the Tibetan side had proved slightly more difficult.
Only two thousand three hundred thirty-one climbers had reached the
summit, while one hundred and six had perished on the steeper and
more dangerous northern route.

Route notwithstanding, not in debate was the fact that most climbers who have perished on Mount Everest are still there. Katherine's father, Malcolm Mandu, was unfortunately no exception.

In less than two hours, at their base camp at the South Summit,
Katherine Mandu was able to find the remains of her father. After removing the snow and his facial windbreaker, she found him frozen in
eternity along the cadaver-littered death zone. She marveled at how he
looked not a day older than the last time she saw him, before the fateful
expedition, the day he and his companions kissed the gods and died on
Mount Everest.

As Kat reached the summit, she instantly understood the meaning of the plaque at the base of the mountain inscribed by Edmund Hillary, the first man to reach the summit of Mount Everest, *People do not decide to become extraordinary. They decide to accomplish extraordinary things.*

Placing her father's wedding ring in the wind-blown snow at the peak of Everest, Kat whispered, *"Christian Roos, Ma Tapailai Maya Garchu."* The words, swept up by the jet stream, usurped by earth's highest vortex, echoed into eternity.

Hearing the words while surfing down China's magisterial Yangtze River, crossing the East China Sea and into an intensive care unit of a Pyongyang medical facility, Carl Strange's eyes miraculously opened and his face smiled. In a drooling voice, he vapidly asked, *"Where in the world is Christian Roos?"*

Hearing the words swooshing down Park Avenue like a Macy's Day float, Alexei Romanov stood ankle deep in financial blood on his gladiator trading room floor. The man, drenched in setting sunlight, still licking his nonfatal monetary and physical wounds, roared, *"Christian Roos, people should know when they are conquered."*

The words slipped down the rooftop opening of Basir Kazim's secret lair like smoke through a keyhole arch, and as he cruised through the sparse uninhabited Registan Desert, Lashkar Gah's new mayor cried out, *"Christian Roos, I am poppyless!"*

The words rippled through the Pillars of Hercules and past the Rock of Gibraltar, across the Mediterranean waters along the northern coast of Africa, turned left up the eastern coast of Spain and passed the island of Ibiza before collecting in the South of France in the Port of Hercules in Monaco, where *Akrep* was at anchor. Christian Roos, who was seated on the aft fly deck, upon hearing the words smiled and turned to the great white pelican proudly perched on the teak stern deck railing below: pinkish bill, three-gallon yellow pouch and marshmallow plumage all ablaze in the resplendent Louis XIV sunset, and said, *"The world is a scary place, but it just may be all we have, so I am afraid we simply must make do — for now."*

# What the Characters Are Saying about *Blood Herring*

*"Extremely informative, wildly entertaining and delightfully fresh,* Blood Herring *delivers the literary money shot. The opening line informs the reader that life isn't as it appears; well neither is this book."*

Christian Roos, Fund Manager and Writer, Washington, D.C.

*"My Lululemons are still twisted in a knot from reading this provocative novel. Love the two sex scenes: on a yacht in the Med and in Pyong-yang on a purple bean bag chair with neon lights flickering to the glow of gooey gelatinous lava lamp bubbles and the smell of kimchi wafting through the air."*

Katherine Mandu, Yoga Maven, Kathmandu, Nepal

*"If this masterful work is fiction, then would someone tell me in what world I am living, If You Please?"*

Carl Strange, Retired Chief Investment Officer of investment bank
Springer and Waldron, Puerto Ayora, Indefatigable Island, Galapagos, Ecuador

*"The author's cynical portrayal of the hedge fund industry may have breached the tipping point at times, but net-net, I think he is spot-on."*

Alexei Romanov, Vengeance Capital Founder and CEO, New York, New York

*"Jules Verne's man, Phileas Fogg, took eighty days to circumnavigate the world.* Blood Herring *does it in twenty-five. Talk about a giant step for mankind."*

Charles MacCormick, Retired Chairman and CEO of Springer and Waldron,
Greenwich, Connecticut

*"If* Blood Herring *were a building, it would pierce the clouds and french kiss a God or two or three."*

Basir Kazim, Poppy Prince and Construction Tycoon, Founder
Registan Realty, Lashkar Gah, Afghanistan

*"Fast-paced wire-to-wire action, filled with suspense and intrigue. I needed to pop a Valium every other chapter just to make it through this spine-tingling read."*

Hard Yang, Thallium Expert, Xicheng Medical Company, Beijing, China

*"This book has more momentum than a shop trading algorithm."*

Dr. St. John Smythe, World-Famous Economist, London, United Kingdom

*"Scene in Tokyo's Michelin Three Star Sukiyabashi restaurant alone makes* Blood Herring *a must read. Can almost taste the iconic eighty-eight-year-old Jiro Ono's succulent, mouthwatering fresh and eye tearing wasabi with the kick of a Fuji eruption. The toro wasn't bad either."*

Sakura Nagasawa, Corporate Strategy Financial Analyst Sony Corporation, Tokyo, Japan

*"James Bond meets Austin Powers meets Marco Polo meets Warren Buffett meets the World's Most Interesting Man in this brilliant pastiche of humanity."*

Frank Harrison, Hedge Fund Manager, Rye, New York

*"About time my country was portrayed in something other than a humanitarian crisis documentary or United States military recruitment video.* Blood Herring, *a book that never jumps the shark, is quickly reaching cult status on the Somali waters."*

Mooge Abdikarim, Pirate and Fisherman, Berbara, Somaliland

*"Despite being characterized as a heartless, currish tyrant suffering from a Napoleon complex, honestly, I couldn't put the book down. It is simply that fascinating."*

Kim Jong-un, Supreme Leader of the Democratic People's Republic of Korea, Pyongyang, North Korea

*About the Author*

**Douglas C. Eby**, a Washingtonian, studied economics at Catholic University and received his MBA in finance from Indiana University. His successful and diverse Wall Street career has focused primarily on the investment management business. He is a venture partner in a firm investing in next generation technology, communications and information companies, and has enjoyed the pleasure of serving on the board of directors of multiple public and private companies in the technology, financial services, real estate and healthcare industries. In addition to writing ***Blood Herring***, he is the author and publisher of ***If You Please*** (www.ifyouplease.com), an online publication of original stories, articles, essays and opinions covering a wide range of related themes that provide a colorful perspective on humanity. Employing his eclectic style, one which emphasizes informative entertainment, Eby has written articles for ***IYP*** about Cuba, Warren Buffett, the Oscars, South Beach, Mick Jagger, and Mars One's planned one-way trip to the mysterious Red Planet. He has attended and written about some of the most important sessions of the Supreme Court of the United States in recent history, including: the same-sex marriage cases, DOMA and Windsor, as well as the constitutional challenge of the Affordable Care Act.